WEDNESDAY

A Novelization of Season One

Random House Children's Books
A division of Penguin Random House LLC
1745 Broadway, New York, NY 10019
penguinrandomhouse.com
rhcbooks.com

WEDNESDAY © 2022–2025 MGM Television Entertainment Inc. WEDNESDAY is a trademark of Tee & Charles Addams Foundation. *Wednesday: A Novelization of Season One* © 2025 Metro-Goldwyn-Mayer Studios Inc. All Rights Reserved.

METRO-GOLDWYN-MAYER is a trademark of
Metro-Goldwyn-Mayer Lion Corp.
© 2025 Metro-Goldwyn-Mayer Studios Inc. All Rights Reserved.

Penguin Random House values and supports copyright. Copyright fuels creativity, encourages diverse voices, promotes free speech, and creates a vibrant culture. Thank you for buying an authorized edition of this book and for complying with copyright laws by not reproducing, scanning, or distributing any part of it in any form without permission. You are supporting writers and allowing Penguin Random House to continue to publish books for every reader. Please note that no part of this book may be used or reproduced in any manner for the purpose of training artificial intelligence technologies or systems.

Random House and the colophon are registered trademarks of Penguin Random House LLC. WEDNESDAY is a trademark of Tee & Charles Addams Foundation.

Cover art by Marcela Bolívar

ISBN 978-0-593-89665-5 (hardcover) | ISBN 978-0-593-89667-9 (ebook)

Manufactured in the United States of America
10 9 8 7 6 5 4 3 2 1

The authorized representative in the EU for product safety and compliance is Penguin Random House Ireland, Morrison Chambers, 32 Nassau Street, Dublin D02 YH68, Ireland, https://eu-contact.penguin.ie.

Random House Children's Books supports the First Amendment
and celebrates the right to read.

WEDNESDAY

A Novelization of Season One

Adapted by Tehlor Kay Mejia

Based on *Wednesday* Season One Episodes

Written by
Alfred Gough & Miles Millar (episodes 101, 102, 108)
Kayla Alpert (episodes 103, 104)
April Blair (episodes 105, 106)
Alfred Gough & Miles Millar and Matt Lambert (episode 107)

Series Created by Alfred Gough & Miles Millar

Based on the Characters Created by Charles Addams

Random House 🏠 New York

FROM THE DESK OF WEDNESDAY ADDAMS

Ask any problem child how they feel about being dumped at their eighth school in five years and you'll get about the same answer.

I'm no exception, though I like to think my expulsions (as well as my taste in curses) tend to be a bit more creative than your average bully's. I can't overstate how little I wanted to be dragged to Nevermore Academy (my parents' alma mater) on the fateful fall day that our family hearse wound up the drive. In my eyes, any institution that could produce my mother's smug superiority or my parents' nauseating obsession with each other was a place to be avoided at all costs.

But as any investigative genius will tell you, it's important to be able to admit when you're wrong. And I was. About Nevermore Academy. About almost everything that happened there that year. In my defense, however, who could possibly have predicted that a campus notorious for housing your garden-variety outsiders and weirdos would play host to a monster mystery so deep, so twisted, that even *I* would be surprised by its conclusion?

If I could go back in time and tell that younger, more naive version of me one thing—well, I probably wouldn't. Pure, unforeshadowed terror is one of life's few true diversions, after all, and I know she'd be furious with me for ruining the surprise.

Instead, let me take you back to the beginning of a story in which I, Wednesday Addams, find a purpose and a home in the very last place I ever expected to find either. Don't worry, it's not a feel-good story. If you should know one thing about me going into this, it's that I detest a story without at least five brutal murders.

CHAPTER ONE

Months earlier . . .

My parents are kissing passionately in the seat across from me. It's a good thing we drive a funereal vehicle, because I'm seconds from expiring. Cause of death: pure revulsion.

I'm convinced a coffin six feet under would be a preferable destination to the one I'm heading for. *Nevermore Academy.* The very campus I swore, as a child, I would never set foot on. Anything that makes my father misty-eyed is something I reject summarily—including my mother, who surfaces for air and turns her imperious gaze on me.

"Darling, how long do you intend on giving us the cold shoulder?" she asks.

I don't turn my gaze from the window. "Lurch," I say in an even tone, addressing the family's monstrous butler in the driver's seat. "Please remind my parents I'm not speaking to them."

Lurch moans, as he's wont to do. Right now I prefer it to the conversation my parents have been trying to have with me since we left home this morning. I know my father understands the warning in his tone, but he ignores it.

"I promise you, my little viper, you'll love Nevermore. Won't she, Tish?" My father is incapable of having an opinion my mother doesn't share. It's unnatural, and it only increases my nausea.

"Of course," my mother says. "It's the perfect school for her."

These words grate against my already frayed nerves. I abhor a cliché, but certain adolescent experiences, I suppose, are universal, and there's nothing I detest more than being told who I am or what's good for me by my mother.

"Why?" I snap, breaking my silence against my will. "Because it was the perfect school for *you*?"

She doesn't even deign to respond, just smirks in that way of hers, nonverbally suggesting that everything she thinks is objectively correct. Baiting me with that knowing silence.

And I bite. Which only makes me more furious at the both of us.

"I have no interest in following in your footsteps," I say. "Becoming captain of the fencing team, queen of the Dark Prom, president of the Séance Society." I try to infuse these accomplishments with as much disdain as possible, but of course she looks even more smug.

"I merely meant that you will *finally* be among peers who understand you," she says. "Maybe you'll even make some friends."

This I don't dignify with a response. Friendship, in my experience, requires opting into a series of identifiers that I have never had any interest in. Psychologists say adolescent friendships are made and broken almost entirely on being in or out of a group. And I've never been part of any group. I don't intend to start with one that would have my parents as members.

Besides, I don't believe my mother has ever had a friend. She's had followers. Sycophants. She's been trying to get me to join their ranks since I was born.

"Nevermore is like no other boarding school," my father says, gazing at her, utterly proving my point. "It's a magical place. It's where I met your mother and we fell in love."

You'd think I would be used to that moony look on his face, the way he takes her hand in his and sighs like the car is powered by his personal carbon dioxide emissions and not fossil fuels that are burning the planet and everyone on it at an alarming rate.

I know there's no use trying to interrupt them. Even my most carefully sharpened verbal barbs have always failed in that endeavor. Instead, I turn back toward the window, taking refuge in the last memory that brought me peace.

I can almost feel the cheap linoleum flooring of Nancy Reagan High School beneath my Mary Janes. See the half-closed locker barely containing my brother, who spills out, red-faced and humiliated, an apple jammed in his mouth. I touch his arm and it happens. A vision. A jolt of past or future that violently overrides my circuitry. It's hard to explain how it feels . . . like electroshock therapy without the satisfying afterburn.

These visions had been plaguing me the past few months. But this one showed something actionable, at least: the identity of my brother's tormentors. From there, vengeance wasn't hard to obtain.

It took me a few days to get the piranhas. My guy at the exotic animal store dragged his feet until I unearthed some photos of him and his current mistress that considerably dampened his curiosity about what I wanted them for.

The memory of standing at the edge of the pool during water polo practice carries me all the way up the drive to Nevermore. The amusement turned panic in the culprits' eyes. The sleek silver bodies of the fish streaking through the overchlorinated water. The way they somehow *knew* to go straight for the family jewels.

I'll never forget the way the vivid red blood contrasted with the blue of the water, or the screams filling the water sports practice center. I couldn't have set the stage better—incredible acoustics.

They lived, unfortunately. My one solace is that their parents didn't press charges for attempted murder. Imagine a lifetime of anyone looking at your record knowing you'd failed to finish the job.

CHAPTER TWO

The Nevermore principal's office is exactly the kind of academic self-importance fest I most loathe. Leatherbound books and furniture, polished mahogany and bronze. The kind of room that makes stupid people feel intelligent and intelligent people want to vomit.

I sit in one of the leather chairs between my parents as the principal examines my file with a pained expression on her face. I know the file contains my transcripts. Probably some warnings from past teachers and counselors. Nothing out of the ordinary—unless you're not used to vigilante justice.

"Wednesday is certainly a unique name," she says at last,

latching on to what is potentially the sole inoffensive detail in the tome. "I'm guessing it's the day you were born?"

"I was born on Friday the thirteenth," I correct her, keeping my stare level to show her this means exactly what she fears it does.

"Her name," my mother cuts in, pacifying, "comes from a line in my favorite nursery rhyme. *Wednesday's child is full of woe.*"

The one time she ever really understood me, I think.

"There's that unique Morticia perspective," the principal says. "Did your mother tell you we were roommates during our time at Nevermore?"

Suddenly, Larissa Weems is more than just a barely distinct talking head to me. I try to imagine her young—was she this prim and uptight then? I wonder. She can't have been popular if she's working here now. In-group adolescents almost never return to the scene of the crime.

So she's reliving something, I deduce. And she doesn't seem to be a sycophant of my mother's, which means she was at least partially immune to the legendary Morticia Addams charm even back then, when it was most concentrated. Perhaps there's something I can learn from this woman after all. Not that I'd give her the satisfaction of telling her that.

"Impressive," I say in my most neutral tone.

"What is?" she asks politely.

"That you graduated with your sanity intact."

Is it my imagination, or does she take another look at me too? If so, she has the good sense to stop before my mother takes notice.

"You've certainly had an *interesting* educational journey," she says, returning to the file. "Eight schools in five years, each tenure ended by an . . . incident of note."

"I'm a strong believer in vigilante justice."

She presses on, ignoring this. "Nevermore doesn't usually accept students in the middle of a term, but you're clearly a bright girl, and your family has a long history with the school. The board understands that students who thrive here are often . . . underserved in other educational environments. We've made an exception in the hopes that will prove true for you as well."

"They haven't built a school yet that can serve me," I parry. "Or one that can hold me, either. I don't imagine this one will be any different."

"What our daughter is trying to say," my father interjects with a pointed look in my direction, "is that she greatly appreciates the opportunity."

"Yes," my mother agrees. "And she'll prove it by being a model student, as well as attending her regular, court-ordered therapy sessions."

"Ah, that brings us to my next point," Principal Weems says brightly. "Many of our students require extra psychological support. We have a relationship with an excellent practitioner in Jericho who can meet Wednesday twice a week."

My stomach clenches at the thought of *therapy*. I avoided the requirement during my last seven expulsions, but this time it was either counseling or juvenile detention. Pity they let my parents decide. I've always been fond of stripes.

"We'll see if your therapist survives the first session," I say.

Principal Weems isn't fazed. It'll take more than a few one-liners to put her off, I see. I'll have to work harder—but I enjoy a challenge. I make a note to find out her worst fear and exploit it before I make my escape. Assuming there's time.

The principal gets to her feet. She's tall. Much taller than I expected. She and my mother look like giants, and I curse my father's genes for my diminutive size.

"I've assigned you to your mother's and my old dorm," she says in that forcedly bright tone—which sounds even more condescending from her twelve-inch altitude advantage. "Ophelia Hall."

My mother gasps, delighted, and claps her hands. I loathe Ophelia Hall on principle before I even set foot in it, but setting foot doesn't improve my judgment one iota.

Later, as we stop in front of what I assume to be my dormitory, I ask my mother, "Ophelia's the one who kills herself after being driven mad by her family, isn't she?"

Principal Weems interjects before my mother can answer—not that she would have bothered. "Okay!" she says with a toothy smile. "Let's meet your new roommate!"

Roommate.

Just the word makes my blood run cold. No one mentioned a roommate. I'd pictured myself in some try-hard, moody room with arched windows, ravens circling overhead. Playing my cello. Writing my next great novel. Plotting my inevitable escape.

I hadn't pictured doing any of that with an audience.

"Here we go!" Principal Weems says, tapping twice before opening the door.

My first thought upon entering the room is that I would have preferred there to be a victim in a pool of blood. A centipede infestation. A cloud of poison gas that causes excruciating pain before it eventually hijacks your nervous system and causes complete organ failure.

Anything but the explosion of *light* and *color* that assaults my eyes as I step into my new residence.

My alleged roommate has papered our round floor-to-ceiling window with a literal rainbow, its glow backlit by the gloomy day outside. The room has been collaged from the kind of magazines that make women feel bad about their bodies in order to sell pink razors and cloying scented soaps and antiperspirant. Her bed is covered in an array of stuffed animals.

"Oh my," my father mutters from behind me. "It's so *vivid.*"

I'm about to enumerate for the tenth time the exact ways in which they've betrayed me by sending me here, when a humanoid figure bounces up to me, blond curls flying, smile showing all her teeth—and not in the predatory way I prefer to view incisors.

"Howdy, roomie!" she says, cementing in those two words the fact that we will never, ever be friends. In case I needed further proof, she steps forward in an attempt to embrace me. A stranger. I step back before I can stop myself.

"Wednesday," says Principal Weems. "This is Enid Sinclair."

"And *you're* not a hugger," says the Enid in question. "Got it!"

"Please excuse Wednesday," my mother says with a smirk that says she pities Enid and her rainbow as much as I do. "She's allergic to color."

I'm trapped in a horrible internal battle now, where both outcomes feel like defeat. Either I force myself to like *Enid Sinclair,* or I share an opinion with my mother.

"Oh, wow, allergic to color," Enid is saying now, looking at me with true concern. "What happens to you?"

I stare back at her unblinkingly. "I break out in hives and then the flesh peels off my bones."

"Well!" Principal Weems says, stepping in with that diplomatic smile. "Luckily, we've ordered you a special no-color uniform.

Enid, why don't you take Wednesday to the registrar to pick it up along with her schedule. Then you can give her the grand tour while her parents and I fill out some paperwork."

She says *schedule* like "shed-dule" and makes doing paperwork with my mother sound like the highlight of her day. Surrounded by adults, I doubt anything less than ritual sacrifice will get me out of this. And at a place like Nevermore Academy, even that might be too pedestrian to work.

"Lead the way," I say, but not before turning and glaring at my parents.

Enid is only too happy to oblige. She insists on giving me a tour, even though I do my best to convince her it's unnecessary. I don't need to know the school was founded in 1791. I plan on taking that many minutes or less to escape from its on-the-nose, Poe-soaked-aesthetic confines.

"Why do you want to leave?" Enid asks when I tell her as much. "This place is great! Way better than normal school."

"This was my parents' idea," I say, noticing a photo of my mother with the fencing team on the wall of the entrance hall. She's wearing her uniform. Her hair is down, a flirtatious smirk on her vivid red lips. "They've been looking for any excuse to send me here. It's all part of their completely obvious plan."

"What plan is that?" Enid asks.

"To turn me into a version of themselves," I say with a sigh. It's the worst fate I can imagine. Except, perhaps, living in the rainbow room for the rest of my life.

"Okay, as long as we're sharing?" Enid says. "Maybe you can clear something up."

"I doubt it."

She plows ahead, undaunted. "Well, rumor has it you killed a kid at your last school, and your parents pulled strings to get you in here even though you're, like, a danger to yourself and others."

"Totally wrong," I say in a bored tone.

Enid looks visibly relieved.

"It was two kids. But who's counting, right?"

For a minute, she seems torn between terror and amusement. Eventually she chuckles, a weak sound that says she hasn't picked a side.

Luckily for her, we've reached what appears to be the social hub of Nevermore Academy, and the sight of this many seething bags of hormones dulls my wit just long enough for her to strike.

"Okay, the layout of campus you can get from your map, so let me give you the tour that really matters. A who's who of Nevermore's social scene."

She seems genuinely thrilled to impart this information, and as overwhelmed as I am by the crowd, I can't give her the satisfaction of receiving it. "I'm not interested in participating in tribal adolescent clichés," I manage.

"Great!" Enid replies, with what I think is a hint of genuine sarcasm. "You can use it to fill your obviously bottomless pit of disdain!"

Touché, I think, and wave for her to continue. It seems better to get it over with quickly.

"So, the four main Nevermore cliques are as follows: Fangs, Furs, Stoners, and Scales."

My pattern-hungry brain has them all mapped out before she can begin to gesture, despite the pedantic nicknames. The Fangs, or vampires, sit at a table out of direct sunlight, looking morosely at their smartphones. I wonder if an immortal life of high school is enough to drive a person mad and vow to find out at my first available opportunity.

"Some of them have literally been here for decades," Enid informs me before waving to a group of people who seem as obsessed with neon as she is. "Those are the Furs, aka werewolves. Obviously that's my crowd." She howls at them, then flashes her retractable claws in my direction.

"I'm sure full moons are a riot around here."

"Already got you some noise-canceling headphones," she says with a grin. "Hope you like pink!"

"Pass. I'm assuming Scales is your little nickname for sirens?"

"Yup," Enid confirms, gesturing to a group of ethereally beautiful people gathered around a water fountain. "That girl in the middle, Bianca Barclay, is basically Nevermore royalty. No one crosses her. Although her crown's been slipping lately." Enid leans in, lowering her voice. "The rumor is that she's vulnerable after she and Xavier Thorpe mysteriously broke up at the beginning of the semester."

"Enid!" comes a voice from behind us, and I turn to see a tall boy in an oversized hat approaching us. The hat seems to be concealing something bulky on his head.

I don't exactly hide behind Enid, but I'm obscured from the boy's view and I do nothing to remedy that. Far be it from me to turn down the gift of invisibility when it presents itself.

"Ajax," Enid says in that flirtatious way people sometimes do. Drawing out the last vowel. I try to get a good look at him without revealing myself, searching for the answer to why she finds him worthy of altered vocal inflection.

My first glance gains me nothing. He appears average in every way. And when you factor in Enid's above-average appeal—calculated by facial symmetry; smoothness, and tone of her skin; ratio of visible skin to clothing; and mastery of beauty product usage—they seem an unlikely match.

"You're not gonna believe what I heard about your new roommate," Ajax says, oblivious to my presence. "She *eats* human flesh. Chowed down on that kid she murdered. You better watch your back."

I sigh quietly, aware that I'm now honor bound to relinquish my convenient observer status.

"Quite the contrary," I state as Enid steps aside to reveal my presence. "I actually fillet the bodies of my victims, then feed them to my menagerie of pets." I hold eye contact with the below-average boy until he drops his gaze. A victory.

"Ajax," Enid says with what sounds like a suppressed giggle. "This is my new roommate, Wednesday."

"Whoa," he says. "You're in black-and-white."

I cross *superior intellect* off my mental list of potential reasons Enid is humoring him, leaving me with exactly zero remaining options.

"Ignore him," she says, turning away with a wave of her hand. "He's cute but clueless. Gorgons spend way too much time getting stoned."

I can appreciate the pun. Enid appears pleased.

"The rumors will clear up once we get you on social media," she says. "There's not much online about you, so people feel free to fabricate. Tell me you at least have an Instagram?"

"I find social media to be a soul-sucking void of meaningless affirmation," I reply.

Enid nods, not knowing what to say. I walk back to our dorm in silence, alone.

My parents and Pugsley leave before dinner, which I consider to be the one positive in an otherwise miserable day. I stand with them in the school's circular driveway, doing nothing to disguise my impatience for them to be gone.

"Why don't you boys wait in the car?" my mother asks the rest of my family after I've said goodbye to them. "Wednesday and I are in need of a moment."

If only to hasten her departure, I swallow my assertion that we have never had—and most likely will never have—any interaction that could be described as a *moment*.

When they're gone, she turns a decidedly unsentimental eye on me. "I want you to know I've told every family member to alert me the moment you darken their doorstep. You have nowhere to go. Try to make the best of this."

Inwardly, I scoff. As if a *family member* would be my first stop. "As usual, you underestimate me, Mother."

She ignores this, reaching into the little purse my father usually carries for her. "I got you a little something."

The necklace she extends is studded with black stones. A silver *W*—or an *M*, depending on which way one turns it—hangs in the center of the pendant. It's hideous.

"It's made of obsidian," she says. "The Aztec priests used this stone to conjure visions. It's a symbol of our connection."

At the word *visions,* I feel myself recoil inwardly. I refuse to acknowledge this emotion as fear, but I'm even more determined not to show it to her. Whatever it is.

"I'm not you, Mother," I say. "I will never fall in love, or be a housewife, or have a family."

She sniffs, as if it's possible to injure her. "I'm told girls your age say hurtful things. That I shouldn't take them to heart."

"Fortunately, you don't have a heart."

At this, my mother smiles. "Why, thank you, my sweet."

She then gives me a bulky crystal ball in a bag and promises to call me at the end of the week (despite my protestations), and then they're gone. I stand in the wind, relief coursing through me. Nevermore isn't the place for me, I know that. But at least without them hovering I won't feel forced into the little box they insist on placing me in.

Immature child. Future psychic. Rebellious daughter. *Addams.* I plan to transcend every one of these labels, and soon.

Lost in my fantasies of escape, I'm unaware that right down the road a mystery is already unfolding. One in which I'm destined to play a part. I don't learn the details until much later. Won't see photos of a hiker's limbs scattered through the trees on the day of my arrival or the cause of his death.

I won't learn of the Jericho sheriff's deeply held belief that this murder—already one of a string of murders—is connected to Nevermore Academy, or the reason for his prejudice.

In the morning, the newspaper will run a mostly sanitized story of a bear attack. I'll take inspiration from the grisly description for a scene in my novel. But the truth, as it so often does, will prove much stranger than the fiction.

CHAPTER THREE

Enid and I are already bickering when Ms. Thornhill, our "dorm mother," taps on the door later that evening.

My roommate is upset that I've taken the rainbow transparencies off my half of the window. I'm irritated by her intrusion into my writing time. Enid's claws are out, and I'm considering which of my decorative medieval torture weapons will be the most functional in an actual combat scenario.

"Girls?" Ms. Thornhill calls as she opens the door, surveying the standoff. "Is this a bad time?"

Enid retracts her claws with a glare.

"I'm Ms. Thornhill. I'm sorry I wasn't here when you arrived. I was out on the grounds dealing with a foliage . . . situation." She gestures down at the mud covering her bright red boots.

"Riveting," I say dryly.

"I trust Enid has been giving you the Nevermore welcome!"

"She's been *smothering* me with hospitality," I say, not breaking eye contact with my flush-faced roommate. "I hope to return the favor. In her sleep."

Ms. Thornhill chuckles as if I'm joking. She steps forward with a plant in a pot. I have to admit it's gorgeous. Dark green leaves and a large bloom that's the perfect shade of freshly spilled blood. "I brought you this as a welcome present. It's from my conservatory. I try to match the right flower to each of my girls."

"The black dahlia," I say, surprised. Almost impressed.

"You know it?" she asks, smiling with an embarrassing amount of eagerness.

"Yes," I say. "It's named after my favorite unsolved murder. Thank you."

I mean it as a compliment, but she falters, setting it on the desk next to my typewriter and then moving toward the door. "Well, before I leave, I have to deliver the house rules. Lights off at ten, no loud music, no boys. Ever."

I fight the urge to scoff at the idea.

"Also, Jericho is a twenty-five-minute walk from campus. There's a shuttle on the weekends if you want to shop, or hang out, or whatever the cool kids are doing these days." Ms. Thornhill laughs. I don't. "The locals are a little wary of Nevermore, though, which means no claws, sleep smothering, or any other stereotypical Outcast behavior while you're there. Are we clear?"

I turn back to my typewriter. Enid flicks her claws out again and begins sharpening them with a purple nail file.

"Great talk," says Ms. Thornhill—clearly a paragon of authority.

When I arrive at the Fencing Hall for my first class, I am forced to admit the facilities are adequate. And more than that, a few of my temporary classmates don't appear altogether hopeless at the art.

The same skills that make you a good amateur investigator also make for a quality swordsperson. You must be light on your feet, have a keen attention to detail, and be skilled at quickly discovering your opponent's weakness. If the sport didn't keep me in shape for my true goals, I wouldn't have bothered for my mother's sake.

Everyone is wearing white, of course, so my all-black attire stands out. People stop their bouts to peer at me curiously. I wish I had put my mask down. Instead, I make a mask of my face, refusing to let them see that I feel at home here. That I like the feeling of the blade within reach.

The bouts continue as if the other students haven't noticed my arrival. I recognize Bianca Barclay immediately—her luminous dark brown skin shines even through the mesh of her mask. Her opponent is new to me. Short. Fifteen years old, I'd wager.

He has terrible form. His steps are wild, desperate. He moves his arms too much. Economy of movement is the hallmark of a good swordsman, and this boy's is worse than a toddler's.

Bianca, on the other hand . . .

The boy goes crashing to the floor. "Coach! She tripped me!"

he calls out, pulling the mask off to reveal his brilliantly pink and sweaty face.

I'm not much for sentiment, but in this moment he reminds me a bit of my brother, Pugsley, shoved halfway into a locker and trying not to cry.

"It was a clean strike, Rowan," comes the ruling from the coach.

"Maybe if you whined less and practiced more, you wouldn't suck," Bianca says. Loud enough for everyone to hear. "Anyone *else* want to challenge me?"

She says it like she's sure no one will be stupid enough to agree. Or if they do, they'll be sorry. I have no desire to upset (or even participate in) a social hierarchy, but I have a problem with people who punch down, and I didn't bring this foil here to look menacing. I might as well get a workout.

"I do," I say, stepping forward. Someone actually gasps.

"So," Bianca says, circling me, sizing me up for weaknesses. "You must be the new psychopath they let in."

"You must be the self-appointed queen bee," I observe, matching her step for step. "Interesting thing about bees: pull out their stingers and they drop dead."

Another gasp. This one is collective. Bianca's expression says she's surprised by my retort—which tells me people usually lie down and let her trample all over them. That's one of her weaknesses, I can already tell. She's been spoiled for lack of worthy opponents.

The other one is how aware she is of her audience. She turns to them now.

"Rowan doesn't need you to come to his defense," she says, speaking at me, but to them. "He's not helpless. He's lazy."

I draw my weapon. The flicking sound it makes against the air is satisfying. "Are we doing this or not?"

"En garde," Bianca says. But she's still paying too much attention to what everyone thinks. It leaves her wide open.

The thing I'll never tell my mother is that there are times when I love this sport. For someone like me, getting out of your head isn't always possible. But in a bout, I can transmute my mental energy into physical force. There's no surrender. It's all about tactics. Control. Like dancing with a deadly edge.

I've always preferred an opponent to a partner, anyway.

A few seconds in, I get my first touch as Bianca considers her angles. Abruptly, she's furious.

"Point to Wednesday," the coach says, sounding almost offensively surprised.

I knew Bianca was good the moment I saw her against Rowan. This is the moment I know she's dangerous. Her whole body seems to home in on me, as if she's taking this seriously for the first time. She *knows* her weakness, I realize. She's just not used to being held accountable for having it.

When she goes on the offensive, I'm barely matching her steps. The fluid feeling of my mind and body connecting is gone. I'm a half step behind.

Bianca's foil makes contact. I barely hear the coach say the score is even. I'm in trouble. Bianca is clearly the superior athlete, but perhaps I can still best her with psychology.

"For the final point," I say from behind my mask. "I would like to invoke a military challenge. No masks. No tips."

A third round of gasps. This time even the coach joins in.

"Winner draws first blood."

I remove my mask. With her queenly face visible, I think, she'll be too aware of the optics. The anonymity of the suit will be gone. Perhaps she'll slip.

"It's up to you, Bianca," the coach says. I can hear the eagerness in his tone for some diversion from the usual hum of competitive teens.

Bianca takes off her mask and begins the bout with a confident lunge. I know in her first step that my trick didn't work. She's more ferocious than ever. Faster. The siren moves like the water that she draws her strength from. She's everywhere and nowhere.

I know I won't beat her without taking a risk, so I do. Leaving myself open. Hoping.

But she parries, takes expert advantage of the ploy. I feel the sting along my forehead that means it's over.

"Word of advice," Bianca says, her tone mean-girl scathing as she revels in my badge of humiliation. "Stay in your lane, which is as far away from me as possible."

I stare at her. There's no doubt Bianca's a worthy opponent. And I'm left wondering if I've underestimated Nevermore's queen in more than just swordsmanship.

The infirmary is empty save for Rowan and me. Coach insisted we be examined, though I tried to explain I've walked away from far more gruesome injuries without faux maternal affection and a Band-Aid.

"You're Wednesday, right?" Rowan asks when the nurse bustles away, leaving me with an embarrassingly large synthetic bandage across my forehead. Broadcasting my defeat to anyone who glances at my face is a dastardly form of torture. I vow to remember it for next time I need to induce humiliation in a foe.

"Rowan?" I reply, and the boy nods. That trembling chin. The weak, bird-boned frame. He's utterly, almost obscenely helpless.

"I know how you feel," he says.

"I guarantee you don't."

"My mother promised I'd finally fit in somewhere," he continues, scattering his pressure points like confetti. He'd better hope we never find ourselves at odds. "I never thought it was possible to be an Outcast in a school full of Outcasts. But it looks like you're gonna give me a run for my money."

I don't bother to answer. People like Rowan always assume my "out-group" status has been forced on me. No one who's involuntarily alone can understand someone who chooses it. It's impossible to explain, so I don't try.

"Uh, sorry about the . . ." He gestures to the place on his own forehead where I'm currently wearing a neon sign that says *Bianca Barclay Was Here.*

"No good deed goes unpunished," I reply, and I walk out of the room before he can make any further attempts to commiserate.

Outside, it's beginning to pour. Typically, I'm not one to try to control public perception, but I take a less traveled path back to my room. I don't want people to know Bianca bested me before I have a plan to even the score.

I'm weighing my options between an insect infestation in her room and a horse head shipped to her dorm when the scraping of stone from high above catches my attention. It's a gargoyle— slightly on the nose as far as decoration goes—but at the moment I'm more concerned with the fact that it seems to be scraping toward the edge of its perch.

And the fact that I'm directly below it.

There's little time to act, and while quick decision-making is typically my forte, I find myself tangled up in the knots of my previous defeat. I experience a moment of self-doubt. And that's enough to snuff me out like a candle. The last thing I consciously think is that the impact is coming from the wrong direction, and then everything goes dark.

The next thing I know, I'm awakening in the infirmary with an awful pain radiating through my head. I've been taught to weather extremes. It's nothing I can't handle. And yet I can't help but wonder how I survived at all.

"Welcome back," says a slightly raspy voice from somewhere to my left.

I sit up quickly, aware that my prone position leaves me at a disadvantage.

"The nurse said you don't have a concussion," the voice continues. "But you probably have a hell of a bump, huh?"

Beside me is a boy. Tall, thin, long hair pulled back. He has a delicate bone structure and sympathetic eyes that look a little haunted—though perhaps performatively so.

"The last thing I remember is walking outside, feeling a mixture of pity, rage, and self-disgust," I say, more to myself than my companion, whom I've already profiled. Not a threat or an ally. "I don't think I've ever felt exactly that cocktail of emotions before."

"Losing to Bianca has that effect on people, I think."

I refuse to acknowledge that my fencing defeat is already school-wide knowledge, but the rest of my memory of the incident is returning to me, and my curiosity is piqued. I turn to look the boy in the eye, hoping to unsettle him into telling the truth.

"When I looked up and saw that gargoyle coming down, I thought, 'At least I'll have an imaginative death.' But the force of the impact came from the wrong direction, which means *you* tackled me out of the way. Why?"

He appears amused by the question. As if people do unselfish things more than 2 percent of the time on average. "Call it instinct."

"I didn't want to be rescued," I say, irritated by his nonchalance and the throbbing in my temples.

"So I should have just let that thing smash all your bones?"

"I was taking care of it." I acknowledge this as a lie. In fact, I remember having distinctly failed to react in a timely fashion, which had contributed to my feelings of self-loathing. "I'm quite used to saving myself."

The boy has the nerve to scoff. "Good to see you haven't changed," he says unnervingly. "If it makes you feel any better, let's just say I returned the favor."

At these words, I'm forced to examine him again. There's nothing familiar, and I pride myself on maintaining an accurate catalogue of names and faces.

"Xavier Thorpe?" he supplies. This does ring a bell, but only from Enid's insipid social-hierarchy speech. I note with mild interest that this is the boy who mysteriously ended his relationship with Bianca Barclay, and then consider bloodletting to rid myself of the impulse to care.

"What happened?" I ask.

"Puberty, I guess?" he replies. "Last time we met, I was about two feet shorter. Cute little chubby cheeks."

"I mean, what happened the last time we met," I clarify.

Xavier leans back in his visitor's chair, as if reliving the memory. I wish, not for the first time, that I could simply read minds. Much more useful than my mother's visions, and it would save so much obnoxious chitchat.

"It was my godmother's funeral," he says. "She was friends with your grandmother. We were ten. We got bored. Decided to play hide-and-seek. *I* had the inspired idea to hide in her casket and the top got stuck on the way to the crematorium."

At last, I remember. The funeral. I'd begged my mother to let me come. I loved the scent of a decaying rose wreath. The grating sounds of grief, like music. The peaceful presence of death so close.

"I heard muffled screams," I say as I recall the details. "I just figured your godmother had cheated death and was trying to claw her way out." I leave out that this was one of my most cherished funereal fantasies, and one I've yet to cross off my list.

Xavier smiles. In it, I see a bit of that round-faced boy. I've always had a soft spot for the underdog. "Well, either way, you hit the big red button and saved me from being flame-broiled. So now we're even."

I don't tell him, but this does actually make me feel slightly less humiliated.

Once I'm finally released from the clutches of the school nurse, I make my way back to my dormitory, delighted to find Enid out and the room deserted. I'm behind two days on my writing, and the familiar clacking of my typewriter soothes me.

I'm deep in this installment of girl detective Viper de la

Muerte's story when I catch a whiff of something familiar. A smell that should be nowhere near Nevermore Academy, because it belongs back at home.

Following my nose, I tiptoe over to the bed, ripping off the quilt dramatically to reveal a severed hand, which cowers predictably in fear as I stand over it, triumphant for the first time today.

The hand in question bolts, making for the iron bed frame, clinging on with three desperate, traitorous fingers. But I've caught bigger rats, and soon this one is clutched in my own hands, trembling in a way I know denotes pleading.

"Hello, *Thing*," I say conversationally. "Did you think my highly trained olfactory sense wouldn't catch the whiff of neroli and bergamot in your favorite hand lotion?"

He struggles, as if I wasn't already overpowering him like he was a toddler in a pram. I tighten my grip.

"I could do this all day," I warn, slamming him down onto my desk. "Surrender?"

Thing taps three times, the signal. I let him up, but I keep my eyes on him. He's a squirrelly one. Presumably that's why he's here.

"Mother and Father sent you to spy on me, didn't they?"

He declines frantically. Protecting them even now, in the hour of his defeat.

"I'm not above breaking a few fingers," I threaten.

Thing begins signing as quickly as he can. I get as far as the word *worried* before I roll my eyes.

"Oh, Thing, you poor, naive appendage. My parents aren't *worried* about me. They're evil puppeteers who want to pull my strings even from afar."

He doesn't sign anything more, but I can tell by his posture that he disagrees. It doesn't matter. He can underestimate me along with them. They'll all be sorry in the end, but I won't be undermined. I seize my desk lamp and turn it on him.

"The way I see it, you have two options," I tell him before pulling open the top desk drawer. It's shallow. Sturdy. Lockable. "Option one, I put you in here for the rest of the semester, and you go mad trying to claw your way out. Ruining your nails. And your smooth, supple skin. We both know how vain you are."

He trembles, and I know he's picturing cuticle damage. Wrinkles. Sagging knuckle skin.

"Option two," I offer magnanimously. "You pledge your undying loyalty to me."

Instantly, he drops to his middle and pointer finger in an unmistakable kneel. The perpetual chessboard in my mind reorients, a new piece beside the queen on the board. My petty loss to Bianca today suddenly seems trivial. The unsettling encounter with Xavier even more so. I meant what I said to Principal Weems during our first meeting. This school could never hold me.

"Our first order of business," I say to Thing. "Escape this teenage purgatory."

Thing begins to sign in response, and I scoff, rolling my eyes.

"Of *course* I have a plan," I say as all its different elements start to become clear in my mind's eye, connections forming, possible futures shifting and settling. "And it begins now."

CHAPTER FOUR

For my entire life so far, I've avoided being truly psychoanalyzed. As I'm sure you can imagine, it hasn't been easy. Someone with my aesthetic and sensibilities seems easy fodder for the bottom-feeders of this profession.

Typically, the plan is simple and effective. Control the narrative from the outset. Prey on the obvious wounds they offer up along with the introductory small talk. Shock and awe so they're too busy reacting defensively to see that you're blocking their attempts to dredge up some petty childhood trauma to earn their bloated paycheck.

This time, things will need to be slightly different. I can't imagine someone whose client list is filled with Nevermore students would be as easy to spook as the guidance counselors I've tried it on in the past. I can't count on her leaving the room screaming, so I'll have to do the leaving part myself.

Dr. Kinbott's office is your classic quirky-neutral space. Probably put together by some office designer. I wonder if these "personal touches" are even personal to her or just things to prompt comment.

"So, Wednesday," she says, coming in and closing the door behind her. "I read the notes from your school counselor."

"Mrs. Bronstein," I offer. "She had a nervous breakdown after our last session. Had to take a six-month sabbatical."

Dr. Kinbott appears unfazed by this. She gestures for me to sit, and I do. If only to lure her into a false sense of security. It's part of phase one. "How did you feel about that?" she asks.

Really reinventing the wheel here, I think. "Vindicated," I say. "But it's not like someone who crochets for a hobby is really a worthy adversary."

She sits down across from me. Blond, thin, dressed in business comfortable. Pretty, but her stare is a little too intense.

"Well, Wednesday, I hope you don't think of *me* as your adversary," she says. "I hope we can forge a relationship built on trust! And mutual respect!"

I scoff. As if I could ever respect someone who coordinates her watch band and loafers.

"This is a safe space, Wednesday," she enthuses. "A sanctuary where we can discuss anything! What you're thinking, feeling, your views on the world, your personal philosophy!" She smiles at me after this, as if she's offered me a real treat.

"That's easy," I tell her. "I *think* this is a waste of time. *The world is a place that must be endured.* And my *personal philosophy* is kill or be killed."

To my extreme annoyance, her eyes light up at this. "Yes, for instance, when someone bullies your brother—your response is to dump piranha in the pool."

How dare she. I'm well aware that my proclivity to protect Pugsley and the other sweaty, inept misfits who remind me of him is my one identifiable weakness. But to bring it up in the first five minutes is bad form, even for a shrink.

"The point I'm trying to make is that you assaulted a boy," she says, "and showed no remorse for your actions. That's why you're here. Because I believe you have deeper feelings than the judge understands. That maybe you're hiding them. From the world. From yourself."

This assessment makes my skin crawl. "He was a vicious, stupid bully," I say. "If you're wondering about my hidden emotions on the subject, allow me to enlighten you. He lost a testicle. I'm disappointed he didn't lose both. It would have been a favor to the world. People like *Dalton* shouldn't procreate. Now I've answered all your questions." I get to my feet.

"We're not done yet," Dr. Kinbott says. There's a thread of steel in her voice that makes me weary. This is going to be harder than I thought.

I sit back down, mentally diagramming a new approach.

"Therapy is a valuable tool to help you understand yourself," she says, back to her kindergarten teacher voice again. "It can help you build the life you want."

"I know the life I want," I say, shaking my head.

"Then tell me about it," she offers, leaning forward. Smiling again. "Everything said in these sessions is strictly confidential. Maybe your plans involve becoming an author? I was sent your manuscripts as part of your evaluation. Do you want to tell me about them? About Viper de la Muerte?"

The intrusion of this stranger knowing about my books, about Viper, is enough to make me fast-track my plan. I give her the bullet points as I look for the exit.

"What about the relationship between Viper and her mother? Dominica? Maybe that would be a good place to start."

"Maybe it would," I say with a smirk. "But would you mind if I use the powder room first?"

In the baby-blue-wallpapered room, I open my bag.

"Nail file," I tell Thing, who passes it to me obediently. I get the window open, near-silently, and squeeze through it onto the roof. By the time Dr. Kinbott calls out to see if I'm okay, I'm already shimmying down the drainpipe to the sidewalk. I will Morticia to stay upstairs with the good doctor. Carrying her around has never done me any good.

I know for a fact Principal Weems is waiting for me out front. She offered to take me for *hot chocolate* after my session. The only reason someone of her pay grade would be personally escorting me to therapy is to prevent an escape attempt. Even *she* wouldn't expect me to get out within eight minutes, though. That gives me a head start—if only a small one.

Luckily, Jericho is the size of a postage stamp. I see the dinky little café she mentioned just up ahead. The Weathervane. I'll get a jolt of caffeine and get some townie to call me a taxi. It doesn't even matter where it takes me at this point.

Crossing the street, lost in my plans, I collide with a farmer carrying a box of apples.

It comes on immediately. Just like it did with Pugsley in the locker. Suddenly, I'm not in my body anymore. I'm somewhere else. Seeing something I didn't ask to see. This time it's the apples, scattered along the side of the road. The farmer's truck is wrecked. His neck is bent at a nauseating angle.

Before I can see any other details, it's over. The farmer in question, with his vertebrae neatly stacked, is staring at me like I've just confirmed every one of his worst suspicions about Nevermore students simply by stumbling into his arm.

You're going to die, I think about telling him.

"Who let you out?" he rasps. "You goddamn weirdo."

I walk away without saying a word.

The bell over the café door rings as I open it, and immediately three pairs of eyes are on me. As predicted, there's a townie behind the counter.

To test him, I stare over the espresso machine until he notices me. He nearly leaps out of his skin when he does, but he turns to face me afterward. *He'll do,* I think. For phase two, anyway.

"I need a quad over ice," I say. "It's an emergency."

Seemingly recovered, he gestures to the massive machine belching steam between us. "Sorry, the espresso machine is having a seizure. Can't do a quad until it's fixed."

"What's wrong with it?" I ask, already cataloguing the parts and the location of the steam emission.

"It's a temperamental beast with a mind of its own," the boy says. "Not to mention the instructions are in Italian."

He watches me slip behind the counter to stand with him. As if a counter that lifts is really so difficult to operate in a hurry. "I need a tri-wing screwdriver and a four-millimeter Allen wrench," I say to him, already pulling off the front to access the machinery inside.

The boy only gapes. Typical.

"Here's the deal," I say slowly. "I'm going to fix your coffee machine. Then you're going to make my coffee and call me a taxi."

He shakes his head, but at least he fetches the tools. "No taxis in Jericho," he says. "Try Uber."

I wave him away. "I don't have a phone. I refuse to allow our despotic tech overlords to mine me for profit. What about trains?"

"Station in Burlington, it's about a half hour away," he replies.

Bingo. The problem with the machine is easy enough to fix. I tinker around more than I need to, just to make it look like I'm really doing him a favor. People don't value efficiency as much as they should. Especially when it comes in diminutive packages with pigtails.

"Valve issue," I say finally. "It's the same one my steam-powered guillotine had. My poor dolls were doomed to partial decapitation until I figured it out."

The steam stops. The mention of decapitated dolls doesn't seem to faze the boy, who shakes his head in gratitude. "Usually the kids from Nevermore don't like to get their hands dirty. I'm Tyler, by the way."

"Wednesday."

"How about I give you a ride to the train station to show my appreciation. I get off in an hour."

My attempt to bribe Townie Tyler to leave work early—before Weems can find me in this very predictable location—gets me absolutely nowhere. I'm inconvenienced, but the tiniest bit impressed by his spine. This is rare enough in adolescent males that it's worthy of note.

I sit with my coffee in a booth by the window. I'm so attuned to the possibility of Weems appearing that I barely notice the strangely aggressive Amish boys who have surrounded my table.

"What's a Nevermore freak doing out in the wild?" one of them asks. "This is our booth."

It's clear they're trying to intimidate me, but I can't get past the costumes. Black pants, shirts with wide, starched collars. Flat-topped captain hats. "Why are you dressed like religious fanatics?" I know I'll likely regret taking the bait, but I have time to kill anyway.

"We're pilgrims," one of them says, and I shrug as if to indicate I see little difference between the two designations.

"We work at Pilgrim World," another says, flipping over the café menu to show me an advertisement for the establishment. People in similar pilgrim outfits, smiling broadly in front of shabby, colonial frontier–themed storefronts. It's local ad quality. The photos are grainy, the smiles forced.

"Wow," I say, perusing it carefully. "It takes a special kind of stupid to devote an entire theme park to zealots responsible for mass genocide." I say it loud enough to make sure they all hear me. Like I said, I've got time to kill. And if these nitwits aren't harassing me, they might move on to someone less capable.

"Hey!" the third one shouts. "My dad *owns* Pilgrim World! Who are you calling stupid?"

"If the buckled shoe fits," I intone; then I get to my feet, sensing that trading verbal barbs isn't all these three are after. And to be honest, after my fencing failure with Bianca, I wouldn't mind besting someone for a change.

"So, tell me, freak," Pilgrim World Junior says, his face close to mine. "You ever been with a normie?"

Ignoring the repellant implication of his words, I maintain his gaze. His fear is tangy in the air. He's only putting on this show for his little friends, who are standing behind me just in case I pull out a magic wand and turn them into frogs.

"Never found one who could handle me," I reply. Then I step forward, right into his personal bubble. "Boo."

This is all it takes for the one behind me to lunge for my arm. I close my eyes briefly, find my center; then I use his own momentum to fling him past me onto the floor without even looking at him. The second one charges in. I'm seeing them all in slow motion now, plenty of time to react. No need to use my own force when your opponent makes theirs so easy to weaponize.

When the second one hits the floor, I decide to have a little fun. I mean, I'm not actually a pacifist, after all. The spin kick hits the third one in the chin. Down before he can even deliver his own clumsy attack.

Several of the gathered patrons murmur worriedly. Most stare at us in shock. This is probably the most entertainment they've had in years, if Pilgrim World is any indication.

I smirk when I see Tyler standing a few feet off, his hands outstretched like he hoped I'd need rescuing. "Don't worry," I tell him. "Steam-powered doll guillotine wasn't my only childhood weapon."

"Apparently not," he mutters.

I'm about to parlay this little scene into an earlier ride to the train when a complication steps through the door in the form of Jericho's sheriff.

"Dad?" Tyler says, and my eyes dart between them. *A sheriff's son,* I think. The plot thickens.

"What the hell's going on in here, Tyler?" his father asks. This time, I think it wise to allow Tyler to jump to my defense.

"They were harassing a customer," he says, gesturing at the groaning and prone pilgrims littering the café's floor. "She put them in their place."

Usually, I try to avoid the eyes of law enforcement at any cost, but I don't have much choice but to let the sheriff appraise me. When he speaks, he speaks to Tyler as if I'm not even in the room. "This little thing took down three boys?"

A second complication follows the sheriff through the door.

Principal Weems is flushed, her hair windswept. I assume the real relief in her face is tied directly to the purse strings of the Nevermore board. "Apologies, Sheriff," she says breezily. "This one slipped away from me. Come on, Miss Addams. Time to go."

I give Tyler a *maybe in another life* look as I prepare to be carted back to the madhouse. But the sheriff stops us.

"Did she say Addams?" he asks. *Now* he can see me. "Don't tell me Gomez Addams is your father."

He asked me not to tell him, so I don't. I have the right to remain silent, after all.

"That man belongs behind bars for murder," the sheriff says accusingly. "I'm guessing the apple doesn't fall far from the tree. I'll be keeping my eye on you."

I glare at him, another diatribe ready to fly, but damn Principal Weems and her superior strength have me out the door before I can say a word.

In the sleek black SUV, my esteemed principal-slash-chauffeur is laying into me about keeping a low profile with local law enforcement.

I interrupt, remembering she was at school with my parents. "What did he mean?" I ask. "About my father?"

"I have no idea," she says—though I don't know if I believe her. "But a word of advice?"

Raising one eyebrow, I wait for this life-changing tidbit to land.

"Stop making enemies and start making a few friends. You're going to need them."

Before she can say more, I see a familiar truck that has rolled onto its side on the road. There are apples spilled across the lanes. The farmer in front of me. His sour breath in my face. *Goddamn weirdo.*

"I hope the driver's okay," Weems says, slowing down as we pass.

"He's dead," I say without thinking. "Broke his neck." I reach surreptitiously to touch the obsidian talisman my mother gave me. The one I've been hiding beneath my shirt.

"How can you tell from this angle?" Weems asks.

But I don't reply. I've already said too much.

CHAPTER FIVE

Back at the dorm, I wrestle my cello outside. As I play, I try to soothe myself to exorcise the feeling that the visions always conjure in me. The feeling that I'm unlike anyone else in the world. That I'm destined to move through it without a single person ever understanding me.

I give myself one playthrough of an orchestral arrangement of "Paint It Black" to wallow; then it's back to business.

Little do I know, as I'm pouring all my inane, pedestrian loneliness into my instrument, I've already begun to make waves in the little community of Jericho. Already tied myself to more than one player in the grand mystery unfolding without my awareness.

I don't see Rowan Laslow descending into a secret library beneath the school as I play. Pulling a book from the shelf with the powers he believes make him an Outcast here. I don't see him opening the book to a drawing of a girl in a striped shirt and a black skirt, standing before a blazing fire. A girl that looks suspiciously like me—thin, deathly pale, pointed features, and dark brows. Dirty-blond hair in two distinctive braids . . .

During the first crescendo, I don't see Tyler Galpin, town barista and sheriff's son, digging through his father's file stash by flashlight. Pulling out a file with my last name on the tab.

During my Bartók pizzicato, which is excellently executed if I do say so myself, I don't see the good sheriff himself. Driven to drink. Approaching a bulletin board in his office, whose contents I'll become quite familiar with in the coming weeks. It's a series of news stories and photos of Jericho residents and visitors dead in alleged animal attacks. . . .

As my music drifts through the Nevermore campus, I won't see it catch the attention of Xavier Thorpe, Principal Weems, and Ms. Thornhill, but they'll all be moved by it too. Just further proof that most people's approach to human communication is flawed to the extreme. That's what art is for.

Thing appears on the top of my music stand to turn the final page of my sheet music. I end on a confident note that might have moved my early instructors to tears. But without the knowledge of the plot deepening at Nevermore, I feel dissatisfied. My instincts are telling me things I don't yet have the evidence to support.

Feel better? Thing signs.

"No, I don't really feel better. There's just something *wrong* about this place. And not just that it's a school," I insist.

Before I can continue to connect the dots, the window opens behind me. I'll never, in a million years, admit I'm glad to see Enid—who looks like she's trying to win a *how many contrasting colors can one person wear at a time* contest.

"How the hell did you get that oversized violin out here?" she asks. I can tell she's trying to hold on to her prickliness from our earlier skirmish, but I'm exhausted. And frankly, I have bigger problems now. Problems that may benefit from an additional ally.

"I had an extra hand," I say, and Thing waves to Enid.

I'm glad not to have underestimated Enid, who steps closer after noticing him. "Whoa," she says. "Where's the rest of him?"

Smiling, I remember asking this very same question of my parents the moment I understood that Thing was a hand, much like my hands, which did not—disappointingly enough—come detached from my wrists.

"It's one of the great Addams family mysteries," I tell her. I'm about to segue into my request for assistance when I hear the unmistakable sound of teen werewolves frolicking outside the dorm. Up in the sky, the ever-present clouds part to reveal a full moon, heavy and low in the sky.

Enid sighs, but for once she doesn't immediately begin to speak.

"Why aren't you wolfing out?" I ask. I'm curious what could have this popular, bubbly girl feeling so morose.

She takes a long time to answer. Also uncharacteristic. "Because I can't," she finally says, pulling out the multicolored claws she's so proud of and flicking them like a switchblade. "That's all I've got."

Enid sighs, staring out at the full moon, listening to the howls of her peers. I have the strange thought that we have something in common tonight: we're both separated from society by our erratically manifesting powers.

"My mom says some wolves are late bloomers," she goes on. "But I've been to the best Lycanologist—I had to fly to Milwaukee, would you believe it?" She smirks, a sad little thing. Clearly trying to cover up the depth of her despair. "She said there's a chance I may never . . . you know."

It's not something I've tried for a long time, but I do my best to picture how Enid must be feeling at the idea of failing to achieve her in-group status. The experience isn't pleasant, and it also doesn't help me decipher her wrinkled brow any better. For at least the twentieth time in my life, I swear off empathy.

"What happens if you don't?" I ask instead.

"I'd become a lone wolf," Enid says, looking longingly at the full moon.

"Sounds perfect," I reply. I'm thinking of my over-involved family. If I could get out of my burgeoning visions and lose all that pressure, I'd throw a party. A subdued affair. Organ music, potentially a saw.

"Are you kidding me?" Enid says, clearly upset. "My life would be over. No family pack. No prospect of finding a mate . . . I could die alone."

"We all die alone, Enid." This comes out more harshly than I mean it to, and I know I'm speaking to myself as much as to her.

To my surprise and horror, Enid begins to cry. "You know, you really suck at cheering people up," she says.

I'm struck by the dual desire to flee as far as I can from this place and to . . . comfort her? Somehow? Even though that would require a skill set I never bothered to acquire and am deeply unlikely to learn in the ten seconds I estimate are remaining before such a gesture becomes inappropriate.

Enid huffs, wiping her eyes. "What? Haven't you ever cried before? Or are you above that too?"

The memory of the last time I cried is easily accessible—I keep all my traumas close for safekeeping. Normally, I would make an off-putting, morbid comment and storm away. But Enid has been vulnerable with me tonight. Perhaps it wouldn't be so awful to return the favor.

"I was six years old," I begin. "The week after Halloween. I took my pet scorpion, Nero, out for a stroll. We were ambushed." I wait for Enid to recoil, or to denigrate my choice of pet. But to my surprise she does neither, so I continue.

I tell her about the boys who called me a freak as I promenaded through town. Held me against the wall of a storefront and made me watch as they ran over my precious Nero again and again with their bicycle tires.

"It was snowing when I buried what was left of him," I say quietly, and for a moment I'm six years old again. Sitting before Nero's grave in the Addams family cemetery. "I cried my little black heart out."

At this moment, with the memory of Little Wednesday and her face streaked with tears, I lock my self-pity up for good. It's cathartic to remember the solemn vow she made that day, and I share it with Enid now.

"Tears don't fix anything," I say. "So I swore never to cry again."

Out on the Nevermore grounds, laughter turns to snarling and howls. Enid looks at me, and I don't see the judgment or distaste most people view me with. "Your secret's safe with me," she says. "I still think you're weird as shit, though."

I look away from her, feeling the moment of vulnerability close between us with distinct relief. "The feeling is incredibly mutual."

She's no longer crying, so I decide this is the right time to make my request.

"How would you like your single room back?" I ask her, relieved again when her eyebrows rise with apparent interest. "You just need to show me how to use your computer."

When Tyler Galpin picks up my video call and appears on Enid's computer screen, I'm forced to admit that two allies are significantly more effective than one. Especially when one of them has a humanoid form and can communicate verbally.

"Uh . . . hi," he says, clearly shaken. It's understandable. While I was sharing the grisly details of Nero's demise with Enid, Thing had found the Galpins' house and let himself in. I imagine having a disembodied hand appear at one's window to arrange a last-minute video call might make one a bit queasy if they're not accustomed to it.

"That's Thing," I say by way of explanation. He gives me a wave from what looks to be Tyler's bedroom.

"Is he, like, your pet?" I can almost hear the gesture Thing must be performing in the background. One that only requires a single centrally located digit.

"He's sensitive," I say when Tyler's look confirms my suspicion. "Are you still willing to help me escape?"

"What happened to resisting our despotic tech overlords?" he asks.

I shrug. "Desperate times. So? What do you think? This weekend. The Harvest Festival. Attendance is mandatory; it'll make for the perfect cover. If you're willing to drive me to the train station, I can make it worth your while."

I can see Tyler beginning to hesitate, but he soon makes up his mind. I find that I like that about him. "I'm in," he says. "And . . . no charge. Consider it a freebie."

My hackles are up immediately. No one does anything for nothing. It's not how human nature works. People who are up-front about what they want can be trusted, but I find those who conceal the cost of their assistance are often charging a much higher fee.

"Why?" I ask.

He looks a little wistful for a moment. I mentally take back what I said about liking him. Wistfulness is not a good quality in an ally. "Because I wish I was going with you," he admits. "At least one of us is getting out of this hellhole town."

CHAPTER SIX

The Harvest Festival is supposed to be a chance for the residents of Jericho and the Nevermore students to mingle. Build connections. Smooth tensions. But it's clear right away where the fault lines are, even amid the kitschy pumpkin décor, the string lights glowing in the darkness. I can tell they're ripe for rupture.

Enid stands beside me as we look out for Tyler down the avenue filled with carnival games. I spot him at last, standing beside his father's police car, engaged in some sort of parental disagreement. From the few words I can overhear, it's about me.

"Are you sure you can trust this normie?" Enid asks skeptically.

"I trust that I can handle myself," I say. But something about that sheriff really irks me. And it's not the fact that he insulted my father. Not exclusively, anyway.

"Well," Enid says with a sigh. "Good luck and safe travels."

She extends her arms in an attempt to embrace me. It's all I can do to not hiss at her.

"Still not a hugger," she says, almost affectionately. "Got it."

As she's leaving, I get my first jump scare of the evening. Weems is sitting at a table just a few yards away, and she's staring right at me with an expression that says she's not going to take her eye off me for the rest of the evening.

I was planning to rendezvous with Tyler as soon as possible, but instead I smile (really more of a grimace) at Weems and turn toward the games. Maybe if she sees me acting like a normal carnival-goer she'll take her eye off the ball. That will be my time to strike.

Of course, being observed never happens in a vacuum. No sooner have I settled myself at a dart-throwing, balloon-popping game than Xavier Thorpe approaches me.

"You should know I'm waiting for someone," I say to preempt whatever remark he was planning to lead with.

"Oh yeah?" he asks casually. "Who's the lucky guy?"

I level a stony glare at him.

"Or girl," he amends.

"What does it matter to you?" This can't be more shared nostalgia over a forgettable experience in our prepubescence, so what does Xavier want from me? And why is his timing so abysmal?

He's about to answer when Tyler approaches, clearly mistaking my relief at the excuse to end my conversation with Xavier as enthusiasm to see him. He smiles. Xavier melts off into the distance—

probably to brood at some other vaguely female-shaped figure.

"So, what's the plan?" Tyler asks.

"I've got to lose Weems," I say, gesturing to where she's pointedly eating a hamburger in my direction. As if she doesn't have hundreds of other students to manage tonight. "Meet me behind the parking lot when the fireworks start."

Bribing the dart booth guy to lure Weems into playing an insipid carnival game proves easy and effective. I'm early to meet Tyler, but he surprises me by being there already. Waiting for me.

"Hey," he says as I approach. "Before we leave . . . I wanted you to have this." He hands me a manila file folder stamped with the Jericho Police Department logo. "It's your dad's file from when he was at Nevermore. I think it's the reason my dad hates him."

I take the file, which will prove useful, but the true mystery is the boy handing it to me. I try again to understand his motivation. Why would he put himself at risk to give this to me when he barely knows me? I've given him no reason to offer his loyalty.

"You okay?" he asks.

"Yes," I reply, peering into his eyes again as if the secret to his goodwill is written there. "I'm . . . not used to people engaging with me. Most of them see me coming and cross the street."

"You don't scare me," he says, holding my gaze. There's something there, behind his eyes. Most people are so easy to read, but Tyler Galpin is a puzzle. I can't figure out what he's thinking, and I do hate an unsolved mystery . . .

But there's no time. I snap his metaphorical case file shut in my head. "My train leaves in an hour," I say. "We're burning moonlight."

Unfortunately, Weems's obsession and Tyler's befogging motivations appear to be the least of the obstacles in store for me tonight. Just as we reach Tyler's car, we're descended upon by the pilgrims from the the café where we first met. Only tonight, those pilgrims are dressed more practically. Not to mention heavily armed with baseball bats.

My mind is already sliding into combat mode, cataloguing pressure points and weaknesses, imagining them on the ground cursing my name for the second time this week.

Tyler, however, has other plans. He pulls on my sleeve, insisting we're better off losing them in the crowd. Much as I hate to back down from a fight, I can't deny he has a point. Three of them will be difficult to defang without drawing attention, and a grudge match with violent townies is far from my main objective tonight.

We make our way through the flashing lights and laughing festivalgoers with the pilgrims close behind. We've almost lost them at the edge of the woods when I collide with an unknown silhouette in my path. I only have a split second before the ache in my temples sets in.

The last thing I feel before I topple is a pair of strong arms catching me on the way down, and then I'm lost to the pull of that other world. The future I can't control.

In terms of visions, this one is clear as mud. An old book with an arcane symbol on the cover. The eye of a beast. A fountain with a corpse floating in it, catching fire in dramatic fashion. A crow caws. The book lands on a tiled floor, emblazoned with a large, white emblem of a blooming flower, as if dropped there.

And then, right at the end, the inciting incident. Rowan's

mouth open in horror as his own blood splatters across his face.

When I come to, Tyler is cradling me in his arms, looking worried. I get to my feet, looking around for the person I collided with. The one who caused the vision. When I see Rowan walking away from the periphery of the crowd, nervous eyes filled with fear, my heart sinks. I've never been able to stop the visions from coming true before, but what if, just this once . . .

I step toward him, planning to warn him, to get him back to school, when he spooks. Looks at me like I'm the scythe and not the sanctuary and takes off running.

Tyler is pulling on my jacket again, reminding me we're running out of time. But here it is again. I find I can't let Rowan die. Not without at least trying to stop the vision from coming true.

"Tyler, stay here." As I take off after Rowan, leaving a bewildered Tyler in my wake, I know I may be dooming my chances of escape. I chase him anyway, out of the festival, into the deep woods, calling his name as he stumbles and gasps his way into the dark.

"Rowan, wait!" I cry when he stops to fumble for his inhaler.

"What do you want?" he cries, refusing to turn around. "Why are you following me?"

I've never tried to explain the visions before. I don't imagine he'll take it well. "I don't have time to explain," I say. "But you're in danger."

The last thing I expect is for Rowan to laugh, but he does as he turns to face me at last.

"I think you've got it backward," he says before flinging out a hand. "You're the one who's in danger." This is how I find out his Outcast ability is telekinesis. It's a truly strange feeling, the pressure wrapping around my waist like a giant invisible hand. Pinning me to the towering oak behind me.

"What are you doing?" I ask him, utterly confused. Of everyone at this school, why would *Rowan* be attacking me?

"Saving everyone from you!" he cries, clearly exerting all his energy to hold me against the tree. "I have to kill you."

Even amid my befuddlement, something clicks into place for me then. "The gargoyle," I say. "That was you?"

He nods. It's always the quiet ones.

A whoosh of air blows my hair off my face. It takes a moment for me to realize Rowan has sent a piece of paper, a page torn from a book, up to my eye level. I struggle to decipher it in the darkness, but it appears to be a drawing of a slender silhouette in black and white stripes, standing before a fire.

"The girl in the picture?" Rowan shouts. "That's you!"

"You want to kill me because of some picture?" I ask, thinking that I should have let Bianca skewer this little runt the first time I saw him.

"My mother drew that picture twenty-five years ago when she was a student at Nevermore," Rowan calls. He's clearly distressed, deeply believing what he's saying. That much is clear. "She was a powerful Seer—she told me all about it before she died."

"Put me down," I say in my most commanding voice.

"No!" he screams, and I know I've made the wrong move. "My mother said it was my *destiny* to stop this girl if she ever came to Nevermore, because she will destroy the school and everyone in it!"

His power surges. The wind whips around us. The pressure slams my head back into the tree and tightens around my throat. If I can't figure out a way to stop him, it'll tear me apart, and

Rowan's psychic mother will get her twenty-five-year-old wish.

I call his name once more, then twice. But it's no use. I close my eyes, and for a moment I'll later deny to my actual grave, I wish I could reach for my mother's pendant . . .

But suddenly, the pressure lessens. I open my eyes to see my assailant's face, a mask of fear, and a hulking silhouette bearing down on him. Bulging eyes glinting in the moonlight. Gray, hairless skin. Fangs. Five-inch, razor-sharp claws. The thing is at least ten feet tall, and it's utterly monstrous.

"Rowan!" I scream once more as the beast attacks. His telekinesis falters and I fall to the base of the tree, where I see the outcome of my vision at last. Rowan's face, twisted in horror and splattered with blood.

By the time I make it to his body, the beast is long gone. Slowly, in the arcane wind still swirling in the clearing, the page that started all this descends, fluttering to land on Rowan's lacerated chest.

The girl. Long hair in two braids. Watching Nevermore burn.

CHAPTER SEVEN

I wake in my dorm room to the sound of my crystal ball ringing. I have no memory of how I got there. The last thing I remember is stumbling out of the woods, having only reluctantly left Rowan's mangled body behind.

Bianca Barclay, I recall vaguely. She was the first person I saw. I asked her to go for help. Most likely I lost consciousness after that. It's not my proudest moment, but the body does strange things to protect itself from trauma. And as much as I've fictionalized death in the past, Rowan's murder was the first time I've ever seen someone torn apart in front of me.

Although hopefully not the last.

"Hello, my little black cloud!" my father says as I wave my hand over the crystal ball to answer the call.

My mother is there, too, of course, pushing him out of the frame. "So tell us, darling," she says. "How was your first week?"

I flash back on all that has happened since I was dropped off on the Nevermore grounds. It feels like so much more than a week has passed. I've narrowly avoided death twice, discovered that my father may be a murderer, learned that I could potentially destroy the school, and was mysteriously saved by a homicidal monster.

"As much as it pains me to admit," I begin, "you were right, Mother. I think I'm going to love it here."

My parents beam. They want details but I can't get them off the crystal fast enough. I need to speak to Weems and the sheriff immediately. Find out what they know already. Offer my firsthand account . . .

"Wednesday," Weems says, alarm on her painted features when I catch her and the sheriff walking into the entrance of the main building. "I'll have to connect with you later. The sheriff and I are on our way to my office to discuss—"

"Rowan's murder," I cut in. "I was there. I saw him die."

The sheriff is already shaking his head. "That girl told us what you said, and we looked all night. But there's no evidence of a murder. No body, no blood, no sign of a struggle. Nothing."

Suddenly, I'm back there. As if it's happening right in front of me again. Rowan, his eyes open in terror. His blood splattering everywhere. No evidence . . . I think. But how can that be?

"Your search party must have left their Seeing Eye dogs at home," I snap. "I saw that monster kill Rowan right in front of me."

The sheriff pauses on the landing of the Nevermore entrance hall stairs. When he looks at me, I see the same suspicion in his eyes from the diner, and I know he's seeing my father in his youth. What I wouldn't give to know what else his recollections are showing him.

"Did you get a good look at this monster thing?" he asks.

Fur, hulking mass, large yellow eyes reflecting the moonlight, strangely intelligent for a brute. "It didn't stick around for a chat," I say. I'm not going to share information if I'm not getting as good in return. This interaction is a transaction, plain and simple.

"Maybe it was one of your classmates," the sheriff says, stepping closer. His eyes are bloodshot. *Grief,* I think. Or self-doubt. Something's eating at him.

"Sheriff, I find that suggestion offensive!" Weems exclaims, escorting us farther up the stairs, breaking this strange staring contest we're engaged in.

"I don't care," Galpin growls. "I've got three other dead bodies in the morgue. Hikers, just ripped apart in the woods."

Flesh tearing. Rowan screaming. Blood splattering.

With us now safely in her office, Weems turns a critical eye on the sheriff. "The mayor says those were bear attacks," she says pointedly.

Galpin finally looks away from me to focus on Weems—she towers over him by at least a foot, but he doesn't look intimidated in the least. "Well," he says, "the mayor and I disagree on that."

I watch like I'm at a tennis match. Weems puffs up to her full height. "Oh, so you automatically assume a Nevermore student is the murderer, though there's no evidence a crime was even committed."

Sheriff Galpin grunts. "I'm sorry, I forgot. You only teach the *good* Outcasts here. Right?"

The moment of tension hangs between them for longer than a beat. It feels thick and storied. I wonder what the history is between these two. Is this just Weems taking Outcast advocacy to the nth degree? Or is there more to it . . . ?

But then, before I can surmise any more, Weems shakes it off. Her countenance settles on coolly professional. "My guess is Rowan ran away. State troopers have put out an alert and I've contacted his family. They haven't heard from him either."

My chest, compressed by telekinesis. Rowan's drawing. His determined, tearful eyes . . .

"Dead people are notoriously bad at returning calls," I say, and the sheriff seems to remember I'm here at last.

"What were *you* doing in the woods with him anyway, Miss Addams?"

"I heard a noise in the forest and went to investigate," I answer promptly. "That's when I stumbled upon the attack." Lying to authority figures has never been a moral qualm of mine. Besides, if Sheriff Galpin thinks I'm an Outcast now, I doubt detailing the neural malfunctions that cause my visions will endear me to him as a reliable source.

"Then what happened?" he asks.

"I left the woods quickly, ran into Bianca Barclay, felt myself becoming faint from shock, and told her to go for help. Next thing I remember, I was waking in my dorm."

"I think Miss Addams is done now," Principal Weems says in

a tone that suggests she's doing me a favor.

"Actually," I interject. "I would like to speak to Sheriff Galpin. Alone."

Weems's eyes narrow dangerously. "I'm not sure I can allow that."

But the sheriff's interest is piqued. "How about I take her down to the station and get a formal statement instead? Come with me, Miss Addams."

I'm about to submit calmly to police escort for the first time in my life and Weems folds like a napkin. "You have five minutes," she says, stepping briskly toward the door. "And everything is off the record." At the door, she homes in on the sheriff with those intimidating, narrowed eyes. "Play nice, or I will call the mayor."

And then she's gone.

I know I need to make the most of my time, so I turn to Galpin immediately. "Someone is trying to cover up Rowan's murder," I blurt out. "It's the only reason to scrub the crime scene."

He looks skeptical to say the least. "As convincing as the opinion of a killer's daughter is, I think I'll leave it to my forensics team. It's been a long night." But he doesn't move to dismiss me, or to leave the room.

"You want to reject my claims, but you can't," I gamble, not letting him break eye contact.

"Why is that?" he asks.

I step closer, lower my voice so he has to lean in to listen. "Because you and I both know there's a monster out there. And that Rowan is its latest victim."

A feeling of power courses through me, electric as the sheriff's expression registers his agreement. I know I have him then. That with his help I can find out what really happened to Rowan. What

the beast is. Why it saved me, and—

"Sheriff?" comes the voice of his deputy as she opens the office door.

"What?" he snaps, still not looking away from me.

"You're gonna want to see this."

The door opens wider, and I can't help but follow his gaze to find *Rowan*. Plaid shirt, hoodie, glasses, an embarrassed smile on his face. He waves, and just like that I've lost the sheriff. Lost my theory. Lost everything but my favorite Edgar Allan Poe quote: *Believe nothing you hear, and half of that you see.*

Poe is Nevermore's most famous alumni.

It's no wonder he became a drug-addled madman.

I'm coming out of Dr. Kinbott's office the next day, ready to purge my tortured brain of her cliché platitudes, when I run into Tyler Galpin as I'm heading for the door.

"Hey," he calls. "Guess you decided to stick around Jericho? I didn't know you see Dr. Kinbott."

I don't bother to stop walking. My head is full of the good doctor telling me that keeping people at arm's distance emotionally stems from a fear of rejection. Revolutionary. The truth is that Tyler is Sheriff Galpin's son. And I just don't want to hear that he thinks I'm as crazy as his father does.

"You should know I'm legally required to be here," I say when he follows me across the street.

"Me too," he replies. Smiling for no earthly reason I can decipher. "Court ordered."

"Look at us," I say, not looking at him. "A couple of teenage tearaways."

He laughs, not taking my very unsubtle hint to leave me alone. "So, when you ran off last night at the Harvest Festival, I wasn't sure what happened. But then I heard . . ." Tyler trails off. He wants me to finish this for him. Admit I was doing it for attention. Prove him right about Outcasts and weirdos and Nevermore.

I whip around to face him at last. If he's going to force this, I'm not going to make it easy on him. "Everyone, including your father, believes I made it all up."

Tyler's cell phone buzzes. Saved by the bell.

"I gotta go," he says. "Time to tame my inner rebel."

I'm turning around, halfway through burning the page that bears his name from my personal history, when he says the last thing I expect to hear: "You know, for the record . . . I believe you."

As much as I loathe to admit it, Tyler's confidence—whatever his reason for offering it—galvanizes me. There's no reason for him to believe me, and yet if my first days at Nevermore Academy have taught me anything, it's that one needs allies to accomplish one's goals.

If Tyler insists on being one of them, perhaps I haven't lost my others, either.

Thing, of course, is eternally pledged to my service on pain of dry patches and hangnails. No need to confirm he's still on my side. Enid, on the other hand, was missing from our room when I awoke this morning. As Nevermore's gossip queen, she'll be essential in making sure I have dirt on all possible suspects—and victims, too, since those seem to be walking and talking and attending meetings with Principal Weems these days.

I find Enid on the grounds, shouting at a group of faux artsy-looking girls reluctantly doing her bidding. Which appears to involve the despoiling of a perfectly good canoe with acrylic paints.

"If Bianca Barclay wins again this year, I will *literally scratch my own eyes out,*" Enid is shrieking as I approach.

"I would pay money to see that," I say.

She whirls around, her smile adorably canine. I can tell she's exercising Herculean efforts not to physically embrace me, for which I am grateful.

"Howdy, roomie," she says. "I'm so glad you decided to stay."

This is the second time today I've been surprised by someone's desire to continue seeing me socially. But it doesn't mean she believes me. And that's the most important thing as far as allies go.

"So, why the change of heart?" Enid asks, turning to walk me past her art lackeys.

"I refuse to play the role of *pawn* in someone else's corrupt game," I say, thinking of Sheriff Galpin's hangdog face. The suspicion in his eyes. The wound I've yet to uncover.

"You mean . . . Rowan?" Enid asks. Her expression looks pitying. My third least favorite emotion.

"I witnessed his murder, Enid." *Twice.*

She smiles. Pity, again. "It's just . . . we all saw him this morning. Very much, like, *not* dead?"

My fists clench in frustration at the reminder. My instincts, finely honed over years of peering into the darkest underbelly of society, scream that Rowan was ripped apart before my eyes last night. I have the mild PTSD aftershocks to prove it.

So the question is, has something paranormal happened to resurrect Rowan—or are my powers getting out of hand?

"I know," I finally admit. "I saw him too. But I know there's more to the story. Even if it's just that I'm losing my mind—and having far less fun than I always imagined in the process."

Enid smiles again. I can tell she wants to help me, even if she can't overcome her disbelief yet. That still qualifies her as an ally, I suppose.

"You know everyone who's anyone around here," I say, now that I'm mostly convinced that she's on my side. "What's Rowan's story?"

"Other than being a weird loner," she says, "he's Xavier Thorpe's roommate. You know, if you had a cell phone, you could text and ask him. . . ."

I refuse to do the mental gymnastics required to decipher this nonsense, but it doesn't take long before Enid fills the silence. "Yoko! Come on! Flare those whiskers! The Poe Cup droops for no one!"

"What is the Poe Cup anyway?" I ask. I've been told it's socially appropriate to feign interest in the hobbies of your social contemporaries. Especially when they've just given you a potentially vital lead.

"Only my entire reason for living right now!" Enid answers with enthusiasm. "It's part canoe race, part foot chase. No rules. All the dorms pick an Edgar Allan Poe story for inspiration."

I nod vaguely at the obvious reference to "The Black Cat," which Enid clearly mistakes for curiosity about the process of painting a boat socially.

"You could grab a brush," she offers. "Ms. Thornhill ordered us pizza. Want to take a stab at being social?"

Dr. Kinbott's words from earlier resurface then. My alleged fear of rejection. But there's a difference between fearing rejection and having better things to do. The mystery of Rowan's unmurdering is far more important than social bonding. Especially when Enid's allyship is all but assured already.

"I do like stabbing," I offer. "The social part, not so much."

"No worries," she replies. "Just as long as you're lakeside cheering us to victory on race day!"

I do my best to convey with my facial expression alone how extremely unlikely my participation in said event is, but I walk away with the sneaking suspicion that Enid's hope will be harder to douse than I thought.

For some reason, I don't immediately go find Xavier. It could just be that he's my only lead. If I strike out, I'll be back to square one.

Back in our dorm, I take out the drawing Rowan had shown me before dying and study it again. There's nothing more than there was last night. A girl who looks suspiciously like me, standing in front of a wall of flame. But when I hold it up to my desk light on a whim, I find something. A symbol, barely embossed into the corner.

There's only one person who can explain this to me. And what kind of detective would I be if I ignored my best lead because he *happens* to have attempted to murder me less than twenty-four hours ago.

When I don't find Rowan on the quad, in the fencing practice hall, or in the library, I make my second visit of the day to Weems's office. She doesn't seem upset when I burst open the door. In fact, she doesn't even pause whatever letter she's writing.

"I need to speak with Rowan," I say in my most authoritative tone. "I can't find him."

Weems, her eyes on her letter, delivers the following devastating blow in an utterly casual tone. "It won't be possible, I'm afraid. He's been expelled."

"For what?" I ask, disbelieving. How could they *expel* my would-be murderer before I even get the chance to question him?

"Never you mind," Weems replies. "He'll be on the first train out this afternoon." She speaks to me as if I'm some disobedient grade school student and not a near-adult who is central to this investigation. At least she looks at me now, appraising. "What *were* you doing in the woods with him?"

I stand up straight. Fold my arms. "I told you already. I heard a noise, and I went to investigate."

She scoffs. The letter she was so intent upon when I walked in is clearly forgotten. "That excuse might have placated the sheriff, but you can't fool me. *You* had a psychic vision, didn't you?"

Of all the avenues of discreditation I've prepared responses for, this was not one of them. I feel myself freeze. Feel my mother's obsidian monstrosity heavy around my neck. I already know it's too late to deny it. That my second of hesitation has spoken for me.

"I realized you might be having them in the car the other day, when you knew that poor farmer had broken his neck."

You goddamn weirdo.

"You know, your mother started having visions around your age," she says pointedly. "They were notoriously unreliable and dangerous."

This is news to me, though I try not to let it show. I won't allow Weems to trade on her adolescent relationship with my mother to force some false bond with me. Especially when she's obstructing my attempts to find answers. Justice.

"I remember at first, she thought she might be losing her mind," Weems muses. "Have you spoken to her about them?"

Of course I haven't. The last thing I need is my mother throwing me some abhorrent *coming-of-age* séance, finding another excuse to act like I'm exactly like her. No thank you.

"Ah," she says, responding to my silence again. "It seems the person withholding information here is you."

"May I go now?" I say curtly. Infuriating as this is, I now know there's a ticking clock on any chance I might have to speak to Rowan. To decipher the symbol in the corner of his mother's drawing.

Weems picks up the page she was writing on when I came in, holding it out to me. "Not until you've picked your extracurricular activity," she says brightly. Back in principal mode as easy as that. "I took the liberty of putting together a list of clubs that have openings."

"How thoughtful," I say through gritted teeth. The only reason I stayed in this sham of a school is to investigate a murder. Not to become Susie Social Chair. But I know any insubordination will only limit my scant freedom, and so I take the list.

The moment I'm out of earshot, I open my bag, letting Thing out onto the parquet floor. "Weems is keeping tabs on me, so I need *you* to keep an eye on Rowan. Got me?" Thing salutes and makes his way out the door.

A silver lining for all this is that two of the clubs on the list are run by people I needed to get statements from anyway. At least it won't be a complete waste of time.

CHAPTER EIGHT

Bianca Barclay, of course, leads the school a cappella group. I approach them in the courtyard, where Bianca is holding a literal conductor's baton. She turns to face me, letting the choir sing on, expression nonchalant.

"Weems said you'd be stopping by," she says, looking me up and down. "But after your performance at the Harvest Festival, I think drama might be more your speed."

I don't have time for queen bee barbs. I make straight for her and speak softly. Urgently. "After I passed out, who did you tell? The sheriff?"

Bianca looks at me like I've grown an extra head. "I don't trust normie cops," she says definitively. "I went straight to Weems and let her handle it."

Weems, I think. She didn't mention Bianca came to her. Did she tell the sheriff before I arrived this morning? Or even last night? The two stories don't quite add up—and I often find the overlap is the place where mysteries get solved. I'll just have to keep an eye on them both.

Xavier Thorpe is standing before a row of archery targets, pretending not to look for me when I arrive. The gothic stone edifice of Nevermore makes an imposing figure against the gray sky. The trees are turning for fall, birds flocking from them.

It's beautiful. Take all the other people out of it and I might stay forever.

"Huh," Xavier says. "You actually showed up. Ever shoot a bow and arrow before?"

I give him my most withering look. "Only on live targets."

He doesn't seem fazed. Between him, Tyler, and Enid, I'm going to have to brush up on my macabre one-liners if I expect to intimidate anyone around here.

"Square stance," he says, taking his position at the line with his left foot too far forward. "Load the arrow like this, yellow side out." His grip is too tense. He's overcorrecting. "Three fingers. Pull back." Too far. He won't have enough control. "And let it fly."

His arrow hits one of the outer rings of the target just where I predict it will.

"Any questions?"

I have several scathing archery questions, but not a lot of time, so I focus on what matters. "When's the last time you saw your roommate, Rowan?"

The look he gives me is half mocking, half pity. His hair is pulled back. His jacket fits well. Against the changing leaves, he could be on the front of the Nevermore catalogue—and I don't mean that as a compliment.

"You mean the one who was killed by a monster?"

I count down from ten in my head. Seething anger and weapons are a poor combination. If I do ever kill someone, it'll be in cold blood, not hot.

"The Harvest Festival," he says, when he's apparently satisfied that I'm not going to dignify his attempt at humor with a response. "I haven't talked to him since, but his side of the room was all packed this morning."

I'm not going to tell him about the expulsion. He'll find out soon enough, and I don't want Xavier to get the wrong idea about how fast this information highway travels.

"Rowan's always been a little bit . . . off," he says, taking the bait my silence lays out. "The last couple weeks, though, he's been more erratic. Telekinesis can mess with your mind, you know, but he really started to freak me out."

A few weeks ago, I note. Likely when Rowan found the drawing of the girl and the flames and vowed to enact his dead mother's vendetta. Interesting.

"So, what's the deal with you and Tyler?" Xavier asks as I pick up the second bow, examine it for structural flaws.

I raise an eyebrow in his general direction, which strikes me as a better option than raising the weapon in my hands. I can practically feel Weems watching me from a high window somewhere.

"Oh, I'm sorry," Xavier says. "Are you the only one who gets to ask non-archery-related questions?"

It's not an unfair assessment. And the information he's asking me for is meaningless, so I see no reason to be adversarial. "There is no deal," I clarify. "He was doing me a favor. Driving me out of town." I choose an arrow carefully.

"Yeah, a word of advice? Steer clear. Tyler and his friends are jerks. They can't stand that this school props up their backwoods town."

I'm aiming at the target but am forced to turn to him in surprise. "No need to be an elitist snob," I say evenly; then I grab one of the apples set out for target practice, toss it up, and take the half second it's falling to skewer it right through the middle with my arrow.

Bull's-eye.

Now that my interviews are finished, I suppose I'll actually have to find an extracurricular activity. Obviously Bianca's singing group is out, and Xavier has nothing to teach me about archery *or* life, despite what he may think.

I skip to the end of the list, assuming that whatever Weems thought of as lowest priority will be the thing that suits me best.

Unfortunately, that thing is beekeeping. It takes place about a mile from campus in an overgrown, muddy field. And it's run by a boy even smaller and snifflier than Rowan.

"Are you interested in the ancient art of beekeeping?" the boy asks. It's an attempt to be pompous, I think, but I imagine it's hard for him to be anything but cherubic with those cheeks, that ringleted hair. Those cartoon character eyes.

"Eugene," he says, sticking out a hand. "Eugene Ottinger. Founder and president of the Nevermore Hummers."

"Wednesday Addams," I say, reaching out to shake his hand. I look around, though I'm not really expecting a crowd. "Am I late? Or is it only you?"

There's a tinge of regret on his good-humored little face when he says: "The hive life isn't for everyone. Most kids are afraid of venomous insects." He steps forward, smiling to reveal a retainer that explains the lisp. "Are you willing to feel the sting?"

As I slowly nod, I feel I may have met the only person at Nevermore who isn't a complete fraud in one way or another. Possibly including myself.

I'm outfitted in a beekeeper's suit a few minutes later, making the rounds as Eugene explains the matriarchal society of bees. The way they work together to achieve their goals. It's interesting enough until I see Thing gesturing to me from between two potted flowers.

He gestures that it's urgent, and I know he's found Rowan. Assuming Eugene won't pause for breath for at least another hour, I sneak off the moment his head is turned. I'll make it up to him at the next Hummers' meeting. Assuming I survive that long.

It's a good thing I didn't wait for a convenient stopping point in Eugene's speech, too, because Rowan is already loading his luggage into Ms. Thornhill's garish purple Volkswagen Beetle— which clashes so horribly with those bright red boots she insists on wearing everywhere—when I reach the front of the school, out of breath.

"Rowan!" I call, and he turns. Locking eyes with me for the first time since he held me against a tree and threatened to kill me. I can see his dead, cold eyes as I look into his unmistakably living ones. See the lacerations across his chest. Feel his heartbeat slowing to a stop . . .

"I'm not allowed to speak to anyone," he says.

I scoff. "You had a lot to say when you tried to kill me." Is it my imagination? Or do his eyes widen a fraction of a millimeter when I say it? As if he's . . . surprised. "You told me I was destined to destroy the school, remember? Where did you get that drawing?"

He doesn't get a chance to answer before Ms. Meddling Thornhill approaches. "Wednesday, you shouldn't be here," she chastises.

"Yeah," Rowan says. "Back off, and leave me alone."

He's in the car before I can say another word, but Thing is one step ahead of me. He clings to the bumper of Ms. Thornhill's motorized anachronism. When they speed off, he does too. And now all I can do is wait.

Later that afternoon, Thing relays what he can to me before my class with Ms. Thornhill, but even with his small stature and penchant for espionage, he wasn't able to see it all. He tells me he followed Rowan into the station and then a bathroom with no windows.

He waited outside for Rowan to emerge, but Rowan never did. There were no windows and no other exits. So when Thing went inside to check on Rowan and found his suitcase perched on a toilet, abandoned, it was a frustrating and infuriating dead end.

With my last lead having abandoned me, I lash out at Thing, telling him a lefty wouldn't have let me down. He scuttles off to nurse his wounds while I'm forced to take a seat next to Xavier Thorpe, of all people, and await Thornhill's brilliant instruction on carnivorous plants.

I feel lower than the lowest disgraced former investigator. Rowan is gone, and with him, my last lead. My last reason for being in this stupid school to begin with. If I can't find new evidence and find it soon, I vow to leave Nevermore just as tracklessly as my lost quarry.

The rest of class passes in a blur. Xavier sulks because I called him a snob, Bianca does her best to compete with me intellectually and forces Ms. Thornhill to break it up. It's not even mildly diverting, because all I can really think about is what the *hell* happened to Rowan.

What I don't know, yet, is what Thing *didn't* see in the train station. Rowan, stepping into the bathroom stall. Adjusting his collar. *Shape-shifting* with a small gesture into a middle-aged man with gray hair in an overcoat.

Because Rowan wasn't Rowan at all.

Who was he really? Thing didn't catch that, either, having lost the boy he thought he was looking for. In fact, no one saw the middle-aged man step into a deserted corridor of the train station. No one saw how he twitched his collar again and became Principal Weems.

But, like I said, I won't discover that particular wrinkle in the plot until later—when it's already almost too late.

Thing is nowhere to be seen when I finish Ms. Thornhill's class, so I return to the canoe-painting ground in search of my only other confirmed ally.

"I have to get back to the woods," I say to Enid without

preamble. Blessedly, her pack of artsy handmaidens seem to have decided to attend class for once. "But Weems has been watching me like a vulture circling a carcass."

Enid doesn't look up from her painting. "And you want me to cover so you can return to the scene of a crime . . . that didn't happen?"

"I don't have time to explain it again," I say. "I have beekeeping club this afternoon and I need you as decoy."

Enid pauses on making sure the pupil of her grotesque cat's eye is perfectly round. "Sorry," she says offhandedly. As if this is a matter of minor importance. "Two strikes. I'm busy *and* bees totally creep me out."

I'm just wondering if I miscounted when I considered her my second ally when she looks up at me with a sly expression. "Why don't you ask Thing? Oh, wait. You can't because he's mad at you."

I'm momentarily distracted from my urgency. Why would Thing be upset with me? And why would Enid know before I do? "Why?" I ask. "He's the one who screwed up with Rowan. If anyone deserves to be mad, it's me."

She shrugs. "All I know is that we spent an hour giving each other manis and he really opened up. He feels like you don't respect him as a person."

"Technically he's only a hand," I point out impatiently.

At this point, Enid abandons her brush and her nonchalant pretense at once. "Wednesday! He's your family! He would do anything for you!" She turns her nose up sanctimoniously. "Go apologize to him and I'll *consider* helping you."

This is absurd, but I storm up to our room without another word. If she insists on putting me through this apology theater when I'm not even to blame, fine. As long as I get my decoy.

I find Thing on Enid's bed flipping through a magazine. He doesn't even register my arrival, a sure sign that he's mortally offended. "I snapped at you," I say as he turns the pages listlessly. Lip gloss. Boy band. Airbrushed starlet. "I'll check my tone in the future. Now, chop-chop before all our leads turn cold."

I'm halfway back to the door, expecting him to follow me, when I hear the magazine pages again.

"What is it that you want?" I ask, exasperated by all of this. "Hand cream? Nail buffer? Cuticle scissors? Consider it done."

He taps the space beside him on the bed, inviting me into his confidence. I'm stretched so tightly I'm ready to snap. Take back my apology and hang Enid's help and go back to doing things alone, as I'm accustomed to. But then I think back to what Enid said. That Thing considers me family. That he would do—and had done—whatever he could to help me.

I sit down with a sigh. "I know I'm stubborn," I say. "Single-minded. Obsessive. But those are all traits of great writers."

Thing begins to sign, but I already know where he's going with this.

"Yes, and serial killers," I allow. "What's your point? I have nothing to get off my chest. I'm not submitting to your emotional blackmail."

He drums his fingers against his reading material, and I know I'm not getting out of here without giving him something. This is the trouble with letting people in. Letting them care. They expect you to *share* things. To be vulnerable. It's exhausting.

"Fine," I say.

I pull Rowan's mother's drawing out of my bag and unfold it

in front of Thing. I haven't shown it to anyone yet, nor admitted what I'm about to tell him. If this isn't enough, I swear it's back to being a lone operative.

"When Rowan showed me this, it confirmed my greatest fear. That I'm going to be responsible for something terrible." As obsessed with the dark and macabre as an Addams is encouraged to be, I've never thought of myself as a villain. Only someone who's willing to look into the darkest underbelly of the world to determine the truth.

"I can't let that happen," I tell Thing. "That's why I need to find out the truth."

Sympathy is practically oozing from his pores already. This has gone far enough. I stand up, glaring down at him. "Breathe a word of this, and I will end you."

He salutes, and I feel my armor snap back into place.

CHAPTER NINE

Once Enid is securely—if not comfortably—installed as my beekeeping doppelgänger, I make quickly for the woods. It's a twenty-minute walk, which doesn't give me much time to investigate.

The woods are gloomy, everything dripping with green in the overcast late-afternoon light. They look different in the daytime, I think. Peaceful. Not a place where something obviously sinister transpired last night.

To my surprise, they're not empty. The sheriff is here with his hunting dog, but interestingly without any of his fellow officers. I duck behind a tree to observe him more closely, but the space behind me isn't empty either.

I'm being grabbed before I can react, my mouth covered insultingly, as if I'm the type to scream. I can't turn around, but the arms pinning me to a tall and slender torso don't feel as though they're trying to squeeze me to death.

"Sorry," Tyler whispers in my ear. "Didn't want Elvis to pick up on your scent."

He lets me go the moment the sheriff and his dog have passed. I turn to appraise him, realizing that he's here watching his father and that he looks none too pleased about what he was seeing. Perhaps he was telling the truth about believing me.

I adjust my official ally count to two and a half, pending further investigation.

"Thanks," I say. "What's he doing out here?" I gesture toward the sheriff.

Tyler's expression at this question makes me wonder momentarily what he did to land in court-ordered therapy. It wasn't something I even thought of asking before. "He doesn't tell me shit," he says. "Like, earlier, he just lays into me about therapy. Tells me he's paying for it, so he deserves to know what we talk about. And then when I tell him that I talk about my mom, he just shuts down. Takes the dog, won't tell me where he's going. I'm on my own for dinner again, big surprise."

This is such an overabundance of words and emotions that I'm momentarily stunned into silence. It takes me a moment to process. Tyler's mother is dead. His father is an emotional husk. Emotional husks don't make great single parents.

I'm just trying to think of something comforting to say when he changes the subject, for which I'm immensely grateful. My conversation with Thing earlier was all the emotional allowance I had for this week.

"So, what really happened the other night at the festival?" he asks. "I swear, I won't say anything to my dad."

I look at him again, trying to detect an ulterior motive. I don't immediately sense one, and as is becoming common in my life lately, I feel compelled to reciprocate the trust he showed me by talking about his parents.

Plus, it might be nice if one person knew the truth. Especially someone who's already proven to have access to the sheriff's personal files.

"I thought Rowan was in danger," I say, sidestepping the how and why of it. "Turns out I was wrong. He proceeded to use his telekinesis to try and choke me to death."

Tyler looks shocked, a little nauseated. Just the way I like a boy to look. I continue my search of the woods as he scrambles beside me. "Holy shit," he exclaims. "Why would he do that?"

"No idea," I keep the part about the drawing to myself too. I don't know if confidential information access goes both ways in the Galpin household yet. "That's when the monster came out of the shadows and gutted him."

"Wow," Tyler says, clearly reeling. "So . . . you really saw it? And it didn't try to kill you?"

It interests me that Tyler speaks of the monster as something he already knew existed. Something he hasn't seen but believes is real. This tells me I was right when I bluffed on his father in Weems's office. He *does* know there's a monster. Which makes the fact that he's out here alone all the more suspicious.

"It didn't try to kill me," I confirm, scanning the ground. The trees. Nothing. "It actually *saved* me from Rowan. That's the part I'm trying to figure out. I came out here to find something that can prove he was murdered. And that I haven't lost my mind."

Tyler looks slightly intimidated by this.

"Yet," I add ominously, and then I see something. Glinting on the ground. Something the sheriff and his dog—as well as whoever is trying to keep Rowan's murder quiet—obviously missed.

Rowan's tortoiseshell glasses look up unseeingly from the ivy-covered ground. There's blood on one of the lenses.

"I knew it was a cover-up!" I exclaim, reaching out to grab them.

It comes on the moment I touch them. The woods disappear, the glasses, Tyler, even my own body. The vision shows me Rowan in the past. Arguing with Xavier about Rowan's obsessive, creepy behavior. Rowan flinging him against the wall with his telekinesis the same way he pinned me to the tree.

I see him moving the gargoyle from his dormitory window and know I'm standing just below it, about to be crushed.

"*I did*," Rowan says triumphantly to Xavier in the vision.

"*You're crazy!*" Xavier retorts.

And then the purple book is back. The one from the vision where I saw Rowan die. Only, this time I can see the cover. On it is the same symbol from the corner of the drawing Rowan's mother did. Only, from this angle I can see words too.

The Nightshade Society.

And just like that, I have my next lead.

The Nevermore library clientele does nothing to disabuse me of my uncharitable notions about the school. The only (debatably) living beings I see as I browse the shelves for the distinct shade of purple from my vision are two vampire students—who are clearly not here to brush up on their philosophy.

Thing and I are making our way through, pushing aside eggplant and lavender volumes in search of that exact, bruise-like hue, when Ms. Thornhill sneaks up behind me. "Oh!" she says, as if I've startled her. "I don't usually find students here looking for actual books."

I think of the vampires and their decidedly extracurricular "research" and suppress a shudder. But then I realize Ms. Thornhill might actually be able to help me.

"Have you seen this before?" I ask, pulling out an etching of the symbol on Rowan's drawing. The one I saw in my vision on the cover of the book. "It's a watermark from a book I'm looking for."

Ms. Thornhill looks thoughtful—or as thoughtful as one can look in a crocheted floral cardigan and what she clearly considers to be her signature red boots. "I think it's the symbol to an old student society," she says. "Um . . . the Nightshades? I was told they disbanded years ago."

I'm intrigued by the name—though a deadly flower name is as likely to be affixed to something try-hard as something legitimately interesting around here.

"Any idea why they disbanded?" I ask.

Ms. Thornhill shrugs. "Sorry. While I have you, though, I was very impressed with your answers in class today."

It's my turn to shrug.

She's given me the information I need. I'm eager to get out of here and continue my investigation. There's little chance that a secret society would keep member materials in the library for anyone to find. "My mother is a carnivorous plant aficionado," I say. "I assume I get my red thumb from her."

The look on Ms. Thornhill's face is eerily similar to Dr. Kinbott's when she mentions Morticia. "Are you and your mother close?" Ms. Thornhill asks.

I wonder what she's imagining. Spooky tea parties. Tending her garden together. My mother teaching me to apply dramatic eyeliner. Whatever it is, I know it's so far off that I can't respond in a way that won't disappoint her.

"Like two inmates sentenced to life on the same cell block," I land on.

"I know it can't be easy, showing up mid-semester," she presses. "I've been here a year and a half and I still feel like an outsider."

It's likely she's only confessing to persuade me to do the same. But this does call back a memory of some gossip Enid passed along when I was pretending to be asleep. "Is that because you're the only normie on staff?" I ask. It's not an accusation.

"To tell you the truth, I've never really fit in anywhere," she says with a self-deprecating chuckle. I take in her red fringe. Her thick, horn-rimmed glasses. It all seems impossibly sad, being a teacher. "Too odd for the normies, not odd enough for the Outcasts," she continues. "I thought Nevermore would be different, but there's still a handful of teachers who will barely acknowledge me."

I wonder what I've done to make three people confess their innermost feelings to me in a matter of days. If I can find out, perhaps I can reverse-engineer the process so that it never happens again.

"I act as if I don't care whether people dislike me," I say, still unused to the exchange rate of vulnerable moments. "Deep down, however . . ." Many possibilities linger on the tip of my tongue in that moment, but Ms. Thornhill's face is so eager, so utterly focused on me, that I find myself withdrawing. ". . . I secretly enjoy it."

"Never lose that, Wednesday," she says, smiling.

"Lose what?"

"The ability to not let others define you. It's a gift."

The words are out of my mouth before I can rein them in. "It doesn't always feel that way."

She gives me a knowing smile, and I'm furious with myself for revealing too much. Damn this strange culture of unearthing your secret wishes and fears anytime someone catches you standing still.

"The most interesting plants grow in the shade," she says with the shadow of a wink. "And if you ever need anyone to talk to, the door to the conservatory is always open."

I make a mental note to avoid it at all costs. Why would I go seeking out emotional interludes when one seems poised to jump scare me around every corner?

In Xavier's dorm, I see the towel out on the bed for his post-run shower. I hide in Rowan's empty closet until he returns, grabs said towel, and disappears for what I hope will be one of those famously long teenage boy showers.

"That purple book has got to be around here somewhere," I tell Thing. "And we don't have much time, so start investigating."

Thing rifles through bookshelves and cupboards while I tackle the desk. Xavier's sketchbook is here. There's a drawing of the gargoyle Rowan tried to push onto me. The one he saved me from against my will. The next page, to my surprise and utter confusion, is a carefully drawn sketch of . . . me.

More to avoid having to confront the potential implications

of this than anything else, I move onto phase two. Turning off the lights, I shine a blacklight along the walls, the bed frame, the floorboards, until *bingo*. A series of fingerprints on a floorboard beneath the bed reveals Rowan's secret hiding place.

Inside it is a masquerade mask. One I don't recognize. "Rowan's full of surprises," I mutter, before two taps on the door have me diving beneath Xavier's bed to hide.

He exits the shower (fully dressed, thank God) and heads for the door. With my luck, it's probably Weems. Or the sheriff.

But it's somehow both better and worse at the same time.

"You're not supposed to be up here," Xavier says, pulling Bianca Barclay into the room by her shoulder. "How'd you get past the housemaster? Use your *siren* powers?"

I hadn't needed any powers to get upstairs, just a penchant for the shadows and an innate ability to predict when someone on guard duty is going to yawn. But there's a disdain in the way he says this. I file it away.

"Not while wearing this," Bianca says, fingering a pendant around her neck. "Would it kill you not to think the worst of me for once?"

"What do you want, Bianca?" he asks. His tone is cold. There's no evidence that these two were once a couple. Not on his part, anyway.

"To see how you're doing," she says, waltzing around the bed to stand in front of him. "I'm sorry about Rowan. I know you guys used to be close."

Close? I think. That's hard to imagine. Is it possible Xavier is covering something up about Rowan out of misplaced loyalty to an old friend?

"Since when do you give a damn about Rowan?" Xavier asks.

"Hey, you were the one who turned on him, remember? You

said you were afraid he'd do something to Wednesday. Isn't that why you've been following her around like an eager-eyed puppy? Or is it something more?"

The insinuation in her voice is unmistakable, and I have a sudden and visceral wish to disappear through the floor. I know most of my peers would give an eye to be able to hear what people really thought about them, but not me. I'm truly relieved when Xavier seems to shut down this line of questioning by maintaining his stony silence.

"Seriously, what do you see in her?" Bianca presses. "You have a thing for tragic goth girls with funeral parlor fashion sense?"

This comment I do file away. It's not often you get a compliment from your nemesis.

"Maybe it's because *she* hasn't tried to manipulate me," Xavier snaps. As little as I want to be party to this, it's impossible not to draw a parallel between his earlier snideness about Bianca's siren powers and this. Did she use them on him? Try to control him?

"I make one mistake and you can't forgive me," she says. "*She* treats you like crap and you can't get enough."

"Why are you so fixated on Wednesday?" Xavier asks.

Silly boy, I think. Queens are always obsessed with subversives. We remind them they're vulnerable.

"Because she thinks she's better than everyone else," Bianca replies, heated. "I can't wait to crush stupid Ophelia Hall tomorrow and watch her werewolf roommate crumble. It's gonna be a Poe Cup to remember."

Suddenly, I'm on high alert for what she says next. I won't let her punish Enid for the crime of fraternizing with me.

"I hate to think what you've got planned," Xavier says, shaking his head.

83

"Oh, my game has already started," Bianca boasts. "I like to win. Is that so wrong?"

It takes me forever to escape Xavier's dorm, but the moment I'm out, I run as fast as I can back to Ophelia Hall, fearing for Enid's safety. I find her weeping on her bed and my heart sinks. Clearly, Bianca's already gotten to her.

"Are you hurt?" I ask, and she raises her tearstained face to look at me.

"Where have you been?" she cries. "I'm literally having a heart attack right now. Yoko's in the infirmary!"

It's funny, I think, a week ago I was ready to strangle this girl with one of her multicolored fashion scarves. Today, I'm relieved she wasn't the target.

"What happened?" As if I don't already know. Bianca sabotaged the Ophelia Hall team. The only thing I don't know is how she did it.

"Garlic bread incident at dinner," Enid moans. "She had a major allergic reaction. She's out of the Poe Cup and I don't have a copilot!"

I can practically see Bianca cozying up to Xavier, looking at him through her lashes. *I like to win. Is that so wrong?*

"It wasn't an accident," I say brusquely. "Bianca's behind it."

Enid's eyes go round. "How do you know?"

"Doesn't matter." There's no chance I'm explaining Xavier and Bianca's little after-hours bickering session to Nevermore's gossip queen. Her head might explode before we get the chance to do what needs to be done. "You and I are going to take her down tomorrow."

To my horror, Enid's eyes—which were on the verge of drying—are instantly tear-filled again. "You're willing to join the Black Cats? For me?"

I don't have time for another emotional interlude right now.

Or to parse out my strange new feelings of concern for and loyalty to Enid. Right now, I'm just thinking of Bianca. Crossing campus and making an against-the-rules visit to her ex-boyfriend just to talk about how I'm better than everyone.

Using her siren powers to manipulate Xavier, and her social powers to manipulate everyone else. Bullies like Bianca are asking for a reality check, and she made it personal.

"I want to humiliate Bianca so badly that the bitter taste of defeat burns in her throat," I say to Enid, who has stepped forward and is dangerously close to hugging range.

She stops when I step back, but her expression doesn't change. "Yeah, but mostly you're doing it because we're friends, right?"

Friends, I think. I'm not certain I've ever had a friend. Not a humanoid one that walks and talks, anyway. I'm not sure how I'd begin to understand it. Enid is my ally. Someone I trust more than most. Is that enough? I'm not sure, so I don't push it by asking.

"Tell me how she keeps winning," I say instead.

"It's a real brain cramp." Enid abandons her pre-embrace posture and begins pacing the room. "The past two years, no other boat has made it back without sinking."

"Sounds like sabotage," I say, thinking of the necklace she was wearing in Xavier's room. The way she admitted to *making a mistake* when it came to manipulating his thoughts and feelings. Clearly, she's not above using her powers to get ahead.

"There are no rules in the Poe Cup," Enid reminds me. "And she *is* a siren, which makes her master of the water."

It's this phrase that gives me my idea. "Then we just need to beat her at her own game," I say. In my mind, I'm already crossing the finish line, leaving Bianca in the dust.

CHAPTER TEN

If you told me, before my first day at Nevermore, that I'd find myself in a skintight black cat suit taking my place in a canoe hand-painted by my peers joining a school-sponsored sporting event . . . I'd probably have taken an eye.

And yet, the next morning, that's exactly where I find myself.

Thing and I were up all night creating a surprise for the Ophelia Hall boat. I haven't even told Enid. But if it works, Bianca will be humiliated and furious, and I will be vindicated.

She's in the boat beside us. I haven't made eye contact. But Xavier, on the other side, turns to glance at me, and Bianca must see it because I hear her voice seconds later.

"What do we have here?" she asks. "The runt of the litter."

Now I do stare her down. "For the record," I say. "I don't believe I'm better than *everyone* else. Just that I'm better than you." I can see on her face that she's rattled. Quoting her from a moment she believed she was alone in Xavier's room? The wheels are turning as she wonders whether I overheard or he told me.

Even I know better than to think that'll throw her off her game, but that doesn't make it any less fun to watch her squirm.

Weems takes the microphone and begins to introduce the teams as I'm sizing up the competitors. Bianca's boat is a clear reference to "The Gold Bug," one of the only Poe stories *not* to end in murder or madness. A truly uninspired choice—not that I should be surprised.

Beside us is a boat captained by Ajax, the Gorgon who told Enid I was a cannibal on my first day. Xavier is also on board this one, which is filled with macabre jesters in honor of "The Cask of Amontillado." Not my favorite Poe story, but a vast improvement over "The Gold Bug"—which seems mostly like an excuse for Bianca and her followers to wear confusing Cleopatra eye makeup.

The last boat is a design after my own heart. "The Pit and the Pendulum." I recognize the two vampires from the library on this one, wearing convenient hoods to block the sunlight. Personally, I always thought the main character should have died in the end. But that's just personal preference.

Weems explains the rules as we all survey the massive, murky lake we'll soon be traversing. No rules, row to Raven Island, pull a flag from Crackstone Crypt. First one back without sinking wins the cup, bragging rights, and the chance to defeat Bianca Barclay.

Game on.

When the pistol fires, we're off. The Gold Bugs fall behind quickly, but I know Bianca is complacent. She has some siren trick planned. Sure enough, the *Pit and the Pendulum* is quickly smashed against a buoy in a way that indicates foul play. I waste no time scanning the water for the culprit—the flicking tail of a siren doing Bianca's bidding.

"Thing," I say under my breath, and he knows what to do. He flips the switch I installed last night in the prow of the boat and fires an underwater projectile net in the direction of the siren's tail. Miraculously, no more boats are sunk before we reach the island, and Bianca is starting to look panicked.

On the shore, I tell Enid to stay with the boat before running as fast as I can toward Crackstone Crypt. Only the jesters are ahead of me.

The woods here are dark and gloomy. Raven Island, living up to its name. I can see how some people might find it unnerving— the mist, the quiet, the darkness that feels out of place on a sunny afternoon. But I love it. I make a note to return when I'm alone.

Right now, it's all business. Xavier and Ajax are ahead, having grabbed their flag. No sign of Bianca, though, and if I get our flag and the jesters' boat is out of commission, we still have a chance.

The Black Cat flag is there, and I jump for it, bracing myself on the stone wall.

That's when it happens. The rushing in my ears. The seizing feeling in my chest. A vision, and at the worst possible time. I'm unprotected, Bianca is getting away, and I'm . . .

. . . I'm in a forest that looks much like this one, only it's all cast in black-and-white. Stranger still, I'm in my body. Normally the visions are like a TV changing channels too rapidly, but in this one I can get up. Walk. Take in my surroundings at will.

All sound is muffled here. I seem to be utterly alone. I turn around, looking for whatever the vision is trying to show me, when I find myself face to face with a girl who wasn't here seconds ago. She looks just like me, only even more ghostly pale. Her hair is a light blond. She's dressed in old-fashioned clothes, and she holds a massive tome under one arm.

The familiarity is so startling I forget the Poe Cup. Forget I'm in a vision at all. I'm locked in the place our eyes meet, unable to look away.

She steps closer. I can't back away.

"You are the key," she says, and then everything is contracting, and she's gone.

I wake face down in the dirt, the flag still clutched in my hand. To my horror, Bianca is standing over me with one of her lackeys. The last person I'd ever want to find me vulnerable twice. "Taking a catnap?" she asks in that snide tone of hers. Then she seizes the Gold Bug's flag and takes off running. Laughing.

With the memory of that other girl still fresh, I can't summon the urgency I felt before. Who was she? Some distant ancestor? A version of myself from an alternate universe? A hallucination brought on by the stress of the Cup?

I remember Weems's assessment of my mother's visions: dangerous and unpredictable. Yet the girl had called me the key. The key to what?

Looking back over my shoulder as I get up, I take in the name on the tomb: Joseph Crackstone. I want to go inside. To understand what about the stone triggered the vision. But then I remember Enid. Thing. I'm not about to abandon them.

This tomb has been here for hundreds of years; surely it'll still be standing when the race is done.

Back at the boat, the Black Cats are panicking. Everyone else has already left the shore. I get back in as quickly as I can and paddle like my life depends on it, despite the clammy feeling left over after the vision.

We're in last place. Out of range of any of my brilliant saboteur plans. But then I notice that the jesters appear to be sinking.

I glance back at Enid—the only member of our team who had access to the jesters' boat.

She smirks before turning back to her paddle. "I just asked myself: WWWD? What would Wednesday do?"

I'll never tell her this, but I'm moved by it. Her trust in me. Even if we don't humiliate Bianca today, perhaps it's worth it to be Enid's ally every once in a while. Hopefully next time, I won't have to wear a costume.

The sinking of the jesters raises everyone's spirits. We're really moving quickly. Bianca and her team aren't strong paddlers. They're relying on her powers alone. But I have more upper arm strength than my silhouette would indicate, and Enid has been training with the girls. We're the superior athletes. Soon enough, we're in range for my final secret weapon. I flip the switch, pleased when the metal spikes extend from the side of the boat as planned.

Sleeping three hours a night has its benefits.

My pleasure is short-lived. I feel a jolt in the boat. The siren must have escaped the net—or Bianca has more than one on the payroll. We're drifting close to the same buoy that took out the *Pit and the Pendulum* when I see Thing leap off the side of the boat.

Moments later, the pressure on the boat is gone. I make a note to buy him some very expensive vitamin E oil supplements. We steer the boat alongside the *Gold Bug* and I hear the tearing that tells me my spikes have found their target.

Bianca's boat is taking on water. We're sailing toward the finish line. I feel . . . elated. I'll deny it later, of course, but gripping the flag with Enid, running across the finish line . . . I can almost see why people participate in social activities recreationally.

Almost.

The trumpets are blaring. Bianca hauls herself out of the water looking deflated. Enid knows better than to hug me, but she's clearly vibrating at a frequency only audible to canines. "This is the greatest moment of my entire life!" She turns to look at me, grinning. "Admit it, you kinda got into the whole school-spirit thing."

I allow her a small smirk. "You didn't say it was a dark, vengeful spirit."

After three minutes of the award ceremony on the quad, I'm ready to take back anything positive I said, thought, or even internally implied about school events.

Weems is beside herself with pride delivering her speech, as if she was coxswaining the boat herself. Enid bounces up and down beside me, her multicolored hair obscuring me partway, but not enough. People are *looking* at me. Cheering. It's unsettling.

The moment Weems has finished her speech and handed the trophy to an ecstatic and howling Enid, I slip away into the blessedly empty entrance hall and sit at the feet of the Poe statue to catch my breath.

There's hardly been a moment to consider my vision. Rowan's book. And yet I feel wrung out like an old sponge.

I tip my head back to see if old Poe has any advice on how to deal with people suddenly being aware of your existence when you prefer the shadows. He doesn't, but what he does have is much more interesting.

I've walked past this statue daily since I started here—seen photos of it at home since I was old enough to scowl. How did I never notice the book? And more importantly, what's on the cover. The symbol of the Nightshade Society.

Suddenly, I'm energized again. Just in time for Enid to come rushing into my sanctuary.

"What are you *doing* down here?" she asks.

I turn away from the statue abruptly. "Hiding," I confess. "People keep randomly smiling at me out there. It's unsettling."

"It's called having your moment," Enid says, bumping her shoulder with mine in a way that's both unexpected and not entirely unpleasant. "You took down Bianca Barclay. Try to enjoy it?"

We head back to the quad. Some of the hubbub has died down, thankfully. People are sorted into their usual social groups at the long tables instead of *milling*.

"The girls want to know if you'll hang out later?" Enid says hopefully.

I let my expression answer for me.

"Oh, come on, it won't kill you."

I'm about to retort that it very well might and that death might be preferable. But then I remember Enid calling me her friend. *What Would Wednesday Do?* There's little chance I'll ever become the type of person Enid looks for in a friend, but if she's willing to accept me for who I truly am, perhaps I can meet her partway.

"I'll think about it," I say. She doesn't push, nor does she try to hug me, much to my surprise. It's a good sign.

When she bounces off to rejoin the team—and the giant trophy—Weems approaches me on the sidelines. "It's good to see you fitting in," she says. "You reminded me of your mother out there."

"My mother and I are two different people-slash-species-slash-everything," I say, quickly and forcefully.

"Hmm," Weems begins. "The last time Ophelia Hall won the Poe Cup, your mother captained the team. And I was her copilot. Maybe you two are more alike than you think."

She's gone before I can tell her that's impossible. That while my mother and I may physically resemble one another, any similarities end there.

As I peer over at Bianca's table, see the siren (back on two legs now) with a black eye courtesy of Thing, I know I'll never be like her. Never.

The moment Enid is asleep, her arms around the Poe Cup as if it's a teddy bear, I make my way back to the entrance hall. The statue.

Edgar Allan Poe's riddles were legendary, and when I step up onto the platform to view the pages of the book he holds, I'm forced to concede this might be his cleverest yet.

It's not one riddle, but a series of them. I pull out my notebook and begin to answer them one by one. Looking for a pattern. Something to convince me this isn't all a coincidence.

The opposite of moon? Sun.

A world between ours? Nether.

Two months before June? April.

A self-seeding flower. Pansy.

One more than one. Two.

Its leaves weep to the ground. Willow.

It melts in the sun. Ice.

Its beginning and end never found. Circle.

Every rule has one. Exception.

When every riddle is answered, I look down at my list. It's not a code, I don't think. And the words spelled backward reveal nothing. But the first letter of every word . . . that might be something. I circle them all, one by one, and when I have my answer, I can hardly believe it.

The answer will make a sharp cracking sound.

I snap twice.

Before me, Edgar's statue becomes suddenly mobile. He slides out of the way, revealing a secret passage at his feet. An entrance to the place where Rowan found the book with his mother's drawing in it. The one where I stand before the flames, destroying Nevermore and everyone here.

This is my chance to change the future she saw.

I descend the staircase. Paintings line the wall on the way down. Shadowy faces. Smirks. Smiles. Hooded eyes. No one I recognize.

At the bottom, the floor is a custom job. A flower with a skull. The symbol of the Nightshade Society. There are cobwebs everywhere. My flashlight falls on a portrait of my parents, and I'll deny it to the grave, but it makes me feel a little less alone down here.

In a recessed shelf in the wall are a hundred purple volumes like the one my vision showed. I step forward to remove the one with the least dust in front of it. There, at the center. A torn page.

The other half of Rowan's mother's drawing.

There's a tingling in the air. An anticipation. After days of hoping, have I finally found the answer? I put the book in my bag and turn to mount the stairs again.

That's when the sack descends over my head, and my ill-timed abduction begins.

CHAPTER ELEVEN

Once I'm wrestled into a chair at what feels like the center of the room, I assess the situation as I always imagined I would when I was eventually kidnapped.

Bag over my head for optimal disorientation? Check. Wrists tied tight enough to cut off circulation? Check. I have no idea whether I'm going to live or die, which feels thrilling after a day of high school social drama.

In short, just the way I like to celebrate a victory.

My mind is whirring with possibilities. Is this someone connected to the monster that killed Rowan? Someone connected to Rowan himself? His psychic mother? Or is the sheriff worried about my insistence that Rowan was murdered—he *was* in the woods alone that day I found Rowan's glasses. Come to think of it, I wouldn't leave Weems off the list. She appears benevolent, but I never trust people who dress that well.

The bag is ripped off my head. Bright lights shine from every direction, causing me to squint, unable to see who's behind them. Hooded figures, I think. No idea how many. If I'm lucky, maybe twenty. I won't break the silence first.

After a long moment, however, one of my assailants speaks, and my hopes of high intrigue and a narrow escape are dashed against the rocks of bitter disappointment.

"Who dares breach our inner sanctum?" The voice is unmistakable. Our resident queen bee, muffled by some kind of face covering.

"You can take the mask off, Bianca," I say, not bothering to hide my regret.

The lights die out. Bianca, in a purple robe, removes a mask identical to the one I found under Rowan's floorboards. Everyone else removes theirs too. It's just the in-crowd of Nevermore. Yoko, Xavier, Ajax. A bunch of other kids whose names I'll never bother to learn. My foe is no psychotic killer intent on psychological torture before the inevitable end. Just a bunch of high school bullies playing dress-up.

"How did you get down here?" Xavier asks.

"Rowan showed me," I say, nodding to my skirt. "Left pocket."

He steps forward to Bianca's obvious and intense displeasure and removes the drawing. Me and the flames.

"I tracked the watermark to the Poe statue," I say. "Then I solved the riddle."

"Wait, there's a riddle?" one of the boys says, looking at Bianca.

It's the siren from the Poe Cup this afternoon, still sporting the black eye that Thing gave him. I think his name is Kent. "I thought we just snapped twice."

"Well, aren't you the brightest in the bunch." I was supposed to be facing off against a famous serial killer dressed like a clown or something by now. This is such a poor substitute.

"The Nightshades are an elite social club," Bianca continues. "Emphasis on *elite*."

I can practically feel her sizing up my outfit. As if we don't all wear a Nevermore uniform.

"We have roof parties, campouts, the occasional midnight skinny-dip."

This girl I recognize as Yoko, the one Bianca put in the infirmary last night with the garlic bread incident.

So much for the enduring bonds of fellowship, I think.

"And Yoko's an amateur mixologist," says another girl in the group, one with a slicked-back brown bob. I later learn her name is Divina.

"She makes a killer virgin mojito. It can get pretty wild," Ajax added.

If anything, this makes me hate the social upper crust of the school even more than I did before. Centuries of history, secret society gravitas, a hideout behind a statue of Edgar Allan Poe and all they can do is throw virgin cocktail parties? It's pathetic.

"Wow," I deadpan. "Do you guys even have a bedtime?"

Bianca sneers at me, but I don't wait for whatever unimaginative retort she's planning. "I thought the Nightshades had been disbanded."

Xavier speaks up this time. "Yeah, the group kind of lost its charter thirty years ago after some normie kid died. But we have a long legacy of wealthy alumni, so Weems looks the other way as long as nobody makes any waves."

"Like Rowan?" I ask sharply. I know he was once a member—I saw his mask. Does that mean the people here know about his mother? Her vision? It came out of one of these books, after all . . .

"We booted that loser last semester," Bianca says dismissively. I remember her feigned concern in Xavier's room yesterday. "The question is, what are we going to do with *her*?" She poses the question to the other Nightshades as if she'd ever consider an opinion besides her own.

"I say we invite her to pledge," Xavier says, still standing next to me. "I mean, she is a legacy." He shines his flashlight on the portrait of my parents in their youth. My mother in a large, circular armchair. My father standing next to her, dotingly holding her hand.

I'm about to say they'd be disappointed at the diluted sham this organization has become, but Bianca is already objecting.

"After the crap she pulled in the Poe Cup? There's no way in hell. Talk about not making waves—Wednesday Addams is a tsunami."

Several students nod in agreement. Xavier is clearly about to speak up in my defense, despite my clear instructions not to attempt to rescue me again.

"Let me save you the trouble," I say before anyone else can speak. "I'm not interested in joining."

Yoko scoffs. "You're *seriously* turning us down?"

"Can you believe it?" I intone, borrowing her insipid Valley girl patois, though I know my sarcasm is lost on her.

Bianca alone seems satisfied. "Untie her," she says, snapping at her siren lackey.

I get to my feet, holding the rope out to him when he

approaches. "I freed myself five minutes ago."

Everyone watches in disbelief as I snatch Rowan's drawing back from Xavier and make for the stairs. I intend to leave them with no further comment, but halfway up the stairs the disappointment and rage are too much to contain.

"You know," I say to the pathetic crowd still gathered below the railing. "It's amateurs like you who give kidnapping a bad name."

Before bed, I pull the book out of my bag, thinking at least one of my objectives was achieved on this disappointment of an evening. I unfold the drawing that caused Rowan to attack me and fit it in with its other half.

The usual dread fills me when I see the flames in the background, myself standing stone-faced in the midst of it all. But the second half of the drawing offers a puzzling context clue. Fire rages, shadows dance, and across from me is the silhouette of a pilgrim.

I may not be able to decipher exactly why Rowan's psychic mother predicted this grisly scene, but perhaps I can at least solve the mystery of the man with whom I'm destined to share the stage.

I've taken to haunting the table on the quad with the exact point of view depicted by the drawing. Imagining it all burning. Today, I'm thinking of the girl from my vision at Crackstone Crypt. The one who told me I'm the key.

Will I ever discover her identity? Or that of the pilgrim silhouette in the drawing?

And if I do, will it be enough to stop whatever is unfolding?

Unfortunately, my musing is cut short as Principal Weems

steps up to address the crowd of blithely ignorant students—much more concerned with their own petty social dramas than anything so dire as the destruction of their little habitat.

"All students will report to their volunteer jobs at ten o'clock sharp, followed by a community lunch at one."

I put away the book for now, shuffling forward to join the crowd. In the disappointment of being inadequately abducted last night, I nearly forgot about Outreach Day. A futile attempt to fuse Nevermore into the Jericho townie culture.

"As you know, this year's Outreach Day culminates in a very special event," Weems continues, sounding as though she actually believes this crap. "The dedication of a new memorial statue in the town square—with performances by several of your fellow Nevermore students!"

At the mention of performances, Enid approaches in her usual bouncing manner.

"As representatives of our school," Weems cautions as teachers begin handing out envelopes in the crowd, "I trust you will all put your best face forward."

Ms. Thornhill reaches us just as this rousing speech ends. Enid and I each get an envelope, and she squeals as she opens hers.

"Yes! I got Pilgrim World! What did you get, Wednesday?"

I pull mine out with some trepidation. "Uriah's Heap," I read out. "Whatever that is."

Enid's look of distaste gives me hope. "It's a weird, creepy antique shop," she says. "You'll love it, though. I'm just hoping Ajax and I will be *outreaching* together, if you catch my drift."

As usual, I don't. Enid's continuing interest in the nondescript Gorgon continues to elude my understanding. But before I can ask her to explain, Weems approaches with a smile that makes me sure I'll regret making eye contact.

"Wednesday, don't worry about your cello," she says. "I'll have it brought to the town square this afternoon."

"My cello?" I ask, nonplussed.

"I caught your rooftop serenade the other night and volunteered you to accompany the Jericho High School Marching Band at the ceremony tomorrow. I'm sure an uplifting Fleetwood Mac medley isn't beyond your considerable skill?"

The steel in her tone tells me it's pointless to argue, and as I'm currently investigating a murder under her nose, I know picking my battles is of the utmost importance.

I grimace in a fashion some people mistake as a smile. "Only if you promise to hang me as a witch afterward," I mutter.

We're bussed into Jericho like cattle. As the adults scramble to get everything under control, I spot Xavier apart from the group, staring morosely at a wall that's been painted white.

He hasn't spoken to me since I left the Nightshades abduction. Not that I particularly miss his attention, but even a lone operative needs allies, and Xavier is the only member of the society who will even look me in the eye.

Plus, he didn't seem surprised when I showed him Rowan's drawing during my brief captivity. There may be something there.

"Why are you staring at a blank wall?" I ask, approaching from behind.

He doesn't look up, just continues staring at the paint bitterly. "It wasn't blank last Outreach Day." Without waiting for a response, he turns and starts back toward the crowd of milling students.

I follow. "You're not still stewing because I rejected your little club invitation?"

He shrugs, not denying it. "I went out on a limb for you."

My eyes roll of their own accord, thinking back to the gathering. Xavier's eyes darting to Bianca and back every time he spoke to or about me. "Please," I chastise him. "I'm just cannon fodder in whatever cold war you're waging with Bianca. Leave me out of it. I have more pressing issues on my mind."

Xavier's feigned indifference drops then. "Like what?"

"Like tracking down the monster that killed your former roommate," I say, exasperated.

It seems I'm not the only one feeling frustrated. "For the last time," Xavier says, throwing up his hands. "Rowan was expelled. We all saw him leave."

And disappear in the train station, leaving his suitcase behind, I think. But I plan to keep this ill-gotten detail to myself for now. I don't need Weems questioning my sources.

Instead, I pull the Nightshades book from my bag, which stops Xavier in his tracks.

"Guess you can add thief to your résumé," he says. "Why did you want this so bad anyway?"

I open the page to the burning quad. Me and the pilgrim wreathed in flames. "You've seen this before, haven't you?" I ask him.

Xavier shrugs. "Yeah. A few days before the Harvest Festival. It was open on his desk. I knew he'd stolen it after he got kicked out of the Nightshades, so I confronted him. He kind of . . . lost it."

The scene replays in my mind without needing to be conjured.

103

The one from my vision. Xavier, shouting at Rowan. Rowan flinging him up against the wall. The gargoyle inching toward the edge. Toward me.

"He attacked you with his telekinesis," I say.

Xavier looks down at me, clearly surprised. "How did you know?"

"Lucky guess."

He takes a closer look at the drawing, which is what I wanted, of course. But at what cost? People and their constant need for sharing. It's exhausting. "It's weird you're in this drawing. This journal is over thirty years old. And what the hell is Crackstone doing in this picture with you?"

I never expected Xavier to surprise me, but this does. I feel the lightning strike of a new clue reverberate through my bones. "You know who this is?"

Xavier looks at me like I've missed something obvious. "Joseph Crackstone?" he says. "Jericho's founding father?" He gestures all around us, to where a crew of workers is hanging banners for Pilgrim World. Each of them prominently features a strong-jawed, paternal pilgrim that—now that I think of it—does resemble the man in the drawing.

Pilgrim World, the banners read. *Where History Comes to Life.*

Now in possession of a more specific mission, Thing and I leave Xavier to his blank wall and take to the crowd with gusto. By the time I reach Enid in front of the Weathervane, I have a plan firmly in place.

"Enid, I need you to switch volunteer assignments," I say without preamble.

"What? Ew," she replies. "Uriah's Heap is *definitely* not my bag."

Having predicted this response, I'm utterly undaunted. "Oh, that's too bad," I say, turning away from her. "I'm sure *Ajax* and I will have a grand old time without you."

Enid lunges. Subtlety is not her strong suit. Before I know it, she's got my Uriah's Heap assignment, I have her Pilgrim World one, and she's screeching in my ear in a way that will probably lead to increased hearing loss in my old age.

If I live that long.

CHAPTER TWELVE

It's hard to imagine Uriah's Heap (or anywhere in the world) being worse than Pilgrim World. If ever there was a historical population that did *not* need an amusement park . . .

Obviously, this is a popular assignment. Almost the entirety of the Nightshades group is here, led by Bianca, who is only pretending to be led by Arlene, our costumed tour guide.

The dirt path forks off to a bunch of run-down thatched cottages. There's a miniature farm, a blacksmith, a bunch of townies in costume getting ready for the two o'clock witch trials. Before today, I couldn't imagine a fate worse than growing up to be exactly like my parents. Now I know I was wrong. There is a single worse fate in the universe, and Arlene is living it.

"Yonder, behold," she says, gesturing up ahead at a dilapidated building not dissimilar to a barn. "The Meeting House. Inside is a collection of artifacts related to Jericho's most beloved and pious founder—Joseph Crackstone."

I've managed to summarily ignore almost the entire Pilgrim World welcome speech, but at this I perk up. The whole reason I didn't use Outreach Day as a convenient cover to flee is my desire to learn more about this very man.

Stepping forward, I do my best to match Arlene's faux pilgrim speech, hoping to get on her good side. "I haveth a query," I say clearly.

Bianca rolls her eyes. Arlene looks like she just noticed we were here. "Pray, be quick, child."

"In the Meeting House," I say, trying to pass off my urgency as casual interest. "What artifacts of Joseph Crackstone's are on display?"

Arlene looks as though she would rather be anywhere but here as she answers in a flat, bored tone: "It is truly a treasure trove, including farm tools, tableware, even the Crackstone family chamber pot."

"Sounds fascinating," I say as the boys behind me snicker. "I volunteer to work in there."

"Pray, no," Arlene answers with a superior little titter that turns my pity to loathing. "That exhibit is being renovated. Today, thou will all be working at the beating heart of Pilgrim World."

She turns to gesture behind her as if revealing a real treat. I imagine the Crackstone family home. Perhaps the schoolhouse, or Joseph's private office. Anywhere I can get the information about the man I'm destined to share an apocalyptic event with.

But when I look behind Arlene, my heart sinks.

"Ye Olde Fudgery?" Eugene exclaims beside me in a tone of utter rapture. And sure enough, I'm face to face with a combination fudge and souvenir shop—not to mention the death of my hope to discover some historical context for Crackstone to aid in my investigation.

Around me, my fellow students are energized, undoubtedly relishing the sugar coma to come. Further proof that I'm as separated from them as fudge is from historical significance of any kind.

Once we've been given our uniforms and instructions— *Samples lead to sales! The tourists are always right! Don't forget to smile!*—we're turned loose on a group of tourists from Germany. All the better for me, as even Arlene doesn't speak fluent German. If I can't research Crackstone, I can at least shed some light on the farce of this fudge operation.

"Enjoy your 'authentic' pilgrim fudge," I tell them in their native tongue. "It's made with cacao beans procured by the oppressed Indigenous people of the Amazon." They start to look uncertainly at each other as I continue. "All proceeds go to uphold this pathetic whitewashing of American history."

I hold out the tray of fudge samples on toothpicks as I see Bianca and the other Nevermore students doing. I paste a gruesome grimace on my face.

"Also," I add, still in German, as one man reaches forward for a piece, "fudge wouldn't be invented for another two hundred and fifty-eight years." He retracts his hand. "Any takers?" I ask the rest of them. They all back away muttering—mostly about me, but a few of them are doubting the validity of Pilgrim World, which is all I can ask for as a humble servant of the truth.

Well, that and Arlene looks irritable as they all leave the store without tasting or purchasing any Pilgrim World Life Blood. When she stalks off—undoubtedly to speak to her supervisor—I'm able to balance my tray on a storage barrel and slip out the side door.

Out in the alley, I stumble upon the only scene that could shake me from my purpose. Eugene, covered in vomit (his own, presumably), being tormented by a group of idiots. I recognize the same boys I took down in the Weathervane on my first day in town—among them Lucas Walker, son of Pilgrim World's generous proprietor.

They're doing their best to force him into the stocks when I sigh and divert my course.

"Howdy, pilgrims," I say, glaring. The more intimidating I can be, the quicker I can get this over with.

One of the nameless ones steps toward me, but I can see the fear in his eyes as he recognizes me. I imagine the bruising on his windpipe is just beginning to heal.

"Let him go," I say.

"You want to end up in the stocks too?" he asks, narrowing his panicked little rodent eyes in a pathetic display of faux toughness.

"Remember what happened the last time we did this dance?" I ask, loud enough for his friends to hear. It has the intended effect. He shoves Eugene out of the way and lunges toward me. From there it's a quick momentum shift—involving a knee to the sensitive bits—to redirect him into the stocks instead. While he's doubled up and groaning, I drop the top, ensnaring him in the very trap he was hoping to leverage against Eugene.

Neat and tidy, just how I like it.

"Those who forget history are doomed to repeat it," I intone as he snarls at me impotently. It'll be a little while before anyone realizes he's not a reenactor. Especially in that getup. Enough time for Eugene and me to get safely away.

The mayor's son and the other lackey are clearly debating what to do next, but eventually caution wins the day. They leave their friend alone and scurry off to avoid more trouble.

Eugene, beside me, is still covered in sick and looks ready to cry. *Caring about people really slows you down,* I think as I help Eugene to his feet. Then I lead him off to get cleaned up. "We have a Meeting House to break into."

Eugene's presence becomes worth the trouble when I realize I left my lockpick set in my Nevermore uniform back in the changing room. Luckily, his mouth has more metal in it than most key rings, and he's obliged to hand over his retainer after my daring rescue at the stocks.

"What if Mistress Arlene catches us?" he asks nervously.

"Hive code," I tell him as the padlock gives. "Deny everything."

He's trying to exclaim that denial isn't an integral part of hive code when I leave him to keep watch and slip inside the dark room. If there's one thing I can count on Eugene to do, it's make a loud, shrill sound if danger approaches.

Inside the Meeting House, light shafts illuminate the dust in the air. It's a long, narrow room. There are—as promised—at least fifty Crackstone family artifacts littering the tables, and old paintings adorn the walls.

In the center of the room is a life-size wax figure of Crackstone. He's dressed in his pilgrim Sunday's best and holds a gnarled oak staff. I think it's about time as I stand before him and his slippery nature. This man lived hundreds of years ago, and a woman still predicted both of us would stand before a destructive blaze.

Could the answers to my future lie in Crackstone's past?

Interrupting my ill-timed musing, Thing pulls at my pilgrim skirt, directing my attention to a large painting affixed to the north wall of the room. It's clearly propaganda of the most insidious kind. Crackstone stands at the head of a group of pilgrims, spreading his arms out in welcome to a colony of Outcasts in front of the Meeting House.

I don't know much about the arrival of Outcasts to settlements like these, but the little I do know doesn't suggest a warm welcome.

"I think it's a little late for me to be indoctrinated," I say to Thing. "What's next? Thanksgiving without the smallpox?"

As I continue to study the painting, I see something familiar. Some*one*. It's the girl from my vision during the Poe Cup. The girl with the long blond hair who looks like me.

"It's her!" I exclaim. "The doppelgänger from my vision!" And as I look more closely, I see that she's holding the same book she was when I saw her then. A black leather volume with an indistinct symbol on the front.

Immediately, I whirl around to the artifact tables. I know somehow that it will be here. The book from my vision. The answer. I can feel the electricity in my veins, telling me I'm close, pulling me onward as I pass clay dishware and woven blankets and . . . *there*. In a glass-topped case. A black, leatherbound book with an embossed gold title and that same symbol, which now looks much more like the compass points than the cross . . .

I'll never admit it aloud, but my fingers are trembling when

I reach in to take the book. It's lighter than I expected. "*Codex Umbrarum*," I whisper to Thing. "It's Latin for *Book of Shadows*."

When I open it, I know I'm breaking all my rules for expectations, and I'm reminded exactly why I have them when the pages are blank. Not only that, but the paper is clearly of the inkjet printer variety.

With a pit in my stomach, I flip it over to find a branded sticker.

"It's a fake," I say hollowly, turning it around to show Thing.

I shouldn't be surprised this place is full of fakes and frauds. I also shouldn't be surprised when Arlene bursts through the door holding Eugene by the stained collar. It's just the kind of day I'm having.

"Mistress Arlene," I say. "How now?"

"How now indeed," she snaps. "What in the *fudge* are you doing in here? And on the wrong side of the velvet rope?"

I turn, clutching the book tighter to my chest.

"Did thou not hear me proclaim the Meeting House under repair?"

Eugene speaks up from her clutches, his face flushed, glasses crooked. "I told her we found the door unlocked and were dying to learn more about Crackstone."

"Well, you're wasting your time," Arlene says, mercifully dropping the pilgrim persona as well as Eugene. "The book's a replica. Original was stolen last month during the two o'clock witch trial."

"It was probably the only authentic thing in here. And you're still charging thirty bucks a ticket?"

Whatever camaraderie Arlene momentarily felt quickly disappears with her disbelieving glare. "Hold thy tongue!" she says. "I'm reassigning you both to fudge-churning duty!"

Sensing I only have seconds left in this room, I point to the painting. "The original Meeting House," I say. "The one in this painting. Where is it?"

This time, when Arlene drops the persona, I can tell she's just exhausted. "How the hell should I know?" she asks. "I only moved here from Scottsdale in April."

So much for authentic pilgrim culture, I think as I'm ushered back outside. It might be time to consult an actual local. If I can't get my questions answered here, I'll need to find out where I can. And soon.

The Weathervane isn't busy, which I count as lucky, but Xavier greets me wearing the red apron, which I don't. I was hoping to see Tyler.

"Aren't you supposed to be at Pilgrim World?" he asks as I approach the counter.

"I deserted while my sanity was still intact."

He nods without further questions, leading me to believe he's experienced the wonders of Pilgrim World firsthand.

"Want a coffee?" he asks. "Only perk of pulling this assignment. Since it's clearly not the company." He mutters this last part.

"I'm actually here to see Tyler."

Xavier visibly bristles at this. "I thought I told you that guy was bad news."

Now it's my turn to bristle. "You did," I say. "Twice. But who I talk to is my business." There's more I could say about this, about his misplaced desire to rescue me, but I'm in a hurry, so I ring the service bell instead.

Tyler appears. Xavier scoffs. I really don't have time for this.

"You want the usual?" Tyler asks, coming out from the back.

"Yes, please. And some help." I take out a map of Jericho and the surrounding area I picked up from the info kiosk at Pilgrim World, spreading it out on an empty table. "The Pilgrim Meeting House—the original one from the sixteen hundreds—do you know if it's still around?"

Tyler looks down at the map. "What's left of it is out in Cobham Woods, but it's pretty much a ruin."

I point at the map. "Show me."

Tyler points to a spot deep in the map's darkest green.

"Thank you." I fold the map and strangely, I think of Enid and Ajax at Uriah's Heap together. Enid's constant plotting to get closer to a boy who smells like some kind of six-in-one soap/gel/spray/mousse.

It's an uncomfortable enough comparison that I turn to leave without saying more.

"Wait," Tyler says. "It's . . . kind of sketchy out there. Squatters and tweakers use it as a crash pad. My dad clears it out every couple of weeks." Tyler moves closer. "What's this really about? Going out there? I know it isn't a history project."

"None of your business," I reply.

There's a knowing in his eyes that makes me distinctly uncomfortable. Perhaps I've divulged too much in my attempt to make use of my one local ally. I resolve to find another. Spread out the information. I don't need his concern, only his knowledge of Jericho geography.

"You're really getting obsessed with this monster-in-the-woods thing."

I level a look at him that I'm ashamed to admit I practiced in the mirror after my mother used it to such great effect in my childhood. At least I know it works. "Would you prefer I become obsessed with horses? Boy bands?"

Tyler chuckles, shaking his head. He appears charmed, which causes me to rethink the glare. "They definitely broke the mold with you," he says.

I make my way toward the door, assessing that this conversation has outlasted its usefulness. But Tyler isn't giving up.

"Listen," he says. "The ruins are kind of tricky to find. I could take you this afternoon? My shift ends at two."

This time, the tone and expression are unmistakable. He might as well be asking me to get a milkshake before the sock hop. I'm relieved to have an excuse at the ready. "Weems will hang, draw, and quarter me if I miss the statue dedication. And anyway, I know my way around the great outdoors."

I'm out the door before he can mount another offensive. Xavier passes me on his way in with that sad puppy look. I'm visited by the fleeting thought that these two should just take each other out for a milkshake and leave me out of it.

CHAPTER THIRTEEN

The ruins are just where Tyler said they'd be—another reason why I have to be careful not to give him cause to abandon me and my pursuits entirely.

The place isn't much to look at. Just a few flimsy walls partially covered in vines. Bottles and cans here and there. Thing telegraphs his disappointment through his slouched posture and general disinterest. I can't say I blame him. This place hardly seems worth the hike it took to reach it. "I was expecting more too," I tell him.

But a voice growls in answer before Thing can respond. "Who you talking to, little girl?"

I turn to take in an unkempt man with long hair and a beard, crouched over his sleeping bag. I'm about to ask his name, or if he's seen anything suspicious, when Thing flings himself at the man like *he's* the intruder, not us. He flees into the woods—a natural reaction to having a disembodied hand attack you, I suppose.

I raise an eyebrow at Thing. "Was that necessary?" I ask. "He wasn't hurting anyone."

Thing doesn't bother to answer, just signs impatiently. A total non sequitur.

"No, I can't just *touch* something and have a vision," I reply waspishly when he's finished. "They seem to happen spontaneously. And before you say it, I will *not* be asking my mother for advice."

He watches, unimpressed. Deep down, I'm starting to feel like I just hiked three miles into the rain for nothing, and Thing's judgment isn't helping matters.

"Fine," I snap. "I'll prove it to you." I step over to the remaining wall corner, covered in lichen, and reach my hands out theatrically. "Ye olde mossy wall! What secrets hold ye?"

Next, I make my way to the fireplace. The doorjamb.

"I can't believe this isn't working! Oh, wait, *this* should give us some real insight." I pick up a moldy Taco Bell bag from the ground and hold it in both hands, bugging out my eyes and grimacing.

Thing is waiting for my theatrics to conclude, tapping his fingers against the ground.

"Satisfied?" I ask him. "I told you these so-called psychic powers are about as predictable as a shark attack."

The rain is falling more heavily now. I feel extremely irritated with myself for coming out here at all. What did I expect to find? A stone tablet carved with the exact information I needed to untangle Crackstone's past? Hardly likely.

"Let's cut our losses and get back," I tell Thing, who is shaking off water like a dog.

It happens on my way back to the door. I touch it as I open the rotting wooden gate, and there it is. The live wire, electrifying my spine, causing every muscle in my body to go rigid as my head is thrown back against my will, my eyes forced shut . . .

I'm standing outside the Meeting House. It's not raining now, and night has fallen. The structure is fully intact. A new kind of electricity fills me now. I'm in the past. Crackstone's past.

The sound of voices draws my attention to the clearing outside the structure. There's a mob of pilgrim villagers here, holding torches and pitchforks. Not a good sign in any era. I don't know if they can see me, so I keep to the shadows, hiding behind a barrel where I have a better vantage point on their victim.

Only, when I see her, I almost wish I hadn't. It's the girl. The one from my vision at the crypt. The one from the painting at Pilgrim World. The one who looks uncannily like me.

The villagers are tossing her back and forth through the crowd, violently, yelling and jeering at her. "Witch! Repent!" The contrast between their sneering, furious faces and the friendly smiling ones adorning Jericho's propaganda couldn't be more pronounced.

It's thrown into sharper relief when Joseph Crackstone strides through the crowd in a long black cape, holding his gnarled staff. The villagers part for him, clearing his path to the girl huddled on the ground. There's no trace of the cheap, cartoon benevolence that saturates his Pilgrim World persona in his expression—there's only viciousness and cruelty twisting his features as he stops before her.

"Goody Addams!" he shouts, pointing down. "You have been

judged before God and found guilty."

The villagers shout their agreement.

"You are a witch! A sorceress! Lucifer's mistress herself! For your sins, you will burn this night and suffer the flames of eternal hellfire!"

The girl, Goody, proves we're ancestors in more than name and face when she tilts her head back and glares at Crackstone defiantly. "I am innocent," she declares in faintly accented English. I can't quite place the accent, but it's distinctive. It sets her apart from the pilgrims. "It is you, Joseph Crackstone, who should be tried." Her face twists with its own self-righteous fury and I feel electrified again. Proud to be related to her. Proud to be here witnessing her bravery. "We were here first," she tells him. Tells the villagers all around. "Living in harmony with the native folk. But you have stolen our land. You have slaughtered the innocent. You have robbed us of our peaceful spirit. The true monster is you. *All of you.*"

From my perch behind the barrel, I see what she's planning to do before Crackstone does. And I know she won't succeed. Know history continues to unfold for this nightmarish man to leave his bloody fingerprints all over Jericho. But I can't help but root for her as she pulls a knife out of her sleeve and lunges for him.

She connects, slicing a gash across Crackstone's cheek that bleeds freely. But he's too quick to recover. He backhands her across the face with a roar that echoes through the woods.

"The devil never sent such a demon," he says. "And I will send you back."

He grabs her, and it's clear her bravery—incredible as it is, given everything she's up against—has deserted her. He drags her through the door of the Meeting House. I follow as quietly as I can.

I can't lose her. I have to know what happened here that night.

The scene inside the Meeting House is a horror. The entire room is packed with Outcasts, bound and chained to the floor. There are people of all genders, all ages. The children weep and the parents comfort them. The whole place smells of fear. Of fast-approaching death.

It's easy enough to meld with the crowd, to keep my eyes on Goody, who Crackstone grabs by the hair, throwing her to the ground. I've never felt so helpless. Doomed to witness the past, unable to change the fate of these people. My people.

"You are abominations in the Devil's grip," Crackstone says to the gathered crowd, the light from his torch dancing madly in his eyes. "I will not stop until I expunge this new world of every Outcast! Godless creatures!"

He storms out of the Meeting House. Before the door is closed, we all hear him say it:

"Set it ablaze."

Inside, fear spreads faster than fire. I keep my eyes on Goody as she runs to a woman chained near the wall, tearing at her chains. "Mother," she says, voice tight with fear. "I'll free you. We must escape."

I can see what Goody can't. The resignation on the woman's face. The acceptance. She puts a hand over her daughter's busy ones to still them. "There is no time, child. Leave me. Avenge us. Save the others and save our future."

"I won't go without you!" Goody shrieks. I can't help but picture my own mother. The most capable woman I've ever known. I can't imagine a world in which I'd ever be responsible for saving her.

Smoke is filling the room. The flames lick through the cracks in the Meeting House's wooden walls. There's so little time left. The iron chains won't budge. The horror dawns in full on Goody. On me. On every Outcast trapped in this place.

"Please, run as fast as you can," Goody's mother begs her. "You are our only hope."

The strength it must take her to walk away, knowing what's going to happen—what's already happening—is unfathomable to me. It makes every act of courage I've ever displayed look like child's play.

I try to follow her into the fireplace. The smoke is everywhere. I can barely breathe until she lifts the hatch and disappears inside. An escape not afforded to the people chained to the floor. To the walls. I give them one last look.

The passage leads to a clearing some ways from the Meeting House. Trees tower above us. The stars shine indifferently.

But there's no time to grieve. There are footsteps behind us. Goody looks at me in alarm, our eyes meeting in a shock of recognition. "He won't stop until he's killed us all."

Shouting. The footsteps are louder now.

"He's here," she whispers, and bolts.

"Wait!" I call after her, some half-formed plan of taking her back with me, of helping her somehow, dies before I can even begin to enact it. Crackstone is in the clearing. He's still holding the torch.

He strides toward Goody with menacing purpose. He's going to kill her. I know it. I lunge forward, out of my mind, willing to do anything . . . but I trip on an exposed root and hit the ground hard. . . .

CHAPTER FOURTEEN

A hand grips my shoulder. I scream, batting it away before I realize it's not attached to an arm. It's raining. The sky overhead is light.

The vision is slow to let go. Thing signs his concern rapidly, but I wave him off, struggling to sit. "I'm fine," I tell him. Physically, anyway. "I saw her again. The girl from the painting. Her name is Goody Addams."

Goody's mother, tears streaking her face. Goody, in Crackstone's grip.

"She must be my ancestor. From four hundred years ago . . ."

I'm interrupted by a noise from outside. A snapping branch. I get unsteadily to my feet, the vision still making me jumpy.

"Must be the bearded man from earlier," I say, as much to myself as to Thing. I cross to a section of the wall and peer cautiously through a crack. "Hello?"

There's nothing out there but rain and trees. Mud puddles on the path back to the road. It's going to be a long, wet walk back to Jericho.

Thing tugs on my pant leg and I look down in time to see him pointing, frantic.

I peer through the crack and meet a pair of enormous, bloodshot eyes. Shock floods my body, making me clumsy as I stumble back. But the monster doesn't pursue me into the ruin. It runs away.

That's the second time it's failed to kill me when it had the chance. But there's no time to think about why, not now. I shout to Thing, who leaps into my bag as we charge into the woods after the monster.

At first, the rain obscures everything. I can't tell which way it went. But then, on the ground. Footprints—huge ones, with claw marks. I follow them without considering the consequences. All I know is that Crackstone is in the past. The monster is killing people *now*. This might be my only chance to stop it. To stop *anything*.

The footprints already lead deep into the woods. I'm starting to realize I'll never catch up to it when I notice something odd. A human footprint, bare. And another. The monster's prints are gone. I crouch down to examine them and it's crystal clear. The transformation.

"The monster . . . it's *human*," I say, revolted but fascinated.

At least it's possible to catch up to it now. I forge ahead, not caring that I'm soaked to the skin and freezing. But another noise from behind makes me jump again. I whirl around, ready to face yet another harbinger of certain death.

But it's only Xavier, holding an umbrella, a strange and mundane reminder of the world in this mythical place.

"What the hell are you doing?" he asks, as if he's the one with the right to be annoyed.

"Chasing the monster," I counter.

Xavier's eyes widen, scanning all around us. "You *saw* it?" he asks. "It's *here*?"

I nod.

He holds out the umbrella to cover me, back at his ease. But I'm far from mine. "What exactly are you doing out here?" I ask.

Xavier has the good grace to look sheepish. "I overheard you say you were planning to check out the Meeting House. Back at the Weathervane? Guess it's lucky I decided to make sure you were okay."

The gears in my head are turning almost too fast to catch up to. "Yes," I concur. "Perfect timing." Almost too perfect. The monster becomes human and Xavier just happens to be lurking right at the place where the footprints shift?

In the world of investigation, there's no such thing as a coincidence.

"The monster is human," I offer, trying to bait him into confessing anything he might know. "The tracks turned from monster prints to bare human ones."

There's no guilt or shiftiness on Xavier's face, just surprise. Interest. "Show me," he urges me.

I look down to the trail I was just following, but there's only a puddle now.

"The rain washed them away. And before you arch your skeptical brow, I know what I saw."

Umbrella be damned, I storm off toward Jericho on my own. But Xavier catches up quickly. "I'm trying to be open-minded," he offers, replacing the umbrella over my head.

"Why now?"

He hesitates. I stop walking, wanting to see if a confession is forthcoming on his face.

"I think you might be right about Rowan," he says.

"Oh?"

Xavier shakes his head. "I texted him, kind of a setup. Told him we could meet up to go snowboarding like we did last spring break. He wrote back, said he wouldn't be able to make it. Only . . . we didn't go snowboarding last year."

This moody boy rises a half step in my estimation. "Clever," I say.

"Now I need you to be honest with me," he says, turning the tables. "Why'd you come out here really?"

After a lifetime of isolation, this exchanging of vulnerabilities is starting to become almost commonplace to me. I understand that it cost Xavier something to come here, to tell me what he told me. But I'm also wary of sharing too much, especially after the way Tyler behaved today.

"I was looking for clues about Crackstone," I say honestly. "After you identified him in the drawing today, I wanted to know more about how he's connected to Rowan's mother's vision."

The knowing gleam. Two people in one day. I consider taking up residence in the cave we pass. Never speaking to another human being again.

"And you were trying to use your psychic abilities?" he ventures.

"What makes you think I have any?" I retort, defensive.

"Lucky guess," Xavier replies, raising that eyebrow, mirroring my dodge from earlier when I knew what had happened between him and Rowan in their room. "When did they start?"

Deflated, I know there's no reason to keep up the farce. I am attending a school for Outcasts. It's only a matter of time before people discover my diagnosis.

"Not long ago," I manage. "When they happen, it's like touching a live wire. I usually enjoy pain, but not in this case."

Xavier resumes walking, perhaps correctly intuiting that I'd rather not be directly perceived in my moment of vulnerability. "You can't control it," he says. "That freaks you out."

Another direct hit. I feel like we're playing a game of psychic battleship and I'm losing badly. I don't say anything, but I can't help looking at him, searching his face for the source of this unexpected insight.

"My dad's a psychic," he says by way of explanation.

Of course, I think. His famous father. "Vincent Thorpe," I confirm. "My brother is his number one fan. Watched the Vegas special so many times I'm surprised it's not imprinted on his eyeballs."

Xavier doesn't take the bait. We have a long walk ahead of us still. "So, I've lived with the self-described master," he says. "And the first thing he'd tell you is that psychic visions can't be trusted. They only show one angle."

"I saw Joseph Crackstone as clearly as I'm seeing you right now," I argue, only aware after I've said it that I'm divulging too much. But now the vision is back, playing across my mind like a strange, ghostly double. I can't help myself. "He locked all the

Outcasts in the Meeting House and burned them alive."

For a moment, the only sound is our footsteps squelching in the mud. Then Xavier speaks, not to condemn me, or tell me I'm crazy, which is a relief. "Okay, he was a sadistic asshole," he allows. "But what does four hundred years ago have to do with now?"

"You saw Rowan's drawing," I say. "That's Crackstone standing in the quad. It's all connected. If I could only find out exactly how . . ."

"No," Xavier argues. "You're telling a story in your head and you're using these visions to support it. They're telling you what you *want* to see."

I can feel it as soon as he crosses the line in my mind, from momentary confidante to uninvited critic. "Wow, are you seriously mansplaining my powers to me?"

He throws up his hands, exasperated. "No! I'm just trying to tell you what I know. My dad says that psychic ability is rooted in emotion, not logic. You can't use emotions as evidence. And let's be real, feelings aren't exactly your strong suit anyway."

At this point, I close off to him completely. Trying to use a conversation about Outcast abilities and investigations to leverage some emotional blackmail is three strikes in one.

Jericho looms ahead of us at last. The rain has stopped for the moment, and I step out from under the umbrella. "Rowan was right," I tell him. "Something *is* going to happen. Something I have to stop before more people get hurt by this monster." I raise my own skeptical eyebrow at Xavier. "Whoever it is."

That night, I lie awake thinking about Goody. About Crackstone and the cruel twist of his features as he condemned a roomful of Outcasts to a fiery, painful death. How helpless Goody was as he loomed over her, and how helpless I feel in the present—the monster attacks, Rowan's mother's prediction, unable to stop what's coming.

And tomorrow, all of Nevermore Academy's blithe little student Outcasts will gather with the prejudiced Jericho normies and celebrate the genocidal son of a bitch.

How can I let that happen, knowing what I know?

The next day dawns sunny and cloudless—perfect weather to memorialize a psychopath. The Jericho town square is lined with bleachers, one side filled with uneasy townies, the other with bored Nevermore students. The divide only highlights Crackstone's legacy of fear and ostracization.

Principal Weems has brought my cello and introduced me to the marching band as threatened, and I sit in my chair serenely, awaiting my cue in more ways than one.

Mayor Noble Walker, father of Lucas, steps up to the microphone with a smiling Weems beside him. The picture of unity and tolerance. He takes the microphone as I signal Thing to wait. It's almost time.

"Hello, Jericho!" the mayor calls out. "It's my honor to celebrate our town's noble forefather, Joseph Crackstone. He believed that with a happy heart and an open ear, there was nothing our town couldn't achieve."

The screams of Crackstone's Outcast victims echo across four hundred years in my memory. I grit my teeth.

"Together as one," Mayor Walker continues, "our community and our Nevermore Academy neighbors have built a monument to celebrate his memory. May the spirit of Joseph Crackstone be remembered for eternity!"

This is the cue, according to the runny-nosed band geek who filled me in on the proceedings. The conductor lifts his baton. The band shuffles and situates in the bleachers while I wait, frozen in my chair, cello between my knees.

I join in with minimal enthusiasm as they begin a truly amateur version of Fleetwood Mac's "Don't Stop"—one of the poorer offerings in an otherwise stellar catalogue, in my opinion. Weems and Walker cross to a podium on the stage, posing before Walker presses a button with a cheesy, all-teeth smile that doesn't reach his eyes.

The crowd oohs and aahs as the fountain beneath the bronze rendering of Crackstone—life-size and smiling benevolently down on the townspeople—erupts, filling the basin at his feet with a clear liquid they all assume is water.

I know better. As I play my quarter notes by rote, I watch Thing scurry off into the crowd unnoticed. From this vantage point, I don't see him strike the match, nor light the trail of gunpowder he laid last night in preparation, but *everyone* sees the results.

The spark travels along gunpowder through the crowd, past the bandstand, snaking its way toward the fountain itself, which is filled *not* with water, as the mayor planned, but accelerant. It catches immediately, and screams rend the air as the flames leap up Crackstone's body in apocalyptic fashion. A much more fitting tribute to his true legacy, if I do say so myself.

Chaos erupts in the plaza. The crowd runs for cover, Jericho residents and Nevermore students comingling at last as they push to be first out of the blast zone. The mayor, campaign-ad smile long gone, pushes past Weems and dives off the stage.

Fleetwood Mac becomes Vivaldi's "Winter," the perfect song for a retributive strike. Mine might be coming four hundred years too late, but there's no doubt it's effective.

No one is even looking at me as I lose myself to the music. No one, I amend a moment later, but Weems, who is glaring daggers at me from beside the stage. Perhaps the Vivaldi was a bit of a giveaway.

The moment we're back on Nevermore soil, Weems has me in her office, sat in a chair placidly as she paces and gesticulates before her massive Medusa fireplace.

"That was a disaster!" she shouts. "The mayor is furious! I've lost count of the number of angry phone calls and emails I've received from Jericho residents, alumni, *and* parents. They want answers"— she crouches down to look into my eyes—"and so do I."

"Well, it looks like Outreach Day was a success, then," I say innocently. "The townspeople and the school on the same side. Wasn't that what you wanted?"

Weems throws up her hands, groaning in sheer frustration that's only too satisfying. "I can't prove it was you," she says. "But I see you, Wednesday. You're a magnet for trouble."

For a moment, it's there again. A flash of Rowan's mother's drawing. Crackstone and me, facing off across Nevermore's five-sided quad, wreathed in flames.

"If trouble means standing up to lies, then I have to agree," I say, getting to my feet as though my five feet of height is anything compared to her six plus. "Decades of discrimination. Centuries of treating Outcasts as second-class citizens, or worse."

"What are you talking about?" Weems asks sharply.

"Jericho!" I exclaim. "You must know it's real history with the Outcasts. The *real* history of Crackstone."

Her face gives her away before she can speak, and I can't believe there was ever a time I thought I might admire this woman. Sure, she may have survived my mother in her adolescence, but she's a coward, plain and simple.

"If you know, why would you be complicit in covering it up?"

130

I ask, hearing the screams again, seeing the terror on Goody's face as she left her mother behind. "They still hate us in Jericho, nothing has changed besides the platitudes and smiles they candy-coat it in. If *you're* unwilling to fight for the truth—"

She steps in front of me, eyes flashing in the firelight. "You think I don't want the truth?" she interrupts. "Of course I do. But the world isn't black and white. Sometimes you have to compromise."

My disappointment only deepens. I shake my head. "There's no both ways about something like this," I tell her. "Either we tell our story or they do."

For once, being alone doesn't feel like a solution. I can't help imagining what the world would be like if more people knew. People in power. People who could actually change something.

Back in my room, Enid's mood—as usual—couldn't be more different from mine. She's choosing between an array of offensively bright outfits laid carefully on her bed. Usually, I subsist fine on four hours of sleep, but right now I feel drained. Exhausted.

I sit down at my desk, trying to get through the latest chapter of my novel, head pounding as Enid recalls the strange roadkill taxidermy she spent the day grooming alongside Ajax. The mysterious *local artist* who scrapes dead rodents off the highway and puts them in doctor lab coats and wedding attire and sailor uniforms.

"Sounds like a perfect backdrop for romance," I say sarcastically, but to my surprise Enid blushes.

"So glad I have my date with him tonight," Enid continues, completely oblivious to my distaste for her hot-pink crop top. "It'll take my mind off that train wreck of an afternoon. I think I have PTSD. I didn't even get to do my jazz-dance routine."

"What a tragedy," I mutter, not looking up from my typewriter.

"What kind of twisted psycho would want to sabotage such a life-affirming event?" Enid laments.

I stop typing. "You're going to be late."

"Wish me luck?" Enid asks as she loops a tiny little purse over her arm.

I wish, for just the slightest second, that anything could divert me from the horrors of my investigation, my worries for the future, like a date with a half-brainless Gorgon can for Enid.

"If he breaks your heart, I'll nail gun his," I say after a long pause. It's the best I can do.

When she's gone, I lie on my bed as rain streaks our massive window. My stunt today with Crackstone's statue felt good in the moment, but what did it really change? I feel like an island—it's usually a role I enjoy, but right now I'm all too aware of how little one person can accomplish when faced with all the monsters of the world.

The past, present, and future monsters. The literal and figurative ones. The monsters hiding in plain sight. The monsters we're all afraid are inside of us, waiting for their turn.

But on that night, there was so much I couldn't see. Namely, I wasn't the only one reckoning with the monstrous as the sky let loose its great torrents. Let me give you a taste from the future. Not too much, mind you. I wouldn't want to ruin the suspense.

Enid, claws politely retracted, waits behind the greenhouse for Ajax as he inadvertently stones himself in the mirror of the boys' shower, never to arrive for their date. As the moon rises, so does her ire, until the monster in *her* erupts, claws gouging the length of a school bus and slashing its tire.

Principal Weems, decompressing from our interaction with a

glass of wine, pages casually through a yearbook until she arrives on the page half filled with a picture of my teenaged mother. Tearing the page from the book, Weems tosses it into her fire, reducing it to ash.

My sanctimonious therapist, Dr. Kinbott, bends over a worktable, stitching diligently at a stuffed, dead squirrel, to which she's lovingly affixing a winter scarf. Once it's finished, she carries it across the room to a locked closet and sets him carefully among thirty of his horrifying, vacant-eyed brethren.

Tyler submerges himself in his bathtub at home, only to scream silently, eyes open and bloodshot beneath the water. Xavier steps out of an overgrown shed on campus, locking it behind him, reaching up to touch three bleeding slash marks on his neck.

Worst of all, the bearded man is being discovered in pieces at the Old Meeting House, his blood soaking the ground where the Outcasts had burned so many years ago. Sheriff Galpin lifts a camera from the viscera. One with only a few photos left on its roll.

Late in the night, the photos are developed. Photos I won't see for a long time yet. Photos of the monster himself, looking right into the lens, smeared in the blood of his latest victim.

CHAPTER FIFTEEN

In our next session, Dr. Kinbott—who I still do not know as the architect of the squirrel roadkill wedding in the window of Uriah's Heap—tells me I should combat my feelings of isolation by *getting out more*.

I don't think an unsanctioned trip to the morgue is exactly what she had in mind, but I can't deny I feel better after I've been. In my dorm, I'm adding new information to the growing board of clues and connections when Enid arrives.

"When I suggested giving your side of the room a makeover, I didn't have true crime Pinterest in mind."

"True crime is for bored housewives who assign more humanity to killers than their victims," I say without looking up. "I imagine it's their colonizer instincts."

"Okay," Enid says. "But . . . what *is* all this? Are these gross pictures the reason you snuck out last night?"

"Yes," I say, connecting a picture of a kidney in a jar to one of a man with his chest torn to ribbons. "I went to the morgue to copy files of all the monster's victims." I don't tell her I can still feel the welcome chill of the body drawer I hid in to avoid the coroner.

"There are so many levels of *ew* here that I don't even know where to begin."

"Enid, if I'm going to stop this monster, I have to get inside its head. I have to figure out the patterns and anomalies in its attack record. And I've already found something huge."

Now that all my connections are accurately represented, I take the extra photos and turn around to show them to Enid.

"Look at this. All the victims have had body parts removed. The first one was missing a kidney, the second one a finger—"

"Uh, Wednesday," Enid says, looking down at them.

"I know, the gallbladder. Fascinating. And the man from the Meeting House was missing two toes." Enid doesn't immediately respond, so I continue. "Don't you see what this means? The murders aren't the mindless work of a beast or animal. The monster is collecting trophies like a seasoned serial killer."

Before I can point out the potential to predict the monster's next victim based on illegally obtained Jericho medical records, there's a thud. Enid and the photos hit the floor.

I experience a pang of guilt as I summon Thing. "Fetch the smelling salts. . . ." I tell him. "Again."

Once Enid has been safely deposited in the nurse's office to monitor for signs of a concussion, I abscond to Ms. Thornhill's class, expecting to be bored to tears by carnivorous plant facts my mother taught me before my fifth birthday.

Instead, Xavier proves a distraction, wincing in pain as he reaches for his notebook.

Noticing my attention, he waves me off. "I tweaked my back fencing," he says. But his movements aren't consistent with avoiding the activation of a muscle strain in the mid-body. The wince seems more consistent with a wound. Somewhere higher.

I'm about to inquire when Ms. Thornhill raises her voice above the din. "Okay, I know you're all excited about the Rave'N Saturday night—which is why I'm *not* assigning homework."

A general cheer goes up from the anti-intellectual masses.

"But I am still looking for volunteers to help with the decorations. Any takers?"

Xavier leans toward me. "You're not pumped about a disco ball and spiked punch?" he asks. "There's even gonna be a DJ."

I roll my eyes. "I'd rather stick needles in my eye than go to a school dance. At least acupuncture is known to promote mental acuity and overall vitality. I've yet to be convinced of the health benefits of spiked punch."

"You know," he says, closing his notebook, "you could just invite someone. Have a little fun for once?"

I believe Xavier has interacted with me often enough to know that I would never voluntarily go to a social event, let alone ask a fellow student on a date.

My lack of response doesn't seem to faze him. He makes to stow his notebook away, but as he bends down to pick it up, my earlier hypothesis is confirmed. Deep lacerations along the left side of his neck. They look a few days old at most.

Straightening up, he flips his collar to hide them. I look studiously down at my own notes so he won't suspect I've seen anything, but he looks at me a long time before hurrying out of the room.

I can't let this go. The wounds on his neck don't look like any archery accident I've ever seen. So I end up trailing Xavier out to the school grounds, where I watch him slip into an unassuming, abandoned gardener's shed.

Thing questions me as I hide in the nearby hedges. I snap, "Yes, we have to do this. Xavier didn't get those scratches fencing—and you saw the pattern same as me. It's close enough to the photos of the victims that I know he's hiding something."

Xavier emerges, eyes shifting back and forth nervously before he hustles away. I duck behind the bramble I'm ensconced in until he's out of sight. And he's left the shed unlocked.

Inside, everything is light and shadow. There's a single lightbulb with a chain attached, and I click it on, only to gasp. I'm absolutely surrounded by artistic depictions of the monster. Large canvasses that are nearly life-size, small ones barely the size of a greeting card. At least fifty of them, and every single one shows its bulging yellow eyes, the rows of razor-sharp teeth.

I think back to my interactions with Xavier. I've seen nothing that leads me to believe he's capable of killing anyone, but I've been wrong before. On rare occasion. Is it possible that Xavier is the monster? He did appear at the ruins exactly at the moment when the footprints turned into human ones. . . .

After I adjust to the shock of what I've found, I notice a pattern. A circular, dark vortex behind at least half of Xavier's pieces. I take two pages from his journal, fold them up, and slip them into my bag.

"Time to go," I tell Thing, who clicks off the light, leaving us in darkness.

The door is closed behind us and we're beelining for the school, but I only get a few steps before I hear a rustling from the path.

"Wednesday?" Xavier says, approaching the door I'm just leaving. "What are you doing?"

"Nothing!" I say brightly. "I just . . . saw you come out this way." He didn't see me exit the shed. I'll pretend I've only just arrived and get out of here as soon as possible.

"Okay, well, this is my private art studio. Weems said I could use it if I cleaned it out."

"Fantastic," I say. "Why don't you give me a tour?"

I know he won't agree, but I'm curious what his excuse will be. He's already proven he's not above lying with that fake fencing injury earlier.

"It's kind of a mess right now," he says.

"I shadowed a crime scene photographer last summer," I assure him. "I'm not squeamish."

Xavier's jaw sets a little more firmly as he says, "Maybe another time." And then, turning the tables on me: "Why were you looking for me anyway?"

I was so prepared to be on the offensive in this interaction that I haven't even considered a defense. "Oh, I wanted to go over Thornhill's homework assignment." Easy enough.

"She didn't give us homework," Xavier says, which is, of course, true. Stupid weekend dance. But he doesn't look suspicious, or angry. Instead, he's . . . smirking?

"Right," I say, feeling wrong-footed. "Well, I should be going."

"Wait a minute." He comes closer, that strange smile widening. "Is this about a certain *dance* that makes you want to poke needles into your eyes?"

It's at this moment that I know I will never understand people. A boy with a secret finds me, a girl with obvious obsessive investigative tendencies, rummaging around his off-limits, monster-filled art studio, and his first thought is that I'm here to make some utterly out-of-character romantic overture? Why?

But as distasteful as this all is, he's offering me an out. A broadly paved, well-lit one with only a single negative consequence.

As if it's not literally killing me to do it, I nod.

His smirk becomes a genuine smile. As he congratulates himself, I console myself. At least I'll get the chance to spend an evening with a potential serial killer. With his guard down, who knows what I might find out.

"I'm all ears," Xavier says.

Sometimes intentions melt in the face of unexpected opportunity. If this is my chance to get up close and personal with a potential serial killer, how can I refuse?

I close my eyes and take a deep breath. "You're really going to make me ask?"

"Oh, absolutely." He steps closer, all puffed up with adolescent male pride. It's all I can do not to deflate him with a sharp jab. *Clues*, I remind myself. *A suspect with his defenses lowered.*

"Would you . . . possibly . . . ," I begin through gritted teeth, "consider going to the Rave'N ... with ... a certain"—*person who would rather do almost anything else*—"... me?"

The cockiness gives way to genuine boyish joy. He reminds me of Enid when she's got a crush, all sparkly-eyed and prone to ignoring red flags. "Yes, Wednesday," he says. "I'd love to go with you. I never thought you'd ask."

I turn to release myself from this social thumbscrewing, relieved that he doesn't stop me. "Neither did I," I mutter under my breath.

The only thing worse than accidentally asking Xavier to the Rave'N is telling Enid I asked Xavier to the Rave'N. I don't even cover my ears. I deserve the pain of the shriek-slash-howl that fills the room.

"I can't *believe* Wednesday Addams is going to a school dance!" she says when she becomes verbal again. "My world just *tilted*."

"So did mine, and unfortunately I didn't fall off into the cold vacuum of space."

Enid ignores this, turning away from her ridiculously overstuffed closet to appraise me. "You know what you need now?" she asks.

"A swift blow to the head?" I ask conversationally.

"A *dress*," Enid corrects me. As if this should have been obvious.

Luckily for me I already predicted this line of inquiry, and I have a rebuttal prepared. "I already have a dress." One, to be exact. But now that Xavier believes he's broken my resistance to his so-called charms, I doubt my outfit makes much of a difference.

Unluckily, I've underestimated Enid's commitment to the makeover montage.

"Oh, Wednesday. Not the dress you showed up here in. That

was a fashion emergency even lightning couldn't resuscitate. Back me up, Thing."

My traitorous underling crosses the room, taking Enid's side as I deeply regret, for at least the fifth time, the day I introduced the two of them.

"You need something that screams 'Eat your heart out, Bianca Barclay, I have arrived!'" Enid exclaims, with Thing offering her a thumbs-up in the background.

I decide upstaging Bianca, my de facto nemesis, is a compelling enough reason to give in. The truth is, I have business in Jericho that has nothing to do with this awful social gathering—except perhaps to make the information I gather there mean something.

Enid chatters nonstop on the way into town as I mull over my ulterior motives for accompanying her. I'd planned on telling her the truth—that I'm only accompanying Xavier because he's a suspect, that this is all part of a larger plot—but the dance clearly means so much to her. Sometimes I think Enid is the only person I've met at Nevermore who genuinely cares for me, and not some projection of me they've invented on their own.

As such, it seems both unnecessary and cruel to take the wind out of her proverbial sails. If Saturday night is as productive as I'm imagining, I can pretend it's all a big coincidence.

Enid has reached the last quarter of the alphabet as she sorts potential escorts in yearbook order when we arrive in Jericho. She hauls me to the front of a store I've never even glanced at before. It looks like the contents of Enid's closet, covered in confetti icing.

"Our first roommate shopping spree!" she squeals, looping her arm through mine, which I endure only because I plan to escape her grasp and this outing as soon as possible. "The dance committee's *suggesting* all white to match the theme, but that's not gonna fly for us."

She takes a step inside, but I dig in my heels. Our locked elbows are now a tether. "Enid, as much as I appreciate the gesture . . ."

Her smile is sympathetic as she releases me. "This really isn't your scene, is it?"

I shake my head, as if it wasn't painfully obvious without my confirmation. "If I'm going to attend a dance, I'd at least like to resemble myself physically while I do it."

Enid's disappointment is palpable. "I just thought we could, you know, bond," she says with a shrug. "But I get it. I don't want you to be someone you're not."

A crowd of girls from Nevermore with the same idea as Enid walk past us without greeting. I recognize Yoko and a few other girls from the Nightshades. One of them eyes Enid's current outfit approvingly.

"We'll find an appropriately compromising bonding activity one of these days," I assure her. "In the meantime, I feel like I'd only slow you down."

A hint of a smile is visible at the corner of her sparkly lips as the compliment lands.

"You're a gazelle," I say, picturing her shopping. Graceful. Confident. "I'm a wounded fawn. Cut me loose and go run with the pack."

Enid is smiling in earnest now. "You know, maybe we were bonding after all. I mean, that is the nicest compliment you've ever given me."

"The bar has been set," I say. "I live to exceed my own expectations."

She bumps my shoulder with hers, a gesture of affection I find much more tolerable than the hugging or elbow-linking or hand-holding girls of my generation seem to find far too many occasions to engage in.

"If I see anything funereal, I'll put it on hold for you?"

"Thank you," I say, and then I turn and walk away before she can change her mind and drag me inside.

I head to the police station, hoping an appointment with the sheriff can shed more light on Xavier's suspicious activities. As I walk down the street, Thing pops out of my backpack and excitedly taps me on the shoulder, pointing to something past me.

"No," I say to him irritably. "I'm going to see Galpin. I'm not stop—"

I pause midsentence. In front of me, through the window of an antiques shop, is a striking midnight-black dress. A high collar sits above a mesh neckline adorned with ruffled black lace. The skirt is tiered with the same material, cascading down to the bottom of the window display. I stare at it for longer than I'd like to admit.

I consider it a minor miracle when I reach the sheriff's office without being waylaid again. Inside, it's dark and musty. Depressing as all hell.

He's at his desk, five-o'clock shadow inching toward seven o'clock. I put my best piece of evidence to date on his desk.

The sheriff's eyes widen momentarily. He immediately attempts to hide his surprise, but I'm quicker than he wants to believe.

"We both know this monster is out there," I say without preamble. "If we're going to stop it, I've decided we need to put our differences, which are insurmountable in the long term, aside for now. Strike a temporary alliance."

Galpin looks amused, which causes me to bristle. He's lucky I'm even willing to lower myself to this point. If I had access to my own forensics lab and search team, there's no way I would be here.

"So, this drawing is your stake for me to deal you in?" he asks.

"Yes, and the gambling metaphor inspires plenty of confidence, let me assure you."

Galpin studies the drawing alongside another picture of a different kind, comparing the two. I can't see what it is, though I surreptitiously try. He intentionally doesn't show me. Two can play at that game.

"Sorry," the sheriff says. "You're going to have to do better than that. Your drawing has some nice detail, though."

"I didn't draw it," I say, almost absentmindedly.

It turns out, it's this admission that piques the sheriff's interest at last. "I need to know who did."

I shake my head. "Unless we start sharing intel, I'm not at liberty to say."

He's irritated now. I see some of the bluster that must have made him a shoo-in for the job when he leans over the desk. "Listen, Velma, why don't you and your Scooby Gang stick to your homework and leave the investigation to professionals."

I snatch the drawing from his hand. Just then, his intercom buzzes. *"Sheriff, it's the mayor on line two."* I take this as my cue to vacate.

"Hey, Addams," he calls out as I'm nearing the door.

Stopping is all the concession I'll give him.

"The person who drew that picture. Is that your suspect?" he asks the back of my head.

I shrug.

"Bring me some more concrete evidence and maybe we'll talk."

I walk out, not dignifying him with a response.

CHAPTER SIXTEEN

I'm making my way back to the Weathervane to meet Enid, no doubt to suffer the consequences of her latest shopping haul, when Tyler waylays me outside the station. "Should I ask what trouble you've gotten into now?"

"Nothing I can't handle," I say shortly, thinking of our last interaction. Tyler's insistence on accompanying me into the woods. Then, out of the goodness of my heart, I warn him: "Your father is in particularly frustrating form today. Avoid."

He chuckles. "Welcome to my world."

I start to walk past him when he stops me with an utter non

sequitur. "You guys have that big dance coming up this weekend, right?"

I do a terrible job hiding my surprise and discomfort with the subject change.

"It was all the buzz at the Weathervane today," he clarifies. It's not a question, but he's still waiting as if he's asked one.

All this talk about the dance is exhausting. "God, I must be the only person in town not obsessed with this ridiculous adolescent mating ritual."

Tyler smiles. He looks relieved, which is more perplexing than anything. "I should have known you wouldn't be going."

It would be so easy to let that be that. To walk away and go about the rest of my life without having the conversation he wants to have. But lying, for the sake of preserving someone's unfathomable feelings, isn't something I would do, and I don't want to let this place, these *people* change me.

"Actually, I was forced to ask someone as an act of self-preservation," I clarify.

His face contorts a little, as if he's experiencing a stomach cramp. "Sure, that happens. I guess." It's clear he doesn't believe it. Even I have to admit it sounds far-fetched. But only if you don't know what lengths I would typically go to avoid an event like this. "So, who is it?"

I took brutal honesty as my weapon of choice in pre-K. I won't abandon my principles now for a boy who got attached to something I didn't promise him.

"Xavier," I say.

This time, the expression is less stomach cramp and more punch to the gut. He doesn't hide it well. "Got it," he manages, his face turning bright red. "I hope you two have fun."

Tyler makes to storm off, once again giving me a perfect out that I, once again, don't take. This day has been such an awful tangle of other people's feelings. Xavier wanting me to ask him to the dance enough that he ignored the obvious red flags. Enid taking me to that ridiculous dress store. Now Tyler . . .

"I don't understand why you're so upset," I say, the frustration spilling over.

"Yeah, that's kind of the problem," he says, whirling back around to face me. "Call me crazy, Wednesday, but I thought we liked each other."

There's something in his eyes as he says it. Something that transcends the sad-boy townie barista category I filed him under on the day we met. Some internal war that I find I can relate to. In that moment, I see someone extremely lonely, afraid of what they're capable of, reaching out to someone they believe could share their pain.

But what secret pain could Tyler Galpin have?

As I'm intuiting, he's ranting: "When you do something like this, like asking *him* to this dance, I have no idea where I stand. Am I just some lackey you hit up when you need local geography knowledge or a ride? Or is there a chance I could ever get into the more-than-friend zone?"

Not when there's a murderer on the loose, and Rowan's mother's fiery vision of Crackstone and me is still looming. But I don't tell him that. "I'm dealing with a lot of other things right now," I say to Tyler instead, trying to make him understand. "I need to prioritize—"

He doesn't let me finish. When he turns away this time, I know it's the end of the conversation. Maybe the end of this friendship, if that's what it was.

"Thanks for clearing that up," he says over his shoulder. "Maybe give me a call when I move up your to-do list."

And then he's gone, and Thing is climbing out of my bag with a finger placement that tells me he's queuing up a lecture, and I'm ready to fulfill my destiny of moving to the deep dark woods and becoming a hag who scares children picking berries.

"Not. One. Word," I tell him, and he disappears back into the bag.

I disappear from the Weathervane before Enid shows up, hoping she'll understand my need to distance myself from the uncomfortable conversation I just had with Tyler.

I take a while to return to Nevermore, and when I finally reach my room, Enid is nowhere to be seen. Instead, there's a note on my bed.

NO LUCK ON A BLACK DRESS—GOING TO RAVE'N WITH LUCAS WALKER—PLEASE GET THIS DISGUSTING SCIENCE PROJECT OUT OF MY EYELINE BEFORE I BARF. XO ENID

Each word is a different color. I'm not sure which news item horrifies me more—the fact that Enid is going on a date with *Lucas Walker* or that my prized investigation board is soon to be homeless.

"Come on," I say to Thing, who still looks ready to lecture. "Let's get this out of here before we have to rouse Enid from unconsciousness again."

Eugene and I are in the Hummers' shed, looking over my case wall. This time, I orient the entire thing around the map of the Jericho woods that Tyler marked the Meeting House ruins on. I add the location of each attack.

Coming up behind me, Eugene says the very words I was just thinking: "That attack pattern is pretty clustered."

"It is," I confirm, pleased that at least one person I've spoken to today has their priorities in order.

He points to Xavier's drawing. The monster with the black vortex behind it. "I assume this is the creature that's been rampaging in the woods?"

Another surprise. This time I look at Eugene, who's leaning in closer to the drawing. "You've heard about it?"

Eugene shrugs. "Only rumors. Mr. Fitts banned me from bug hunting in the woods until further notice. He claimed a bear was on the loose, but I knew that was a lie. The attack pattern didn't match their hibernation schedule."

"Exactly what I said," I murmur as Eugene takes his shoulder bag from the shelf behind him.

"Speaking of monsters with sharp claws," he says, handing me a jar of honey from the hive outside. "Could you give this to your roommate and put in a good word for me? Buzz around school is that she's still sans date for the Rave'N."

If I was expecting more surprising insight on the investigation, the world has just righted itself again. Eugene and everyone else in the world, obsessed with this dance.

"Eugene . . . ," I say as kindly as I can manage. Despite my earlier commitment to the cold, hard truth with Tyler, I can't bring myself to tell Eugene that Enid will be attending the dance with none other than his tormentor from Outreach Day.

There's honesty, and then there's brutality.

"I know the chances of her asking me are next to zero," he assures me, though the hope in his chubby face belies this reasonable sentiment. "I'm just gonna keep putting myself out there until she sees me."

Enid's patterns of male attraction have never been more befuddling to me than they are today, but I know one thing for certain. Eugene is not on the list. "What if she never does?" I ask.

"She will," Eugene replies confidently. "My moms say people will appreciate me when I'm older. Till then, I'm playing the long game."

The thin layer of bravado issued through the mangled retainer is just about all the sad and pathetic I can handle for one day. I don't blame Eugene for getting his hopes up—far from it. I blame a society that's made in-crowd norms the barometer for happiness when they're unachievable for so many of us.

"Eugene," I tell him. "People like you and me . . . we're different. We're original thinkers. Pioneers. Intrepid outliers in this vast, stinking cesspool of adolescence. We don't need these inane rites of passage to validate who we are."

His face grows more hopeful as I speak, but then he points out an obvious flaw in my hyperbole without knowing he's doing it. "So you're not going to the Rave'N either?"

My heart sinks. This time, a lie of omission wouldn't do, and an outright lie isn't ethical, so all I can do is tell the truth. "Actually, I am," I say. "With Xavier."

As predicted, Eugene's momentary confidence disappears, leaving him glum and defeated. "I see. So some of us are the kind of different where we end up with the most popular guy in school taking us to the inane rite of passage, and some of us are the hopeless, forever-alone kind."

In that moment, I have to wonder if the information I might gather from attending this idiotic dance with my number one suspect is more trouble than it's worth. Tyler, Enid, Eugene, even Xavier. They all have the entirely wrong idea about why I'm doing this.

But Eugene doesn't appear to be interested in my potential reasons for not skipping out on the school dance. Instead, he's peering through his smudged glasses at the drawing. "This circle," he says in a faraway voice. "I think I know where it is."

A jolt of electricity runs through me. A potential investigative discovery *and* the chance to drop the subject of the odious Rave'N? I'd call it a miracle—if I believed in those.

"Show me," I demand, and Eugene leads the way out of the Hummers' shed, into the woods beyond.

An hour later, Eugene is ruddy-faced and sweating, and the two of us are standing before a natural rock formation that's eerily similar to the vortex in Xavier's drawings.

It's a cave, hidden at the base of an overgrown outcropping. The sole entrance is about four feet wide. Plenty big enough for the monster to squeeze inside. I hold up the drawing again to confirm.

"There's no doubt it's a match," I say to Eugene, who is huffing and puffing beside me. "What were you doing all the way out here?"

Eugene's face lights up in a way that can only signify insect factoids are forthcoming. "Collecting specimens! This place is ground zero for horny spongy moths."

One thing I've learned with Eugene is not to ask follow-up questions when it comes to bugs. I take out a flashlight, peering into the darkness of the cave mouth. I can't see anything, even with the light pointed directly inside.

"You think it's in there?" Eugene asks, a trembling in his voice.

"Only one way to find out." I take a step forward, feeling electric all over. Could it be this simple? The monster's lair, at last?

Eugene hasn't ventured any farther toward the entrance. I look back at him questioningly. Who would want to miss an opportunity like this?

"Not a big fan of confined spaces," he admits. "I'm claustrophobic."

I shrug. "Suit yourself. If you hear me screaming bloody murder, don't come in after me. There's a good chance I'm just enjoying myself."

When I step into the cave, I hear Eugene's timid boots following and I smile.

The cave inside isn't large, but it's clear something's been living here. A crunch underfoot prompts me to redirect the flashlight, revealing a carpet of bones.

I think of Enid finding the perfect outfit. The smile that spreads all the way to her eyes. This must be the same feeling. "This is definitely its lair," I say, doing my best to mask my enthusiasm out of deference for Eugene's obvious terror.

"Are these . . . human?" he asks, gingerly moving a tibia with his toe.

Reaching down, I retrieve a skull. Fractured eye sockets, antler stubs. "Looks like it's got a taste for venison."

The cave appears deserted, so I move more boldly to the middle, shining the flashlight on the walls to discover a tapestry of frenzied scratches in the stone. They remind me of the scratch marks prisoners made in the stone walls of Alcatraz, only I don't think whatever made these was cognizant enough to be counting the days.

"Wednesday, look," Eugene calls. He's holding up a manacle attached to a heavy-duty chain that's bolted to the stone.

I start to move toward him, and that's when I catch it. Something embedded in the wall at the end of one of the deepest gouges in the stone.

"Bull's-eye," I say, pulling out my penknife to retrieve it from the stone. It's a claw. At least three inches long. Broken at the place it should attach to a digit. It's yellowy-white, and the tip is incredibly sharp.

Unbidden, the image of Xavier's supposed fencing injury returns to me. Gashes along his neck. When I came out here, I only had a vague hope. Now I have a plan—or two more steps of one, at least.

"What is it?" Eugene asks, creeping closer.

I smile in the beam of his flashlight, the bones beneath my feet. "Concrete proof," I reply.

Thing and I make it back to the shed before we lose the light. It's deserted and unlocked. I'm almost embarrassed by Xavier's carelessness as we enter his strange shrine to the monster.

"Keep a lookout," I tell Thing before heading inside. "I won't be long. I just need something to match against the claw's DNA."

Thing gives me a thumb-up and closes the door behind me. This time I take no chances with the overhead light, clicking on my flashlight instead. At least fifty of the monster's horrible yellowish eyes follow me as I approach the trash can.

There are empty paint tubes, candy wrappers, an encrusted

paintbrush. I'm about to give up hope when I spot it near the bottom—a rag streaked with blood. I use the paintbrush to extract it and place it in the specimen baggie I never leave home without.

In and out in less than three minutes. Sometimes I even surprise myself.

Stowing the bag quickly, I get to my feet. But it seems even my three minutes was too long, because the door is opening and the silhouette is much too large to be Thing.

"Wednesday?" Xavier sounds shocked, hurt. When he closes the door behind him, I can see his expression matches his voice. "What the hell are you doing here?"

There's no convenient dance invitation in the world that could get me out of this one. Instead, I remember something my mother once said. *The best defense is a good offense.*

I point to the paintings all around us. "How do you know what the monster looks like?" I ask in my most accusatory tone. "Or are these *self*-portraits?"

The hurt and shock persist a moment longer before morphing into unmistakable anger. At least this way, we won't have to dress up and parade around in front of our classmates before I get my answers.

"You seriously think *I'm* the monster?" he asks. "I saved your life!"

"So did the monster," I parry. "It was you, wasn't it? The night Rowan was killed? And again at the Old Meeting House. The monster leaves me alone and then you mysteriously appear right where its tracks turn to human?"

Xavier rolls his eyes, as if it all doesn't make perfect sense. "You are so out of line."

"I'm just trying to get to the truth," I say. "And you have to admit this particular showing of your work doesn't paint you in the best light."

He steps forward, his eyes intent on mine as he points to the closest monster. "This creature has been haunting my dreams for weeks, okay?" he says, on the defensive now, right where I wanted him. "I try to block it out, but I can't. The only thing that helps is painting it. Over and over."

Xavier walks to the largest canvas, the one closest to me. I resist the urge to step away from him. I need to look him in the eye to know for sure.

"When I was drawing that one . . . its claws reached right out of the canvas and took a swipe at me. That's how I got the scratches. I was going to tell you at the dance."

His face and body language display none of the tell-tale signs of dishonesty—but that doesn't mean he isn't simply schooled in the art of deception. "I thought you could control your ability," I say, stalling for time.

"Not when it comes to this thing," he says grimly.

"Maybe it's your guilty conscience," I reply, knowing I'm pushing too far. If I anger him enough, will he transform here and now? Add me to the monster's ever growing victim list?

"I told you!" he shouts. "I'm not the monster!"

Again, no sign of an obvious lie. No darting eyes or nervous tics or twitches or sweating. But this is the closest I've been to solving this mystery in months. I can't back down. There's still every chance he's hiding something.

"You just happened to draw pictures of the monster, down to the location of its lair in the woods?" I press. "Those must be some pretty vivid dreams."

But instead of an expression of guilt, I see one of suspicion bloom on his angular features. "Wait," he says. "You were in here before, weren't you? When I caught you outside. The only reason you asked me to the dance was to try and cover . . ."

I don't meet his eyes this time. I'm not proud of it, but a brilliant investigator goes to any lengths to get to the truth.

"You're unbelievable," he says. As if I'm somehow the monster in this scenario.

"It's nothing personal," I tell him. The same thing I've been telling everyone all day. Tyler, Enid, Eugene . . .

"It never is with you," he bites back. "Do you actually care about anyone? Are we all just pawns to you?"

The question is eerily similar to the one Tyler asked me earlier. I didn't know how to answer it then, either. Aren't we all just pawns to each other? Isn't everyone simply moving toward their own goals and clumsily bumping into each other along the way?

Xavier scoffs. He's still hurt, but now he looks disappointed too. Disappointed in the person he thought I was—as if he ever made any attempt to separate me from his projection.

"Get out," he says, and I'm only too happy to oblige.

The following morning, I'm up before the sun to arrive at Galpin's office first thing. I storm in, stopping only when I hear him on the phone. Listening at the door:

". . . I know she's usually three sheets to the wind, but she keeps calling the mayor and telling him there are lights on at the old Gates place. Just do a drive-by, make sure it's not squatters."

I throw the door open without knocking.

The sheriff doesn't even seem surprised to see me. I drop the baggies of evidence on the desk.

"That's the monster's claw," I tell him, pointing. "And that's blood from my suspect. Run a DNA test and see if there's a match."

He squints at me, irritated as always. "I'm sorry, are you under the mistaken impression that I work for you?"

"You said to bring you concrete evidence. I did. What's the holdup?"

Sighing, he picks up the baggies, peering into them against the light of the window. "How the hell did you get that? And who's the suspect?"

"Run the test," I order. "Then I'll tell you everything." Of course, I have no intention of doing so. Any information Galpin brings me will only further my own investigation. I have no intention of being useful to him, only making him useful to me.

"I'm not playing games, Miss Addams," he growls. A tactic that might be effective on a lesser mortal.

"Neither am I, Sheriff," I retort.

He blinks first, then sighs again, pushing down his intercom button. "Bernice, bring me a DNA authorization form."

The thrill of victory tastes better than any watery spiked punch ever could.

CHAPTER SEVENTEEN

Back at the quad, I beeline for Eugene, who's looking glumly at the reflecting pool. It's packed with students chattering inanely about tonight's festivities.

"Why so glum?" I ask him, as if I don't already know.

"Saw Enid this morning," he says. "Asked if she got my honey."

I sit down beside him. "I tried to warn you."

"She said you and Xavier had a big blowout," Eugene says, gesturing to where the suspect in question is working on a mural across the quad.

The last thing I want to do is discuss social drama with the only person at this school who seems to have a single reasonable priority. "Well, since neither of us have dates..."

"We should go together!" Eugene exclaims.

I'm not quick enough to hide my surprise, or my displeasure. "No!" I exclaim. "That is, I meant to suggest we go stake out the cave. Try to ID the monster..."

I cast a dark look at Xavier, who returns it until he's engaged by a sashaying Bianca, flanked by her sycophants. *Perfect,* I think as Eugene rambles on about tonight's plans with a passable attempt at enthusiasm. Bianca and Xavier will reunite over dance remixes and mocktails. Meanwhile, I'll be where I belong, on a stakeout staying three steps ahead of the sheriff.

All is right in the world again.

Later that night, I prepare for my outing with Eugene. Enid left earlier to meet Lucas Walker. I told her it would be cruel not to be gone before Eugene arrives. Especially in a dress like the one she's wearing—a shimmering silver above-the-knee thing with white fur at the collar and sleeves. She's luminescent. His heart wouldn't be able to take it.

I have everything I need, and the dull thump of an unimaginative pop music bassline rattling my floor does nothing to disabuse me of the opinion that getting out of this dance is the best thing that has ever happened to me.

There's a knock on the door. Eugene, right on time. "I'll be right there," I call out. "Did you bring the flash—"

It takes me a moment to process the scene outside my dorm. My visitor is not Eugene, as I predicted, but Tyler Galpin. Wearing a white suit. Holding a black rose corsage.

"I don't understand," I say blankly. Our last conversation was outside the station. Tyler, storming off with hurt feelings after I told him about my plans with Xavier.

He holds up a note that clearly came from my typewriter. "I got your invite," he says with a half smile. "I'm . . . guessing you had Thing drop it in the tip jar."

It's at this moment that it all clicks into place. Thing, overhearing my fight with Xavier. The dissolution of my plans to go to the dance. Could he have possibly done this to me?

"Great guess," I say through gritted teeth.

"After our last conversation, I didn't know if I'd ever even speak to you again," Tyler says, and there's something soft in his eyes. So different from the way he looked outside the station, like he was at war with some secret pain. "But your note was so genuine . . . sweet. It totally took me by surprise."

"Yeah, me too," I say, loud enough so that Thing can hear me wherever he's cowering in the room.

"Now that I'm here, I'm really glad I came," Tyler says. I feel it again in that moment. The relief at feeling normal that I've given in to my weaker moments. It gives me pause enough to consider this from another angle. Tyler has been my most steadfast ally since I arrived in Jericho, willing to risk his reputation and even his father's ire to help me, time and time again.

Tyler didn't understand why I needed to flee Jericho on my first day here, but he offered to take me anyway. He didn't understand why I needed to investigate the ruins of the Old Meeting House, but he offered to make sure I could without getting hurt.

I don't understand why he wants to take me to this dance. There's little chance I ever will. But I've been twice accused of using people as pawns this week, and I do try to address my flaws when I discover them. Is this part of reciprocal allyship? Doing things for people that are meaningful to them, even when you don't understand why?

"I'm . . . not quite ready," I tell him after a long pause. "Meet me downstairs."

Once the door is closed, Thing creeps out of the closet looking guilty and self-satisfied all at once. "Genuine and *sweet*?" I hiss. "How could you do this to me?"

He scuttles over to a magazine splayed open on Enid's floor. The visible headline reads: WHY I REGRET MISSING MY HIGH SCHOOL PROM.

"This is a disaster," I say, rolling my eyes.

With Tyler still waiting on me at the door, I frantically rifle through my closet, looking for something I can wear to this dreadful occasion. Then Thing snaps and points to a vintage black dress, laid out plainly on my bed. It's the one from the shop window. He must've caught me staring at it.

The sentimental fool.

"How'd you pay for it?" I ask. Thing holds up five fingers. "Five-finger discount. Of course. Thank you."

It's a dress that was created for walking down old-fashioned stairs. I can feel the material floating around me as I descend.

Unfortunately, it seems to be equally compelling an image to Tyler, who's waiting at the bottom of the stairs.

"Wow, Wednesday," he says. "You look . . ." There's something soft and wistful in his eyes that makes me think of an animal seconds before an unseen predator severs its spine with their teeth. They never see it coming.

"Unrecognizable? Ridiculous? Like a classic example of female self-objectification for the male gaze?" I ask, holding up a hand.

Tyler smiles. Still wistful. Almost like he's nostalgic for the moment before it even happens.

"No, I just wanted to say you look beautiful," he says.

I'm about to tell him this compliment means nothing to me. That it's exactly the kind of perception I was asking him to refrain from engaging in. That I'd much rather be called brilliant, or ruthless, or something that actually *means* something.

But before I can open my mouth, Eugene appears behind Tyler and my heart sinks. "Eugene," I say. "Hi."

He's looking between me in the dress and Tyler holding a corsage with dawning awareness. I was so focused on what Tyler wanted that I forgot to consider the promise I'd made to my most loyal ally.

"What happened to staking out the cave?" he asks. He's dressed in camo pants and a puffer jacket. He's wearing a heavy backpack. Amid all the Rave'N latecomers in their gossamer and suits, he looks woefully out of place.

"Something came up," I say, and his jaw tightens against an emotion I can understand for once. "I'm sorry, Eugene."

"I get it," he says, attempting bravado again. "I'll just go alone."

The idea of tender-bellied Eugene in the woods alone with the monster on the loose makes me feel something akin to panic. "Don't you dare," I tell him sternly. "It's too dangerous. Stand down and we'll go together tomorrow night. Promise?"

With another look at the dress, he nods reluctantly. It never occurs to me that he'll do anything but obey.

Once he's gone, Tyler raises an eyebrow. "Staking out a cave?" he asks.

"An alternate evening plan," I say. "For if you didn't show up."

I expect him to welcome the change of subject, but his eyes are no longer soft. They're intent on mine. A little too intense. I prefer this expression immensely. "You're not hunting down the monster alone at night with *him,* are you?" he asks.

"What I do is my business," I tell him. "Now, let's go in there before I change my mind."

The prospect has never seemed more likely than when I look through the doors to the event room. It's dark. Flashing lights and music pour out along with synthetic fog from one of those rentable machines.

"Ready?" Tyler asks as we face it down.

All in all, I think I'd wildly prefer the monster's lair and its threat of imminent disembowelment to this.

Inside, everything is stark white and vaguely smokey. The whole room seems to have been transformed into some foggy, ice lair. Everyone else is wearing white, or some shade of ice blue.

Enough heads turn to look at me that I'm ready to flee after a millisecond, but Tyler steadies my arm. My classmates are all dancing, sipping horrid-looking blue drinks, smiling at each other. Even the teachers are dressed up for the occasion.

Right on theme, Ms. Thornhill approaches then. She's dressed in some frumpy monstrosity, but you can tell she used to be pretty. Foxy-faced with dark eyes.

"What a lovely surprise," she says.

In the woods a few miles from here, the monster's lair sits

unobserved. I turn to my teacher and say stiffly: "Ms. Thornhill, this is Tyler—"

"—Galpin," she finishes for me. "I know."

For a moment I'm surprised. How would Ms. Thornhill know a random townie? But then Tyler smiles his barista smile and says, "Yeah, that's right. Double cap. No foam. Two pumps of vanilla."

Ms. Thornhill smiles ruefully. "Hard to keep secrets from anyone in a town this small."

Before I can attempt to figure out why a coffee order should be a secret, I hear Enid screech from a few yards away, and soon I'm bombarded with the sparkles and feathers of her own ensemble as she cuts in with no regard for Ms. Thornhill.

"I'll get us some punch," I say, walking off toward Enid, posted at the bar—which appears to have been carved from solid ice.

"OMG, I love the look!" Enid says. "I can't believe you decided to come. I have *so much* to tell you. Did you know Xavier is here with Bianca? I can't believe he would hop over to her after everything that happened with you guys."

Coming up for air, she catches her first glimpse of Tyler.

". . . But it seems like you've made your own interesting choice of date," she says with a sly smile.

"I could say the same to you about your date choice," I say. Lucas is sitting at the table where Enid probably left him. "You know that pilgrim already has two strikes in my book."

Enid shrugs it off. "He's trying to make his ex jealous. I'm trying to make Ajax jealous. It's a win-win. Although I have been surprised! He likes hockey *and* kung fu movies, so we've low-key been bonding. Maybe he just needed to see we're all people like them."

I roll my eyes. "You sound like Weems with all that unity crap.

Watch your back, that's all I'm saying."

"You too," Enid says, turning the tables as she catches Tyler staring from across the room. "That boy looks like he wants to devour you whole."

"If he tries, it'll be him you should worry about," I say.

As Enid excuses herself back to her date, I stand waiting for Tyler. I can't stop thinking about Eugene, all alone in his dorm, and the unattended monster cave where absolutely *anything* could be happening, when a shadow cuts across my path.

"I can't believe you brought him," Xavier says with a glower. "Let me guess, he caught you breaking into his room and rifling through his diary."

I whirl around. "Why do you even care?" I ask him pointedly. "Why did you come all the way over here to start this conversation *again*? As if this dance wasn't tedious enough."

The glower only grows more pronounced. "You wouldn't ask that if you knew what Tyler did to me."

This piques my interest. "Fine. Enlighten me, then."

When I've heard the end of Xavier's sordid tale, I excuse myself, weaving through the crowd until I find my way to an exit and a place to sit.

It's not that anything Xavier told me is particularly shocking, more that I'm disturbed that there's a darker side to Tyler. An explanation of sorts for what sometimes seems to be lurking behind his benign smiles.

Before I can analyze further, the boy in question approaches. "Was it the Yeti-tinis or the thin mountain air that got to you?" he jokes.

"Xavier told me what happened last year," I say as he sits down beside me on the stone bench. "How you and Lucas and your friends trashed his mural on Outreach Day."

This time, I watch his face closely. I don't want to miss anything. I see embarrassment. Shame. Nothing more twisted.

"Can't believe it took him this long to tell you," he says, looking at his shoes. "I'd like to say it was an accident, or it wasn't that bad. But I'd be lying. It was bad. And he could have made things a lot worse for me than he did."

"Why did you do it?" I ask. I'm still trying to connect the person I've gotten to know with some prejudiced bully who would destroy artwork out of ignorance.

Tyler sighs. He looks out across the quad to where the moon is just visible. "I could give you a thousand excuses, but the truth is I'm still trying to figure it out. Court-ordered therapy, remember?"

I nod, recalling the day we bonded over our outlaw status. I had no idea . . .

"My dad sent me away to this wilderness school for troubled kids, and while I was out in the woods, I realized the person who did that isn't who I want to be. Some bitter townie who blames everyone for the shitty hand he's been dealt."

It's there on his face now, plain as day. The war I sometimes see him fighting. The haunted memory and the cheerful, helpful barista battling it out for dominance. It makes sense now. And more than that, it's relatable. Perhaps Tyler and I have more in common than I thought.

"I did a terrible thing," Tyler says, meeting my eyes again. "But I'm trying not to be a terrible person."

In that moment, I think of my own worst instincts. Treating people as disposable. Being single-minded to the point where I forget the humanity of those around me. Hurting Enid, Thing, Xavier, Tyler... even Eugene.

"I believe people can change if they want to," I tell him. "And that the worst choices we make shouldn't define us."

Tyler smiles, looking genuinely moved by my most embarrassingly hopeful belief. Then he bumps my shoulder with his. "You mean like putting piranhas in a swimming pool?" he teases. "I may have done a little digging on you after we met."

I shake my head. "That's not the worst choice I've made. In fact, I feel no remorse about it whatsoever."

He shakes his head. Back to soft nostalgia again. "I knew there was a reason I liked you."

It's probably time to make some sort of declaration about what kind of *liking* is permitted, but in this moment I feel something I haven't in a long time—if ever. The sense of a kindred spirit. Someone who's working hard not to let their monstrousness define them.

I tell myself there'll be time for boundaries in the future. Right now, I prefer the shared silence.

Eventually, I've had enough of the so-called dance music and miserable trap of shoes on my feet. I excuse myself from Tyler's company and head out of the dance hall for some air and blessed silence.

My sanctuary of the bench is already occupied by Bianca Barclay, who clearly wasn't expecting anybody else to try to claim her spot.

I gesture to the shoes in my hand. "Whoever invented heels clearly had a side hustle as a torturer."

"As my dear mother always says, 'Fire tests gold, suffering tests a woman.'"

"Speaking of suffering, where's your date? I thought you and Xavier would be giving our entertainment-starved peers something to talk about."

Bianca raises an eyebrow. Her eyes are so blue, like the ocean on a clear day. "We had a little tiff," she says. "About you, actually."

It makes no sense that Bianca would confess something vulnerable to me. And yet, here we are. I have no idea what to say in return. I've been doing my best to meet vulnerability with the like in the name of allyship, but I can't bring myself to make a confession to Bianca, so I stay silent.

"You don't know what it's like," she says after a long pause.

"Being beautiful and popular?" I ask sharply.

She shakes her head impatiently. "Never knowing people's true feelings. I can never trust that people like me for who I am."

For the second time since I sat down on this bench, I find I can relate to the person beside me. People want to conquer my indifference much more than they want to know me. It's been that way since I arrived here. They want me to be who they think I am.

But with Bianca's power, it would be so much more literal. I stop myself short before I can start feeling sorry for her.

"You're lucky, you know," she says.

"How's that?"

"You don't care what people think of you."

Once again, my mind is drawn to the friends I've alienated, the people I've hurt in my single-mindedness. "Honestly," I say, "sometimes I wish I cared a little more."

Back inside, the DJ decides to play some real music for once, so I enter the crowd and let myself dance.

I've always enjoyed dancing, for all the same reasons I like fencing. A physical expression of the tension in my body is much easier than trying to put it into words.

Tyler loses the hopeful glance he followed me onto the floor with and contents himself with shuffling in my orbit. This is when it's nice not to care what people think, when I'm moving however it suits me and The Cramps are echoing through the hall.

When they see I don't care about their tittering, most people join in. Enid bumps shoulders with me after Lucas excuses himself and for a moment, I'm not sorry I came. As often as I've danced alone in my room, there's something about collective movement. About feeling the rhythm of music as a whole . . .

"Yo, yo, yo," calls the DJ as the song is winding down. "It's almost closing time, so haul it out onto the dance floor one last time before the Rave'N says *Nevermore*."

"That's my cue," I say to Enid as a house beat replaces the eccentric bassline of "Goo Goo Muck." But she clings to my arm.

"Don't go!" she cries. "Lucas still isn't back yet and it's the last song of the night!"

"Fine," I say. I'm still full of endorphins from dancing; that's the only explanation I can offer. Enid gasps, tilting her head up and prompting me to do the same as glittering snowflakes begin to swirl down from a hidden machine in the rafters. The light from the disco balls reflects off of them, and the room is momentarily transformed into something vaguely magical. Even I'm not totally immune.

But then the fire alarm begins to sound, and the sprinklers splutter to life. I wonder if they've taken it a bit too far. I won't be thrilled to be blasted with actual hailstones, no matter how realistic they want this winter wonderland to be.

The first drop on my face is lukewarm, but when I touch it with my finger, it comes away red. Soon, the prank is revealed, as the entire fantasy and every all-white outfit herein becomes a gorescape.

Blood rains down as people begin to scream, to push past each other, to run for the exits.

I put the blood drop to my tongue. "They couldn't even spring for real pig's blood," I say, before I realize I'm the only one not screaming or running. "Calm down!" I shout. "It's only paint!"

But no one seems to care what it is. Faces are smeared with blood tears, outfits dyed crimson with fake blood that won't brown as it oxygenates. Despite the cheapness of the material, I can't deny the effect is rather spectacular.

Someone shoves me from behind as they slip on the now sodden floor. I feel more hands, more bodies pushing past me. I see Tyler and Enid but neither of them stop, and then, in the onslaught of bodily contact, I feel an all-too familiar jolt down my spine.

This time I'm not transported to a period in history. I have no agency. No voice. I'm seeing everything through night-vision goggles. Eugene. He's in the woods, at the mouth of the monster's lair. An explosion of light overwhelms everything. Orange flames are billowing from the cave. Then Eugene is running for his life, stumbling backward in the woods, before the monster descends on him in snarling fury.

I'm back in the present before I can even memorize his location. Panic seizes me as the screaming and blood tells me I haven't been out long.

"Wednesday!" Ms. Thornhill calls, slipping and sliding to my side. "Are you hurt?"

"No!" I call out over the chaos. "It's Eugene! He went to the woods alone. He's in danger. I have to find him!"

There's no time to wait for a response. I don't know how far in the future the vision was. Xavier, Weems, and even my mother would tell me I'm being driven by emotion, not logic, but right now it doesn't matter. Eugene went to the woods alone because of me. Whatever happens to him will be my fault.

I get to the vortex cave, where I found the claw, as quickly as I can. All is quiet for now, but there's no sign of Eugene.

"Eugene!" I call into the night. "Where are you?"

From across the glade I hear scrabbling. "Wednesday?" Eugene's voice calls.

Relief floods me. I take off running toward the sound of his voice. I'm not too late. My dress is shredded quickly in the underbrush, but I don't care, I just have to get to him.

But before I can, I hear a snarl. Too familiar now. "NO!" I shout, running faster, barefoot on the carpet of fallen leaves. "Eugene! EUGENE!"

I burst into a clearing up ahead and see a lifeless form on the ground. The monster is nowhere to be seen. I approach Eugene's body feeling heavy as cement. His face is stained with blood, his eyes closed. I can't tell if his pulse is weak or—if it's not there at all.

More footsteps enter the clearing. I snap my head up, expecting the sheriff, Xavier, even Tyler. But instead, it's Ms. Thornhill, still streaked in paint from the prank at the dance.

"Oh my god," she breathes. "Is he alive?"

Only I can't answer, because I don't know. All I can think is that if he isn't, it's all my fault.

CHAPTER EIGHTEEN

The first days of Eugene's coma are hard on me. I won't pretend otherwise.

I wonder, as the near-constant rain streaks my window and even Enid makes herself scarce, whether I've gone too far this time. Whether my unquenchable thirst for the truth is worth the results when its damage extends beyond the monsters I'm hunting.

But the longer I stare at the mist-wreathed campus of Nevermore, the more defined my problem becomes, rising from the muck like a swamp creature from the black-and-white bogs of an old horror movie.

Pursuing justice is not the problem. The problem arises when I attempt to compromise my fervor for truth-seeking with the impossible-to-navigate quagmire of social relationships. If I hadn't been determined to give Tyler what he wanted the night of the dance, I never would have abandoned Eugene.

If I hadn't abandoned Eugene, he wouldn't be lying comatose in a hospital bed right now.

A commitment to simplifying my life and prioritizing the pursuit of the monster's identity is enough to break my multiday doldrums period, but unfortunately all my evidence is in the Hummers' shed, and curse my sentiment—I can't bring myself to go inside.

It's inconvenient, but I suppose more seasoned investigators than me have needed a break from the horrors. And with Parents' Weekend coming up at Nevermore, I think I can use said break to solve another mystery instead. One that's been haunting me since the moment Sheriff Galpin uttered my father's name in the Weathervane on my first day in Jericho.

To that end, I spend the morning of my family's arrival studying the Nevermore quad. I'm trying to replicate the events of the report Tyler stole for me. The one in my father's police file.

It's the night of the Rave'N, 1990. Larissa Weems, then a presumably unpopular Nevermore senior, walks out of the dance holding an umbrella, only to witness a body free-falling from the second-floor balcony.

She screams, alerting the dance-goers to the tragedy unfolding outside. But she's the first to see him. My father, Gomez Addams, then a dapper teenager in a pinstriped suit. According to her statement, he's standing right in the place the body fell from, holding a sword covered in blood, peering over the balcony in horror at the lifeless form beneath.

The report picks up in the Nevermore drive. My father is escorted to a police cruiser as the sheriff of the time—a younger Mayor Walker—takes Larissa Weems's statement.

There's a certain passage that stands out to me. One typed out verbatim in the report:

"I don't want to tell tales, Sheriff Walker"—I can almost hear her whispering it—"but it's all Morticia Frump's fault. They were fighting over her."

My father was taken away in the police cruiser after that. I can only imagine the nauseating things my mother said to him as they walked him past her in cuffs—accused of murder . . .

"Miss Addams!" A modern-day Weems's voice cuts into my dramatic re-creation.

The quad is still here, just as it was the rain-soaked night my father was arrested. Only today the sun is shining for once. My mother will be horrified.

"I've just been told your parents have arrived out front," Weems says.

Narrowing my eyes at her, I nod, but I can't help but speculate. Weems and my mother were roommates. Close friends, if Morticia's tales can be believed. So then, what would lead Weems to blame the death of the normie boy on her?

I may not be able to stomach the monster investigation with Eugene hooked up to a ventilator, but I plan on uncovering plenty of truth this weekend regardless. Starting with my father.

Weems is swept away by the crowd, and I'm forced to break my stare. Rather than greet my parents in the drive, I plan to wait here. Hopefully they'll get their sentimentality out of the way during their walk through the entrance hall.

Enid finds me in the crowd before there's any sign of my family, and we stand together, bonded in our trepidation as Weems begins her speech to the gathered crowd of Outcasts and the freaks who spawned them.

"As you all know, Nevermore was created as a safe haven for our children to learn and grow—no matter who, or what, they are," she begins. The parents applaud wildly. I can practically see them holding her up as the gold standard of educators.

Meanwhile, her past is seething with secret resentments . . .

"I realize most of you have heard about the unfortunate incident involving one of our students," she continues in a more somber tone.

Worried muttering ripples through the crowd. My stomach is uneasy as I picture Eugene in the hospital I can't bring myself to set foot in. Weak and helpless—well, more than usual, anyway.

"But I'm happy to report that Eugene is on the mend and is expected to make a full recovery. So let's focus on the positive and make this Parents' Weekend our very best yet!" Weems enthuses.

All the parents are pacified by this diplomatic sandwiching of Eugene's attempted murder. I scoff in disgust.

"'On the mend'?" I say under my breath to Enid. "Try 'in a coma.' She's so full of it."

"Have you been to see him?" Enid asks sympathetically. She's looking nervously around for her parents, too, and I can't help but notice her claws are out.

I throw her a look.

"He's your friend," Enid chastises gently.

"I'm also the reason he's in the hospital," I retort. "It doesn't feel right that I should assuage my conscience with a tearful bedside visit when he won't even know I'm there."

At this, I get Enid's full attention. "It is *not* your fault, okay? And on the bright side, that monster thing hasn't attacked anyone in a week. Maybe you finally scared it off."

Looking around, I locate Xavier on the balcony and Bianca at the foot of the stairs. I still haven't figured out which of my blood-soaked classmates triggered my vision during the Rave'N, but someone on this quad knows more than they're letting on—I know that much at least.

As I'm scanning, I spot my family at last. My mother in the showstopping black gown she's infamous for. My father in that same pinstriped suit. My brother, Pugsley, striped shirt and black shorts. He's taller, but he looks even weaker somehow.

"Maybe the monster went into hiding to avoid this weekend," I say to Enid, projecting wildly. Even if the monster *had* parents, I doubt they're as embarrassing as mine.

A howl tears me from my examination of them. I follow Enid's eyeline to a wolf pack on the opposite side of the quad. Three boys, all howling. Two parents, observing with pride.

"Would you look at them?" Enid asks in a smaller-than-normal voice. "Talk about toxic pack mentality. I give my mom thirty seconds before her judge-y claws come out." She sighs. "Let's get this over with." And we go our separate ways for now.

"There she is!" my father calls as I approach them, stowing his police file in my bag for later shock value. "How we've missed those accusing eyes and youthful sneer."

My mother opens her arms for a hug. "How are you, my little rain cloud?" she asks with motherly concern and affection.

I step back, crossing my arms. "Why ask? I thought *Thing* was filling you in on my every move," I say. They look at each other guiltily. "Yes, I uncovered your feeble subterfuge almost immediately."

My mother raises her eyebrows at my father as if to say, *You deal with her.*

"So, how is the little fella doing?" he asks. "Does he still have all his fingers?"

I roll my eyes. "Relax," I tell him. "He's doing my bidding now. He'll join us later in the weekend."

"Delightful," says my mother, now that any possibility for recourse has passed. "So, tell us everything. I've left at least twelve messages on the crystal ball. You never call back."

"Yes," I say as the rest of the school mills around us, absorbed in their own familial mini-dramas. "I've been rather busy being hunted, haunted, and being the target of an attempted murder."

Both my parents' eyes go wide. My father places a hand over his heart. "Ah, Nevermore," he says in a tone of rapture. "I love you so!"

As my parents entertain each other with nauseating tales of their adolescent romance within these very stone walls, I watch my classmates and their families. Everyone seems a smaller, less certain version of themselves today. A mark of the coffins our family names lock us all in if we're not careful.

Bianca's mother is a stunning siren woman in a gold dress that dims even Bianca's shine by comparison. Enid's mother barely gives her an inch of space, firing question after inaudible question as her daughter shrinks further in on herself.

Only Xavier stands alone, still on the upper balcony where my father was once spotted with a bloody sword. He's alone, staring moodily down on all the happy families. But I can't help thinking he might be the lucky one.

Eventually we're issued a *special invitation,* which lands us in Weems's office before lunch.

I sit stiffly in my chair as my mother fawns over the yearbook on the principal's desk. There's a roaring fire in the Medusa's mouth fireplace, and the mahogany and leather of it all is just as pretentious and irritating as ever.

"Our old yearbook," she says in that dreamy voice of hers. "I haven't laid eyes on this in over twenty years. Such good times we had, didn't we, Larissa?"

This time, I know to watch for the tightening of Weems's jaw. The slight narrowing of her eyes. "Some of us better than others," she says in a light tone.

"Don't be modest," my mother says, waving a hand in her direction. "You always filled a room with your presence. Like a stately sequoia."

So I was right about Weems's lack of popularity. If I didn't loathe the woman, I might sympathize.

"And I guess that would make you the lumberjack," she says. This time the bite in her tone is unmistakable. I shouldn't be surprised, after what I read in the police report, but the question is: Which came first—Weems's hatred for my mother, or the murder accusation?

"There's that biting sense of humor I always adored," my mother says, oblivious, as always, to anything but praise. "Oh no!" she exclaims next, glancing down at the yearbook again. "My picture's gone!"

"Really?" Weems asks mildly. "That is odd."

I can't be certain, but I swear I see her eyes flick down and to the left as she says it. Which means that Principal Weems knows exactly what happened to my mother's yearbook picture. Yet another secret for the list.

"Let's get to the matter at hand, shall we?" Weems asks then, shifting into brusque school administrator mode. "Unfortunately, Wednesday's assimilation has been rocky at best."

Finally, time to discuss Weems's hatred of me instead of Morticia. "Because I refuse to embrace the culture of dishonesty and denial permeating this school," I say in my own defense, getting to my feet. "Starting with the monster that killed Rowan and landed Eugene in the ICU. Even though I hear he's *on the mend.*"

I glare at Weems for this last part, and she glares right back. My father, ever the diplomat, attempts to cut in and defuse things.

"We've always encouraged Wednesday to speak her mind," he says. "Sometimes her sharp tongue can cut deep, but she always gets to the heart of the matter. Don't you, my little vampire bat?"

Weems doesn't give me a chance to answer. "Apparently, Wednesday's therapist doesn't feel she's been very open to the process. Their time together has not yielded the results we hoped for."

Traitorous Dr. Kinbott, I think. Discussing my sessions with this two-faced snake.

"I'm not a lab rat," I deadpan.

Weems doesn't even acknowledge this. "Doctor Kinbott and I have spoken, and we both agree it would be very beneficial for you all to attend a family therapy session while you're here. She can fit you in this afternoon."

My initial response is to refuse outright, but then I see how uncomfortable my parents seem. I'm going to have to talk to the good doctor whether they go along or not. At least this way I can see them squirm for a change.

"I'm afraid we won't have time," my mother says graciously. "After all, we're only here for the weekend."

But my father must have seen some assent in my expression, because he changes tack quickly. "Oh, come on, what can it hurt? I've always been a big fan of head shrinking."

"It's not *that* kind of head shrinking, Querido," my mother corrects him.

"Well, that's disappointing. But anything for our little girl, right, Tish?" he asks.

To my surprise, she nods.

For my part, I'm fingering the police file in my bag, thinking I may just have found the perfect backdrop for my long-awaited confrontation with my parents.

"So, who wants to start?"

Dr. Kinbott is sitting across from the Addamses looking just the way she always looks—altogether too cheerful for the situation at hand. We've been here for ten minutes of our designated fifty. No one has said a single word, and this question doesn't prompt anyone to change that.

"Maybe we can discuss what it's like to have Wednesday away from home?" she suggests. Still nothing. Pugsley reaches out to the bowl of potpourri in the center of the table between our family and the doctor and takes a handful, crunching on them as if they're chips.

I stifle a laugh.

"I mean, for me . . . ," he says when he's swallowed half a cinnamon-scented pine cone.

"Yes, Pugsley?" Dr. Kinbott asks with too much enthusiasm.

"It's been really hard not having Wednesday around," he says. His lower lip is trembling. "I . . . I never thought I'd miss being physically tortured so much."

Again, I have to suppress a smile. We'll always have our memories.

"Okay!" It's clear Dr. Kinbott is reaching her limit. "Morticia, Gomez? How have you been coping?"

My mother leans forward in her chair. I can feel a scene coming on. "It's been *torture* for us too," she says. "We've really had to *lean* on each other."

At this, my father reaches across me, taking my mother's hand and kissing it passionately. "Times like these really highlight the strength of our connection, don't they, mi amor?"

"Absolutely," my mother breathes. His caresses become more enthusiastic as the room melts away for them once again. I might as well not even exist, let alone Dr. Kinbott and her sterilized therapy room.

"Enough!" I shout over their passionate kissing noises. "I have something to say."

"Wonderful, Wednesday," Dr. Kinbott exclaims. "I don't know that you've ever volunteered information in this office before."

Ignoring her, I stride to the front of the room with Gomez's police file in hand. "It's high time my parents faced the music," I say. "It seems they've been lying to me for years. Keeping secrets. Murderous secrets that need to be addressed."

I brandish the file in front of me, open to a photo of my father's alleged victim. He looks like your typical jock, 1990s edition. His hair swoops. He smirks.

"Who is Garrett Gates?" I demand. "And why were you accused of murdering him?"

My father has never once failed to make a comment, or a pun, or a joke, or a new nickname out of anything I've ever said to him. It's almost satisfying to see him lost for words.

"Those charges were dropped," my mother says, her face a mask. "Your father is an innocent man."

"The local sheriff isn't convinced," I tell her, thinking of the look on Sheriff Galpin's face when he first heard my name. *Your father's a murderer* echoing in my head for months.

"Whoa," Pugsley exclaims, looking between my parents for an explanation.

"Wednesday, I demand you stop this at once," my mother says. The mask is cracking. "This is neither the time nor the place."

"Actually," Dr. Kinbott cuts in, "I think this is *exactly* the place. These sessions are—"

"Doctor, this doesn't concern you," my mother snaps. The temperature in the room seems to drop ten degrees—an effect I'm well accustomed to. "Wednesday, I refuse to debate a decades-old witch hunt with you right now."

She gets to her feet, towering over me, my father, Dr. Kinbott, everyone. Gathering her long dress into one hand. I stand my ground, though I feel myself shrinking on the inside. Instincts screaming at me that my cause is doomed. That giving in is the only option.

"Darling," my father offers. "Maybe we should—"

"No." She sweeps toward the door like an overgrown bat,

taking all the air in the room with her. "This session is over."

"Have it your way, Mother," I say as she reaches the door. I shove the photo and the file back into my bag. "But if you won't tell me the truth, I'll have to excavate it myself."

She gives me a withering look, and then she's gone. If I were anywhere else but Dr. Kinbott's cursed office, I might hide out until she's gone, but I've never stalled in leaving this place and I'm not going to start today.

Unfortunately, Morticia is waiting for me by the car, positively vibrating with fury. "What were you thinking?" she demands in front of the whole street. "How could you ambush your father like that? In front of a stranger. A *therapist*, no less."

"How could I?" I ask, stepping closer. "You're the ones deceiving me. You insisted I go to this school; you know who I am. Did you really think I wouldn't experience the consequences of your erstwhile wrongdoings?"

"You don't know the full story," my mother says imperiously. "Your father did nothing wrong."

But she doesn't elaborate further. Because she doesn't trust me with the truth. "I'll be the judge of that," I tell her, and when she throws herself into the family hearse, I don't follow.

"I need some space," I say brusquely before storming off down the street. Past all the Nevermore Academy students and their families who I'm sure *think* they're having a terrible time. But none of them have any idea.

I try to take refuge in Eugene's hospital room for the first time, bringing him the jar of honey I harvested from Hive Three. Thing is in the room keeping watch, but I'm soon joined by Eugene's two tearful moms, who call me his friend.

After that, I have to make my excuses quickly. He didn't deserve this, and I don't deserve the thanks and affection of his parents. It's my fault he's here. I can't forget that.

Ousted from even my second most loathed location in town, I make my way back, dreading tonight's family dinner. I stop when I reach Crackstone's statue, melted and horrifying after the fire. I hear the city can't afford to replace it, so it's still here, making a much more powerful statement than the original.

Movement on the other side of the square catches my eye. Or maybe all daughters are drawn to their mothers by some magnetic biological imprint. Either way, I catch her stealing down the street alone, holding a single rose, and I can't help but follow.

She leads me to a cemetery—one I've never been to before. Creaky little gate, crumbling tombstones. I take cover behind one of them and watch, not knowing what I'm expecting.

Morticia stops in front of one of the graves and stands there, utterly still, for what feels like an hour. When she's finished, she snaps the head off the rose she brought and tosses the empty stem onto the grave before leaving through another exit.

Only when I'm sure she's gone do I find my way to the gravestone she came to visit.

GARRETT GATES, it reads. BELOVED SON AND BROTHER. TAKEN TOO SOON. FOREVER LOVED.

CHAPTER NINETEEN

Back at Nevermore, the family comes together to join the crowd for the big Parents' Weekend dinner. There's a lavish spread, of course. Weems would never skimp on such an important alumni weekend.

"Darling, aren't you hungry?" my mother asks as I sit with my arms folded in front of the buffet.

"My appetite eludes me, Mother. Just like the truth. Perhaps you'd care to enlighten me."

She shows no signs of relenting, but my father leans over and whispers—as if I haven't been able to read lips since I was five.

"We need to tell her."

So I was right. There is something to tell.

My mother turns her head away, but I can just make out her return whisper. *"She would never forgive us."*

I'm about to unleash a new and unrelenting assault upon their blockade, but just then, every head turns to look at something behind me. All the talk quiets. I hear the clomping of Sheriff Galpin's boots before I see him, flanked by three deputies.

Weems attempts to head him off, her voice ringing out through the quad as she asks: "What is all this about, Sheriff?"

I shouldn't be surprised when his eyes find our table. My father in particular. The sheriff's been nursing this grudge a long time.

"Gomez Addams!" Galpin calls, ignoring Weems's attempts to move this somewhere more private.

My father gets to his feet, an expression of mild amusement on his face. "How can I help you, Sheriff?" he asks jovially.

I can see it on Sheriff Galpin's pathetic, has-been face. He's savoring this moment. The crowd. The humiliation.

"You're under arrest," he says. "For the murder of Garrett Gates."

My mother gasps dramatically, as if she wasn't at the alleged victim's grave just an hour ago. My brother looks like he might cry. I feel a hatred curdling in me. For Galpin, and for everyone who could have helped me understand and didn't.

Galpin reads my father his rights. Enid looks at me sympathetically, while Bianca stares, incredulous. I'm sure she can't wait to spread the news that Wednesday the Freak has a murderer for a father. Though who she'll spread it to, I don't know. Everyone is already here.

My father is handcuffed in front of the entire Parents' Weekend crowd. There's nothing I can do to help him. And then they escort him away.

I get to Jericho's pathetic excuse for a jail before they even have my father booked. I have to wait in a molded plastic chair, seething, until they let me in to see him.

Thing accompanies me, summoned back from the hospital in the family's time of need.

"My little tormenta," my father says as he's seated roughly across the glass from me. "How's your mother?"

"Devastated," I reply. "She hates you in orange."

He smiles. "She's right. It's an accent color."

I don't have the time or the patience to engage in further small talk. "Yesterday I caught her laying a rose on a grave," I inform him. "The name on the headstone was Garrett Gates. The very boy you've been arrested for murdering. Care to explain?"

This is the best chance I've had all weekend to uncover the truth. My parents are a united front, stronger than the bars of this jail or any other. But without my mother's steel spine to fortify him, my father has always folded surprisingly easily.

"Garrett was infatuated with your mother," he begins. "They met on Outreach Day, and he mistook her kindness for interest. She told him politely that she had a lover—we'd been together over a year. But he was rich. Entitled. He wasn't deterred. His infatuation turned to obsession. He began stalking her."

As easily as I expected my father to give in, this surprises even me. "Why didn't you go to the police?" I ask.

"We tried," my father assures me. "But Garrett's family was the oldest and richest in Jericho. We couldn't get them to take us seriously."

His eyes mist over at the memory of this past injustice. I wait for him to continue.

"It all came to a head the night of the Rave'N dance," he says, and I recall the report. Weems discovering the body falling from the balcony. "Your mother and I snuck upstairs to catch our breath. That's when I saw him."

I can picture Garrett, the handsome boy from the picture, watching my parents maul each other. It fits the picture I painted this morning with the police file almost exactly.

"He'd broken into the school," my father explains. "And he shouted my name, his eyes brimming with nefarious purpose."

As he continues, I can see the scene unfolding in my mind's eye. Garrett taking a ceremonial fencing saber from the ornately decorated Nevermore wall. Advancing on my teenaged parents, filled with jealousy and rage.

My father, bravely stepping in front of my mother until she pleads with him to leave her to talk Garrett down. Gomez, unable to refuse her anything, leaving by way of the stairwell, but not going far in case she needs him.

"She shouted his name," my father says. "And I knew he was coming after me. It was raining on the second-floor balcony, lightning crashing in the distance. I knew it was fight him or die, and I would have done either for your mother, but she never would have forgiven me for leaving her."

I can practically see Garrett, the superior athlete, getting the best of my father quickly. Forcing him against a column but dropping the saber in the process. The sword, skittering toward the edge as the rain continues to fall.

The fistfight, then. Ever closer to the scaffolding leading

down to the quad. Garrett pummeling my father to the brink of unconsciousness.

"Driven by hate and rage, he had the upper hand," my father says. "My life flashed before my eyes like an epic poem, destined to remain unfinished, when the gods intervened."

Lightning, forking the sky, striking the metal of the scaffolding and shooting up blinding sparks. My father, crafty, using the distraction to break away. To retrieve the sword. To point it at the boy hell-bent on his destruction.

"I told Garrett to stop," my father says, barely above a whisper. "But he charged me. I didn't have time to move the blade out of the way. It went right through him."

Our tale catches up to Larissa Weems's statement in the police file. Walking through the quad with her umbrella as Garrett falls to his death, my father standing above him with the bloodied sword.

"Now you know the truth," my father says ruefully.

If I'm being objective, his confession sounds reasonable. Sincere. "Thank you for being *honest* with me," I say, and he nods magnanimously.

But there's the matter of his tells to parse.

The way he smooths his mustache. Quirks a brow. Delivers a timely wink. I've been playing roulette with him since I was twelve. I know them well.

"I'm sorry that I haven't been a better father," he says, and the tears in his eyes now are not the crocodile kind.

"You could take it easier on the overt displays of affection and emotion," I say honestly. "But how many fathers give their daughter a fencing blade at five?"

"Your saber strokes were an essay in perfection," he says,

his face lighting up even as the horrible orange washes out his naturally glowing skin tone.

". . . Or teach her how to swim with sharks?" I add.

"They found you as cold-blooded as I do."

". . . Or show her just the right way to flay a rattlesnake?"

"They really do taste just like chicken when prepared properly."

I steel myself for the sincerity I'm about to display. Especially knowing what I know. But he deserves it, in his way. "The point is you taught me how to be strong and independent," I tell him. "How to navigate a world full of treachery and prejudice. Showed me that no matter how weird people think you are, being true to yourself is the greatest of strengths."

He's looking at me with such genuine emotion on his face. Tears once again collecting in the corners of his eyes.

"As far as fathers go"—the coup de grâce—"I'd say you've been more than adequate," I finish.

"Gracias, Wednesday," he says, his voice breaking on my name.

A deputy comes in then, separating us, leaving me alone with my thoughts. Every crime novelist knows that a killer's unforced confession isn't the end of the story. It's just the beginning. This fact, coupled with how well I know Gomez Addams, makes me suspect he's lying through his teeth.

The only question left is why.

"We need to talk," I say, appearing in the sheriff's office doorway before he notices me. He jumps, nearly spills his coffee.

"Dammit, Addams, you can't just sneak in here like that." Sheriff Galpin doesn't look surprised to see me. Annoyed, yes. But not surprised. And I don't mind being a thorn in an embittered cop's side.

"My father didn't kill Garrett Gates," I inform him, not bothering to explain why his reception desk was unattended.

"I don't have time for this," he says. "I have his signed confession *and* he identified the murder weapon. I'm about to deliver both to the district attorney."

"Why now?" I ask him, stepping forward, blocking his exit. "What did you find that allowed you to move on him this particular weekend after decades of holding a grudge?"

Sheriff Galpin sighs, scrubbing a hand over his face. "The coroner killed himself last night. Did you know that?" he asks.

I didn't, but I endeavor not to show my shock. I saw the coroner only last week when Thing and I snuck into the morgue. He bragged about his imminent retirement. The cruise he was going to take his wife on. Hardly a man who was planning his own death.

"Why?" I ask, hating that I need to rely on him for information.

"Guilt," he says. "Over a decades-old case. Apparently, he falsified a report. Let a guilty murderer walk free. Three guesses which case that was."

It's clear to me immediately that someone killed the coroner. Faked the suicide note. But why? I don't have much time to untangle the knots, not with the sheriff none-too-subtly edging me toward the door.

"Don't you find the timing a tad too convenient?" I ask, stalling.

"What do you mean?" Galpin asks.

I'm not sure what I'm going to say until I'm saying it, but the path lights up ahead of me one step at a time and it all fits. It seems my father's history won't be quite the detour from the monster hunt I anticipated after Eugene's attack.

"The coroner happens to 'kill himself' out of remorse for a

decades-old murder case the very weekend my father, your prime suspect, deigns to return to town?"

The sheriff interrupts, raising a hand. "All I see is a guilty man who's finally going to pay for his crime. The fact that I got to cuff him myself was just icing on the cake."

I narrowly resist the urge to stomp out of sheer frustration. "Wake *up*, Sheriff!" I shout. "Someone is desperately trying to derail my investigation. I found the monster's cave, I gave you the DNA evidence. Did you even bother to test it?"

Galpin sits back down behind his desk. I can tell from the look on his face I won't like the answer, but I wait for it anyway.

"I know this is going to come as a shock, but I do have other things to do besides follow your teenage hunches, Miss Addams." He pulls a file from his desk, sliding it toward me. "The DNA came back. Inconclusive. No match."

This stops me in my tracks. It's the last thing I expected. Xavier, the drawings of the monster, the scratches on his neck. The way he appeared at the ruins just after the monster turned human. Something isn't adding up.

"You really think this is all some coincidence?" I ask, almost in disbelief. "Whoever hurt Eugene killed the coroner. Someone doesn't want this truth getting out."

There's a glint in Sheriff Galpin's eye as he leans over the report. "I'd like to help you prove that, but *someone* sabotaged the morgue's security camera so there's no way of knowing. They stuck bubble gum on the lens. *Black* bubble gum. Maybe I ought to run DNA on that."

I hate that horrible smirk on his face. "Somebody wants to throw me off my game. Stop me from uncovering the truth. This ridiculous accusation against my father is proof that I'm getting too close. That they want me distracted."

The sheriff is on his feet again, and this time I can tell he won't stop until I'm on the sidewalk out front. He holds up my father's confession, as if it proves a single thing. "This is justice being served," he says. "Garrett Gates' family deserves to have closure. Even if none of them are around to take comfort in it."

More to forestall my inevitable ejection than anything, I ask: "What happened to them?"

There's a haunted look in the sheriff's eyes as he answers—leaving more questions than closure. "His mother hung herself in the backyard while his father drank himself into an early grave. Even Garrett's little sister didn't escape. When she was orphaned, she was sent overseas. She drowned. Every last one of them is gone. Your father doesn't have just Garrett's blood on his hands—he has the whole damn family's."

I think about Garrett's unfortunate family all the way back to Nevermore. The mother in the noose. The little sister drowning. But then I think about what my father said about them being one of the most powerful and influential families in Jericho.

Something doesn't add up. I just wish I knew what.

Then there's my father, his sad excuse for a confession. If I've learned one thing in my life, it's that anyone who willingly confesses to a crime they didn't commit is hiding something worse . . .

And there's only one person in the world who will certainly know what it is.

But before I track down my mother, it's time for a little heart-to-heart with my little brother.

I find him sitting on the dock, the happy families of Nevermore Academy socializing in the background.

"Go away," he says as I approach.

"You forgot your fishing gear," I tell him, handing over a bag I found in my dorm.

"Stop trying to be nice," he says glumly. "It doesn't suit you."

He's right, of course, but he's the only one I've ever attempted to soften myself for. "Father packed your favorite bait," I tell him.

He opens the bag, finds the grenades that have always been my father's tried-and-true fishing secret, and smiles a little.

I take it as an invitation to sit. He doesn't object. Nothing like a few explosives to bring a family together.

"What will happen to him now?" Pugsley asks, looking at the water beneath his dangling feet.

"Well, he's confessed, so there won't be a trial," I say. "After he's sentenced he'll be sent to a state penitentiary, where he'll lose his mind being separated from Mother." The idea is revolting. The two of them pining for each other is almost worse than the way they carry on when they're together.

Pugsley doesn't seem to have an opinion. I've never asked how he feels about their constant, overwhelming displays of affection, and I don't think today is the day.

"Did you know they haven't spent a night apart since they tied the knot?" I ask him.

But Pugsley has something else on his mind: "I always thought I'd be the first one in the family behind bars," he says morosely.

I nod. "Lurch and I had a bet going," I tell him to cheer him up. "Come on, let's see if the fish are biting."

Pugsley looks sadly down at the grenade and I'm sure he's thinking of all the times he's pulled a pin with my father by his side. I must make a poor substitute, but eventually he pulls it anyway, chucking the live explosive right into the center of the pond, where it explodes satisfyingly.

My father's methods are nothing if not effective. A whole school of silver-scaled fish floats to the surface of the pond.

"That's quite a catch," I tell Pugsley.

He looks at me with those desperately sad, soft eyes that led me to empty an entire bag of piranhas into a pool on his behalf. "I'm gonna miss him, Wednesday," he says.

"It's not over yet," I say, trying to be bracing. "He's innocent."

"Well, if anyone can find out who really committed the crime, it's you. You have to find the truth and free Dad."

I think of the attempts I've made to do exactly that. The frustration of being obstructed by the very wrongfully convicted criminal I'm trying to free. "Until that happens, we both know Mother will be falling apart," I tell him, dodging the subject. I don't want to make a promise I can't keep. "We have to be strong. And by 'we,' I mean you."

His jaw clenches stubbornly and he nods once. Hopefully this man-of-the-house assignment will keep him from falling apart too.

"Now give me one of those," I say, putting my hand out for a grenade and pulling the pin. We watch it explode together. Bonding, I suppose.

But I can sense this heartwarming sibling moment drawing to a close. Pugsley may need me, but he doesn't have the information that can help me prove my father made a false confession. Only one person has that. The woman he tells everything to.

"Where is Mother, anyway?" I ask Pugsley as casually as I can.

"She said she wanted to be alone," he says, befuddled.

"Somewhere no one would find her."

And where else to disappear to, I think grimly, than the library of a secret society...

The entrance hall is deserted, all the happy Outcast families cavorting around the grounds and another catered buffet courtesy of Weems. I know my brother is out there moping about our father's arrest, but Morticia would never brave the unwashed plebians without my father as her honor guard.

As often as I claim to have been body snatched or switched at birth, it's probably not a coincidence that I find her in the first place I look.

She looks at home in the Nightshades library as she surveys the memorabilia around the room.

"Hello, Mother," I greet her.

My mother turns immediately at the sound of my voice. "Hello, Wednesday. So, you're a Nightshade. That didn't take long."

"Actually, I turned them down," I say casually.

"Why? Because I was a member?"

Of course that's most of the reason, but for some reason I feel as if confessing that to her will only make me seem petty and childish. "I'll never live up to your legacy here, so why even try?" I ask. "I win the Poe Cup, you claimed it four times. I join the fencing team, you were its captain. Why would you send me to a place where I could only ever exist in your shadow?"

It's probably the most vulnerable I've ever let myself be with her.

"It isn't a competition, Wednesday," she says reproachfully.

"*Everything* is a competition, Mother," I tell her.

For a long moment, we only survey each other in the light of my confession. I break first. This time, I don't even condemn myself for it.

"Mostly I didn't join because the Nightshades are a pointless social club."

She takes the peace offering, turning to look nostalgically around the room. "We used to be so much more," she says wistfully. "Our mission was to protect Outcasts from harm and prejudice. In fact, the group was started by an ancestor of your father's from Mexico. One of the first settlers in America."

My jaw drops. Is everything interconnected? "Goody Addams?" I ask eagerly, before I recall that I've never told my mother about my visions.

She raises an eyebrow as if to suggest I'm hiding something. But I didn't come here to give up my secrets. I came to extract hers.

"I saw her in a painting at Pilgrim World," I lie.

Morticia takes it in stride. "Ironic," she says. "Since she's the one who killed Joseph Crackstone. The Nightshades were her secret but deadly answer to his oppression."

"Like the poison it's named after," I muse, thinking it's even more depressing what Bianca and her ilk have done to this group and its legacy.

My mother is watching me. I know I have to ask what I came here to ask, but it's occurring to me that she knows more than I gave her credit for. More than just the truth about my father, but possibly the truth about me. About my visions, and Crackstone, and Goody . . .

"I know why you've come here, Wednesday," she says, her voice echoing strangely off the checkered tile floor. "So go on. Ask."

There won't be a better moment. I push the rest aside and meet her gaze. "Father didn't kill Garrett Gates, did he?"

She's quiet for a moment, her eyes distant as if she's reliving something painful. Then she comes back to the present. To me. "No," she says. "It was me."

I hardly have time to process before she begins her tale, but as she does, I realize this was the obvious answer. Of course my father would do anything for her. Even confess to a crime he didn't commit and risk life in prison for it. Of course.

"When I made it upstairs, they were already at each other's throats," my mother says in that faraway voice. I know she's seeing it, same as me. Young Gomez and Garrett fighting for dominance in the rain, on the edge of the rail-less balcony.

I can see her too. Coming onto the scene. Her one true love, defending her honor.

"Garrett got the upper hand," she continues. "The thunder was crashing all around, but just then a bolt of lightning struck the roof right above us. Chaos."

Divine intervention, my father had called it. But it wasn't divine. It was my mother.

"I screamed at him to leave your father alone. To stop all of this. But he wouldn't listen to me. Wouldn't even look up from where he was trying to kick your father off the scaffolding. Not until I picked up the sword."

It's easy to picture her in her long black gown, young and beautiful and tragic. She was always an expert swordsperson. Garrett would have looked up to see her standing there, lightning reflecting off the blade, willing to do anything to save my father.

"I'll never forget the way he looked at me," she says. "It was like staring into the eyes of a rabid beast. He was even foaming at the mouth in his jealous fury."

This detail pulls me from the past back into the present. Foaming at the mouth? I've seen a few jealous boys in my time, but mouth foaming isn't usually a symptom of jealousy as far as I know . . .

"He lunged at me. All I did was hold the blade steady. When he fell, your father came to me, told me to run back to my room and lock the door. I was so afraid, but I knew he would never let any harm come to me. It was that night I knew I would love him forever."

A tear streaks down her cheek as she remembers it. Replacing the sword, running back to lock her door. There's something about this story that puts my parents' love into context for me. It would be difficult not to bond over something like that.

"Your father took the blame in order to protect me," she says, more tears joining the first. Silent. Even her crying is somehow beautiful. "I was so grateful when he was cleared of any wrongdoing. But I knew someday this would come back to haunt us."

The nightshade flower in the middle of the floor pulls my attention from her. The symbol of the secret society. I turn the details of my mother's story in my mind like a Rubik's Cube until something clicks.

"You said Garrett was foaming at the mouth," I remind her. "That his eyes didn't look human."

"Yes," my mother breathes. "I've never seen someone so blinded by rage."

"Maybe it wasn't rage at all," I say grimly.

She looks at me, confused but not dismissive. "What do you mean?"

"Foaming saliva," I say, ticking off one finger, "dilated pupils, mental confusion. What are those textbook symptoms of?" I know she knows. She's the one who taught me.

It takes her a moment, lost as she is in the past, but eventually she gasps, putting a hand to her mouth. "But . . . how could that be?" she asks.

I smirk, holding out a hand. "There's only one way to find out."

CHAPTER TWENTY

The cemetery is peaceful at this time of night. A frosted half-moon hangs in the starless sky. The smell of soil surrounds me, comforting as I dig with ruthless efficiency.

My mother stands outside the grave, looking down as I near the mark. "This reminds me of when you got your first grave-digging kit," she says nostalgically. "You were so happy you nearly smiled."

I look up, wiping my sweaty brow with a sweater sleeve. "You sure you don't want to help?" I ask. "The exercise is invigorating."

She examines her nails fondly before shaking her head. "I'd

love to, darling," she says. "But I wouldn't want to ruin your fun."

I don't need to be told twice. In another two minutes, the shovel thunks satisfyingly against a casket lid. One of my favorite sounds. "Moment of truth," I tell my mother.

Using the shovel's edge, I pry the twenty-year seal open. I'm consumed with my victory at the sight of Garrett's unusually well-preserved face—the tinge of blue, the lack of decay, it's all here.

"I was right," I murmur.

But before my mother can look at what I've found, a flashlight beam bathes the graveyard, utterly ruining the moment. My only cold comfort is that it's Deputy Santiago, not Sheriff Galpin, who finds us.

"Got a call someone was digging up a grave," she says, shining the light between my mother and me. "You're both under arrest."

As my mother puts her arms up in surrender, I have a few seconds with no eyes on me. I reach into Garrett's casket to secure the proof I'll need to exonerate my father—then and only then do I go willingly.

I always thought there was nothing worse than watching my parents maul each other at home, or in the car, or in the grocery store. Turns out it's worse through the bars of a holding cell.

My mother and I are secured in one while my father inhabits the adjoining cell. Even with my eyes closed, I can hear the sounds of their passionate reunion.

"Even the long arm of the law couldn't keep us apart!" my father says, enraptured.

"At least we'll get to spend this last night together before they take you away," my mother moans.

It's the last straw. "I've seen jackals with more self-control than you two," I snap.

They turn to look at me a little guiltily. It's not going to last, but at least I can explain my plan now that they're mostly two sentient beings again.

"Neither of you are built for hard time," I say witheringly. "And thanks to me, you won't have to find that out the hard way."

My father's attention is fully on me now. "I knew my little jailbird would have an escape plan! Does it involve a non-extradition country?"

"I know of several," I say. "But luckily this escape will be perfectly legal." I pull my handkerchief out of my pocket. Garrett's unnaturally blue finger rests inside it. I hand it to my mother. "A souvenir from tonight's outing. I borrowed it from Garrett."

As they examine it in vague confusion, I narrate:

"*Atropa belladonna*. Nightshade poisoning. The remarkable preservation of his soft tissue and the blue tint confirm it."

Understanding dawns on my mother's face first. "Which means Garrett was dying—"

"—*before* you stabbed him," I confirm.

The look on her face is one I've never seen before. No performance, no sly smile, no disappointment. Only relief. Twenty years of it, stripping her bare.

My father's arms encircle her again through the bars. "You look even more ravishing as an innocent woman!" he cries.

Groaning aloud, I stalk over to them. "For once, can you two keep your hands off each other and *focus*?" I reach out to snatch the finger back from my mother, but as I do, I make physical contact for the first time without the barrier of the handkerchief.

Electricity, shooting up my spine. My whole body going rigid with it. Before I know it, I'm in the back of a pickup truck, in the dark. Garrett Gates sits in the front seat. An older, raging man who can only be his father hands him a vile of glowing blue liquid. Nightshade elixir.

"Quit whimpering over some Outcast girl!" he says as his son shrinks in the seat beside him. "I told you they're not human. Prove to me you're still worthy of being called my son. Sneak into that dance, spike the punch. Kill them all, boy."

A flash, and we're outside the Nevermore gates, Garrett and I. He jumps the wall and approaches the school, looking magnificent in the moonlight, the rain just threatening overhead.

Garrett glances down at the vial in his palm, then puts it in his breast pocket as the sky opens up and the rain begins to pour.

Another flash, this time of lightning. We're on the roof, and my father, seventeen and limber, slams Garrett into a nearby column. Inside his pocket, the vial shatters against his skin. The nightshade elixir seeping in. Poisoning him before he has a chance to poison a whole generation of Outcasts . . .

Gasping, I return to the present. The jail cell. My parents worried glances.

"What just happened, Wednesday?" my mother asks.

In this moment, I don't even remember that I'm trying to keep the visions from my mother. That I'm afraid this is just another way I'll never live up to her expectations. I only know I need to purge what I've learned, as if I'm the one who's been poisoned.

"Garrett . . . that night," I begin. "He wasn't just there to kill Father. He planned to use the nightshade poison to murder the entire school."

My mother and I are released the next morning on bail. For once, we're united in our purpose as we enter the mayor's office, Garrett's finger still stowed carefully in my bag.

"Thank you for seeing us on such short notice, Mr. Mayor," my mother says in that flattering, sultry voice of hers.

The mayor doesn't appear susceptible to her charms. He glares at me instead. "Veiled threats have that effect," he says. "Now, what's this all about?"

Rather than explaining with words, I step forward and deposit Garrett's finger onto his important mayoral paperwork. As I hoped, he recoils in disgust.

"Garrett Gates wasn't killed by a stab wound," I inform him, though he clearly already knows, having been the sheriff on the day of Garrett's death. "He was dead before that blade ever touched him."

My mother sweeps forward now, looking down on Mayor Walker with her most withering look. "The blue sheen is a telltale sign of nightshade poisoning."

"But you already knew, didn't you?" I ask him, stepping up to join my mother, feeling her threatening aura envelop us both for once. I feel three inches taller as I glare at the mayor, waiting for him to crack.

It's a long staring contest, but eventually he slumps over the finger. "Garrett's father, Ansel Gates, hated Outcasts and Nevermore. He claimed the land the school was built on was stolen from his family over two hundred years ago. Garrett went there that night to kill all the kids at that dance. Ansel confessed the whole thing to me in a drunken stupor."

It's one thing to know this information myself. It's another to hear an elected official confirm it. "Why did you instruct the coroner to falsify the autopsy report?"

Mayor Walker appears to have aged ten years in a matter of minutes. "How could I punish Ansel Gates any more than the loss of his son? My job was to keep the peace. If there had been a public trial, both Jericho's and Nevermore's reputations would have been trashed."

I'm about to interject, but my mother beats me to it.

"I think the only reputation you were worried about ruining was your own," she says. "Garrett bragged to me that his father had the sheriff in his pocket. A year later, you were elected mayor. No doubt with the full support of the prominent and respected Gates family."

What little is left of Mayor Walker's spine seems to stiffen at this. "I resent your implication," he says.

But my mother leans across his mahogany desk, her eyes flashing. "What *I* resent," she says in a low, dangerous voice, "is that you could have prevented all of this if you'd done your job when I filed my complaint about Garrett stalking me. But men like you have no idea what it feels like not to be believed."

For the first time, in this moment, I see my mother as more than an impossible standard to live up to. A standard by which I must measure myself a constant disappointment. I see her as the girl she was. The events that shaped her into this woman who does not yield.

The mayor isn't equal to her. Not by any measure. "What do you want?" he asks, broken.

I'm starting to feel auxiliary to this conversation. To all of it.

But to my immense surprise, my mother yields the floor to me.

"All charges dropped," I say without hesitation. "My father released immediately with a full and unequivocal apology from you and the sheriff's office. Do we have a deal?"

I don't even have to wait for a response. His posture says it all.

We make our way to the courthouse in silence. But not the adversarial kind. The kind that allows room for adjustments within it.

"You were very impressive in there," I say when we arrive. Pugsley and Lurch came over in the limo, but for once, my mother deigned to walk with me.

My mother smiles at me, but I know a compliment won't get me out of the question she's poised to ask next. "When did your visions begin?" she asks, not ungently.

There's no point in lying. Not now, when I could actually use her guidance. "A few months ago," I confess. "Before I left for Nevermore Academy."

She leans against the retaining wall, surrounded by flowers. It's a sunny, beautiful day in Jericho. Such a contrast to the dark odyssey we've been on the past twenty-four hours.

"I'm sorry you didn't feel you could tell me," my mother says. "I know we've had difficulties navigating the treacherous shoals of our mother-daughter relationship lately, but I'm always here for you, Wednesday."

So I say the things I haven't been able to solve on my own. My own kind of olive branch.

"Sometimes, when I touch someone or something, I get a glimpse of violent things in the past or future. I can't control it."

My mother looks at me with kindness. Without judgment. "Our psychic ability is filtered through the lens of who we are.

Given my disposition, my visions tend to be positive, which makes me a Dove."

No need to ask whether I'm a Dove as well, I think gratefully. "And someone like me?" I press. "Who sees the world through a darker lens?"

This time, there's pride in her eyes as she answers. "You're a Raven," she says. "Your visions are more potent, more powerful. But without proper training, the things you see can lead you to madness."

I think of Rowan, driven to murder by his telekinesis. His mind warping him from the inside until he no longer knew the difference between using and abusing his power.

"Tempting as that sounds, I would like to learn to master it," I tell her. The way things have been going this weekend, I consider learning from my mother. It doesn't sound like quite the torture I might have assumed last week.

My mother looks at me more intently. Up the stairs, the doors to the courthouse remain closed as my father waits for release.

"If I could help you, I would," she says, real emotion in her voice. "But we aren't trained by the living. Someone from our bloodline reaches out from the beyond when we're ready. A relative, most often, who shares a particular bond."

Goody, I think. Her strange likeness to me. The way she can see me in visions when no one else can. "Goody has," I tell my mother. "She's been appearing in my visions. She warned me that something terrible is coming."

There's no doubt that this is bad news to my mother. She shifts, turns to the courthouse doors, then back to me. "Be careful, Wednesday," she tells me. "Goody was a witch of great strength, but her vengeance pushed her too far. She couldn't save herself . . ."

Just then, the doors open. My father is escorted out in his pinstriped suit by Sheriff Galpin, who looks like he's swallowed something bitter. He shakes my father's hand and they exchange some words. I can't see my father's face, but as the sheriff speaks, I can make out *your daughter* and *my son*.

I grimace.

They shake hands, and then my father is returned to us. The mystery of my father's murder accusation is solved. But the mystery of the monster looms closer than ever. And now I know how far someone will go to keep me from discovering the truth.

The only question now is who?

There's palpable relief in the air as Parents' Weekend comes to a close. In the drive, students of all stripes bid goodbye to their families. My own stands before the family hearse, and I can't help but feel we've grown closer over the weekend. Nothing like wrongful arrests, jail visits, and grave robbing to bring people together, I suppose.

My father approaches me before he gets into the car, hugging me closely, which I endure just this once. "Well," he says as he pulls away. "We can't say Parents' Weekend wasn't a nail-biter!"

I survey him in return. "I knew you didn't have it in you to be a murderer."

He smiles, putting a hand to his heart. "As much as that stings, gracias, my little death trap."

My father gets into the car, my brother follows with a wave, and then it's just Morticia and me in the drive once again. She steps forward, holding the yearbook she took from Weems's office on the first day.

"As I leafed through the pages of this book, I was reminded

of all my wonderful times here," she says, handing it to me. "But they were just that. Mine. You have your own path to blaze. I don't want to be a stranger in your life, so if you need me for anything at all, I'm just a crystal ball away."

I take the book and nod, stepping forward to accept her classic double air-kiss. Something has shifted between us, but she's still Morticia, and I'm still me.

"Thank you, Mother," I tell her. As the car pulls away, I open the yearbook absently, flipping until I find my mother and Judy Garland on a page near the middle.

It takes me a moment. Then the truth hits me like a sledgehammer.

Weems is at her desk when I storm in with the yearbook, slamming it down on her desk, not waiting for her to react to my presence.

"I knew it," I tell her. "I did see Rowan murdered that night in the woods."

"Excuse me?" Weems asks, the picture of the British stiff upper lip.

"The 'Rowan' who showed up the next morning when the sheriff was here was *you*." I jab a finger down on the photo of Judy in the yearbook. "At that talent show, you didn't only impersonate Judy Garland. You *became* her. You're a shape-shifter."

In the photo I'm pointing to, it's undeniable. The bone structure, the skin texture, the hair thickness and length. It's all different. Far beyond the possibility of a costume.

"That's a fascinating theory," Weems says, completely unruffled.

I won't let her throw me off the trail. Not this time. I straighten up, channeling Morticia as best I can as I glare down on her. "I'm sure there are plenty of people invested in the monster attacks who will be very interested to find out you actively aided a cover-up."

The placid façade breaks at last. Weems's intense stare is much more feral than my mother's. Fire rather than ice.

"You won't tell a soul, Miss Addams," she hisses. "And it wouldn't matter much if you did. Rowan's father already knows what happened, and he fully supports my decision not to involve the authorities."

This stops me in my tracks. "Why would he agree to that?"

"Because Rowan was not in his right mind," Weems says, as if this somehow justifies her actions. "His telekinetic ability was driving him mad, and he attempted to murder you twice. His tragic death allowed us to rectify the situation without casting the school or Rowan in an unflattering light."

Unflattering light, I think, nausea setting in at the sheer audacity of this woman. Of everyone like her, who prioritizes public opinion over the truth. Over justice. "You and Mayor Walker are exactly the same, aren't you?" I ask, not bothering to hide my disgust. "Burying bodies to cover up your secrets."

She doesn't even look conflicted about it. That's the worst part. "I did what I needed to do to shield this school from controversy and protect its students from harm."

"The monster who killed Rowan is still out there!" I cry, furious at the hypocrisy. "And because of you, it'll be that much harder to find it. You say you're protecting the students of Nevermore but what about Eugene? You didn't protect him—you directly endangered him with your lies."

At first, I think I've finally gotten to her. Her face begins to show the first creases of concern as my words linger in the silence.

But then I hear the screams from outside, and shouting echoing across the grounds.

Weems reaches the balcony first. As she looks down over the side, an orange, flickering glow reflects off her face. She recoils in dread. "What on earth . . . ?" she whispers.

I advance until I'm standing beside her, surveying the scene below. Large, flaming words are burning in the well-manicured grass leading to the archery targets.

FIRE WILL RAIN, reads the ominous message.

I look up at Weems, who won't meet my eyes, transfixed by the warning below. "Looks like the past is coming back to haunt us after all," I tell her.

CHAPTER TWENTY-ONE

I've never done a séance before, but there's no time like the present. Especially when the present contains a homicidal monster hell-bent on serial murder and madness making visions rapidly increase in frequency.

Enid wasn't in the room when I started the ritual. Probably for the best—I'm out of smelling salts. I'm surrounded by burning candles, chanting, and feeling slightly silly. I've been drawn to the macabre since birth, but communing has never been a strong area of interest. I can barely tolerate the living. Why would I want to talk to the dead?

Despite my divided focus, a few moments into the chant, the door behind me flies open. The candles all extinguish at once. I don't feel the electric current that signifies a vision, but I whirl around anyway, expecting Goody in the doorway, ready to help me control my visions . . .

"Sorry," Enid says sheepishly. "Didn't meant to interrupt your . . . Do I even want to know?"

Defeated, I slump back into my now-useless candle circle, fanning away the smoke. "I was reaching into the black maw of death to contact a relative."

Enid seems unruffled by this news. She's wearing another eyesore of an outfit, but I find I'm getting used to them. There's something to the way her skin glows against a backdrop of hot pink.

"Black void of death feels very on-brand for you," she says. It's the closest thing I'll get to her blessing.

Before I can ask where she's coming from in her incredibly vivid ensemble, the sound of paper sliding across the floor distracts me. Enid turns to look as well.

"Maybe your relative answered you after all," she says.

I open the door quickly, scanning the hallway outside. Empty. The note itself is a hack job. Magazine letters. So passé. "I don't think Goody Addams's communiqués involve scissors and glue sticks," I say, flashing her the note.

"'If you want answers, meet me inside Crackstone Crypt,'" I read. "Midnight."

The real surprise is when Enid offers to accompany me. It's also when I should know something is wrong, but I'm too eager to uncover these so-called answers.

Our canoe ride to the island is much less eventful than the

time we traversed it during the Poe Cup. The water is dark and glassy. The woods embrace us on the shore. We arrive at the crypt with only a minute to spare—Enid insisted on reapplying her sparkly eyeliner and lip gloss twice before departure.

Joseph Crackstone's name greets us as we approach, etched into the aging marble, just visible in the light of Enid's phone. It seems unbelievable that the last time I was here, I didn't even know who he was.

A twig snaps as we approach the entrance. Likely wildlife. I pay it no mind. Enid, however, looks terrified. She extends her claws, peering around. The glitter eyeliner does little more than accentuate her terror.

"You insisted on coming," I chastise her. "I was fine on my own."

The cracked marble door is ajar. Our mystery note author is most likely already inside. I wonder who it will be. Another student? Unlikely. Perhaps someone who knew the coroner. Or a relative of Crackstone's with access to the real *Book of Shadows*.

"Ew," Enid says as we step inside the musty tomb. "What died?"

I take a deep breath. "Smells like childhood," I tell her. "Come on. And kill the phone light."

We advance in pitch darkness. My eyes adjust slowly to the hulking shapes inside. No one is immediately visible. I don't hear anything until there's an echoing footstep that didn't come from Enid or me.

"Whoever you are, show yourself," I call out. I'm tired of waiting for answers. It's one minute after midnight. I abhor a lack of punctuality.

In response to my words, I'm stunned by flashlight beams. At least five of them. There are silhouettes behind them. Humanoid.

Still silent. I crouch into fighting stance, determined to protect Enid from whatever's summoned me here, but before I can land a single blow, a most unwelcome sound rings out:

"SURPRISE!"

Whirling around, I see Enid holding a birthday cake. Black. A fondant Grim Reaper with a scythe in one hand and a pink balloon in the other.

Happy Birthday, Wednesday, reads the icing. How the hell did they find out?

They begin to sing. Thing conducts them, the traitor, so that's an answer to one of my many questions. Xavier is here, along with Ajax, Yoko, and two other Nightshades who must have been bullied or tricked into attending.

When the song is over, Enid holds the cake close, the sparkler candle flickering on the walls of the crypt. "Make a wish!" she exclaims.

But I'm seeing beyond the candle now, to where it's illuminating an inscription behind my party guests. I forget the cake and the party as I approach it.

It's in Latin. Mostly overgrown. But I can still see it just well enough. "Fire will rain . . . when I rise," I read aloud.

"Okay?" Enid's voice from behind me. "Not really a wish."

I whip around to face her. "The first part of that phrase was burned into Nevermore's lawn. That can't be a coincidence."

From behind Enid, Ajax mumbles something whiny. I don't have time for him. I don't have time for any of this. I turn around, reaching out instinctively to run my hand along the letters in the wall.

The moment I do, electricity. My spine lengthens, I feel myself falling but I never land, the world rotates instead until I'm rising out of damp grass. The stone is gone. I'm at the edge of a misty forest with the moon glowing overhead. This one's waxing, not waning. I've traveled back in time again.

"Crackstone is coming," comes a voice to my left.

I get to my feet, looking around until I find Goody, standing at the tree line.

"Goody?" I ask.

She observes me with those otherworldly eyes. I hear my mother's voice in that moment. *Her vengeance pushed her too far. She couldn't save herself.*

"You're the Raven in my bloodline," she says. It's not a question.

I know I don't have much time. I step forward eagerly, feeling as always like I'm looking in a mirror that's just a little off. "I was told you could teach me to control my ability," I tell her.

"There is no controlling a raging river," she intones. "You must learn to navigate it without drowning. Time is not on our side."

Goody gestures in front of her, and the landscape of the vision changes as I turn. From a dark forest to a massive wrought-iron gate. Rusted, leaning, secured with a padlock and chain. Through the ornate bars I can see a dilapidated mansion surrounded by an untamed garden. It's clearly been abandoned. But what does this old house have to do with my visions? With Crackstone? With anything?

"To stop Crackstone, this place you must seek," Goody says in that breathy, ethereal voice.

"Do you always speak in riddles?" I ask, irritated. Just once it would be nice to get a clear instruction and a reason for it.

"Do you always seek simple answers?" Goody fires back. "The path of the Raven is a solitary one. You will end up alone, unable to trust others . . . only seeing what is monstrous within them."

I shrug, though the words cut me deeply. If this is the path to being a Raven, it seems I began walking it the day I was born. "Is that supposed to scare me?"

The smile Goody gives me is cruel. Condescending. For the first time I can see what my mother meant about her. How she let her rage twist everything inside her.

She disappears into the fog. The mansion, the gate, the forest, even Goody herself all vanish in the darkness that overtakes me.

I spend the next morning refusing to speak to Enid or Thing. They're both complicit in the birthday debacle. Instead, I focus on my attempted drawing of the gate Goody showed me. The mansion behind it.

Thing hops tentatively onto my shoulder. Enid, who has so far taken her punishment with good grace, focuses on the little clip things she insists on arranging in her hair.

"Careful," I say to Thing. "That's my cold shoulder."

"Don't blame Thing," Enid says. Their alliance continues to be a perpetual thorn in my side. "The party was my idea. I think everyone deserves to be celebrated on their birthday."

I glower in her general direction. "I prefer to be vilified."

She ignores this, coming closer, apparently bolstered by my first verbal response in hours. "What happened to you down there?" she asks. "You looked like you were having a seizure."

I don't answer. I only shake my head. A seizure would have been a picnic compared to what really happened.

"Can I at least get some kudos for pulling one over on you?" she asks, hopeful.

The truth is that with the new information from the crypt and the directive from Goody, I don't have much time for petty birthday-related grudge-holding. Pity.

"Your subterfuge was impressive," I admit.

The atmosphere in the room becomes immediately less chilly. Thing pulls a massive box out from under my bed. There's a card attached from my parents.

"'May your sixteenth be as sour and misery-filled as you desire. Your ever-doting mother and father,'" I read.

"They asked Thing to hide it before they left on Parents' Weekend," Enid says, bouncing on the balls of her feet as if this is a truly exciting diversion.

I open the box right there on the floor. "It's a taxidermy starter kit," I say to Enid as I remove the chemicals and open the frozen area that holds two dead squirrels. "I would have preferred live ones."

"Okay, ew," Enid says. "But while you're accepting presents!" She hands me a black-wrapped gift with a bow. I'm immediately thankful for her apparent ability to avoid neon in honor of my birthday.

When I unwrap it, however, the gratitude is replaced with confusion. It's black, and it's made of yarn, but beyond that I can't distinguish its purpose.

"Well?" Enid asks, bouncing again. "Do you like it?"

"What is it exactly?" I ask, as inoffensively as possible.

I immediately regret asking. "It's a snood, silly!" she says. "I made it in your signature colors. And do you know what the best part is?"

Not trusting myself to speak, I wait for an answer.

"I have one too!" Enid cries, pulling on her own *snood*,

which appears to be some mixture of a scarf and a hood. Hers, of course, is vivid magenta with rainbow tassels. "We can wear them together to class!"

Her expression is so expectant that despite my vow not to let the social tail wag the truth-seeking dog, I do my best to navigate the situation carefully. "Enid," I say solemnly. "This is far too unique to wear to class. We should wait for a special occasion. Like a funeral."

Enid's face falls a little, but she lets the subject drop, for which I'm thankful. I put the snood into my backpack and make my way toward the door, having had quite enough birthday for one morning.

Thankfully, no one follows me to the site of the fire. The flames died down before Weems could even organize a task force to put them out, but the charred letters remain burned into the lawn.

People are creeped out by it, so it's usually a decent place to think, but I've only been there a few minutes when someone tall and broody approaches from behind me.

"Last night," says Xavier without greeting, "in the crypt, you had another vision, didn't you?"

I don't look away from the letters. FIRE WILL RAIN. "Didn't realize we were back on speaking terms," I tell him.

"Well, I showed up at your surprise party, didn't I? Figured that would have been a hint. So what did you see? In your vision?"

I refuse to look at him, frustrated anew about the DNA non-match. My best lead and Galpin insists it's a dead end.

"Who said I was ready to speak to you?" I ask him.

He scoffs. "You *still* think I'm the monster."

"Haven't ruled it out," I say coldly.

"Fine," he says, throwing up his hands. "If you change your

mind and want my help, you know where to find me."

Since my thinking place has been compromised, I choose a place I'm even less likely to be interrupted. The hospital staff know me by now and don't bother me as I make my way to Eugene's room and settle in. The beeping of the life-support machine comforts me.

"I haven't always hated birthdays," I tell Eugene's unconscious form. "Each one reminds me I'm a year closer to death's cold embrace. What's not to like about that? And when I was young, my family always made sure my birthdays were memorable."

I lose myself in the memory now that I'm safely alone. Eight years old. A cake where a fondant version of me is decapitated by a mini guillotine and strawberry jam comes out. My parents commissioned a piñata in the shape of my favorite creature—the black widow. Several of my classmates came to the party, and as I hit at it, they chanted, *Candy, candy, candy.*

When the papier-mâché broke open, there were live spiders inside. A delightful surprise. But the children from my class didn't see it that way. They screamed, cried, threw up, had nightmares. And every last one of them blamed Wednesday the Freak.

"Parties, presents, and games, they all seem so trivial," I tell Eugene when the memory ends. "Goody said I was destined to be alone. And that I would be sorry for it. But sometimes—"

My unwitnessed confessional is cut short by the sound of a throat clearing. I expect one of Eugene's effusive mothers, but instead a most unwelcome sight greets me.

"Dr. Kinbott," I say coldly. She's standing there in one of her boring young professional outfits, holding a bouquet of peach roses.

"Hello, Wednesday," she says cheerily. "I haven't seen you since our session with your family, which is certainly one I won't forget. How are things going with them?"

She's blocking the door. It seems the quickest way out is to answer her inane questions, as ever. "My mother and I spent some quality time together. Got our hands dirty."

"Gardening?" Kinbott asks hopefully.

"Grave digging," I correct her.

She shakes her head, seeming almost amused before crossing the sterile room to Eugene's bedside, placing her roses in a vase on his side table.

"Why are you here?" I ask suspiciously.

"Eugene's moms," she answers, without addressing my veiled accusation, whatever it is. "I'm working with them. This kind of trauma leaves emotional scars on the whole family. They had to head home for a few days, so I promised to check on him."

Finally, an appropriate exit. "I'll leave you to it, then." I make my way toward the blessedly unblocked door, but Kinbott stops me in my tracks.

"Who's Goody?" she asks innocently.

I turn to face her, shutting down any and all expressive movement in a snap. "A distant cousin," I say. "Very distant."

Dr. Kinbott knows I'm lying, I can see it in her pitying expression. "It sounds like she doesn't see you for who you really are," she says gently.

"She sees more than you think," I snap, forgetting the cardinal rule of therapy and police questioning. Never volunteer information. "I want to assure you that I remain as cold and heartless as the day we met."

The good doctor only shrugs, making her way toward my vacated visitor's chair. "I doubt a cold, heartless person would be sitting by her friend's bedside feeling guilty about his condition."

I roll my eyes, desperate to get out from her clinical gaze. "I didn't ask for a free session."

She smiles. "Consider it my birthday gift."

Only then does she pipe down and permit my long-awaited escape. Of course, if I'd known then what I would come to know, if I could have seen what Mayor Walker was surveying at that moment in his office, I never would have left her alone with Eugene for a single second.

CHAPTER TWENTY-TWO

Twice thwarted in my attempt to be alone, I give up the dream and head to the Weathervane for a caffeine infusion.

I'm sitting in my usual booth reading *Joseph Crackstone: A Pilgrim's Journey* in search of clues when Tyler arrives with something I absolutely did not order. Something with *foam* that has *writing* in it.

Happy Birthday, to be precise.

"I know you're usually a quad girl," he acknowledges, sliding into the other side of the booth uninvited. "But I've been working on that all week."

Glancing at it, I don't bother to put down the book. "Birthday, yes. Happy, never," I say. "Is there anyone Thing didn't tell?"

"He and Enid needed someone to deliver the cake," he says ruefully. "I went with dark chocolate ganache to stick to your preferred color palette."

I wonder for a fleeting moment whether that's all anyone knows about me. That I prefer the color black. It would certainly explain a lot about their behavior.

"Don't you like a day that's all about you?" Tyler asks, pushing through my silence. My head is starting to hurt. I want to read my book in peace.

"Every day is all about me," I say. "This one just comes with cake and a bad song."

Undeterred, Tyler leans across the table into my line of vision. "So, if I asked you out for a non-birthday, song-free dinner . . . would that be something you'd be interested in?"

Soft eyes. All I want to do is look away. "I can't, I'm on a tight deadline," I tell him.

"Term paper?" he asks hopefully.

I nod, hoping the lie will end this conversation more quickly. It seems the more I give, the more he wants from me.

"It's about how whitewashing the sins of the past will doom us all," I tell him; then I pull out my inexpert drawing of the rusted gate from my vision. Maybe there's a chance to get things back to the way they were. Tyler, my local intel. Me, the strange girl he doesn't mind helping from time to time.

I liked it that way.

"Have you seen this place before?" I ask him.

He shakes his head. "What's that supposed to be?"

I take it back frustrated. "Never mind." I raise my book again, the universal signal for *Conversation over.* Tyler doesn't take the hint.

"Did I do something?" he asks in a voice to match those soft eyes. "I feel like ever since the Rave'N you've kinda been ghosting me. Am I wrong?"

From what I understand, the process of ghosting is intended to avoid a conversation exactly like this one. One with hurt feelings and messy emotions. One that precludes the possibility of future allyship.

The bell jingles, forcing his eyes off me. Saved by the bell.

"Guess that's my answer," he says. He appears downcast, but how could I have been clearer about my intentions? Yes, he occasionally intrigues me with his unexpected inner rage. Yes, I appreciate his local geography knowledge and the fact that he drives. But have I ever given him reason to hope for more?

Sheriff Galpin walks past our booth as Tyler gets to his feet. "Tall, black, two sugars to go?" he asks his dad, who nods.

Suddenly, the mystery of Tyler's misplaced hopes is of minimal importance by comparison. I chase the sheriff to the counter. "The threat burned into the lawn at the school," I say without preamble. "It's also etched on the wall inside Crackstone Crypt."

He looks at me with that familiar expression. Bemused and exasperated. "Don't tell me you've been out there digging up more bodies."

I ignore this pathetic attempt at humor. "There's a connection, I know it," I tell him urgently.

He only rolls his eyes. "Great, I'll put out an APB on a dead pilgrim."

"I figured now that you don't have an old vendetta to obsess over, you're free to solve actual crimes."

When he turns to face me, I know I've pushed him too far. I'll get nothing more out of him today. "Your father and I buried that hatchet. Maybe you should do the same." His tone says it's not a suggestion.

"I never bury hatchets," I promise him. "I sharpen them."

But quips aside, if neither Tyler nor the sheriff can help me carry out Goody's instructions, I have the distinctly unpleasant task of finding someone who can.

Xavier's shed is lit up against the gathering darkness in the forest. One day he'll learn to lock it. I open the door without knocking to find him standing before a massive canvas, paint splattered across his face and the work alike.

He turns to face me, the intensity still there in his eyes as he disengages from the world of his art.

"I need your help," I tell him, and then, before he can even smirk: "Don't gloat."

From my bag, I pull the inexpert sketch I made of the gate Goody showed me. I hand it to Xavier without comment.

"Want some drawing lessons?" he asks, teasing as he looks down at it. "Your line work is a little shaky."

The last thing I need is a good-natured ribbing about my lack of art skills. "I saw this place in one of my visions. Do you recognize it?"

Xavier turns back to the drawing with a more serious expression. After a few seconds of studying, his eyes go wide in a way that tells me I came to the right place. Wordlessly, he carries my drawing over to a wall layered with his own. With his free hand, he moves one aside to reveal the source of his surprise.

It's a drawing of the same gate Goody showed me, much more expertly rendered than my own, of course, but unmistakable.

"When did you draw this?" I ask.

Xavier stands beside me,. "A couple of days ago. I started having those dreams again, like before . . ."

It's not the first time his dreams have lined up with my own experiences. I think of his father, the famous psychic. Xavier has the ability to bring his drawings to life, but did he inherit more than just that?

"Was the monster in your dreams?" I ask, its eyes still peering down at me from canvasses around the room.

"Not this time," Xavier admits, shaking his head. "But I could feel it in the shadows the whole time. Like it was lurking in my mind." It's clear he's not comfortable confessing this. That the recollection haunts him still.

"Where is this place?" I ask, pointing to the wrought iron in his pen stroke. I expect the same shrug I received from Tyler, but Xavier surprises me again.

"It's the old Gates Estate," he says, almost casually. "I pass it when I go running."

The Gates Estate, I think, the information fizzing through my veins like sparkling cider. Another connection. If only I could see the bigger picture.

I'm about to tell Xavier exactly enough of this to prompt him to divulge more information about his dreams, the house, the monster, when I hear Thing snapping from across the room. He's standing beside a painting covered in a tarp.

"What is it?" I ask impatiently.

"Wait, don't—" Xavier says, crossing the room in three long strides.

But the damage is done before he can reach his secret work. Thing pulls at the corner of the tarp, revealing a giant canvas. A strange sensation fills me. Flattery mixed with discomfort. I can feel myself freezing up.

"Let me explain," Xavier says.

Only how can he explain better than his painting can? It's nearly life-size, rendered in black and white. Eerily lifelike. In it, a thin, pale girl with dark pigtails plays a cello beneath the night sky. It's a painting of me.

"After our last blowout, all I wanted to do was forget about you," Xavier says in a low, husky voice. "But I couldn't. And when something's eating at me, this is the only thing that works. I started painting and that's what came out."

I have no idea what to say.

"Sometimes I hear you up there playing," he continues into my silence. He waves a hand, and my delicate arm in the painting begins drawing the bow over the strings, a haunting melody drifting out. "I can sense how you get lost in the music. When you play, I feel like I'm seeing the real you."

He drops his hand. The picture goes still, but as it does, the friction within me only grows more intense. I don't have time to think about this right now, or to reckon with the discomfort of being seen deeply.

So I don't. I take the drawing and exit into the night.

I bury the scene with Xavier somewhere deep in my

subconscious the moment he's out of my sight. It doesn't matter what he thinks he sees. I got the information I needed from him—and even without a location, the Gates Mansion is easy to find.

The house is a mile or so outside of town. It doesn't take long to walk, and the brisk morning air clears my head.

It sits on a massive, overgrown lot with weeds taller than I am. The gate looks just like it did in the vision: rusted, moss covered, slightly crooked on its post. The house isn't in much better shape. Dilapidated, peeling paint, sagging lines. There's a metaphor here for this prominent family of Jericho and their bigotry aging poorly, but I don't quite have my finger on it before I make another discovery.

I'm not alone. It seems I wasn't the only person interested in a jaunt into the past today.

I duck into a bush just in time to avoid the man himself coming out the front door. He's on the phone, and Thing and I are close enough to hear every word.

"Sheriff, pick up your damn phone. It's Noble. I might have figured out who's behind all this. It's a long shot, so I have to lay it out for you in person."

He's heading for his car, and I know this might be my only chance to hear his theory. To add his clues to the ones I've gathered myself in the hopes of cracking this thing open. "I need a distraction," I mouth to Thing, who salutes and disappears silently.

"I'll fill you in over pie at the Weathervane just like the old days," the mayor is saying as he approaches the driver's side door. "See you there in half an hour."

Before he can get to the car, a pebble hits him in the back of the head. He spins around, on high alert, and I take the opportunity. I open the hatch in the back, then dive in and settle behind the last row of seats like a bag of groceries. I'm followed shortly by Thing.

By the time Mayor Walker reassures himself that the attack came from a wayward squirrel, we're out of sight, and a few minutes after that we're on our way back into town. I'll have plenty of time to investigate the house later. Discovering the mayor's theory may be a once-in-a-lifetime chance.

To my dismay, he doesn't make any more phone calls on the drive, and he's not the type to talk himself through a theory out loud. We pull up in front of the Weathervane in utter silence.

I stay behind the car for a beat, clocking Sheriff Galpin in the window of the café, waiting just as the mayor asked.

They exchange a wave from across the street before Walker steps off the curb.

That's when it happens. An old blue Cadillac makes the turn onto Main Street at a breakneck pace. Instead of slowing down when the mayor comes into view, the driver accelerates. I don't even have time to shout a warning before Walker is ruthlessly struck by the speeding vehicle, sending his body up and over the hood and onto the concrete with a sickening crunch.

The car doesn't even stop. Just hits the gas again and peels off into the distance.

I've seen a lot of horrors in my short life, but the callousness of the attack, the intentionality, the total lack of hesitation haunts me. Walker's last words before this were that he might've figured out the person behind the attacks. That can't possibly be a coincidence.

And yet a hit-and-run doesn't remotely fit the killer's pattern of attack. Even if the monster can become human, why use a car when those two-inch, razor-sharp claws have been serving them so well?

I'm barely aware of being led to a booth inside the Weathervane. Of watching Walker being taken away in an ambulance. The lights are on, I think numbly. That means he's still alive. Maybe all hope isn't lost.

When Galpin returns to the booth, he looks years older. His face sags, his eyes are bloodshot. He and Walker were old friends. It makes sense.

"Well?" I ask.

"He's alive," Galpin says. "Barely. I'll take you back to school after I get your statement."

"I already gave it to your deputy," I inform him, remembering the last visitor to this table as if through a misty veil. "Blue Cadillac. No license plates. Hit him at full speed."

The sheriff takes out his voice recorder. The light blinks red as he sets it down between us. "I want a better statement," he says.

I shrug. My strategy regarding to Galpin hasn't changed since we first encountered each other. Do what it takes to stay in the loop. No more, no less.

"For starters, what were you doing in the back of the mayor's SUV?"

"I saw him coming out of the Gates mansion," I say promptly.

Galpin rolls his eyes in exasperation. "The Gates mansion? What in the hell were you doing out there?"

"House hunting," I quip. The feeling is starting to return to my extremities. A good sign. A healthy dose of mortal terror is good for the immune system.

The sheriff gives me a pointed look.

"I overheard the voice mail he left you," I admit. "I was intrigued."

He shakes his head. I can tell he's still rattled. That it's making him more confessional than he would normally be.

"When the mayor had my job, he always had a lot of wild theories on cases he couldn't solve," he says, his eyes unfocused. "We'd discuss them over pie, sitting in that booth right over there. Most of the time they went nowhere."

I lean across the table, smelling blood. "Call me old-fashioned, but when someone is run over on their way to give the police key information, it usually means they were onto something. All signs point to the Gates family and that house."

The faraway look in the sheriff's eyes focuses. He seems to remember who he is and who he's talking to at last. "How could they be responsible?" he asks. "The Gates are all dead. Every last one of them. And I don't believe in ghosts."

I reach forward and click off the tape recorder, sliding it back to him. "Maybe you should," I say.

Of course, being returned to school in a police cruiser lands me immediately in the principal's office. By the time I return to my dorm, Weems has yelled at me, accused me of being a magnet for trouble, and revoked my off-campus privileges until further notice.

Which is incredibly inconvenient, given the fact that I was planning to return to the Gates mansion tomorrow night. It doesn't stop me—at this point, I doubt anything could—but it does make the planning a little more difficult.

Despite the embarrassing obsession my generation has with palm-sized technology, Nevermore still has a pay phone near the quad. It's a good thing, because the next morning's subterfuge precludes me from the usual strategy of borrowing Enid's cell. I ensconce myself in the booth and dial Tyler's number.

I haven't slept all night. I just keep seeing the car hit the mayor again and again. If this is the fate of someone who insists on finding the truth, I may have less time than I thought.

He answers on the third ring despite the unknown caller. "Hello?"

"I've reconsidered your offer," I say without preamble.

"Offer?"

"The non-birthday dinner," I inform him. "We'll do it tonight. Pick me up outside the Nevermore gates at eight o'clock. And be sure to cut your lights."

I hang up before he can do more than confirm. My hands tremble a little as I replace the receiver. Normally I wouldn't lie to an ally, but truth-tellers are being hospitalized left and right, and desperate times call for desperate measures.

Unfortunately, I can't track down Enid until close to go time. She's sulking on her bed, as she's taken to doing since the non-starter of a birthday party.

Tyler was easy enough to get on my side. The promise of anything remotely date-adjacent is good for at least twenty-four hours of diminished insight from Tyler. Enid is a tougher nut to crack. She can sniff out dishonesty, so I had to dig deep for things that are true—if not necessarily relevant to this situation.

I take a deep breath, then step across the duct-tape border that's separated our sides of the room since the first week. This gets her attention. She pauses on her sulking and looks up at me.

"I've been thinking about my less-than-enthusiastic response to your surprise soiree," I inform her. "And I will admit that I regret not properly expressing my gratitude to you."

Her eyes go extra round. I can see a smile threatening. "You really mean it?" she asks.

The clock on her bedside table reads 7:55 p.m. "Take the win, Enid," I tell her, impatience creeping in.

She smiles. "Apology accepted," she squeaks.

I step closer to her bed. "If only there were a way to get off campus and have a little birthday redo. Just two best friends."

Her expression changes again at the utterance of those two, long-awaited words. This is the part that's true but not relevant. If I have a single true friend in this world, it's Enid. That makes her my best friend by default under the terms of any reasonable ranking system.

"Too bad the school's on lockdown." I sigh dramatically, looking out the window to where the moon is just shining in. "Would you look at that full moon," I opine. "So bright, isn't it?"

Enid gets excitedly to her feet. I can see the connection forming just as I knew it would. "Wait," she says, as if I positively won't believe what she says next. "I could tell them I'm about to wolf out and get a pass to the lupin cages right off campus! And we could say you volunteered to lock me in!"

It's amazing how closely she sticks to the script I wrote for her in my mind. "My deviousness has finally rubbed off on you," I compliment her.

Thing is already prepared. I point at him. "You know what to do, right?" He gives me a thumb-up as Enid and I make our way to the door. Her enthusiasm is almost infectious. Almost.

"Wait!" she says, doubling back, spending precious seconds

during which Tyler could be caught by Weems or leave in confusion. "We should wear our snoods!"

She pulls her own out of her dresser, so pink it makes my headache worse. Panicking, I realize I have no idea where mine is. I can't hold up the show while I tear this place apart looking for it, but I also can't tell Enid why.

"I think I left mine at fencing," I invent. Anything to get us out the door.

But when Enid makes it back to the door, she's holding my knitted monstrosity as well. "Actually, you left it at the Weathervane. Luckily, Bianca brought it back."

"Wonderful," I say through gritted teeth. "Can we go now?"

Enid wraps the snood around my neck and pulls the hood up. I look like I'm about to flee a war-torn country ravaged by Western imperialism. "Best friend birthday redo, here we come!"

CHAPTER TWENTY-THREE

Tyler is waiting outside the gate, sans headlights as directed, which means exactly one part of this has gone to plan. Luckily, it's the most important part.

He doesn't see me right away, and I watch him checking his hair. Testing his breath against his hand. When he finally does look up, he jumps. Even if this were a date, it's the way I prefer to be greeted.

"Let's get moving," I say, getting into the front seat.

"Uh, hi," Tyler says. "Good to see you too."

Enid opens the back door as he's looking at me, confused.

They exchange looks. I meant to explain, but everything feels so urgent now, like there's a heart beating alongside mine counting down the seconds until I'm found out for being too close to the truth.

"Wait, *he's* our Uber driver?" Enid asks with a tone of condescension.

"Uber driver?" Tyler asks, rounding on me. "I thought we were going on a date?"

"A *date*?" Enid's voice shoots up an octave. "This was supposed to be a girls' night out!"

I close my eyes against the headache. "Change of plans," I say. "Let's go."

The drive is a little awkward, but the cobwebs in my mind are clearing bit by bit the closer we get to the mansion. Tyler and Enid might be upset with me for the subterfuge, but is this really different from tricking me into a surprise party? Apparently, it's what friends do.

The grounds are even more ominous at night. Skeletal trees reach for the foggy sky. Brush and brambles have overtaken the place. The house rises from the chaos like a decaying monument to what the place once was. Dilapidated. It looks like the scene of every low-budget horror film ever made. Standing out front, I can practically hear Mayor Walker speaking into his phone.

I might have figured out who's behind all this.

"Door's locked," I say after trying it. "Let's try the garage."

They follow me to the double doors. I can't get them open, but Tyler—despite his stony silence on the drive—steps up to help, but after a few attempts, his ego gets the best of him.

"This is pointless," he says. "Why do you even want to—"

Enid stands beside the now open doors.

"How—" Tyler begins.

Enid flashes a smile. "It's a werewolf thing."

My flashlight is barely equal to the darkness in here. Dust coats everything, floating and glinting in the beam. I find a lamp in the center of the ceiling and pull the chain. It flickers to unsteady life, bathing the space in a crimson glow.

Now I can see the shelves lined with old, rusting tools. Beer bottles that are twenty years old, and a car covered with a tarp. I know what I'll find before I even reach it, and I'm not disappointed. When I whip the cover away, the blue Cadillac comes into view.

Engine revving, tires squealing, the crunch of bumper against bone.

I shut my eyes tightly to push it all out. "This is the car that hit the mayor," I say in the most controlled voice I can manage.

"Okay," Enid says in a panicked voice. "This whole *birthday* excursion just took a super-creepy turn. We need to call Tyler's dad right freakin' now."

"No!" I snap, turning to face her. "He'll only take us back to Nevermore and have me expelled. And they've been useless in this investigation so far, anyway. I need to take matters into my own hands."

They exchange a look, but no one argues. At this point I don't mind if they leave me alone here. I already got what I needed.

The inner garage door leads into the kitchen. We make our way through the dilapidated, cobweb-coated interior visible in the flashlight's beam. In the hallway, I stop in front of a large painting of the Gates family. Ansel and his wife, flanked by their children, Garrett and Laurel. They're posed in the yard. The rosebush behind them is heavy with peach flowers.

I move on, padding across the rotting, pest-ravaged carpet into a once-grand library filled with ruined leatherbound tomes. Everyone knows old-money families hide their best secrets in their libraries.

At random, I begin pulling on individual books, looking for a lever. Every house of this caliber that survived the Prohibition era had a secret room or speakeasy in the house.

The books do nothing. Instead, I start looking for patterns. A single thing out of place among them. I find it at last on the top of a shelf. A ship carved into the wood where the rest show only sunbursts.

I can practically feel Tyler and Enid exchanging looks behind my back as I reach up to press it.

"Bull's-eye," I whisper as the wall slides away on its old-fashioned mechanism.

Instead, there's a shrine. An oil painting of Joseph Crackstone is the focal point. I can feel the victory waking me up, the adrenaline of knowing Goody was right. That I'm on the right track. Crackstone's likeness is surrounded by dripping candles and roses and various offerings. Painted on the wall beside the painting is a message in dripping red:

FIRE WILL RAIN on one side. WHEN I RISE on the other.

"Who doesn't have a spooky built-in altar in their library?" Enid asks nervously.

I'd all but forgotten I wasn't alone. "Ours is in the living room," I say absentmindedly. "More seating. We practice Día de los Muertos all year round."

Before she can react, I notice something odd. The candle wax pooling in the top of one of the larger pillars, glinting in the light like it's wet. Following a hunch, I kneel down, pinching wicks, confirming.

"They're still warm," I say. "Which means someone's still here—or they had to leave in a hurry. We still have a chance to catch them."

I make a dash for the hallway, casting the flashlight beam everywhere, looking for a creeping shrine-builder among the ruin and dust. There's no one here. The stairs spiral invitingly into the darkness upstairs.

"Tyler, you check the rest of the ground floor. Enid and I will search upstairs."

There's a moment when I'm sure he'll refuse. Maybe I'll see the glint of that internal war in his eyes, hinting at a deeper anger. But instead, he only nods, taking off down the hallway. I find myself feeling strangely let down.

At the top of the stairs, a wide hallway patterned in yellowing floral wallpaper banks left and right. "You go this way, I'll go that way," I tell Enid.

She's nothing like Tyler. She stands her ground. "You can't seriously be telling me we're splitting up. Here. That's how literally every best friend dies in a horror movie."

I know the only thing Enid wants more than to stick together is to get out of here. I use it. I'm not ashamed. We're running out of time to catch whoever extinguished those candles. "The faster we search, the faster we can leave," I say as enticingly as I can.

"Ugh!" Enid grunts, stomping her foot before turning on her heel and taking off in the opposite direction from the one I sent her in.

No matter, I make my way down the other expanse of hallway,

shining my light into more empty, dust-coated rooms. Furniture broken or rotted or covered in sheets. No sign of the Crackstone devotee.

But only a few minutes after we split up, I hear Enid's voice calling out: "Wednesday! I think you should see this!"

When I reach her, she's standing in the doorway of a bedroom much like the others. Small, dark wood and floral wallpaper. The only difference is this one is spotlessly clean. The bed is made neatly, and a vase on the nightstand is filled with peach roses.

"Look at this," Enid says, directing my attention to a jewelry box on the nightstand. It's one of those classic little girl affairs. The kind that plays music when you open it.

Enid's hot-pink fingernail is pointing to two golden letters lacquered onto the lid. LG.

"Laurel Gates," I say, feeling the certainty fill me. I touch it, half expecting a vision. Goody telling me I've come to the right place. But nothing happens.

"Looks like someone moved back into their old room?" Enid suggests.

I shake my head. The urgency is lessened in here. Like time itself has stopped. "She can't have," I say. "She drowned twenty years ago. She was the last member of the Gates family left alive."

There's something in this, I know it. Some connection I'm not seeing. Who would be staying in Laurel's room? Who would have a shrine to Crackstone? It all feels right on the edge of fitting together but I can't . . . quite . . .

From downstairs, a guttural snarl interrupts my attempts to reason through what I've seen here tonight. Tyler screams. The adrenaline is back.

"The monster," I say, locking eyes with Enid. "It's here."

I shove the music box into my backpack for later study. Enid and I race to the door, shoulder to shoulder.

The snarling grows louder as we reach the landing. At first, I don't see anything, but then a shadow begins to grow on the wall opposite Enid. Bristling, hump backed, terrifyingly enormous. Its massive, clawed foot hits the bottom stair. It's looking for us.

I grab Enid's hand and pull her back upstairs as quietly as I can, but I know it's only a temporary measure. We're trapped unless we can discover an exit that doesn't require the stairs—or we can distract the monster while we escape.

"Wednesday!" Enid whispers. "Look!"

She's pointing at a roll-up door in the wall just ahead. Relief surges through me. A dumbwaiter. Now, if only we can fit inside together.

Enid throws the door open as the monster's footsteps ascend the stairs. It's moving slowly now. Sniffing loudly. Tracking us. It's left me alive more than once, but I can't guarantee it won't break its pattern now—or that it'll spare Enid. I won't be able to live with myself if something happens to her.

I motion for her to climb inside first, then follow and close the door behind us. The space is tiny. I can smell her shampoo.

Every one of my nerves is at attention while we listen to the footfalls, coming up the stairs, turning our direction, then stopping cold. Enid opens her mouth and I put a single finger to her lips to stop her. I'm trying to listen for its breathing. For anything in the charged silence.

And then, just as the quiet becomes unbearable, five claws rip across the metal door just a few inches from our faces. Enid screams. I can see the monster's eyes through the slashes it made, bulging and furious and horrifying.

There's nowhere to go but down, but the dumbwaiter's ancient rope is fraying. We can't trust it to lower us safely. Quiet is no longer required as the monster rages and snarls and strikes outside. The metal door rattles. My brain races for a solution, stumbling, faltering until—

"Enid! Give me your snood!" I cry, tearing my own off my head. She looks hurt, but passes it over. I tie them together using a simple sailor's knot and try to use them to tie the door closed on the inside.

The monster can hear me. It backs up and I know what's coming is worse than scratching.

When its head rams into the door, it buckles. One more hit like that and we're toast.

I turn to Enid, feeling death stalking me like a specter, drawing ever closer. Our eyes meet in the darkness and I'm struck by the thought that this might be the last time I see her. The last time I see anything.

The rope holding us up snaps at last. We're plummeting before I can begin to react, and I'm not proud of the scream that escapes me, or of the way Enid and I cling to each other's hands as we fall.

It's a miracle we don't break our necks, but with minor battering and bruising, we make our way out of the dumbwaiter on the ground floor. We're in a laundry room. An ancient washer and dryer stand sentry. My flashlight is gone. The only light in the room is moonlight coming through the single window. As Enid and I stumble across the room in the darkness, my hand brushes on the pull cord of an overhead light. I yank on it.

The ancient enamel pendant sways, casting hideous, warping shadows through the basement.

I let my eyes adjust. When they do, I forget the monster. My moment of confronting my own mortality. I forget everything. Because in front of me is a metal shelf lined with glass jars. Each one contains a preserved body part—a finger, an ear, two toes . . .

"These are the body parts missing from the monster's victims," I say, more to myself than to Enid, who I've nearly forgotten along with the rest.

"Wednesday!" she shrieks, just as the growling begins again. The monster is slamming into the door of what I now know is the basement of the Gates house. "Let's go! The window!"

She's right. The hopper window is the only exit from this room that isn't currently being rammed by a monster. We run across the room to reach it, but I can feel the pull of the evidence in this room, the nagging feeling that if I leave, it'll all be a dream.

"You first," I tell Enid, boosting her up, making sure she's out before I take one last look at the shelves. Could I grab just one jar before the monster breaks the door?

The answer comes in the form of the monster itself, barreling into the basement, its features twisted in rage. It crashes into the shelf, sending everything flying, and I know the evidence is no good if it's found on my corpse.

They'd never know what to do with it.

I pull myself up onto the window ledge as the monster spots me. For a moment, we lock eyes, and then it's lunging for my legs, which I pull out the window just in time.

It howls in impotent rage, smashing its face against the window, which is much too small for it to fit through.

"Come on!" Enid shouts, just a few feet away, as the monster breaks the basement's only lightbulb in its tantrum, disappearing into the dark along with the evidence.

Enid is ready to run, but I can't. "What are you doing?" she shouts as I turn back toward the main drive. "The freakin' monster is back there!"

"So is Tyler," I tell her. "I can't leave him behind."

When she joins me, despite her distaste for Tyler and everything else I've put her through tonight, I know I was right about exactly one thing in all of this. Enid really is my best friend.

"Are you okay?" I ask her as we creep along the house in the shadows.

Her answering scoff surprises me. "Since when do you care?"

Once the monster's furious grunting has ceased, we find Tyler on the porch. He's curled around a wound to his chest, panting in fear and pain. I know the wound before I even turn him over. Five slashing claw marks rending his flesh.

I kneel down beside him. "I'm here, Tyler," I say. "Enid, help me."

But when help comes, it's not from Enid. Xavier, pale and disheveled, passes me his scarf to mop up Tyler's blood. "What happened?" he gasps, as if he's just been running. Or something worse.

"You didn't see the monster?" I ask as skeptically as I can manage while applying pressure to a deep laceration.

"Monster?" Xavier says, his eyes going wide. "I just got here. I heard him scream."

My silence appears to be too much pressure for him, because he continues: "I went to your room to apologize. Thing was there. He told me you'd be out here."

It's a likely enough story, but as we help Tyler back to his car, I reflect that this isn't the first time Xavier has shown up just as the monster disappears. Is it possible the sheriff is covering for him? Or that Xavier found a way to falsify the evidence? Either way, I can't help but feel like the lack of a DNA match between him and the monster isn't the whole story.

We're in the sheriff's living room, patching up Tyler's chest as best we can after he refuses to be taken to the hospital. The Galpin house is nothing special. Single level, root-beer-brown carpet, wood paneling. Tyler seems embarrassed even as he bleeds.

The sheriff provides a distraction by being livid before he opens the door. "What the hell, Tyler? I thought I said—" When he sees me, the typical fatherly frustration turns more pointed.

He takes in the group of Outcasts around his coffee table—Enid, Xavier, and myself—then the deep gouges in his son's chest that I'm currently attempting to close with suture tape.

Accusing, his eyes land on me. "This was your fault, wasn't it?"

"Dad, please," Tyler says weakly. "I'm okay."

I stand up, abandoning my suturing project. I understand as the person who roped Tyler into tonight's escapade, I'm responsible for him, but now that his father is here, all I can think about is the blue Cadillac. The body parts in jars. With the resources of the sheriff's department, we might have all we need to close this case once and for all.

"Sheriff, I understand you're angry," I say in my most respectful tone. "But believe me when I say I have something you really need to see."

The drive back out to the Gates house in the cruiser makes all of the night's earlier silences seem benign. Sheriff Galpin's lips are a line, his knuckles white on the steering wheel. But I'm as composed as ever. This is so close to being over I can almost taste it.

"Right through here," I say when we arrive, directing him into the basement door that still has the monster's claw marks all over it.

The sheriff shines his flashlight around the basement, and my heart sinks suddenly. Horribly. The room is entirely empty, stripped as if no one was ever there.

"It was all there," I say in disbelief, after the garage, library, and Laurel's room are similarly stripped. "The body parts, the altar, the Cadillac. The bedroom with the fresh roses."

It's clear Galpin doesn't believe me, and this time I don't blame him. The exhaustion is back, filling my limbs like cement.

"Well, it's gone now," he says, and from his tone, I can tell that's not all he has to say.

"Enid saw it too," I protest feebly. "Someone cleaned it out after we left."

"Do you have any proof of that?" Galpin asks as we stand in Laurel's empty room. He shines the flashlight in my eyes. "Any idea who this mystery person you're accusing is?"

He knows I don't. I feel rebellion rising in me again. "Yesterday I told you everything pointed to this house," I say. "And I was right."

This is what it takes to push him over the edge. He steps closer, the light growing brighter until I can barely see his expression besides two angry eyebrows. "Is that your justification for nearly getting your friends and my son killed?"

I open my mouth to defend myself, but he doesn't wait for a response. He only leans in closer.

"From this point forward, you are forbidden from seeing

Tyler," he says. "And, probably more importantly to you, you are forbidden from having anything more to do with this case. Do we understand each other?"

He doesn't wait for a response now, either, but as he escorts me back to Nevermore, I think it's possible we've never understood each other less. And that's saying something.

Sheriff Galpin leaves me at the front door. The entrance hall of the school is deserted when I arrive. I have no illusions about the consequences of tonight's outing, so I'm unsurprised to see Weems standing at the stairs the moment I begin to ascend.

"You directly violated my express orders and left campus during a lockdown," she says in that measured, school administrator voice. "Not to mention putting your peers and yourself in grave danger."

The cement feeling is still there, weighing me down as she drowns me in accusations. But I have to get through this next part before I can rest. "All grounds for expulsion, I know," I assure her. "And you have every right to exercise that option. But I believe it would be a grave error on your part."

Her eyebrows shoot up in disbelief. "I think contrition is in order right now, Miss Addams, not hubris."

Contrition. The only reason I'm even considering remaining in this absurd monument to administrative ineptitude is because it's where the monster is. But she doesn't need to know that. Not yet, anyway. "I'll never apologize for trying to uncover the truth," I say instead. Which is also true.

Before she can parry, I hold up the drawing Rowan's mother did. Myself and Crackstone in the flames. Taped together in the center but well-worn on its creases by now. Weems steps down a stair to examine it.

"What is this?" she asks.

"A warning from Rowan," I reply.

Her face creases with concern as she studies the drawing. No doubt she recognizes myself, Crackstone, the quad, and the implications.

"Is this why he tried to kill you?" she asks. I'm momentarily startled by the fact that she knows, but then I remember. The day "Rowan" left school. I confronted him outside Miss Thornhill's car and demanded an explanation. Of course, it wasn't really Rowan. It was Weems's ear I was whispering into.

"Yes," I tell her. "His mother drew it. She told him I was going to destroy the school . . . but I think I'm meant to save it."

The stairwell is dark around us, all rich mahogany and priceless artwork. Things that wouldn't fare well in a fire. I can tell Weems is intrigued, though she tries not to show it. Caring about this school is her one weakness—at least the only one I've found.

"Now you know what's at stake," I tell her solemnly. "Everything you vowed to protect, nothing less. I believe that warrants another chance." I swallow, hard, knowing what she's waiting for. *"Please,"* I manage.

Weems weighs her options carefully. A distant grandfather clock chimes midnight. Somewhere out there, the monster is loose, and someone is relocating victims' body parts in jars. An old blue Cadillac.

"One more infraction," Weems says, resigned. "One more step

out of line and you *will* be expelled. No ifs. No buts."

I would be relieved if there wasn't still so much work to be done.

"Enid and Xavier will also be spared," I tack on.

"And *no more negotiating*! Good night!" She turns on her heel and sweeps back up to her office. But I have no doubt she'll be thinking about what I showed her tonight for a long time. Long enough to keep me at Nevermore just a little longer.

Back in Enid's and my dorm, I'm looking forward to sleep. If I'm lucky, there'll be a nightmare involved.

But when I enter the room, it's clear I haven't had my last confrontation of the evening. Enid, her expression closed off in anger, is packing a large duffel bag. I know it must be serious.

"Where are you going?" I ask carefully.

"Yoko's room," she says in a stiff, cold voice. "Ms. Thornhill said I could crash there for a few nights."

This is incomprehensible to me. Why would Enid willingly choose to spend days with Yoko? "You don't need to worry about being associated with me. I worked it all out with Weems—you and Xavier won't be punished either."

She turns, her eyes flashing. "Am I supposed to thank you?"

"Why are you so upset? I apologized. It's over."

"Over?" she asks in disbelief, stepping toward me with a furious expression on her face. If I didn't know her so well, I wouldn't know that beneath it is a deep hurt. One I caused. "Tonight was just the icing on the birthday cake you couldn't be bothered to cut. You will use *anyone* to get what you want, even if it means putting them in danger. We could have died tonight because of your stupid obsession."

I step forward too. We're toe-to-toe on the duct-tape line. "I needed to investigate," I tell her. "That house is the key to everything. Without you and Tyler, I could never have gotten there."

Enid shakes her head slowly. "It never even occurred to you to ask me, did it?" she says. "You had to lie and manipulate me. Even though I've tried really, really, *really* hard to be your friend all month. I put myself out there for you, I think about your feelings, I defend you to people who think you give off serial killer vibes! Which is *a lot* of people, you know."

"I never asked you to do that," I counter, ignoring the first part. How can I explain that I couldn't risk her saying no? That in a situation this mired in life or death, with Walker and Eugene both in the hospital, it was better to ask forgiveness than permission.

"You didn't have to," Enid says, her voice cracking. "I did it for you because that's what friends do. They consider each other. They do things to make each other's lives better, not worse. And the fact that you don't know that says everything."

I know at that moment that I won't be able to stop her. She's seething with anger, but the hurt goes deeper.

"You want to be alone, Wednesday?" she asks, grabbing her bag. "Be alone."

And she's gone, the door bouncing off its hinges behind her.

In order to put off the moment I'll have to process this, I walk to the window, sitting down, pulling out Laurel's jewelry box. The little ballerina spins, its quiet tune loud in the now empty room.

Goody warned that I was destined to be alone. Maybe it's inevitable, that my hunger for justice will eclipse all my other relationships, leave me isolated, the truth my only mistress. I always thought Enid was right—that I liked being alone, that I preferred it.

Only right now, it doesn't feel good. I put my friends in danger. And for what? What did it even get me?

I squeeze the box, willing a vision to come. To explain what Goody wanted me to see in that place. Make it worth everything I did to get there, and everything that happened when I did.

Nothing comes. The stupid box is just a box. Some keepsake meticulously tended to by a psychopath whose identity still eludes me, even after everything I've sacrificed to discover it.

Suddenly, a hidden drawer pops open at the bottom of the box and something falls out. Papers . . . no, photos. A stack of photos. Not the old-timey ones that would have been taken years ago. These are recent.

And they're all of me.

In my lonely room, the moon hovering outside, I sift through the stack. Here's Tyler, Enid, and me in the car. Enid and me outside Crackstone's crypt. My family by our car in Jericho.

Me, alone on the roof, playing my cello, an expression of peace and serenity on my face.

They've all been taken at a long distance by an impressive telephoto lens, from the looks of it. Which means that whoever has been living in Laurel Gates's room has been watching me. I stand up, staring out the round window with Enid's rainbow transparency still covering half. Almost daring the mystery photographer to capture me again. I'm more convinced than ever in that moment that it's all connected. The monster, that house, the Gates family, Crackstone and the killer . . .

If I had known that at that very moment, someone was

creeping through the halls of Jericho Hospital, I might not have worried about presenting my good side. But I wouldn't find out until morning, when Mayor Walker would be found intentionally unhooked from his life support.

Killed, before he could ever tell his story. Luckily, tracking down a killer is one of my top three favorite recreational hobbies.

CHAPTER TWENTY-FOUR

The funeral takes place the following week. It rains all day. I've always enjoyed graveside services. I've been crashing them since I was old enough to read the obituaries section.

But this one feels too personal to enjoy.

The cemetery is filled with black umbrellas. For once, I don't stand out amid the sea of mourning clothes. A minister spouts empty platitudes about God's strength. I can't imagine it's much of a comfort to Walker's wife or Lucas, who don't even bother to protect themselves from the rain.

What's even more ironic is that the entire police force is here, standing behind the family as if they can keep them safe when they couldn't even keep an unconscious man in a hospital safe.

I barely knew Walker, but I am mourning today. I'm mourning the information that died with him. Whatever he saw in the Gates house that day was a truth he paid for learning with his life. A truth I'm still trying desperately to uncover.

As everyone sniffs and sobs, I'm on alert. I know the killer is here, standing innocently among us, plotting their next move. That's what I'd do, anyway. The only question left is . . . who is it?

The service breaks up soon after. I scan the crowd for anything suspicious beneath the cover of my own umbrella. Tyler nods my way, Xavier averts his eyes as he walks off with the Nightshades. Enid, sharing an umbrella with Ajax, does the same.

When I turn toward the trees, I catch a glimpse of a man in a dark coat, a fedora pulled over his eyes. Who is this mystery man, and what connection did he have to Walker? I dart off after him. The thrill of a lead after the disappointment in the Gates house almost makes up for the fact that no one will speak to me.

Almost.

We play cat and mouse through the trees, him darting behind trunks, moving quickly enough that I can't track him from a distance. I stop in the last place I saw him, spinning around, looking for anything moving.

Behind me, a branch snaps. My instincts take over as I pull a narrow sword from the handle of my parasol. A tenth-birthday gift from my father. Following the source of the sound, I'm able to get the drop on my quarry the moment he steps out into view.

But the last sound I expect to hear with my blade at his throat is a chuckle. An all-too-familiar one at that.

"Still as sharp as ever, my pigtailed protégée."

I'd never admit it to anyone, but an unparalleled elation rises in me as I realize who's in front of me. A feeling that belies the growing loneliness I've been doing my best to ignore.

"Uncle Fester!" I cry, releasing him.

He turns to face me, doffing his hat to reveal his pasty bald head, his deep-set eyes with their perpetual dark circles, his prominent nose, and crooked, slightly feral smile.

"How long have you been stalking me?" I ask delightedly as we fall into step, making our way toward school.

"Just blew into town this morning!" he says, tucking the tail of his scarf into his long coat. "Got hit by a wave of nostalgia."

"I thought you didn't go to Nevermore," I say, puzzled.

He chuckles again. "I didn't. Your dad got all the brains. But I used to drop in on him." Fester smirks evilly from under his hat brim. "Usually from the ceiling with a dagger between my teeth, just to keep him on his toes."

"Naturally." For a moment, I wish Pugsley was capable of such a feat. It would certainly break the monotony of my solo existence now that Enid has left me for greener social pastures.

"Your dad filled me in on what's going on here," he continues, his tone turning more serious now—or as serious as it can be for someone with the cadence of a deranged clown. "Monsters, murder, and mayhem, what fun! I had a job in Boston, but I told him I'd check in on you afterward."

It's only then that I notice the satchel he's carrying. Fester's not the type to pack pajamas and a toothbrush. "What kind of job?" I ask.

He smiles, noting my suspicion. "The kind that means I need

somewhere to lie low for a few days," he admits.

I'm sure he expects a lecture, but for once I'm not going to give him one. It's not because I approve any more of his lifestyle than I did the last time he escaped prison. It's just that I don't mind the idea of a friendly face nearby for the short-term.

"Come with me," I say as we reach the edge of the Nevermore grounds. "I know of a place that's not being used."

Fester follows along cheerfully enough until we reach the Hummers' shed; then he goes on alert—eyes darting, hackles raised just in case.

"Don't worry," I tell him. "It's not currently in use, but it belongs to a friend."

His eyes bug out as he sets his satchel down amid Eugene's beekeeping accoutrement. "You actually made a friend?" he asks. "That poor kid will be going home in a body bag."

It's typical Addams' family repartee, but given the coma Eugene is currently in and my culpability in the matter, it hits a little closer to home than it might otherwise. I can practically hear Enid's words echoing through my mind. *You will use anyone to get what you want, even if it means putting them in danger.*

Fester has already moved on, not noticing my discomfort— which tells me that my mask is still functioning at the very least. He's currently perusing my case wall, which is now outdated. I haven't been able to update it since Eugene was hurt, a secret shame I will take with me to my grave.

"So," he says, scanning the autopsy reports of the first few victims. "What kind of monster are you dealing with?"

Digging into my own bag, which is *not* filled with heisted jewels or whatever is currently inhabiting my uncle's, I pull out

Xavier's sketch of the monster. It's hard not to picture it tearing through the doors of the dumbwaiter, or chasing me and Enid through the basement, but I've been told I have a near sociopathic ability to compartmentalize.

"I haven't been able to identify it," I say, handing over the sketch. "It's frustratingly elusive, and there's someone in town doing quite a cover-up job."

Fester takes the page, and my heart leaps at the look of recognition in his eyes. He whistles, long and low. "This puppy is called a Hyde," he informs me, and just like that I'm back in the game.

"As in Jekyll and Hyde?" I ask, and he nods. "You've seen one before?"

Another nod. "It was 1983," he says with a wistful smile. "My vacation at the Zurich Institute for the Criminally Insane. That's where I got my first lobotomy, you know. They say you never forget your first—even if it does take most of your hippocampus."

"But the Hyde," I remind him, too aware of his penchant for long stories. Most of which could make the listener an accomplice.

"Yes, yes," he says, returning reluctantly to the point. "Olga Malacova. Jeez, she had it all. Beauty, brains, *and* a deep interest in necromancy. Olga was a concert pianist until one night she transformed in the middle of a Chopin sonata. Massacred a dozen audience members—and three music critics."

I recall the basics of Jekyll and Hyde, not having read it since kindergarten. The man who transforms into a monster. I can see the Hyde's tracks now, bestial, then human in the span of a footstep.

"Something has to trigger them to make them transform, right? Could she do it at will or did something have to set her off?"

Fester shrugs, clearly immune to the urgency in my tone. "No idea. I only saw her in group electroshock therapy. The rest was just institute gossip."

Frustrated, I take the sketch back. Another dead end. "There's no mention of a Hyde in any of the books in the Nevermore library, and we're supposed to have the most extensive collection on Outcasts in the world. If we can't find out here, I don't know where we will."

Fester grimaces sympathetically, leaning against the table. "I assume you already tried Nathaniel Faulkner's diary."

Faulkner, I think. Nevermore's founder. If I had seen his diary, I would remember. "What diary?" I ask. "What's in it?"

"Oh yeah, it's real page-turner," Fester says excitedly. "Before Faulkner founded Nevermore, he traveled the world, cataloguing every Outcast community. Vamps, sirens, lycans, witches, yetis before they went extinct. I'm sure he had a section on Hydes."

"How do you know all this?" I ask him. In my family, Uncle Fester is the one you call if you need a safe cracked without a code. A sensitive government document lifted by someone who won't bother to read its confidential contents. He's never been known as a keeper of history.

He laughs, as if to acknowledge it's not in his usual wheelhouse. "It's kind of a funny story," he says. "You think your parents can't keep their hands off each other now—you should have seen them as teenagers. Oy vey. I showed up unannounced one night in Gomez's dorm room and saw—"

"Enough reminiscing!" I wave my hands in panic. "The diary. Where is it?"

Fester holds up his own hands in surrender. "Nightshades library.

I'm sure you've wormed your way in there by now, haven't you? Your dad parked me in there until he'd concluded his ... ahem ... business. Naturally my first instinct was to look for something to fence. I found this safe behind a portrait on the wall. I was hoping for cash or jewels, but the diary was an interesting diversion."

"And it's still there?" I ask him, thinking of the stolen codex. "You put it back?"

Fester rolls his eyes as if he's insulted I have to ask. "I wasn't going to walk around with a *book* if that's what you mean. It's bad for business."

Finally, a potential lead. It's been so long since I made any tangible progress, I'm close to cheering aloud. Not literally, of course. "We'll sneak into the library tonight when everyone's asleep," I tell him. "In the meantime, stay out of sight."

My uncle gives me a small salute, then begins to make himself comfortable in the shed. With Eugene gone, no one will find him in here—even if they are looking, which is likely if he's just finished a job.

"If you're discovered," I say over my shoulder, "I will disown you and collect whatever reward money is tied to your capture."

I swear his eyes mist over as he smiles. "You make me so proud."

The most difficult part of chasing this lead is sitting on it until nightfall. With Enid out of the room and everyone disbursed for Walker's funeral, the campus is quiet.

I work diligently on my novel, which is fast nearing completion with all the real-world inspiration I'm getting here. But I keep getting tangled up in reality, unable to escape into my fictional world as I used to so effortlessly.

At my desk, I take the music box out again, turning the lacquered wood over and over in my hands as if it has another secret to reveal. It seems to mock me with the questions it leaves unanswered. If Laurel Gates died twenty years ago, who was sleeping in her room as of last week? And what is their connection to this Hyde?

Whoever they are, they're obviously willing to kill to keep their secret. And more than that, they have their eye on me. How much longer until they decide I know too much?

I'm not proud of it, but lost as I am in the weeds of this particular train of thought, I jump slightly when the door opens.

"Oh . . . hi," says Enid, shuffling in still wearing her funeral garb. "I figured you were still at Mayor Walker's wake."

"I go to funerals for the dead, not the living," I say. "Once the dirt hits the coffin, I'm out." I try to keep my tone neutral. A few minutes ago I was focused on my novel and unraveling the building case. Now that Enid's here, I wish she would leave again, or forgive me. This limbo takes up too much space in my already overtaxed brain.

"I can't seem to find my bottle of silver moon nail polish," Enid says when the silence has stretched out too long. "Mind if I look around? Yoko is hosting a mani-pedi party for her crew."

"It's still your room," I say, gesturing to her side. The mattress is stripped, but the inordinate number of stuffed animals remains. A presence all its own.

She meanders slowly over to her side as I turn to face her from my side, crossing my arms as I watch her lackluster search commence.

"So . . . ," Enid says. "How's it going?"

If she thinks I'll be the first to break, she's got another think coming. I'm sure only one of us learned the ins and outs of resisting psychological torture before middle school.

"Solitude suits me," I tell her. "Without any annoying

distractions, I've almost finished my novel."

She whips around, nail polish forgotten. "Is that what I was? An annoying distraction?"

I shrug. "No. But you do have some very annoying habits."

Enid steps closer. "Such as?" Her eyes flash. It's a dare, and I know I shouldn't take it. Not if I'm being contrite. But I'm sick of being punished. I've never had a best friend before Enid, and twelve hours after I finally admit it's her, she wants out of my life? It won't be so easy to waltz back in.

"You giggle when you text," I inform her, "which, by the way, is a twenty-four-seven addiction."

Her nostrils flare, a sure sign she's ramping up to furious. "At least I keep my phone on silent, unlike that migraine-inducing typewriter hammering in my head."

I don't hesitate before loading another harsh truth into the chamber. "When you're not grinding your canines, you growl in your sleep. It's impossible to get my four hours."

"Oh, and it's so easy for *me* with your late-night cello solos?"

I don't even notice myself taking another step until we're practically nose to nose across the duct tape line again. "You overcommit to clubs and activities and then complain about it nonstop."

"I'd take that over your obsession with all things creepy and dead!"

"You could choke an entire concert hall with the amount of perfume you spritz," I say. "And those are just off the top of my head."

Enid's face flushes. She looks more angry than hurt this time. "Guess I'm lucky to be with a new roommate who doesn't find ways to literally endanger everyone she comes into contact with."

This is an escalation, and her expression says she knows it. Listing off irritating habits is one thing. Part and parcel to the whole girl-best-friend experience, at least as it's been marketed to me. But this is personal, and it goes beyond our roommate spat.

I can't immediately parry, because I'm too busy hearing it again. From Tyler, from Xavier, from Sheriff Galpin and Kinbott and Weems. Even from Thing. Single-minded, obsessive, selfish, unconcerned with the well-being of others. Never mind that I'm trying to save the whole town from a vicious killer. No one ever seems to remember that part.

Enid flips her hair. Her tone goes haughty and cool. "Yoko and I are so in sync, she's begging me to be her roomie. Permanently."

Another blow. No matter how angry Enid was, I always assumed our estrangement was temporary. Goody warned me I was destined to be alone, but I'm not going to beg Enid to stick around. Even if the thought of spending the rest of the year alone in this room hardly appeals anymore.

"Don't let me hold you back," I manage.

She scoffs. I've said the wrong thing, somehow. The trouble is, I don't even know what the right one would have been.

"Enjoy your solitude, Wednesday," she says.

Enid has almost made it to the door—sans nail polish, I note. "It's not solitude if you're still here!" I shout, just before the door slams behind her again.

CHAPTER TWENTY-FIVE

The entrance hall is empty, as I predicted when I reach the Poe statue. I descend the stairs on alert for anyone following who might be concerned about my non-member status, but I don't encounter anyone.

In the library, all is dark. I click on a lamp, illuminating the geometric floor with the Nightshade bloom and skull spreading across it. Before I can get to work looking for the safe, a silhouette steps out of the shadows.

"Uncle Fester?" I ask.

The figure steps into the light wearing a quizzical expression.

"Who's Uncle Fester?" asks Xavier, eyeing me suspiciously.

It's all I can do not to roll my eyes. "What are you doing down here at this time of night?"

He turns his back on me, slotting a book back onto the shelf in front of us. "Since I'm an actual Nightshade, I don't have to explain myself," he says, turning back to face me. "What's your excuse for creeping around in the middle of the night?"

I drop his gaze. Evasive maneuvering. "Research," I say vaguely.

Xavier isn't fooled. "On the monster?" he asks. "I'll save you some time. I've already scoured every book. There's nothing here matching that thing."

I picture Xavier, haunted by dreams of the monster, coming down here to comb through old journals, books, student records. Looking for anything that would explain what he's seen. I don't doubt he's been thorough, but Hydes are a type of Outcast. If their existence has been scrubbed from even this secret, forbidden knowledge cache, it has to be intentional.

Which means a member, or someone with access to this library, could be involved in the cover-up.

"Convenient," I say to Xavier. I'm hoping if I can end this conversation, he'll leave me alone to wait for Fester, but of course I'm not that lucky.

"You know what your problem is?" Xavier asks, his eyes still on me.

I whirl around to face him. "I can't wait for your piercing insight."

Ignoring my sarcasm, he continues in a tone much like Enid's. Anger, covering hurt. "You don't know who your real friends are," he says. "I've been on your side since day one. Hell, I saved your life! I believed your theories when no one else did. I told you things about me I've never told anyone else. And what do I get in return? Nothing but suspicion and lies."

It's clear he's been building to this speech for a while. But I've been keeping a list of my own—and it's not all the ways Xavier has wronged me.

"You want honesty?" I ask him, doing my best to make my eyes flash like Enid's do when she's angry. "Here it is."

Xavier opens his arms, welcoming it. A mistake, and not his first.

"Every time the monster has attacked, you've been right there."

I can see every instance as I list it, my mind racing ahead to make the connections along with my words.

"First with Rowan, at the Harvest Festival, you were watching Tyler and me when I ran after him into the woods. You saw right where we were headed and minutes later, he was dead."

Xavier's face is impassive as I continue.

"On Outreach Day, you showed up at the ruins of the Meeting House barely minutes after the monster disappeared. And yet you claimed not to have seen it at all."

This was the moment I began to suspect him, I remember. The bestial prints turned human, and Xavier, the only person around.

"Didn't realize proximity was a crime," he says smoothly.

"Then there's your little drawing obsession," I continue, unable to stop now that I've started. "You drew the monster dozens of times without ever having seen it. You even drew where it lived. And then, when Eugene went to investigate, you tried to kill him, so he'd never spill your secret."

This time, Xavier looks offended. It seems I've finally gotten a rise out of him. "You really think I would hurt Eugene?" he asks.

But I'm not finished. "And then, the most recent clue on the list," I say, stepping ever closer. "Your oh-so-convenient appearance minutes after Tyler was attacked by the monster at the Gates house."

Having presented my evidence, I stand accusingly, waiting for him to respond. I don't mention the DNA match, or lack thereof. In my mind it's not even relevant. If I've learned one thing during my tenure at Nevermore, it's that local law enforcement is far from infallible.

To my surprise, Xavier steps closer to me, halving the distance between us. He looms over me, looking down with an inscrutable impression. For a moment I imagine his eyes bulging out into those of the Hyde. His teeth turning to razor-sharp fangs. My blood, splattered across the checkered floor . . .

"If I'm the monster," he says in a low, dangerous voice, "then why haven't I killed you?"

It's the question I've most often asked myself, during my long, sleepless nights. Turning over every clue. Plenty of people have been attacked simply for being in the monster's path. Others have been silenced for knowing too much. I've been guilty of both, and yet I'm still breathing.

But now, standing here in the dim light with Xavier's dark eyes intent on me, I realize something damning. "Because," I begin, a little breathlessly, "for reasons I cannot fathom or indulge, you seem to *like* me."

It's clear that this cuts deeper than any of my other accusations. He scoffs, but a beat too late, not covering his hurt. "What's to like," he says darkly, then sweeps up the stairs without another word.

Alone, Xavier's denouncement would scarcely have bothered

me. But Xavier's words add to the rest. Weems, Galpin, Enid. I hear Goody's voice in my head again, reminding me my path is a lonely one. And it just got a little lonelier.

I shake it off after a moment. If my unproven suspicions are correct, if Xavier *is* the monster, then good riddance, right? I vow to learn whatever I can in this journal of Faulkner's. To give myself the best possible chance of catching him. Stopping his reign of terror . . .

"Wowee," comes a voice from above as Fester drops down to the floor into the pool of lamplight.

"How long have you been lurking?" I ask, irritated and a little embarrassed.

"Long enough to feel the tension between you two," he says, putting his electric fingers together and zapping for effect. "You could have cut it with an executioner's axe."

"Yes, well, if I can prove my suspicions about him, there may be one of those involved in due time," I say. "Where's the safe?"

But rather than answering, Fester turns to where Thing has just appeared on the shelf behind me. His face splits in a delighted smile.

"I'd recognize that patter of fingertips anywhere!" he exclaims. "Hello, Thing!"

But Thing clearly doesn't reciprocate Fester's positive feelings about this reunion. He taps his fingers along the shelf, indicating that he's waiting for something.

Fester's eyes widen in surprise. "Come on, you can't still be mad about the Kalamazoo job. That wasn't my fault!"

Thing lunges for Fester's throat and locks on. I know from experience that the best thing to do is let them resolve it. That intervening will only prolong things. But somewhere in this room is the information I need to prove that Xavier is the killer.

"You said you could crack that safe in thirty seconds!" Fester is saying, his voice strained as he attempts to pry Thing off. "Five minutes later, we were still standing there! You were all thumbs!"

Thing only tightens his grip in response, indicating he saw things differently.

"Enough!" I say, stepping between them. "Let him go, Thing. You can adjudicate this family squabble on your own time. For now, show me where the diary is."

Thing lets go of Fester, whose lips are turning slightly blue. As I walk away, Thing sticks his finger in Fester's ear. He receives a well-deserved zap.

Fester makes his way across the library to a portrait of someone with a long curtain of gray hair. He wears a bow tie, wire-rimmed glasses, and a bowler hat.

"'Ignatius Itt,'" I read aloud. "'Supreme Shade, 1825 to 1850.'"

"Iggy was Faulkner's right hand," Fester informs me. "He trained a generation of Nightshades."

He reaches forward with his pale, pudgy hand and pulls the portrait back on its hinges. Inside, as promised, is an old-fashioned wall safe. Fester turns to Thing with an eyebrow raised.

"Do I have time for a snooze, or can you crack this one quickly?" he asks.

Thing ignores the dig and gets to work. In under a minute, the door is open. Inside, to my surprise and delight, is an old, leatherbound diary. Fearing the arrival of any more Nightshades, I stuff it in my bag and head back up to Ophelia Hall with Fester and Thing in tow.

One positive about no longer having a roommate is that there's no one to explain Fester to. We settle in before the spiderweb window.

"These are some sweet digs," Fester says. "Easy access to the roof for a midnight rendezvous. How'd you swing your own single?"

I glance over to Enid's side of the room, to her nauseating collection of brightly colored stuffed animals. Ignoring the pang in my chest, I say casually: "My roommate couldn't handle my toxic personality."

Fester isn't surprised enough to comment, so I turn my full attention to the diary in my lap. There are vampires, lycans, sirens, and Gorgons here, of course. Some of the lesser-known types of psychics and visionaries. Telekinetics. And then, right there on a middle page. A Hyde.

The drawing looks almost identical to Xavier's drawing when I compare them. The smooth, gray skin. The bulging eyes. The pointed teeth and long, razor-sharp claws.

"Here it is," I say to Fester, who approaches to peer over my shoulder as I scan the entry—which includes notes as well as a few more drawings. "Faulkner says Hydes are artists by nature, but vindictive in temperament."

Artists, I think, picturing Xavier's hideout on the grounds. His drawings of the monster, of the Gates Estate, of me . . .

The next portion, I read aloud: "'Born of mutation, the Hyde lies dormant until unleashed by a traumatic event, or unlocked through chemical inducement or hypnosis.'"

The drawing in this section is a Hyde performing a simpering bow to a humanoid figure, who extends a hand as if controlling it, or appeasing it.

"'The act of unlocking causes the Hyde to develop an immediate bond with its liberator,'" I continue, "'who the creature now sees as its master. It becomes the willing instrument of whatever nefarious agenda this new master might propose.'"

Even Fester, who I know for a fact has eaten human flesh, looks disgusted by the prospect. "Anyone willing to unlock a Hyde is a real sicko," he says, but I'm already two steps ahead of him.

"This means I'm not looking for one killer," I say, more to myself than to my uncle. "I'm looking for two—the monster *and its master.*"

A knock at the door makes my heart jump into my throat. For a moment I picture whoever hit Walker with that car and unplugged his life support, advancing into the room now that I've discovered the secret identity of the monster . . .

But it's only Ms. Thornhill. I stow the journal quickly, unsurprised to see Fester has disappeared into some hiding place in the room.

"Didn't mean to startle you," my dorm mother says with a sheepish smile. "Do you have a minute?"

"Of course," I say calmly, turning to my desk. "I was just working on my novel. It's almost finished."

"Wonderful," Ms. Thornhill says. There's something sad in her expression. I can still feel my pulse racing. "Listen, Wednesday. Enid asked to room with Yoko for the rest of the school year."

This is the last thing I expected. Amid my discoveries tonight, it shouldn't even register. But I find it does. The rest of the year isn't a momentary problem that can be solved. It feels permanent.

"She did?" I ask, trying to disguise my disappointment.

I can tell I'm not fooling Ms. Thornhill, who sits down on the end of my bed and addresses me with the particular brand of adult female pity I most loathe. "Whenever there's a falling-out, I like

273

to get both girls' perspectives. So what happened, Wednesday? I thought you and Enid were thick as thieves!"

Refusing to meet her eyes, I look down at my lap instead. "Thieves ultimately turn on each other," I tell her. "I've seen it with my own eyes."

Ms. Thornhill only leans closer. "Deflect all you want, but we both know you care about Enid. And you have to admit, she's managed to bring out a spark of warmth in you!"

I serve up my most withering glare at the accusation.

"Don't worry," she says with a conspiratorial smile. "It's a tiny spark. Barely perceptible to the average eye. But I noticed."

For a moment, I reflect on whether what Thornhill is saying is true. Certainly, my relationship with Enid has shifted something, but right now it feels as though she's only opened up a part of me that feels sadness rather than relief when I'm left alone. I can hardly thank her for that.

"I'll survive alone," I tell Miss Thornhill. "I always have."

She stands up, disappointment clouding her usually cheery expression. *Welcome to the club,* I want to tell her. "If that's your choice," she says, "then I'll submit the room assignment forms to Principal Weems."

As she heads to the door, I think briefly of stopping her. But what would be the point?

When she's gone, Fester emerges from Enid's pile of stuffed animals before I've had time to lock this new disappointment away in the casket where I keep all my other inconvenient feelings.

"Hey, being a solo lobo has its perks!" he says. "You get to live life by your own rules, do whatever you want. Just look at me!"

It's clear he thinks his own life is a selling point, but being a nomadic, deranged criminal hardly appeals. But I also feel disgust at the idea of living like my parents, joined at the hip and the heart with someone you'll never truly understand. Tying your own happiness and freedom to their whims.

Is there no happy medium? I wonder. No compromise?

But it doesn't matter. Not right now, when any one of us might be the monster's next victim. "Thanks for the advice," I say. "But right now, we have a Hyde to catch."

The first step of the plan is simple: placing a tracker. I make my way to Xavier's art studio the very next morning. I wait on the side of the shed for him, and I hear him approaching while talking to someone on the phone. He sounds distressed.

"I need to see you," he says urgently, then: "No, it can't wait!" A longer pause, then he speaks again, a little more calmly. "Yeah, I know where that is. See you there in twenty."

The moment he hangs up, I make my appearance. "Who were you talking to?" I ask before he can react.

On his face is an expression I haven't seen before. He's agitated, but there's also none of the affection he usually greets me with. It's as if some switch has flipped from liking to loathing in the span of one conversation.

"None of your goddamn business, how about that?" he says, pushing past me.

"I know what you are, Xavier," I say, almost willing him to get angrier. To lose control.

He turns at the door, his hair wild, his eyes too wide. "Seriously, Wednesday, stay the hell away from me." And he slams the door in my face.

No matter. Our conversation gave my accomplices plenty of

time to place a tracking device on his bike. Now I'll be able to place him at the scene of the next attack definitively. The truth is finally within my grasp.

I rendezvous with Fester and Thing behind the shed and we watch together as Xavier climbs onto his bike and pedals off down the path.

"You placed the tracker?" I ask, and Fester looks offended that I even had to ask.

I pull the tracking device out of my backpack. It's active. I can see the red dot that indicates Xavier moving away.

"Okay," I say, satisfied. "Let's hit the road. You *do* have some sort of vehicle, don't you?"

He smiles. "Don't worry, Uncle Fester's got you covered."

My uncle's so-called vehicle is a vintage motorcycle with a sidecar. It wouldn't be so bad if it wasn't painted white with Dalmatian spots. Or if it didn't say PENNY'S POOCH PATROL! DOOR-TO-DOOR DOG WALKING!

I give him my best withering glare as he hands me a helmet with dog ears.

"What?" he asks. "I picked it up on my way out of town. You know me, I like to travel incognito."

The red dot representing Xavier's bicycle is getting farther away by the second. There's no time to argue. For that reason *only*, I put the helmet on and climb into the sidecar.

"Let's roll!" Uncle Fester cries, kicking the engine to life and following my directions through the quiet streets of Jericho.

We track Xavier to a lakeside park a little ways outside of town. It's a cloudy day, the water is windswept, the trees standing sentinel around it. In the distance, a raven caws mournfully.

There's no doubt this is a strange place for a student to be meeting with . . . who?

In the trees, I watch through my spyglass as Xavier approaches a Prius, the lone car in the lake's day-use parking lot, and opens the passenger door. I'm almost too far away to see the identity of the driver, who from this distance looks like a vaguely blond blob.

"Come on," I whisper, twiddling the focus until at last, the lines become crisp.

I nearly drop my spyglass when I recognize the driver.

It's Dr. Kinbott. And she looks worried.

CHAPTER TWENTY-SIX

Back at Nevermore, I make my way to Weems's office on a mission. At the very least, I know Dr. Kinbott is having unsanctioned meetings with students in her car by the lake, that should, at the very least, be enough to get Weems to look into things.

There's no doubt in my mind that once the first thread is pulled, the whole thing will unravel like a cheap sweater.

"Principal Weems," I call, pushing open her office door. "It is imperative that I speak to you about Dr. Kinb—" I stop short when I see who Weems is entertaining.

"Wednesday!" Weems says. "We were just talking about you."

I shouldn't be surprised when Kinbott turns around from the chair facing Weems to smile at me. "Speak of the devil," she says sweetly.

"And she appears," I reply, narrowing my eyes.

Kinbott leans forward to pour tea from a china pot into Weems's cup. Weems, however, is looking right at me.

"It's good you're here," she says, possibly for the first time ever. "Dr. Kinbott was just discussing your assessment. I need to sign off on it before she hands it into the court."

I find it so ironic that this psychopath is allowed to evaluate anyone. Let alone someone she's actively stalking. "What's the verdict, Doctor? Am I cured?" I ask, my voice oozing with sarcasm. With any luck, I'll have her license before our next session is scheduled.

She narrows her eyes at me. "I'm glad you find it amusing, Wednesday," she says. "Because I can assure you the judge assigned to your case won't."

Weems puts on her *protecting the students of the school* voice as she offers Kinbott a refill on her tea. "And *I* was just explaining that you've recently been taking small, but meaningful steps to embrace your new Nevermore family," she says pointedly, her eyebrows disappearing into her hair.

She's clearly encouraging me to go along with this lie, even though we both know that the closest thing I've ever had to a friend requested a room reassignment just yesterday.

"I'm more at the half-hug stage, not a full embrace," I say, and then inspiration strikes. If I have to participate in this farce of a conversation, at least I can get something out of it too. "But I'm working on it. Speaking of which, I've been reading about *hypnotherapy*. Thought that might be a technique to unlock my inner Wednesday. Are you a devotee?"

Watching her carefully, I see the moment when her face lights up. "Very much so," she enthuses, confirming my worst fear. "I applaud your new willingness to delve deep into yourself. I have you on my schedule for Monday. We can start then."

Not if I can help it, I think, but I give her my fakest smile instead. "Can't wait."

With a self-satisfied little clap, Weems gestures to a chair. "Now, Wednesday, what did you so urgently need to discuss with me?"

For a long moment, I don't look away from Kinbott. I want to know if she knows I know. I want to know if she's scared. But she looks as placid as ever, with that vague smile on her face I've come to loathe so much.

"It can wait," I tell Weems. "Now, if you'll excuse me, I have some homework to do."

Of course, I'm not planning on wasting time on something as pedestrian as homework with a killer and her monster on the loose. Fester accompanies me to the Weathervane, sitting in the booth opposite as I attempt to process the implications of what I've seen today. It means nothing to my uncle, who is drinking ketchup from a bottle without a care in the world—besides the probable bounty on his head.

After checking to make sure no one from Nevermore is here, I open Faulkner's diary and focus in once again on the Hyde page.

"Kinbott has to be Xavier's master," I mutter under my breath. "She must have figured out he's a Hyde and used hypnotherapy to unlock him. That would explain his phone call and their secret sessions. . . ."

The only answer is the squirting of the ketchup bottle. But then Fester's eyes go wide.

"I think the kid behind the counter has clocked me," he whispers. "Yep, he's walking over. I'm gonna put him in a Romanian sleeper hold. Cover me."

I follow his eyeline to where Tyler is approaching our table. "Relax," I tell Fester, suppressing an eye roll. "He's not interested in you."

As if to prove my point, Tyler arrives at our table with a single coffee cup and smiles at me. "Made you a quad," he says. "On the house."

Fester lunges for it. "Thanks, kid!" he says, slurping at my drink with a happy smile on his face. Next, he hands off the now-empty ketchup bottle. "Gonna need a refill on this puppy too."

Tyler looks supremely confused until I take pity and interject. "Tyler, this is my uncle Fester."

Fester offers his hand with a mischievous expression Tyler clearly can't read. He takes it, only to withdraw a second later from Fester's signature electric shock. My uncle laughs. Tyler, more confused than ever, puts some distance between them, only to catch sight of the diary on the table in front of me.

His eyes go wide. "Is that . . . ?" he asks.

I nod. "I found out it's called a Hyde."

Without waiting for an invitation, Tyler slides into the booth next to me.

Stiffening, I look around for other Galpin. "Your father gave us explicit instructions to stay away from each other," I tell him, somewhat regretfully. It's been a while since anyone my age spoke to me with anything other than disdain or fury.

Tyler shrugs. "My dad's not here and I'm on a break as of now," he says. "What else did you find out?"

Part of me wants to let him in, but the other part is remembering all the condemnation I've received lately for putting people in danger. The more Tyler knows, the more danger he's in—especially if Xavier, who has never been Tyler's biggest fan, is the monster.

"Hey," Tyler says, correctly interpreting my hesitation. "C'mon. It almost gutted me, remember? I'm in this whether I like it or not."

It's true, and as justifications go, it's good enough for now. "Okay," I say, pointing to the drawing of the Hyde bowing to its master. "Apparently a Hyde has to be unlocked by someone."

Tyler leans in closer, his arm bumping against mine. "Whoa," he says, looking at the picture. For once, his expression is inscrutable. It makes him look different. Less soft.

Before I can explain further, the elder Galpin strides by the window on his way to the door. Fester gets up immediately—he's allergic to law enforcement—and disappears into the back somewhere.

I expect Tyler to make a break for it, but it's too late. The sheriff opens the front door and eyes the proximity between the two of us just as Tyler stands up to meet him.

"For the record," he says hastily. "Wednesday wanted to keep her distance. I was the one who sat down with her."

Galpin is holding a stack of flyers. He shakes off his son's justification like it's a bothersome fly. "I've got bigger problems today." He hands one of the flyers to Tyler, avoiding my gaze entirely. "We're putting these up around town. Bank robbery suspect. A real creep by all accounts. You haven't seen him, have you?"

Even from a blurry upside-down security camera, it's still impossible not to recognize Fester's signature fedora angled over his brilliantly white face.

Now Galpin looks at me. I shake my head. Addams family

code is never to give up your own unless they're stupid enough to get themselves caught. But I imagine I've seen the last of Fester in Jericho—Tyler has no reason to protect him, and there's no way he doesn't know the man guzzling the Weathervane's ketchup and his dad's bank robber are one in the same.

But he shakes his head too. "He'd be pretty hard to miss," he says. "I'll put this on the notice board, though."

Galpin nods, then turns to exit the café without another word.

I turn to Tyler, surprised. "Thank you," I say. "You didn't have to do that."

He waves a hand, as if it's nothing. "Your family's very . . . colorful," he says with a chuckle.

"Ironic," I say. "Fester's always been the black sheep." I put the diary back into my bag, grateful Galpin had other things on his mind besides examining my belongings or my proximity to his son today. Turning for the door, I plan to reconnect with Fester at the Hummer's shed, but Tyler stops me.

"So," he says. "About rescheduling our date . . ."

I'm surprised again. Enid was so furious about me tricking her after my birthday that she permanently relocated. And Tyler just wants to try again?

"Between the Hyde and my uncle . . . ," I begin, trying to give us both an out.

But Tyler doesn't back down. That strange look is still in his eyes, something like determination. "No excuses," he says. "After what happened last time, I figure you owe me."

Normally I would heartily object to the idea that a person could ever *owe* another person a date, but I'm too caught up in the contrast. After the Gates house, everyone in my life took a distinct step away. Tyler, for some unknown reason, is trying to step closer.

I've discounted him before, just a silly townie who doesn't know who he's attaching his affections to. But doesn't he know me now? Hasn't he seen me at my worst? And isn't it vaguely human of me to want there to be one person in the world who doesn't detest me on principle?

"I can't get off campus," I say, giving him one last off-ramp. "All eyes are on me now."

He smiles. The smile of someone with a plan. As smiles go, the scheming ones are my favorite kind. "You won't have to," he says. "I'll come to you. Crackstone Crypt. Nine o'clock."

Later, I'll blame the isolation. The disappointment of Enid's departure. The fact that I've been sent to live in a pressure cooker of adolescent urges. In the moment I simply say yes.

At least one good thing has come of Enid deserting me—the only person here to watch me getting ready to meet Tyler is Thing. And he has enough opinions.

It starts when I discover her silver moon nail polish on the floor near her desk. As I retrieve it, Thing begins to sign.

"No, I don't miss her," I say curtly. "Friends are a liability. Liabilities can be exploited, which makes them a weakness."

He starts back up again as I place Enid's nail polish on the little table by the door—in plain sight, in case she returns for it while I'm out.

"It's not a *date*," I snap back at Thing. "He's relentless. I'm doing penance for almost getting him disemboweled."

Thing doesn't buy it. I leave in a huff as he winds his index and middle fingers around each other in a crude pantomime. I'd call the whole thing off if it wouldn't let him know he got to me.

Tyler is waiting for me outside Crackstone's crypt as promised. He smiles at me as I approach, and I'm struck again by how *not* awful it feels to have someone glad to see me.

"Last time someone lured me here for a surprise, it didn't end well," I say by way of greeting.

He doesn't seem intimidated. In fact, he rarely does lately. When I first met him, he was all blundering and stuttering and self-conscious, but lately it's like he's discovered some hidden wellspring of confidence.

I guess having your flesh shredded has that effect on some of us. I just never thought Tyler would be the type.

Ahead of me, he opens the crypt door and motions for me to enter first. "Close your eyes," he says.

I hesitate. It doesn't seem like a great idea, especially since I know there's a killer on the loose. What evidence do I have that Xavier didn't follow me here? Or Kinbott?

"Please," Tyler says when I don't comply. It doesn't sound like a question.

I close my eyes.

He leads me inside, telling me when to step, one arm on mine and one on the small of my back, guiding me. It reminds me of the night we danced at the Rave'N. I was extremely uncomfortable then too.

"Okay," he says. "You can open them now."

When I do, the crypt is transformed. I can't honestly say the twinkle lights are an improvement over the original moss and mold and Latin inscriptions, but he certainly went to some effort.

The whole place is bathed in a golden glow. In front of us, there's a black-and-white blanket on the ground, surrounded by candles. Anywhere but a crypt it would be unbearable. Here it's . . . tolerable. At best.

"What?" Tyler asks, bemused. "No one's ever taken you on a picnic inside a crypt before?" I don't have time to answer before he reaches up behind him and pulls down a white sheet, then gestures for me to sit on the blanket.

I do. I've come this far. And as strange and awkward as this whole thing is, I can't deny it's a semi-welcome distraction from sitting in my room alone, waiting to be murdered.

"How do you feel about scary movies?" Tyler asks, firing up a projector that's sitting on top of Crackstone's tomb. The screen flares to life.

I smirk at Tyler. My favorite films list would send him scurrying home to his daddy in tears. But before I can tell him Japanese filmmakers make American horror films look like child's play, the opening credits of the movie he's selected begin.

In that moment, I know I was wrong. The true meaning of horror wasn't invented until someone turned on a camera and started making *Legally Blonde*.

Tyler laughs as I cover my eyes. Sorority sisters, heart-shaped sunglasses, a little dog in a purse. Soul-chilling in the worst possible way. Enid would love it.

To my immense surprise, I make it to the end of the movie without bolting or losing the popcorn-and-candy contents of my stomach. Tyler maintains a respectful distance, and somehow so do the details of the case.

But as we pack up the picnic, I can sense a change in atmosphere approaching.

Sure enough, as soon as he shoulders the backpack, he turns to face me. "I have to say something," he says. "And don't hate me, okay? But . . . I want us to be more than friends."

It makes no sense, but I can tell from his expression that he's sincere. And more than that, he's expecting a positive response. This part is the most unbelievable, especially considering how crystal clear I've been on the subject.

"You'll snap out of it," I tell him.

His eyes flash then, a little of that anger that so intrigued me at the Rave'N. The internal war. It seems I've triggered something with these words, but what? "Don't do that," he says impatiently. "Don't discount my feelings."

I don't, for the record. I just know he's feeling these things for a fantasy version of me who will never exist. One who cares more about having a boyfriend than staking out a cave in the woods. It's partially my fault. I've compromised more than once when it comes to Tyler. He's started to believe I'm like him. Like the girls at school. But I'm not.

Taking a deep breath, I force myself to look him directly in the eye. "Look, I'm not even friend material, let alone more-than-friend material. I will ignore you, stomp on your heart, and always put my needs and interests first. You've already seen it firsthand. What makes you think this will change anything?"

Tyler shakes his head, smiling as if the devastating truth I'm telling him is just another inconsequential quirk of mine. "You can keep trying to push me away," he says in a low voice. "But it's not going to work."

"I already almost got you killed."

"Well, I survived," Tyler says, moving closer to me, even though he's already well within my personal space bubble.

But in this moment, I don't mind. There's something about the way Tyler looks at me that makes me feel like a shaken soda can, overflowing and expansive and out of control. The same way I feel when I'm on the tail of a vitally important suspect—which is the best compliment I can give.

"This is a mistake," I tell him, but I don't move away. It seems only fair to give him one more chance to change his mind.

"Probably," Tyler says with a smile, closing the now negligible distance between us a millimeter at a time.

"Definitely," I counter. Not stopping him. The bubbles continue to fizz, to threaten the limits of their container.

But before we can cross that final distance, the door to the crypt slams open and we're being blinded by a flashlight beam so bright it could only belong to one person in town.

"What the hell, Tyler?" the sheriff shouts.

"Dad?" Tyler replies, shielding his eyes with his arm. "What are you doing out here?"

Sheriff Galpin looks both embarrassed and exasperated. "The Nevermore groundskeeper found a motorbike by the lake. Matches the description of one the bank robber stole. There was a canoe missing, so I thought he could be holed up on Raven Island."

I take a step back from Tyler.

The sheriff points his flashlight between the two of us. "I'm not even gonna ask what this is, but I never saw you two here, and I'm never gonna see you here again. Got it?"

Tyler nods.

"Addams, with me," he says. "I'll take you back to school. *Again.* Tyler, back to the house and stay there. Understood?"

Another nod, and my first date with Tyler Galpin is unceremoniously over.

CHAPTER TWENTY-SEVEN

I manage to convince the sheriff to not accompany me inside, and the moment he's out of sight I double back to climb through my window. The last thing I need tonight is Weems knowing I made another extracurricular nighttime outing.

But before I even enter the room, I know something's amiss. The window is open, for one, standing ajar to the chilly night air. If it were Enid, the lights would be on, but they're not. I step inside hesitantly, my head on a swivel.

The sight that greets me is pure catastrophe. The room has been ransacked, and thoroughly from the looks of it. The pages of my novel are strewn all across the floor. My records. The taxidermy kit my parents got me for my birthday. Everything.

I've barely catalogued half the damage when I realize something even more horrifying than the loss of my novel.

"Thing?" I call out. "Where are you?"

No answer. I make my way to the light switch by the door, bathing the mess in a light that throws the chaos into sharper relief. I know whoever was here was looking for Faulkner's journal. And from my preliminary scan, they found it.

But none of that matters when my eyes land at last on Thing—pinned to one of the room's columns by a dagger.

"*Thing*!" I shout, running to him. He's been fully impaled, and he's deathly still. Fighting back the panic clawing up my throat, I free him as quickly as I can. Blood is pooled beneath him. How long has he been like this?

Even freed from his pinning, he's limp and lifeless. I don't know what to do for him. I don't even fully understand his anatomy or what keeps him animated. Suddenly the words I've always been told—*It's one of the great Addams family mysteries*—seem horribly inadequate.

Then I remember: the Addams family. Fester. With any luck he's in the Hummers' shed right now. He'll know what to do. It can't be too late. It just can't.

"Help!" I shout as I plow through the door of the shed with Thing wrapped in a towel. It's already soaked through with blood.

Fester has been eating one of Eugene's prized honey jars with his filthy hands, but the moment he sees me, he's on his feet.

"What happened?" he asks as I unwrap the towel.

"He's not moving," I say through gritted teeth. The rest is self-explanatory enough. Fester's eyes widen at the sight of the stab wound.

"Lay him flat on the table," he says in a businesslike tone that comforts me. I do as I'm told, and Fester rubs his palms together. Electricity crackles between them, a faint blue glow in the low light of the shed.

He motions for me to stand back, then puts two fingers on Thing's palm and jolts him.

I flinch as though I'm the one being shocked. But Thing, aside from reflexively jerking upward and falling back, doesn't move.

Fester shocks him twice more, each time with the same result. Then he stands back, his usually jackal-like expression mournful and drooping.

"Try again," I demand.

The mournful eyes fill with pity, which only angers me more. I feel tears welling in my eyes, threatening to break the pact I made with myself at my scorpion's snowy graveside ten years ago.

"He's gone, Wednesday," Fester says, and the tears spill over at last.

"No. He's. Not." I throw myself down on my knees, eye level with Thing, who's pale and limp on the table. "Thing, if you can hear me," I say urgently. "I want you to know that if you die, I *will kill you.*"

I stand up, giving Fester my most no-nonsense glare.

"Do it now! Please . . ."

It's not lost on me that Fester doesn't believe this will work. That he goes through the motions only for the love of his favorite niece. But it doesn't matter why he's doing it, only that he does.

He jolts Thing again, the most powerful shock yet. Thing jerks up, falls back. Lifeless. Gone.

But then, after the longest minute I've ever lived, his little pinky finger twitches, and slowly, slowly he wiggles the rest of his digits.

Relief surges through me like I've never experienced. I feel like I'm the one being subjected to Fester's voltage.

When he waves feebly, I wipe away my tears, swearing that no one will ever know I cried. Fester kneels down and greets him joyfully, and by the time he steps aside, I'm composed again.

"Who did this to you?" I ask him.

He signs gingerly, the wound obviously still causing pain.

I scoff in disgust when he's finished. "Knife from behind the back. Cowards." I'm down on my knees, looking right at him. "When I find them, I swear they will suffer. And it will be long, slow, and excruciatingly painful."

After a beat, he extends just his pinky toward me. I lock mine with it and squeeze, burning the promise on my heart like a brand, before standing up to face Fester.

"I'll stitch him up," I say. "They found your motorbike—you need to go. Next time, maybe steal something a little less conspicuous."

Fester smiles, but there's a tinge of sadness to it. "Where's the fun in that?" he asks. "I'll lie low here tonight, keep an eye on the patient and skedaddle in the morning."

I nod. "Well, I'll see you at your arraignment or the next family reunion. Whichever comes first."

Shaking his head, he chuckles. "You'll always be my favorite, Wednesday."

There's no more room in me for sentiment tonight. "Make sure to tell Pugsley next time you see him," I say. "It'll give him a complex."

Once Thing is stitched and resting, it's time to cope with the rest of the fallout from the break-in. Ms. Thornhill surveys the damage and insists on taking me directly to Weems's office for the second time today.

After she's been apprised of the situation, she paces, deep in thought. "I'm guessing this wasn't some random prank?" she asks at last, sounding almost hopeful.

I shake my head. "Whoever ransacked my room stole Nathaniel Faulkner's diary," I tell her. Thornhill looks confusedly back and forth between the two of us as Weems straightens up in fury.

"That diary is supposed to be safely locked in the Nightshades library!"

And abruptly, she's not the only one who's furious. "So you know about the diary. Which means you also know the monster we're after is a Hyde."

Thornhill looks truly confused now, and Weems seems to notice, because she turns with a completely different expression than the one she was just directing at me. "Thank you, Marilyn," she says. "I can take it from here."

"Oh!" says Ms. Thornhill, clearly taken aback. "Of course. If you need me, I'll be right down the hall." The firelight flickers on those shiny boots of hers as she exits. I'm seriously starting to wonder whether she owns another pair.

Weems's smile disappears before the door shuts behind her. Instead of rounding on me, she wanders to the Medusa fireplace, leaning on it, staring into the flames. "Faulkner spent years studying Hydes," she tells me. "He wanted to determine if they were just mindless killers, or if they were conscious of their actions."

"And his conclusion?" I ask in a neutral tone. I don't care if she's angry at me, so long as she tells me what she knows.

"He was killed by a Hyde before he could reach one," she replies. "Others tried to carry on his research, but the Hydes were too unpredictable. Too violent. Lives were lost, the whole experiment was chaos. They were officially banned from Nevermore thirty years ago."

I step closer, feeling the heat of the fire on my face. "All this time . . . you knew it was a Hyde. Why didn't you tell anyone? The sheriff?"

Weems turns toward me. "Because if I do that, Nevermore is finished. Over. Shut for good. The normies won't care that Hydes don't attend Nevermore anymore. All they'll care about is the fact that an Outcast is responsible for a killing spree. And I'm not letting that happen on my watch."

So it's back to appearances, I think, bitterly disappointed. It's one thing for Weems to cover up the atrocities of the past, but to ignore the murders of the present seems nearly as monstrous as committing them.

"But I'm not the only one withholding," she says. "If you suspect someone, you need to tell me."

I scoff, turning away from her gaze, more blistering than the flames. "Why would I do that? All you've ever done is gaslight and obstruct me. You don't care how many people die as long as you get to protect your reputation."

The moment she closes herself off to me, it shows on her face. Like a door slamming shut. I should know, I've seen plenty of those lately. "I am protecting our Nevermore family, which also includes you, Miss Addams. For the time being, anyway."

The next day, I attend classes in a haze. Fester is officially gone, which means I'm on my own again. Sheriff Galpin and Weems won't take me seriously, Enid is gone, Xavier the Hyde is probably being controlled by Kinbott, but I have no proof. No allies. No nothing.

It's surprising, therefore, when Bianca Barclay approaches me between classes on the quad. "Come with me," she says. "I have information on something Mayor Walker was looking into before his murder."

"Why would you tell me?" I ask suspiciously.

Bianca rolls her eyes. "Look, don't make a big thing of it? But I've been sort of . . . hanging out . . . with Lucas Walker. He was telling me some stuff about his dad; he doesn't trust the sheriff with it and I know you're fully obsessed with this kind of thing. Thought you might be able to help him figure out what to do with it. But if you'd rather I tell someone else—"

"Show me," I say before she can change her mind.

She leads me to the Nightshades library, where Lucas Walker of all people is waiting for me.

"I come in peace," Lucas says when he sees me, raising his hands. In one of them is a stack of papers.

"I knew it wasn't an accident," he says with a slight nod in the direction of the papers. "So I started looking through the files on his computer to figure out what would have made someone want to kill him."

He hands over the papers, looking relieved.

"This is some stuff from his computer. Someone he was trying to track down right before he died. Laurel Gates. Ring a bell?"

My heart is already pounding as I leaf through them. "She's supposed to be dead," I say.

"That's just it," Lucas says, stepping over to point at the page I'm reading. "According to the British police report, she's *presumed* drowned, but her body was never recovered."

I can see it in my mind's eye. Laurel's room, pristine, roses on the bedside table. There are property records along with her death certificate and the police report. "Strange," I say. "Apparently the Gates mansion was bought last year by a ninety-year-old candy heiress who then died mysteriously, leaving everything to her caregiver—Teresa L. Glau."

Bianca and Lucas are both staring at me blankly.

"It's an anagram for Laurel Gates," I explain. "Keep up."

A look of recognition hits Bianca's features first. "So Laurel secretly buys her old house, then comes back to Jericho as someone else? But why?"

For a moment I pause, impressed by her ability to parse the situation so quickly with no prior knowledge. Then I remember what's at stake.

"Revenge," I say. "On all the people she blames for her family's misfortune." I think of the victims, it all makes sense. Right down to Weems's speech about the Hyde's discovery being the end of the school. "Lucas's dad, the coroner, my parents," I say. "But most of all . . . Nevermore."

Lucas looks totally out of his depth, but Bianca is sharp. Her eyes find mine. "This all has something to do with the monster, doesn't it?" she asks. "How does it fit in?"

"The monster is called a Hyde," I tell her, putting the pieces together as we speak. "And I think it's been doing Laurel's bidding."

"You know who Laurel is, don't you?" Lucas asks.

For the first time in longer than I can remember, I know *exactly* what to do next.

Dr. Kinbott's door is closed when I arrive. I open it noisily. My heart is beating so hard I can feel it in my scalp. Today is finally the day this ends.

She's on her phone when I enter; her expression changes quickly from concern to alarm. "Wednesday? We don't have an appointment scheduled today."

I feel like every cell in my body is vibrating in anticipation of this moment. "I wanted to return something," I say, stepping forward to cross the distance between us. "I found it in your old bedroom."

My hands are steady as I reach into my bag to pull out the music box. LG lacquered into the top. I hand it to her and she takes it with a quizzical expression on her face.

"I know you're Laurel Gates," I tell her. There's no turning back now. "Mayor Walker figured it out too. He was on his way to tell the sheriff. That's why you killed him."

Kinbott's mouth drops open. She's a hell of an actor, I'll give her that. "You're not actually here to accuse me of *murdering the mayor*?"

I stay laser focused on her face, watching for any twitch of her expression that might give her away. "Who better to slip in and out of a hospital undetected than a psychiatrist under the guise of visiting another patient? The roses you brought Eugene were your mistake. They were the same variety I discovered in your old childhood bedroom."

Her expression of disbelief doesn't crack. No visible ticks or tells. But of course, she's been lying a long, long time.

"Wednesday," she says slowly, as though I'm a deranged patient and not a warrior of justice. "I honestly have no idea what you're talking about, but if you're experiencing paranoia as a result of the disturbing events lately, we can talk about that."

I scoff. "Please. There's only one reason an overqualified psychiatrist like you would settle in this inconsequential backwater, and that's Nevermore. Here you got to crawl through troubled young Outcast minds until you found a Hyde you could manipulate to extract your revenge."

She still seems torn between pity and disbelief. Her phone buzzes and she glances down. "If you won't let me help you with these delusions, then I'll have to go. There's another patient in crisis who *does* want my help."

"Xavier?" I ask, stepping to block her when she attempts to move toward the door.

Her eyes widen in surprise.

"I know all about your secret sessions in your car. I also saw the cave in the woods where you conducted your other 'sessions' to unlock his Hyde."

For the first time, Kinbott appears angry. *Good,* I think. Angry people are sloppy. "You are out of line, young lady," she says through gritted teeth.

"Did you know that a Hyde is dangerously unpredictable?" I ask conversationally. "Or is your plan to have Xavier committed before he can turn on you?"

She shakes her head, face sagging in an incredible imitation of genuine horror. "Wednesday, you are scaring me right now. You need help. More help than I can give you."

Pulling out her phone and dialing, she backs slowly away from me.

"Calling your little beast to finish me off at last?" I ask. "I bet you've both just been waiting for this moment."

"No, Wednesday," Kinbott snaps. "I'm calling Judge Reynolds to recommend that you're committed to a psychiatric facility for observation."

It's so funny I almost laugh out loud. She'll be hard-pressed to find an institution within a hundred miles that an Addams hasn't ruled with an iron fist.

"Please," I say. "We both know I'd be running a place like that in a week. Time's up, Laurel." And I walk out without another word.

My next stop is even more important than that one, because as much as Kinbott likes to pretend to have my well-being and safety in mind, we both know she's going to sic Xavier on me the first chance she gets. And if Faulkner's diary is correct, no amount of affection he's ever had for me will stop him from obeying a direct order.

But I don't make it halfway back to Nevermore before I'm intercepted by Weems in her shiny silver SUV. From the look on her face, I know something is horribly wrong.

"Get in," she says tersely. "We're going to the hospital. Dr. Kinbott was attacked."

I sit with Weems outside the emergency room. As we wait for news on Dr. Kinbott's condition, she tells me about Kinbott's call to her after I left. The one where she told Weems I'm irrational. She asks more than once what our conversation was about, but it seems Kinbott was attacked before she could explain the reason I was there.

Another curious wrinkle in the narrative I've been crafting. Hydes are known to turn on their masters eventually, but was it a coincidence that Xavier attacked her before she could implicate me?

We wait at the hospital for over an hour, but when Sheriff Galpin appears, he only shakes his head. Kinbott is dead. Which means that Xavier is now a monster without a master, and more dangerous than ever.

It's time to stop him once and for all.

CHAPTER TWENTY-EIGHT

I wait in Xavier's shed for nearly an hour before he arrives. By then it's all in place, and I know everything I need to know.

When I hear him coming, I kill the light. Sit at his workbench. Usually he's the one appearing in places he shouldn't be, but tonight I plan to beat him at his own game in more ways than one.

The door opens. The light clicks on. Xavier jumps, startled when he sees me. "Seriously, Wednesday, you need to stay out of my space!" he shouts.

"You should stay out of mine," I say, holding up the dagger that nearly killed Thing. Stabbing it into the tabletop right in front of him. "You left this in my room."

"I don't know what you're talking about," he says, but he's not as good at hiding his emotions as his master was. His eyes dart all over the place. He's defensive right away.

"Why didn't you tell me you were seeing Kinbott?" I ask, not bothering to address the obvious lie.

Xavier's eyes widen. "Have you been spying on me?"

I shrug.

"What am I saying? Of course you've been spying on me. I'm the villain in your little story now." He begins pacing around the room. Gesturing wildly as he speaks. More tells. He's giving himself away completely. "The dreams have been getting to me, and my father sees my mental health as a PR problem he needs to manage. He wanted to keep his *troubled son* out of the tabloids. Okay?"

A suspiciously rehearsed backstory. And if he was really the offended innocent he pretends to be, why would he bother to give his wrongful accuser a detailed alibi? His guilt makes him talkative. I can use that.

"I wasn't in your room," he says when I don't respond to his desperate storytelling. "Believe me, don't believe me. I don't care."

But every line of his agitated form, his panicked expression, says he does care. And he should. There's no one calling the shots anymore. No one to direct his monstrousness.

In the corner of the studio where there was once a painting of me and my cello, another large canvas sits beneath a tarp. I point to it, trusting that I still have his attention.

"Your technique has improved," I tell him. "I particularly enjoyed this new piece."

Before he can stop me, I cross the room to unveil it. It's a portrait of Kinbott. Her long blond hair. Her delicate features. The silver moon necklace she always wears. In Xavier's rendition, she's bathed in red light and harsh shadows. Five claw marks rip across her face.

Faced with proof of his monstrous deeds, Xavier sags. "What do you want?"

"Answers," I tell him, returning to his worktable. The tackle box of art supplies I rifled through while I waited for him. I pick up the orange inhaler right on top. "Let's start with how Rowan's inhaler wound up in your shed."

Xavier's brows knit in confusion. Maybe Kinbott taught him more tricks than I thought, but it won't stop me. I pull out the next item, and the next.

"Or how about Eugene's glasses? The stalker images you took of me?"

"I don't understand," Xavier says under his breath. His eyes are dilated, all pupil as he looks down in horror on the trophies in a neat line on his table.

"Or your latest addition." I reach in for the final item. The coup de grâce. Kinbott's prized half-moon pendant, flecked with blood. "How about Kinbott's necklace?"

Now Xavier is indignant. He stands up. "Somebody planted all this stuff!" he shouts. "Was it you?"

He takes one step toward me before the shed doors burst open. Sheriff Galpin enters, flanked by two of his deputies. His gun is pointed right at Xavier, who puts his hands up, his face slack with horror.

"Cuff him," the sheriff says. Xavier doesn't resist, just continues to look as though he's fallen into one of his own nightmares. I wonder for a moment why he doesn't transform. Free himself. Especially now that he has no orders to the contrary.

But who can decipher the mind of a monster?

"Xavier Thorpe," Galpin says, advancing on him. "You're under arrest for the murder of Dr. Valerie Kinbott."

"Murder?" Xavier says, his voice shooting up an octave. "No! I'm being set up!"

The officer who put the handcuffs on Xavier hauls him toward the door. Normally I would never involve law enforcement in one of my investigations. They're notoriously sloppy and prejudiced. Plus, I believe in the old adage: *Snitches get stitches.*

But in this case, Xavier's killing spree had to be stopped. Weems wouldn't help me. I'm disconnected from my usual network back home. For the time being, a Jericho jail cell is the safest place Xavier can be.

We all have to make compromises from time to time.

The flashing of the squad car lights fill Xavier's studio, bathing the depiction of Kinbott's slashed face in eerie blue and red. I stand with my arms crossed, watching as they escort him roughly to the car.

"You framed me," he says, his face twisted with loathing. "I should have just let Rowan kill you."

"You have the right to remain silent," Sheriff Galpin says. "You have the right to . . ."

His voice trails off as they exit the shed, leaving me alone with the relics of Xavier's killing spree. I expected to feel relieved. Kinbott is dead and her Hyde is in chains. The people of Jericho are safe.

So why do I still feel so unsettled?

After a while I make my way back to my room, surprised to find it's not empty and dark as it's been on my recent homecomings.

Enid stands at her bedside, the visually assaulting patchwork quilt back on the mattress. She's just hanging up the last of her clothes.

"Hey," she says when she sees me. Her tone is casual, as if she's been greeting me this way every day of her absence.

"You're back," I observe, trying not to attach any value to the statement, in case she's only looking for her nail polish again.

When she rolls her eyes, it seems affectionate. A tiny flicker of hope catches in my chest.

"I'm gone for a few days and all hell breaks loose," she says. "The place gets trashed. Thing is almost killed. Someone needs to look out for you two."

It seems inconceivable that it can really be this easy. That she's just back.

"What about Yoko?" I ask.

Enid shrugs, replacing her prized rainbow wolf-icorn on her pile of stuffed animals. "Yoko's great. Just decided I need a few more boundaries."

She holds up the roll of black tape with which once divided our room, back on that fraught first day.

"Let's skip the tape," I say, hardly believing the words are coming out of my mouth.

It's worth it when Enid smiles. "Don't tell me Wednesday Addams is mellowing out?"

I think of the last twenty-four hours. Bianca and Lucas's information. Confronting Kinbott. Xavier, being led off campus in handcuffs. The unsettled feeling I had when it was all over. Like I don't know what to do with myself if I'm not tracking a gruesome killer.

"Mellowing?" I reply. "Never. But maybe evolving."

Enid giggles. I find I don't mind the sound. "One inch of duct tape at a time."

There's a pause then. A shared but comfortable silence. It's a new phenomenon for me, but once again, I can't relax until I understand it thoroughly.

"Why the change of heart?" I ask when I can't take it any longer. What I really want to know is that she won't change it again, but I can't bring myself to ask that.

Enid shrugs. "We work," she says simply. "We shouldn't, but we do. It's like some strange friendship anomaly. Everything you said about me the other day is true. I giggle, I'm obsessed with texting, I love bright colors and pop music and perfume. But I don't apologize for that. Not anymore. If you want to be my friend, that's just part of the deal."

It's the second time this week I've seen someone I know to be soft and timid and overly concerned with the opinions of others (namely me) sprout a backbone seemingly overnight. It looks good on Enid. Maybe someday I'll find the words to tell her so.

"Thing missed you," I say instead. It's the best I can do for now.

Enid's smile says she understands what I really meant, and for once I don't mind someone reading between the lines. "I missed *him* too," she says. And then: "Sorry about Xavier."

"I'm not," I reply too quickly. "He's a liar and a killer. Besides, there's nothing quite like the feeling of being right about someone." Or at least, I imagine there won't be. Once it sinks in.

"Sure, besides maybe having someone to share it with." She says this in the long-vowels teasing tone she usually applies to Ajax.

At first I think she means herself, and I think she's right. It does feel better now that she's here, and she's the only person I've ever been able to truly say that about. I'm about to muster the courage to put the sentiment into words when she continues. "Thing may have blabbed about your date with Tyler. How did it go?"

This is such a hard one-eighty that it takes me a moment to calibrate. It's certainly no longer time for a compliment. I haven't thought about Tyler all night, even when I was coordinating Xavier's arrest with his father. But Enid seems to want to discuss the date.

"It was... interrupted," I say. It's the only word that feels honest.

Enid's smirk widens. "Maybe it's time to finish it? I heard Tyler is working the late shift..."

It would never have occurred to me to do any such thing, but then I think maybe this is what Enid wants from me. Someone to discuss boys with. Dates. All the trappings of adolescent girl friendships I've always avoided like the plague. Maybe this is what she shared with Yoko. The thing that made the other girl the more attractive option when all I could do was fixate on attack patterns and organs in jars.

There's more to parse out, of course. Part of me wants to confess that I'd rather stay here. Discuss Kinbott's death and Xavier's activation. See if Enid thinks stopping Laurel and the Hyde is enough to put the kibosh on the vision Rowan's mother had of me and Crackstone in the flames...

But there will be time for all that, now that she's back. And tonight, the Hyde is behind bars, his master in the morgue. The streets are safe.

"I'll tell you all about it when I get back," I promise her, and I head out for the Weathervane.

It's closed, of course. Snow swirls in the streets, just a little dusting to signify fall is over.

Inside, I see Tyler sweeping in the low light. He's alone. I realize I should have asked Enid what to do, because right now nothing is occurring to me. We tried to kiss after our last date—are we supposed to do that again? Do I want to?

Rather than stand out here in the cold overthinking it and risking having nothing to report when I return, I decide to be bold. I open the door.

"We're closed," Tyler calls, not looking up from his task.

"Then you should lock your doors," I tell him. "There are all kinds of crazies out there."

He looks up, his face splitting into a genuine smile. But beneath it he looks tired—dark circles beneath his eyes. He's pale like maybe he hasn't been sleeping.

I suppose we've all been stressed with a killer on the loose. Maybe now we can finally relax.

"Hey," he says, stepping closer. "My dad told me what happened with Xavier. That's pretty nuts. The guy always seemed so normal . . . well, for an Outcast." He smirks.

There are several ways I could refute the idea that Xavier was in any way normal, but I didn't come here to talk about him. "It has made me reevaluate some things," I say carefully.

"Oh yeah?" Tyler asks with a smile. The distance between us seems smaller all of a sudden, though neither of us has moved. "Like what?"

There's that look in his eyes again. Almost confidence. That lost little boy stare is gone. It intrigues me.

"Like who I can trust," I say.

"Does that mean you're ready to be more than friends?"

I've answered this question already. I've given him every warning I can think of. I've told him exactly how this will most likely end. If he's still here, it's with his eyes wide open. If he wants to kiss me and I want to kiss him . . . well, I've never done it before. And shouldn't every good investigator be willing to have new experiences?

For scientific purposes, of course.

Tyler steps in closer. I look up, moving closer to him, wanting to do it right. To have the full experience. His expression is eager. It looks familiar in a way I can't quite pinpoint.

Finally, I cross the uncrossable line, pressing my lips against his. They're soft. Responsive. I pull away, looking at him, at the wonder in his eyes. I know I have my data now. That there's no need for further testing. But the fizzing-soda-can feeling I had during our date is back. The feeling that I'm close to something that's always been just out of reach.

I kiss him again, more eagerly this time, chasing the feeling. My favorite feeling. As we kiss, deeper this time, electricity takes root at a point in my spine and begins to radiate upward. This is how they described it, right? Sparks? Fireworks?

My body goes rigid. The scene in front of me disappears, replaced by a horror beyond imagining. Claws tear into flesh. Kinbott's bathroom tiles are splattered with blood. She screams, begs as the monster bears down on her with an expression that holds only rage.

I become Kinbott in the vision, and I see the thing looming over me is no longer a Hyde, but Tyler. His eyes vacant, his bare skin streaked in Kinbott's blood.

I snap back to the present. Tyler is holding me in his arms.

I need to get out of here, now.

"Wednesday?" Tyler asks. "Are you okay?" His eyes are concerned, but if I look deeper, I can see that emptiness. That rage lying in wait.

"I . . . I have to go," I blurt out, and before he can say anything else, I throw myself out the double doors of the Weathervane and into the street. Outside, the snow is falling again, thick and fast. I run into the night, terrified that Tyler will realize what I saw . . . chase me down . . .

But he doesn't. My lungs are screaming in the cold. I slow to a jog, finally allowing the truth of what I've seen to hit me full force. It's Tyler. It's been Tyler the whole time. That means I've been wrong about so many things, but worse, I've been a complete fool.

CHAPTER TWENTY-NINE

It takes me some time to figure out how to confront him. First, there's my own embarrassment to contend with. How could I have let this happen right under my nose? Tyler was there every step of the way, yet I discounted him. Of course the first person I ever kiss would turn out to be a psychotic, serial-killing monster. Let it never be said that I don't have a type.

But there's still the fact that I helped the police lock up the wrong person.

Not to mention the monster is still out there. And whether or not he likes me or just wants me under his spell, he's dangerous.

Unfortunately, I was wrong about more than Tyler. More than Xavier. I can't believe I let myself trust Sheriff Galpin, of all people. I spend the whole next day wondering if he knows his son's secret. If that's why he was so intent on derailing my investigation—keeping me away from Tyler and the case.

It hardly matters except in the logistical realm. When I falsely accused Xavier, I had institutional power on my side. Now I have nothing. In fact, it's imperative that law enforcement does *not* find out what I'm planning. If I know one thing, it's that humans are tribal. They protect their own. Sheriff Galpin will never put his son away.

Which means I'm on my own.

But when I walk across the quad, I realize I'm not alone anymore. Enid and Ajax wave from their lunch table. Bianca nods from her perch on the upper balcony. Even Yoko doesn't look displeased to see me.

Maybe there's some truth to what Weems said when I first came to school. There's something to having a community. Having friends. Knowing you don't have to deal with the consequences of your past mistakes alone.

One of the most insidious things Tyler did was make me feel like *he* was the only person I could count on. Just one more thing I plan to punish him for.

I wait until enough time has passed since our disastrous kiss. I stand in the woods on Nevermore's grounds, waiting. I can see my breath in the fog.

Tyler's a punctual monster, at least, I think as he approaches, looking around nervously as if there's anything in this entire town that poses a threat to him.

Other than the truth, that is.

I step out from the shadows, doing my best to hide the way my hands are trembling in fury. The only thing I hate more than an unsolved mystery is being made a fool of. But it's not quite time for that punishment yet. First, I have to set the trap. Then I have to coax him into it.

We'll see how Tyler feels about being tricked.

When he sees me, he smiles, and I wonder how I ever could have thought it genuine. It looks so false to me now, the way it doesn't reach his cold eyes.

"Thing gave me your note," he says, stepping closer, as if he has any right. "I was kind of surprised you wanted to see me again after you ran off the other night."

The urge to attack him bodily is strong, but I swallow it, remembering what he is. What he can do.

"Is this a date?" he asks when I don't immediately reply.

"It's a surprise," I say, deadpan.

Obviously misreading this statement, Tyler closes the distance, making as if to kiss me. I sidestep him.

"When I came to Nevermore, romance was the last thing on my mind," I tell him. "But then you kissed me, and suddenly it all made sense."

Kinbott, screaming in the bathroom of her office. The monster tearing into her flesh. Tyler, splattered in blood, staring into his own dead eyes in the mirror.

Tyler looks bemused, waiting for what's next.

"Xavier warned me about you," I say, crossing my arms. Leveling him with a stare worthy of my mother. "But I didn't listen."

There's no doubt he's uncomfortable now. He shifts from foot to foot, half chuckling. "Ironic now, isn't it?" he asks.

Still trying to hide behind a wrongful accusation, I think. Like father, like son.

"*Ironic* would be Xavier getting charged with murder while the real Hyde helps me put him away," I say.

Tyler laughs again, but he must see something in my expression that tells him I'm not joking. The smile fades. "Wait," he says. "You don't think—"

"I don't think. I know," I say. "Kinbott must have learned your dark secret in therapy and unlocked you." A pause, during which he does nothing but stare in disbelief. He's a much better liar than I thought. "Why'd you kill her? I thought Hydes were loyal to their masters. Unless you got tired of doing her bidding."

He puts his hands up, shaking his head slowly, taking a step back as if I'm the dangerous one. "Wednesday, seriously, this is nuts. I don't know what you think I did, but—"

"Outreach Day," I interrupt, my rage harder to control as he attempts to gaslight me. "I told you I was going to the Old Meeting House. Did Kinbott tell you to spy on me?"

I can see the monster's eyes peering at me through the slats in the boards. Xavier had shown up moments later, but I never saw Tyler, of course. Not in his human form, anyway.

"And the night of the Rave'N," I continue when he stands, frozen in disbelief. "You heard me and Eugene talking about your cave in the woods. You must have warned Kinbott. When Eugene saw her torch it, she sent you to clean up her mess."

"Wednesday—" Tyler begins, but I cut him off once more.

"I must admit," I say loudly, "wounding yourself at the Gates place was a masterstroke of misdirection. I never thought you had much in the way of brains, but I was clearly wrong."

"Okay, stop!" Tyler says, taking another step back. "Do you know how insane you sound right now? I'm not a monster! And if you really thought I was, why the hell would you risk bringing me out to the woods to confront me alone?"

He says this with concern in his voice. As if he's worried about my safety. I don't know that I've ever hated anyone more than I hate him in this moment.

"Who said I was alone?" I ask him as Yoko, Divina, Kent, and Ajax emerge from the shadows of the crypt, surrounding Tyler. Outcasts versus normies again, I think. What else could it ever have been?

For the first time, Tyler looks genuinely afraid. "I don't know what kind of sick joke you're playing, Wednesday," he says, throwing up his hands. "But I'm out of here." He turns to storm off, coming face to face with Bianca, who is sans pendant tonight—meaning her siren powers are at full potency.

"Actually," she says, staring right into his eyes. "You're coming with us."

A tendril of barely perceptible red mist issues from her mouth. I can see it spiral in Tyler's eyes as his jaw goes slack. He would follow her off a cliff if she asked, but I only need him to make it to a certain remote shed.

When Tyler comes to, he's chained to a chair in Xavier's art studio. I stand before him, wanting to be the first thing he sees. He blinks drowsily as we come into focus—the Nightshades and me. His worst nightmare.

"Where the hell am I?" he asks.

"Somewhere no one can hear you scream," I reply without missing a beat.

He rattles against the heavy chains crossed over his torso. "What's with the chains?"

I narrow my eyes. "We both know the answer to that."

Tyler's expression is pleading now. "Wednesday, this is crazy. You know I'm a normie."

"That's only half true," I reply, reaching out a hand. Yoko puts a folder in it, which I open to the photo of my mother's fencing team. She stands front and center, demanding all eyes on her.

But she's not the only girl in the photo. Near the back, there's a girl with a long face. Reddish brown wavy hair. "Recognize her?" I ask Tyler, pointing to the girl's face. His eyes go wide, but he doesn't answer.

"If I hadn't been so fixated on my own mother, perhaps I would have noticed yours sooner," I say. "She taught fencing at Nevermore. Your father fell in love with and married an Outcast."

Tyler goes from helpless to indignant. "Fine, she was an Outcast!" he says. "Now she's dead. That doesn't make me a monster."

"She wasn't just any Outcast," I say, feeling the thrill of having him here, captive. Finally about to pay for what he did to me and all those innocent people. "She was a Hyde. According to her medical records—" I return to the file.

"You stole her medical records?" Tyler asks, disgusted. As if paperwork theft is equal in scope to the crime of murdering multiple people.

"Technically Thing did, from your garage," I admit. "Your

father is quite the pack rat. It seems her postpartum depression triggered her condition."

"My mother was bipolar!" Tyler shouts. He's getting angry. Good.

"We both know that's a lie," I say, pressing in, giving him nowhere to escape my gaze. "She was a Hyde. All these years your father must have been living in dread, wondering if she'd passed her condition along to you."

He leans his head to the side, beseeching the others: "You're all really just gonna stand here and let her do this to me?"

No one intervenes. No one even replies. They know what's at stake. Well, up to this point, anyway. I may have omitted a few key details.

I reach into my backpack, pulling out the supplies I'll need for phase two. A Taser, pliers, a staple gun, a hammer.

"Wednesday," Bianca hisses, stepping close. "What are you doing?"

"A Hyde only understands one thing," I say without looking up. "Pain. This is how we prove he's a monster. That Xavier's innocent."

Before she can stop me, I turn and tase Tyler in the neck. He roars in pain but remains a human boy in chains. No matter, I never expected the first attempt to do it. That's why I have so many other tools.

"That's it," Yoko says from back near the door. "I'm out."

The other Nightshades go, too, even Ajax after a long look. "Enid just texted," he warns. "Thornhill's suspicious we all missed dinner. Whatever you're doing, do it fast."

I make a mental note: Ajax is more loyal than the rest. Either that, or he's mortally afraid of pissing off his girlfriend.

Bianca is the only one left, and she levels me with a look. "I didn't sign on for this," she says. "Let's just take him to Weems. Explain everything."

But I've had enough of institutional interference. The school, the police, the city government. All of them have already failed. I'm the only one who can solve this.

"Weems won't help us prove an Outcast is responsible for murder," I say, but I can't look away from Tyler. From the agony on his face. "And Galpin would be useless even if Tyler wasn't his son. I'm on my own."

"You sure are," says Bianca. "I hope you know what you're doing."

And then she's gone too. Tyler screams in panic: "No! Don't leave me with her! I'm begging you, please!"

"What did I say about screaming," I say, closing back in. The Taser sizzles, ready to strike again. "What was Kinbott—or should I say Laurel Gates—using you for?"

"Wednesday, please," Tyler pants.

I tase him again. He should know what it feels like to hurt. How much pain has he caused other people during this mad killing spree?

"The body parts in the basement at the Gates' house—what was Laurel collecting them for? What was her plan? Was it something to do with Crackstone? Rowan's mother's vision?"

"I don't understand," Tyler sobs. "Why are you doing this?"

Anyone else might be fooled, but I'm not. No tears.

I slam the Taser down on the table in plain view. "If you won't cooperate, I'll have to go old-school." I pick up the hammer and the pliers, pretending to agonize over which to choose.

That's when I hear the sirens. Of course one of those marshmallow Nightshades went to Weems. None of them would dare call a normie sheriff, but Weems would, if it meant staying in Jericho's good graces.

No matter, this is only an obstacle. Sooner or later, the truth about Tyler will come out. I don't plan to rest until it does.

The red and blue lights bathe the shed through the windows. Tyler's face sags in relief. "HELP! I'M IN HERE!" he shouts, as if they don't already know.

Sheriff Galpin bursts in a few seconds later, gun drawn, surrounded by officers. He looks haunted, his eyes bloodshot and his face sallow. "Drop the Taser and step away from my son!" he shouts in a hoarse voice.

I do, reluctantly raising my hands. "This isn't over," I say to Tyler out of the corner of my mouth.

Weems is waiting for me at the station, shock of all shocks. I overhear her conversation with the deputy. Apparently, the Nightshades went to her together, said I'd gone too far.

Traitors.

The two of them approach me together.

"Sheriff Galpin isn't going to press kidnapping charges," Weems says in a tone of barely repressed rage I'm becoming all too familiar with. "Which I'm sure you know is a *miracle* given the circumstances."

But I know it's much more than a miracle. It's a cover-up. "How long have you known?" I ask him, ignoring Weems's attempts to lick every boot in the place.

"Excuse me?" the sheriff asks, whipping around to look at me.

"When I gave you that claw from the cave, did you already know the truth about Tyler?"

"Wednesday!" Weems cries, scandalized. "That's enough!"

But Galpin doesn't look surprised. He regards me as one might an irrational child. "Xavier Thorpe is our Hyde," he says. "We've got the evidence. All thanks to you, which is the *only* reason I'm giving you one last pass."

It's bullshit and we both know it. No wonder the sheriff was so eager to arrest Xavier. It must have been a massive relief. The only question is whether he's lying to himself or just the rest of us.

"Tyler's going to turn on you," I say, staring him down. "And when he does, you'll wish you'd listened to me. But only for a few seconds, because then you'll be dead."

Weems gets to her feet, grabbing me by the arm and hauling me toward the door. Galpin watches me go with an unfathomable expression on his face.

We're almost to the door when I hear the last voice I expected to hear tonight. "Wednesday, wait."

It's Tyler. He approaches me across the checkered linoleum floor of the waiting room, but is intercepted by his father before he can reach me.

"Ty, what are you doing?" he asks in a low voice.

"I need to talk to her, Dad," he says. That fake boyish expression. The round eyes, the mouth puckered as if he's about to cry at any moment. "She was my friend. And I'm in a police station—what's gonna happen?"

To a privileged son of the sheriff? Probably nothing, I think. Unless I can reach my boot knife in time.

Galpin steps out of the way. "Make it quick," he says. How

touching, his concern for his monster son's wishes while another boy is imprisoned for his crimes.

Weems follows Sheriff Galpin's nod, accompanying him into the open office on the left. That leaves Tyler and me in the police station, the fluorescent light flickering overhead.

"What do you want?" I ask. He's already too close for comfort.

"To ask a question," he says, and a smirk overtakes his features. One I've never seen before in all the time we've spent together. "What does it feel like?"

"What does what feel like?" I ask, revolted.

"To *lose*?" he asks.

The smirk turns into a truly deranged smile as he moves closer, leaning in as though embracing me one last time. My skin crawls. I hold my breath, staying as still as I can. It occurs to me, for the first time, what it means that Tyler's the monster. What he could do to me if he decided to.

"At first, I'd wake up naked," he says to me. "Covered in blood. No idea what happened. But over time, I started to remember. Everything. The sound of their screams. The panic in their eyes. A fear so primal I could taste it." He pauses. "And it was delicious."

The coldness and rage I occasionally glimpsed in Tyler's expression have overtaken everything else. In that moment, I forgive myself for being fooled. I remember Faulkner's words in his journal: *The Hyde is an artist by nature.*

"You have no idea what's coming," he whispers into my ear, and goose bumps sweep across my skin.

I see it all in real time. The Tyler I knew returning to his face. The wounded look. The distant eyes longing for escape. A victim, forgiving the girl he once wanted for mistakenly accusing him.

Having been face to face with the Hyde several times, I can say unequivocally that I would prefer the gnashing teeth and bloodied claws of that monster to the lethal human coldness of this one.

I'm numb until I'm sitting across from Weems in her office, lost in the memory of Tyler's shifting persona. His father's staunch denial of his son's involvement. Everyone will be watching me now. Every avenue ahead of me is closed.

So consumed with Tyler, Sheriff Galpin, the Hyde, Xavier's wrongful imprisonment, and everything else, I forget to worry about Weems until she's across the desk from me. Even still, nothing she says comes as a surprise.

"The quid pro quo for Sheriff Galpin not pressing charges is your immediate expulsion from Nevermore. I've informed your parents," she says. Is it possible there's a tinge of regret in her words? It doesn't matter in the long-term; this is exactly what I expected.

"I acted alone," I say as my sole defense. "The others had nothing to do with it."

Weems arches an eyebrow. "For someone who claims to have no friends, you certainly go out of your way to protect them."

The truth is, I wouldn't claim to have no friends anymore. That's one thing that happened to me here. But I certainly wouldn't include the Nightshade marshmallows who abandoned me and ran to the principal tonight.

"They didn't have the stomach for what had to be done," I say matter-of-factly.

"You mean kidnapping and torture?" Weems asks. She's angry again. "I should hope not."

I stand up, leaning across the desk to look her in the eye. "You realize Tyler brutally disemboweled five people, then harvested a variety of their body parts for good measure."

Weems stands up too. It ruins my gesture, as she's probably twice as tall as me in heels.

"If only you had come to me with your suspicions instead of taking matters into your own hands," she says.

I scoff. We both know we still would have ended up here. Except I wouldn't have Tyler's confession. "Yes, trust and cooperation have always been hallmarks of our relationship," I say sarcastically. If there's someone to blame for the lack of those between us, it certainly isn't me.

Weems gives me a half smile of acknowledgment. "I admire your ability to be your own person and follow your own instincts," she says. "But those things also make you impatient and impulsive. Your actions have put me and the school in an impossible position."

"*Tyler is the Hyde,*" I say, infusing every ounce of urgency I can into my words. "He framed Xavier. If you're going to ship me out, someone has to know the truth."

Weems's smile turns pitying. "I wish I could believe you."

Panic starts to spread. How can I leave if no one knows the truth? Sheriff Galpin will cover for Tyler. Walker is gone. Kinbott is dead. How many people will die before Tyler gives himself away?

"His mother was an Outcast," I tell Weems. "She was a student here. You must remember her. She was a Hyde."

"Yes, Françoise," Weems says. "She was a lovely woman. I didn't ask what she identified as."

"Just give me some more time," I demand, thinking the truth will help my case. "I can prove they're both Hydes."

But Weems is done humoring me. Her face is calm but stern as she delivers the final verdict. "There is no more time," she says simply. "There are no more deals. Pack your steamer trunks, we'll have them shipped. You can say your goodbyes in the morning. You'll be on the afternoon train tomorrow."

Every instinct I possess is telling me not to walk away without convincing her. Without finding someone who can keep trying to get Tyler off the streets when I'm gone. Only, it seems I've finally reached the end of her patience.

"I'm sorry Nevermore didn't work out for you, Wednesday," she says. "Your mother will be very disappointed. And so am I."

She dismisses me then to go and pack my trunks as instructed. But I don't. Not yet, anyway. It's a long shot, but there's still one more person I might be able to convince to help me—not because he owes me anything, but because he has as much to lose as I do if Tyler isn't caught.

CHAPTER THIRTY

The local jail is as easy to break into as ever. I see Xavier before he sees me. He's alone in his cell—whether for his privacy as the child of a celebrity or as a precaution in case he transforms, I don't know.

His hands and feet are secured with heavy chains. They're bolted to a waist belt and tethered to a metal ring in the middle of the floor. He turns slowly when he hears me entering, and then he rolls his eyes.

"How the hell did you get in here?" he asks.

"Thing distracted the guards and is looping the camera," I say matter-of-factly. The truth is, I've never felt quite as guilty in my life as I do seeing him there, chained up because I bought Tyler's act.

But apologizing isn't going to fix anything. All I can do for Xavier now is try to get him out of here.

"So?" he says. "What are you doing here? Did you come to gloat?"

"No," I say.

He looks gaunt and haggard. Like he hasn't been sleeping or eating enough. It would have been a bad enough fate for a Hyde who hadn't asked to be unlocked for nefarious purposes—but for an innocent boy, it's beyond imagining.

"I know you're not the monster," I finally manage to choke out. "Tyler used me to frame you. *He's* the Hyde."

For just a second, the loathing parts to reveal shock. Curiosity. Hopefully I can use this to get him to help me free him. "I saw it in a vision," I say. "He kissed me, and I saw him murdering Kinbott."

The curiosity is gone in a flash. The sneer returns. "Glad you were getting some action while I was wrongfully imprisoned."

I don't bother to counter. He has every right to be angry with me. "I should have believed you," I tell him as sincerely as I can. And then I get down to the business that brought me here: "You have a psychic connection to the Hyde. Have you dreamed anything recently that could shed some light?"

His expression says exactly what I feared. That he'd rather rot in here than help me again.

"You seriously think I would tell you?" he asks. "After you ruined my life? I tried to help you, Wednesday, and look where it got me." He rattles his chains for emphasis. There's no doubt it's effective.

"This isn't about helping me," I say. "It's about getting you out of here and protecting all the people Tyler's going to attack next. It's bigger than us."

Xavier lurches to the end of his chains. His face is right across the bars from mine. I don't back away. "It's about you," he says in a low, deadly voice. "Every time you get involved, someone gets hurt. You're *toxic*, Wednesday. All you ever do is make things worse."

I understand he's angry, but this calls it all back. Goody's warning. Enid's departure. The various times I've been warned that I'm a terrible friend, that all I do is endanger everyone around me...

There's one more thing I have to try. My last-ditch effort before I get on the train tomorrow and leave Nevermore and Jericho to their fate. I pull out Rowan's mother's drawing, unfolding it so he can see.

"Tyler told me something bad was coming when he confessed," I say in the steadiest voice I can manage. "I think he m—"

But Xavier is done listening to me. "No, stop," he says. "You've already shown me this, and you know what? I don't care. You want to stop this?" He points at the drawing, the chains clinking again. "Then leave. Go far away, and never come back. It can't happen if you're not here. *That's* how you save everyone."

This time, his words cut too deep to shrug off. I don't know if what he's saying is true—whether this prophecy can come true without me present. But I do know that if Xavier won't help me, I'm officially out of allies. And I tried long enough to know I can't solve this by myself.

If Xavier is right, if all I do is hurt the people who try to care about me, maybe it's better for them if I'm gone. At least then they'll only have one monster to contend with.

"I'm—" I begin, but Xavier turns his back on me.

"Leave," he says. "Now."

What else can I do but obey?

The packing process is more emotional than I expect with Enid. She's helping me, but I can tell she's sad. Mourning. I struggle to come up with parting words worthy of what she's meant to me, but everything feels inconsequential compared to the feeling.

"I assume you'll move in with Yoko now," I say instead. "Forget all about me."

Enid looks at me, earnest as always. "Never *ever*," she says, but then a little of the old insecurity flickers back into her eyes. "What about you? Will you forget about me?"

I ponder for a moment, then decide maybe sometimes there are no perfect words. There's just whatever you say and how it makes the other person feel. "You've left an indelible impression," I say. "Whenever I get nauseous at the sight of a rainbow or hear a pop song that makes my ears bleed, I will think of you."

Enid smiles beatifically. "Coming from you, I know what a compliment that is."

I put the last of my outerwear into my last trunk and close it. There are just minutes left now before I leave this place, never to return.

"The truth is, I always believed reliance on other people was a sign of weakness. Or that they would inevitably disappoint me. Turns out I've been the disappointment."

Enid crosses the room until only the trunks are between us. "Are you kidding?" she says. "I've learned so much from you! I mean, some of it is admittedly criminal behavior, but, Wednesday—most people spend their whole lives pretending to give zero effs. You've literally never had an eff to give. You're my hero."

For once, I don't drop her bright blue, overly earnest gaze. I've never been anyone's hero before. I find it . . . strangely emotional. Is it possible I could have had something to do with her newfound confidence? Perhaps my time here wasn't utterly wasted after all.

"So . . . ," she says. Those long vowels of hers again. "Any chance you've got some sneaky plan to elude Weems? Move into Crackstone Crypt? Keep solving mysteries?"

Earlier today I would have jumped at the chance, but after seeing Xavier . . .

I shake my head, pulling out the drawing. Crackstone and me. The flames dancing in the quad. "I think Xavier might be right," I tell her. "If I'm not here, the prophecy can't come true. And even if I'm not right, at least I won't be able to hurt anyone else. If I have one regret, it's leaving while Tyler's still walking around free."

Enid waves a hand dismissively, her claws popping out for emphasis. "If he tries anything, we've got a school full of werewolves, vampires, Gorgons, sirens, and psychics ready and waiting. We got this, Wednesday, I promise."

I appreciate the confidence, but the idea of Enid getting involved, getting *hurt,* is the thing that makes it hardest to leave. Still, I smile like she's reassured me, and I don't tell her to be careful. I know she'll want to be brave. I'd never take that away from her.

"On the good-news front, I got a text from Eugene's moms!" Enid says. "He woke up late last night!"

"He did?" I feel positively weightless with relief. I'm not sure I even realized how heavy the guilt was on my heart. The fear that he would never wake up and it would all be my fault. But he's okay.

"Yep!" Enid says. "Maybe Weems will let you drop by on your way to the station."

Weems. The station. The reality comes crashing back in. I organize my things and pull on my backpack as Enid and Thing share an emotional goodbye, and then it's time. It feels so surreal to think I'll never be back in this room again. That if I ever see Enid, it'll be somewhere else.

"I guess this is goodbye," I tell her.

"So . . . are we gonna . . . ?" Stepping around my trunks, Enid opens her arms.

I step away instinctively, but this time there's part of me that wishes I hadn't.

She laughs, dropping her arms. "Yeah, okay, no. *Not* hugging is kind of our thing now anyway."

And I suppose she's right. Although I like to think there's still potential for things to change. Someday.

I know Weems is in the entrance hall, but I don't expect to see Bianca, Ajax, and Yoko waiting for me downstairs. "We're sorry," Bianca says, ever the mouthpiece. "We didn't know you'd get expelled."

Waving her off, I lock eyes with each of them in turn. "I don't know what's going to happen when I leave. But the Nightshades need to be ready, whatever it is, or a lot of people could die."

Bianca nods. She looks capable in that moment. I nearly tell her to watch out for Enid, but in the end, I decide it might embarrass her, so I simply walk away.

But there are more surprises in store. Ms. Thornhill approaches with a potted plant, covered in mud. She smiles widely. "I'm so glad I was able to catch you!" she says, a little out of breath. "I was weeding my wolfsbane beds and lost track of time." She pushes the plant into my arms. "A little going-away gift for you."

"White oleander," I say. "One of nature's deadliest. I accept."

Ms. Thornhill shakes her head affectionately. "*Actually*," she says, "it symbolizes destiny and renewal. You're a very talented young woman, Wednesday. The world is at your feet, and I can't wait to see what you do next."

It's a nice sentiment, and for a moment I feel guilty for so often reducing Ms. Thornhill to her easy-to-mock red footwear. She really has tried to make me feel at home here. It's not her fault it was an impossible task from the start.

Weems approaches then, and Ms. Thornhill clears out. "I will be personally escorting you to your train today," she says with a vaguely threatening aura. I'm almost flattered that she thinks so much of my escape proficiency.

"I have one final favor," I tell her.

Eugene is sitting up in bed in his hospital room. His moms are down the hall at the nurses station, and they beam and wave as I enter the room. I won't deny that the sight of him, awake, rosy-cheeked and smiling, has a powerful effect on me.

"Wednesday!" Eugene cries joyfully, answering once and for all my question of whether he'd blame me for deserting him that night. "I heard you visited me all the time."

I give him a smirk. The honey jar I brought is already empty. "Hummers stick together, right?" I say. And then: "I'm sorry I wasn't there to protect you that night."

His answering shrug makes me feel even worse. "When the dance floor calls, you gotta answer, right?"

Eugene's forgiveness is more ironically heartbreaking when I reflect on what I was doing the night he was attacked. Not only choosing an empty social tradition over him, but also engaging in said empty social tradition with the very monster who would critically wound him just a few hours later.

My inner censure must show on my face, because Eugene puts a pudgy hand on my shoulder. "It's not your fault," he says. "It's the monster's."

Suddenly, I realize just how much Eugene doesn't know. How long he's been gone. "It's a Hyde," I tell him, "and it's still out there. You have to promise you won't go back to Nevermore. Not even to check on your bees."

I can see rebellion warring with confusion on his face as he looks away, but I can't tell him it's safe to see his bees any more than I can confess Tyler's true identity. Not without putting him in even more danger than he's in. Tyler has gone to great lengths already to protect his secret, and I can't prove the sheriff isn't in on it. Eugene deserves to be innocent of all that.

At least I know Enid will protect him.

"You have to listen to me this time," I say. "Hummer code."

When Eugene speaks again, his eyes are far away. Like he's reliving that night. "In the woods . . . ," he begins. "I saw someone set fire to that cave."

"I know," I tell him. "Dr. Kinbott."

"It's so crazy that it was her," he says, squinting against the memory. "I don't really remember any of it. I just saw someone wearing all black. And these boots . . ."

At this, I perk up. In all my time knowing Dr. Kinbott, I've never known her to wear boots. At least not any distinctive enough to form a core memory in the mind of a monster's victim.

"What about her boots?" I ask sharply. Even an hour from my

permanent departure, I could never let a good clue go to waste.

"There was an explosion of light," Eugene says slowly. "I was on the ground, so all I could see was her feet. The boots weren't black like the rest of her outfit. They were bright red."

Bright red boots, I think, the image blocking out everything else. The hospital room. Eugene. The fact that I've been expelled from Nevermore and am on my way home.

None of it matters. Because I was wrong again. Disastrously wrong. Wrong in a way that puts everyone I've come to care about at Nevermore in horrible danger. And I may have only one chance to make things right.

The conservatory is empty but for Ms. Thornhill. The gray Nevermore afternoon filters in through the high windows. The sheen on the leaves of the plants reflects it back.

At a long table in the center of the room, Ms. Thornhill hums a little tune as she crushes something in a mortar.

"Wednesday!" she says when she looks up, clearly startled. "I thought you'd be halfway to New Jersey by now. Did you forget something?"

I narrow my eyes. Now that I know the truth, this flustered-schoolteacher-just-trying-to-fit-in act is clearly a poor one. I'll have time later to berate myself for being fooled twice.

"You can drop the act, Laurel," I say. "I should have known it was you. Many poisonous plants masquerade as harmless ones." I cross half the distance to the worktable. Now I can see the boots. Bright red. Splattered in mud. Her signature, and her last mistake.

To her credit, she betrays nothing. Her hand disappears into her pocket, then returns empty and meets me in the middle of the room.

"I should applaud you," I continue. "Faking your death, securing a job at Nevermore, unlocking a Hyde. I have a soft spot for well-executed revenge plots, but yours was extreme even by my high standards."

Ms. Thornhill's eyes go wide. The same soft, faux innocence that so fooled me when Tyler used the same expression. Curse my eternal weakness for the underdog.

"Oh dear," she says in that high, worried dorm mother voice. "Weems was right. You really do need psychiatric help. You can't throw around wild accusations without consequences."

It's so easy to hear it now. The loathing beneath her sugary-sweet affect. The disdain. The dangerous edge of sanity she tipped over long ago.

"They may be wild," I concur, "but they're also true. Tyler confirmed everything."

I gesture behind me to reveal the first of several surprises I planned on my way over. Tyler steps out from the shadow of a massive monstera. His eyes flicking between the two of us.

Ms. Thornhill, or should I say Laurel, is clearly an expect liar. She schools her features so well I barely detect a hint of surprise. Tyler stands wordlessly beside me.

"I assumed Kinbott unlocked him with hypnosis," I say. "But I was wrong, wasn't I? You must have used a plant-derived chemical."

Her eyes are perfectly still on mine, waiting for the end of my history lesson. The stillness is what unnerves me, much more than the jars and vials of concoctions lining the walls. But I have to know I'm right this time.

"I'm sure your Outcast-hating father told you the Galpin

family secret when you were a little girl," I continue. "So when you returned to Jericho, you targeted Tyler. Preyed on the fact that he was a troubled teen with anger issues. *You* had answers to all his questions. Little did he know, the truth you told him wouldn't set him free. It would enslave him to you. It was scary for him at first, hence the cave and shackles, but over time Tyler became a willing servant. Kinbott must have been on the verge of discovering the truth, so you had Tyler kill her and pin it on Xavier."

When I finish, her expression finally shifts. From wide-eyed, in-over-her-head, caring normie teacher to Outcast-loathing villain in a single smirk.

"That's enough!" she says in a harsh voice, nothing of that breathless, bumbling wonder in it. "I can't believe I tolerated you for this long." Her eyes shift to Tyler's. "Tyler, sweet pea, make Momma happy and shut her up. Permanently."

Tyler doesn't move, but I'm chilled to the bone by the casual tone in which she issues the command. Like she's done it a hundred times before.

"He's not on your side," I say. "Not anymore."

Ms. Thornhill rolls her eyes. "Please," she says. "Tyler would do anything for me."

When she turns to face him again, her expression has shifted once more. This one is loving. Maternal. And it's just as false as all the rest.

"Remember what we talked about," she says in a low, hypnotic tone. "I showed you who you truly are. What they did to your mother. I'm the only one who cares about you. The Outcasts destroyed your family. They made you a monster."

Still, Tyler doesn't budge.

"If you hate Outcasts so much, why is he killing normies too?"

I ask urgently, sensing that my ruse won't last much longer.

She scoffs, taking her eyes off Tyler for a second. "They're pawns in a much bigger game," she says. This is the most terrifying version of her yet. Her face is twisted with some kind of awe. Like a zealot in a church pew. "Just like you, Wednesday. You underestimated the situation again. You were never getting on that train. I sent Tyler to intercept you."

This time, I'm the one surprised. But not as surprised as she is when I say: "I never made it to the station."

I can see the gears turning, wondering why Tyler would disobey her orders, how I ended up here if not by the kidnapping she ordered him to carry out.

"Heard enough?" I ask him casually over my shoulder.

"Plenty," Tyler says, just as his hair begins to lighten, his form growing taller and broader shouldered. Within seconds, Weems stands before us in her camel coat, looking horrified but determined.

"Gotcha," I say to Ms. Thornhill. "The real Tyler is probably still waiting for me at the station."

Weems takes a step toward Ms. Thornhill, towering over her. "Please, don't make this more difficult than it already is, Marilyn," she says.

For the first time, Ms. Thornhill loses control. Her face becomes a feral mask of rage as she cries, "My name is *Laurel*!" and lunges for Principal Weems.

It's done before I can even process what's happening. Ms. Thornhill's syringe is in her hand, and then it's in Weems's neck. She doesn't drop my gaze for a second as she depresses the plunger, emptying the chamber of that toxic blue liquid.

Weems drops to the floor instantly, gasping. I drop to her side, feeling panic spread through me as her mouth begins to foam and she gasps futilely for breath.

"Nightshade poison," I say, recalling Garrett's leathery skin, this same shade of blue. If it's true, she'll be dead in seconds. If it's true, there's nothing I can do.

"A fitting end, don't you think?" Laurel asks from behind me. The next thing I know, there's a sharp, explosive pain at the back of my skull, and all goes black.

CHAPTER THIRTY-ONE

When I come to, my head is killing me. The first thing I notice is that I'm hanging from the ceiling. My arms are tied. Manacled, to be specific, above my head. There are angels on either side of me. Stone ones. Candles flicker all around.

After a few seconds, it all becomes clear. I'm in Crackstone Crypt again. The candles are placed around his sarcophagus like offerings. I yank on the heavy chains binding me, but they don't do more than rattle.

Tyler steps into view. His expression is cold and cruel, devoid of any of the tenderness he showed when we were here a few days ago, watching a movie just over there.

Or the confusion and hurt he displayed when the Nightshades captured him in the woods.

"Kind of a déjà vu thing we've got going on, huh?" he asks, smirking.

I picture him, chained to the chair in Xavier's office, the Taser in my hand. It calms me. "Except you won't catch me crying and whimpering," I say.

His smirk fades then. A small victory. I don't get to savor it for long.

Laurel approaches, looking dismissively at Tyler. "Go wait by the boat," she says.

"Better listen to your master like a good little Hyde," I say in my most venomous tone.

He bares his teeth before storming off, unable to defy her.

I might feel more pity for him if I didn't remember how he sounded that night at the sheriff's office. How he boasted about loving the taste of his victims' fear. Remembering everything . . .

The question is, will he remember mine after tonight? Or am I enough of an Addams to escape with my life?

Alone with Laurel, I wait for her to slip up, to make a mistake. The fanatic expression makes more sense now, in this shrine to Crackstone. I remember her altar in the Gates house. So lovingly attended.

"I have to admit, that shape-shifting stunt with Weems almost worked," she says, making her way around the base of the sarcophagus, setting down glass containers I can't quite see the contents of. "But as my father used to say—if you want to outsmart an Outcast, you've gotta outthink 'em."

As she finishes speaking, she brings the last jar right to the front. I can see it clearly. A cross-section of a human head. The same one I saw in the basement of the Gates house that night. It's easy to assume the rest of the jars contain the other body parts.

My head swims. I feel nauseated. My chains are hooked to a bolt in the ceiling, my feet barely skimming the ground. It's hard to imagine any way to escape this, and yet I have to, or die.

"Father was such a clever man," Laurel says, stepping back to admire her handiwork. "A real history buff. He traced our family roots all the way back to Joseph Crackstone himself, you know."

"Wow," I deadpan. "Being a psychotic killer must run in the family."

The illuminated look of a fanatic returns to her features. "Joseph Crackstone was a visionary," she says. "He dedicated his life to protecting normies from Outcasts. That is, until his life was cut short by your ancestor, Goody Addams."

Pouting now, she turns to face the tomb. "Then, to add insult to injury, his land was stolen and used to build that abomination of a school."

"A settler having his land stolen," I say. "What a karmic reversal of fortunes."

Laurel ignores me. She's looking around at the jars, the candles, like a cat who's just dropped a decapitated bird carcass at the feet of its master. "Outcasts have always had an unfair advantage over normies," she says. As if institutional power, privilege, and representation aren't advantages far beyond the occasional psychic vision. "So I decided to harness the supernatural for my own purposes."

That's when it becomes clear, even to my potentially concussed brain. The candles, the body parts, the location. This isn't some kind of shrine to Crackstone. This is a ritual.

"There was nothing random about Tyler's murder spree," I say, realization dawning. "He was collecting body parts so you could try to raise Crackstone from the dead."

Rowan's mother's picture comes back to me then in vivid detail. Crackstone's figure, as corporeal as my own, the two of us facing off across Nevermore's burning quad.

"The one man who nearly succeeded in destroying all Outcasts," Laurel says, confirming my worst suspicions.

"You can't raise the dead," I inform her. It's one of the first rules they teach us about using our supernatural powers. Of course, a normie would have no idea.

"Your ancestor Goody Addams would disagree," she says, holding up a book I recognize all too well. It's the book from my visions. The book that Goody was holding in the portrait at Pilgrim World. Laurel must have stolen the original from the fake Meeting House.

"Goody's *Book of Shadows*," I say, my heart sinking.

"It wasn't enough for Goody to kill Joseph," Laurel says. "She had to curse his soul as well."

My head is swimming again. My entire body aches, my wrists chafing against their chains. It's hard to keep it all straight, and even if I can, what does it matter? I'm helpless. Strung up like a pig for carving. No one even knows I'm here besides Weems, and she's dead.

"What does any of this have to do with me?" I ask.

"My dear Wednesday," Laurel says, approaching me, flicking one of my chains. "You are the key. Your arrival at Nevermore set the wheels of my plan in motion."

She crosses back to the sarcophagus. To a white marble rondel on its front I hadn't noticed before.

"Goody sealed Crackstone in here with a blood lock. Which means only a direct descendent can open it."

For a moment, I flash back to Xavier in his cell. Sneering at the drawing. Telling me the prophecy can't come true if I'm not here. He was more right than he knew. And Goody knew too. She told me the first time I ever saw her, my vision on this island during the Poe Cup.

You are the key . . .

"Why not just have Tyler kill me the first time we were alone?" I ask, not understanding. "You could have stolen a vial of my blood. Saved yourself a lot of trouble."

She shakes her head, as if she regrets not doing just that. "The lock can only be opened by a living descendent on the night of a blood moon."

My mental math is slowed, but even so it doesn't take long to realize. The blood moon is tonight. And Goody made sure one of her descendants would be alive if and when Crackstone exited the tomb. Which means it's up to me to stop him before he destroys another generation of Outcasts.

"I've been biding my time," Laurel says. "Trying to make you feel special. But tonight, time's up, Wednesday."

This so eerily echoes what I said to Dr. Kinbott before her death. Of all the times to be wrong. I do my best to strategize with the limited agency I have left. If I were Laurel, I'd kill me the moment the tomb was open, which means I'll have to act fast when she lets me down . . .

Within a minute, she's approaching to do just that. Blood returns painfully to my arms as she unhooks the chain—but of course she doesn't release me, just grabs the chain and jerks me forward, closer to the seal that only I can open.

I'm just considering how best to strangle her with my weak arms and impaired motor skills when she spins me toward her, grabbing my palm and slashing it open before I can react.

With gritted teeth, I bear the additional pain, but there's so little space left in my mind for planning. I feel like a puppet, set up to do her bidding, as much a weapon as Tyler.

I fight tooth and nail as she grabs my wrist, dragging my bleeding palm closer to the rondel. Kicking, screaming, biting, but Laurel's dark determination leaves no room for distraction. I'm moved inexorably toward the seal until at last, my palm connects with it. My blood.

The pain I've experienced thus far is nothing compared to the white-hot agony that burns through my blood at the contact. I can hear myself screaming. Feel my consciousness fleeing to protect me from the damage the pain could cause.

My vision is darkening around the edges. A soft, inviting darkness. Everything pulses in front of me as I slide down the sarcophagus to slump against it on the floor.

Laurel has the book in hand. Goody's book. She speaks a spell that ripples unnaturally through the air, opening the book to the page she's marked. The resurrection spell, I have no doubt.

She reads in Latin. Her pronunciation is abysmal, but I can understand every word. She's summoning Joseph Crackstone from the dead.

I'm losing the fight to remain conscious. Symbols around the edge of the sarcophagus begin to glow. Twisting cords of energy crackle between the jars, like a circuit, connected at last to a power source.

The light builds in intensity as my own pain ebbs. Laurel has forgotten me. I use the distraction to attempt to pick the lock on my manacles, but I'm so clumsy. My fingers are numb.

Tendrils of black smoke seep from under the lid of Crackstone's not-so-final resting place. They snake and twist together at the foot of the pedestal, filling some invisible outline until a large human shape stands in the room.

Laurel's face is ecstasy, lit from below as she lays eyes on her idol. The culmination of her plans. I pick at the lock with increasing desperation, making no more headway.

The chaos in the crypt crescendos. Laurel shields her eyes. My stomach turns.

And then, silence.

The smoke figure is no longer smoke. I can see the long wood staff. His pilgrim's garb. But nothing compares to his face. Bone-pale, a ghoulish horror. Nothing like the square-jawed mascot of Jericho at all.

Time seems to stretch and bend. I remember him from my vision. Torching the Meeting House full of Outcasts. For a moment I don't know whether I'm here or in the past.

"Who freed me from eternal damnation?" he asks in a booming voice.

Laurel steps forward and bows. Crackstone extends a ringed finger and she kisses it without hesitation, turning my stomach again. "I'm of your blood," she says in a sickly, supplicant's voice. "I summoned you so that you could rid us of the Outcasts once and for all."

His horrid, ghoulish flesh stretches into a smile. *"My vengeance will be swift and true."*

Just then, at long last, the lock on my shackles gives. I get to my feet, pain screaming through every cell, upright due to sheer force of will. "As will mine," I declare as the chains fall to my feet.

But I don't have a chance to approach before Crackstone's awful visage is glaring down on me. He raises the oak staff, the end of which glows green in the dark of the tomb. The energy coming from it holds me still.

"Goody Addams!" he cries, face twisted in hatred. "You haunt me still. You will suffer the same fate you bequeathed me." From his belt, he pulls an ancient dagger. I'm immobile, even having escaped my shackles, and Crackstone doesn't hesitate.

The blade is plunged into my stomach. For a moment, the pain is unimaginable, and then it begins to fade. My body protecting me once again. But this time, from agony at the end.

"Now burn," Joseph Crackstone says, his eyes fixed on mine in malignant hate. His knife still in my flesh. "In the eternal fires of damnation where you belong."

All is fuzzy and blurred as he releases the knife, as I fall to the ground with it still inside me. I can feel my blood leaving me. My flesh growing cold. Indifferent, Crackstone and Laurel exit the tomb, slamming the stone door shut. Every candle extinguishes, leaving me to die in the dark.

Dying is much slower and more painful than I imagined it when I got my first coffin as a child. I'd lie in there for hours, arms folded, imagining the peace that would overtake me. The welcome chill. The snuffing out of my light like a bright candle, leaving a beautiful ribbon of curling smoke.

Instead, I fold over my wound, hands futilely clasped in front of it as if I might will my blood not to abandon me so soon. I'm not even strong enough to remove the dagger.

Alone as I am, I could never have imagined what was happening outside. Eugene calling Enid. Ajax summoning the Nightshades. If I had known what a force my friends and community were, marshaling to save me and protect the school at that very moment, I might have fought harder.

Instead, I'm ashamed to say, I was ready to give up. Perhaps that's how Goody finds me so quickly at the door between the world of the living and the spirit world where we met.

"Wednesday!" she calls.

"Are you here to take me to the other side?" I ask weakly.

"Listen," Goody says urgently. "Crackstone must be stabbed through his black heart. It's the only way to vanquish him now and forever."

I do my best to glare. "Is your spectral vision impaired? I'm *dying*."

Goody reaches forward, gesturing at the hideous necklace my mother gave me. The one I haven't been able to bring myself to take off. "Your necklace," Goody says. "It's a powerful talisman."

I want to say it wasn't powerful enough to stop the knife from going in, but I have little energy left even for snark.

"It's also a conduit for spirits," she explains. "It will allow me to pass through you and heal you. But once I do, you will never see me again. The school needs you, Wednesday. The Outcasts need you."

I think of Goody, who dedicated her entire life to protecting Outcasts. Who created the Nightshades for that very purpose. I understand in that moment, as she looks into my eyes, that this is what she wants. That whatever it means for her life as a spirit, it's worth it to her.

In the end, I can't bring myself to ask her to heal me. To sacrifice any part of what she has left. But I don't tell her not to. And so, after a long moment, she leans over my splayed form, grips the knife, and pulls it free with a strength I couldn't muster. Quickly, she places her hands over my wound and closes her eyes.

There's no way to describe the sensation of your ghost doppelgänger entering your blood, your consciousness, passing through you and knitting your injuries back together in their wake, so I won't try. But when I sit up, there's no doubt that she's done it. The pain is gone. The wound is gone. My head no longer aches. Even the place where Laurel cut my palm is smooth and unblemished.

Goody did it. And that means I owe her my life. Or at least Crackstone's ghoulish, sneering head.

CHAPTER THIRTY-TWO

I'm passing Lake Jericho when I hear it—the first howl of the blood moon. It's expected in a place like Nevermore, but what's a wolf doing this far from campus?

What's more than that, the howl sounds vaguely . . . familiar. Like I've heard it a hundred times before, though I can't place how or why that would be.

As I'm stopped, contemplating, Tyler steps out from the trees behind me, taking advantage of my distraction. By the time I see him, he's already too close. Maybe Laurel told him to guard the crypt in case I made an unlikely escape. Or maybe he wants me gone for his own sake by now.

Either way, he's here, in front of me, and I don't need a vision to tell me I'll have to tread very carefully now.

"Thornhill said you were dead," Tyler says, sounding disappointed.

I shrug, trying not to show how aware I am of the dire nature of this situation. Alone in the woods with a monster who no longer has any reason not to kill me. "I'm feeling much better now."

He sneers, his expression hateful. "You're like a cockroach," he says. "Do you have any idea how hard it was not to kill you all this time? Thornhill said we needed you. But we don't need you now."

"This won't end well for you," I promise him, and then the skin of his face begins to bubble.

Despite Goody's healing, I'm weak from the events of the evening. Once he transforms, I won't be able to outrun him or fight him off. His entire body tenses as he roars in agony. I know what's coming next. Is it possible Goody saved me just for me to die a mile to the west? With Crackstone and Laurel on the loose?

I scrabble backward on the leaves as Tyler completes his transformation. The Hyde stands in his place, saliva dripping from its teeth. Its bulging eyes glint with cruelty—the same cruelty I've seen in Tyler's, but more terrifying now. More deadly.

The monster lunges, and I do my best to get out of its way but it's no use. It was created for killing. It reaches forward with vicious accuracy, wrapping its long, knobbed fingers around me and lifting me into the air.

In a burst of speed, it smashes me against a tree. The arm that's not holding me raises high, moonlight glinting off five razor-sharp claws. The same ones that left deep and deadly gouges in the chests of many victims before me.

Having so narrowly escaped death, I know there are no more

miracles coming for me. I struggle, refusing to let anyone say I didn't fight to the last.

But before the Hyde can disembowel me, finishing the job its master couldn't, something huge, white, and furry flies into my line of vision, colliding with the monster, forcing it to drop me.

The Hyde growls in frustration, turning its sights on a fellow predator much more equal to the task of killing it than I am. It's only when the white beast enters a shaft of moonlight that I see the pink and purple tips of its ears. The eyes I could never mistake, no matter the fanged and monstrous face they're peering out of.

"Enid?" I say, and I can almost see the girl in the wolf. She's easily three times her normal size, a full werewolf with all the weapons at her disposal. Despite the circumstances, I feel a rush of intense pride that nearly knocks me off my feet.

But then the monster hulks into view behind her.

"Enid!" I shout, pointing behind her. "Look out!"

The Hyde crashes into Enid, sending her wolf form flying. I'm terrified until I see her right herself almost immediately. Unharmed by a blow that would have killed me or any other human. She appears almost pleased as she rounds on the Hyde, charging in for a second hit.

I've never felt so superfluous in my life. Even if I stayed, Enid doesn't need my help. And back at the school, Crackstone is ready to unleash biblical levels of destruction on the students.

"I've gotta get back to the school!" I shout, hoping Enid's supercharged hearing will pick it up, and then I turn and run toward Nevermore.

The school has clearly already been breached by Laurel and Crackstone. The halls are empty. I can only hope the Nightshades heeded my warning and got everyone out safely.

There's smoke in the entrance hall. I go up the stairs, feeling the history, knowing this was the way my parents went the night they fought Garrett Gates. I only want a bird's-eye view of the quad, to get eyes on Crackstone before he has eyes on me. But as I make for the balcony, I see it. Glinting in the moonlight through the archway up ahead.

It's a ceremonial fencing saber. Probably a prize from some long-ago event held at the school. It's the same one my mother used to kill Laurel's brother. To set all of this in motion. I can hear Goody's voice in my head:

Crackstone must be stabbed through his black heart. It's the only way to vanquish him now and forever.

I've spent most of my life trying to chart my own course. To not linger too long in the shadow of my mother's deeds or my father's name. But tonight, I feel their legacy can only strengthen me, as Goody's has.

Laurel and the Gates family have Crackstone. I'll show them what can be accomplished when one has ancestors worth honoring.

With the hefty weight of the sword in my grip, I move forward more confidently. It's time to end this, once and for all.

It only takes a brief glance to see the chaos that Crackstone is wreaking in the quad. I make my way stealthily down to meet him, sticking to the shadows until the moment is right to reveal myself.

There aren't many students in this part of the school, but Crackstone raises his staff to blast two of them just as I reach the edge of the quad. The moonlight is bright, bleaching the stone to a bone white. Everything flammable has caught, casting flickering light and dancing shadows.

Crackstone's staff is still up. The students, who I don't

recognize, scream and turn to flee. This is the moment I abandon the shadows. Face Crackstone at last.

"Howdy, pilgrim," I say, raising the saber.

As I hoped, Crackstone turns in disbelief at the sound of my voice, allowing the other students to flee to safety. Facing him across the burning quad, I know the events of Rowan's mother's vision have come to pass. If only she'd drawn the end. I suppose I'll have to be the artist of that scene.

"How can your heart still beat?" Crackstone asks. "What demon's sorcery is this?"

He raises his staff to dispatch me for a second time. This time, I raise my sword to meet him, but I know giving the students a chance to flee has lost me my surprise. If he restrains me again with his strange magic, this scene will end much differently from the one I want to ink.

"Stay away from her!" comes a voice from behind me.

I don't dare take my eyes off Crackstone, but when I hear an arrow nocking in a bow behind me, I feel a rush of emotion. Is it possible? How?

The arrow flies straight for Crackstone's horrible eye, but at the last minute he raises his hands, slowing the arrow to a stop, then allowing it to hover in front of him for a moment. The irony of this man, raised from the dead by supernatural means, wielding magic to destroy the magic-wielders he claims to be beneath him, is punishing.

He laughs as the arrow spins itself in midair, pointing back at the archer, then flying back at considerable speed.

I whirl around just in to time to see Xavier, shock on his face, looking worse for wear after his long days of wrongful imprisonment. In an instant, his speech to me in the Nightshades' library comes back to me:

I've been on your side since day one.

Before I decide to, I'm diving. Placing myself in the arrow's path. The pain when it drives into my shoulder is only the third worst agony I've felt today. I'll survive.

I take a knee, gritting my teeth against the pain, knowing I have seconds before Crackstone takes advantage of my vulnerability. But from this angle, I can see another group of terrified students huddling behind an arch. Xavier is looking at me in disbelief.

"Get them out of here!" I cry.

He hesitates, clearly unwilling to leave me here on my own.

"Go!" I urge, and he turns at last, running toward the students and then out of sight.

Once I can't see him anymore, I grit my teeth, wrench the arrow out of my shoulder, and take up the sword again. It's just Crackstone and me now. I face him as he approaches with no thought of surrender or backing down.

He swings with his staff. No more preamble. I block, absorbing the immense strength behind the blow. I won't be able to do that all night. It's imperative that I force an opening, and soon.

Another attack. This time I parry, sending his arm back with impeccable timing, if I do say so myself. With any normal opponent, this would create an opening. Especially a wide and powerful swing like that.

But Crackstone is supernaturally fast as well as strong. He's back in position before I can advance with a clear path. I steel myself, knowing I can't let him keep me on my heels. I have to show him what I can do.

With the historical saber in my hand, I stare down the corrupted visage, the glowing eyes, the fetid smile. And then I throw myself forward, blade first.

It's one of the most graceful attacks I've ever made. I can almost feel my mother in the stands, doing her polite little clap, her eyes sparkling with pride. But Crackstone raises his staff to meet the blade, and as they collide for the third time, the blade of the saber shatters.

My heart sinks as the pieces clatter to the ground. There's barely an inch of jagged blade protruding from the hilt. All the rest is gone. In pieces on the ground between us.

When he points his staff this time, I have no counter. I feel myself lifted off the ground, flung backward to slam into a burning picnic table. Sparks explode from where I land, but I don't fall. I stay pinned against it, feeling the heat growing unbearable at my back.

Crackstone stalks across the quad, staff aloft, until he's towering over me.

"I will send you back to hell!" he roars.

Only once again, my imminent demise is interrupted. An intact blade, thinner and more lithe than my own, appears through Crackstone's shoulder. He roars again, this time in pain, and drops the staff.

I'm freed from its grasp, dropping to the ground, rolling to extinguish any embers attached to my coat. When I rise, I see Crackstone facing Bianca, her chin jutting proudly, her sword back in her hand.

Before I can make it to her side, Crackstone backhands her brutally, sending her flying into the stone bench around the reflecting pool. But her stunt has given me just enough time to recover. On the ground at my feet is a shard of my sword. I don't know if it's long enough to reach his heart, but it's my only chance.

It cuts into my palm when I grip it, but when Crackstone turns back to face me, I'm ready. Before he can retrieve his staff, before he can say another word, I step forward and drive the shard of metal into the place his rotten heart should be.

His eyes go wide, his mouth moving in soundless rage. Despite the way it cuts into my hand, I drive it deeper. As deep as I can. Once it's in as far as it will go, I lock eyes with Crackstone and twist for good measure.

As the light shifts in his eyes from a supernatural glow to the blue of his human gaze, I think of the Meeting House. The Outcasts trapped inside. Their screams as they burn. I think of Rowan's mother, who had this vision twenty years ago. Of Rowan, who died so I could be here, finishing this monster for good.

I think of Goody, who taught me. Who saved me. Who wanted only this.

Crackstone looks down at me. The small, cruel eyes of a bigoted man whose legacy is prejudice and murder. I twist the blade. Black blood runs out of his mouth.

He staggers backward and I lose my grip on the shard, but there's no doubt it's done what it needed to do. There's an incredulous look on his face as he reaches for the weapon fragment protruding from his chest, pulling it out with a sickly sucking sound.

From the wound, a carpet of necrotic festering begins to spread immediately, leaving burning ash in its wake that flakes away on the wind. When it reaches the borders of his reconstructed form, energy begins to gather, then explodes outward in a supernova of blue energy, expelling itself with such force that the flames in the quad are extinguished.

Bianca gets to her feet, meeting my eyes over the small pile of ash that was very recently Crackstone. In that moment, I know we're seeing the same thing: a girl with a hell of a lunge attack, cinders blowing across her in the hellscape that was once our school, proud that because of us, a monster is dead for good.

Before I can say anything, however, I hear the unmistakable cocking of a gun behind me. I turn to find Laurel Gates stepping out of the smoke and shadows, pistol aimed right at my chest. Bianca steps forward in my periphery, but Laurel waves her menacingly away.

"You brought a gun to a sword fight," I say, trying to be casual. "First smart move you've made all day." Even as I say it, I'm wondering how many more miracles are left to me. At least if I die now, I can die knowing Crackstone will never return.

"I may not get to kill all the Outcasts," Laurel hisses, "but at least I'll have the satisfaction of killing you."

Closing my eyes, I wait for the impact of the bullet, trying not to anticipate the pain. Instead, I hear the buzzing of a bee.

I open my eyes gingerly to see Laurel waving away at least ten bees that have inexplicably found their way to the quad. Before I can see where they're coming from, ten bees become fifty. Then a hundred. Within seconds, Laurel is engulfed, screaming from sting after sting. She drops the gun. Only then do I turn to the source of the commotion to find Eugene, approaching from the east entrance, his hands raised as every bee from the hive obeys his command.

"Yes!" he shouts. "That's what you get for messing with Nevermore, bitch!"

Laurel is on the ground, shrieking in pain, curled around herself in a fetal position. I imagine right about now she's wishing she'd actually drowned all those years ago. It would have been a much more peaceful way to go.

Eugene approaches, a proud smile on his face. "Hummers stick together, right?"

It's at that moment that I realize I didn't experience any

miracles tonight. Simply the solidarity of a community who cares whether I live or die. It's an invigorating realization. It makes me feel almost as invincible as I've always pretended I am.

When we're sure there's no more danger from Laurel, Bianca leads us out to the water tower where the rest of the student body is gathered. The moment I have time to think, I know I need to find Enid. To make sure she prevailed in her battle with the Hyde.

My stomach is in knots the entire walk there. Flanked by Bianca and Eugene, I try not to think of what will happen if she's not there. How long it will take me to find her in the woods.

The huddle of students is visible in the torchlight above. I see the hats of Gorgons, the flashing eyes of sirens, and then, finally, a shock of bright blond hair. A patch of pink. A patch of purple. A whole lot of blood.

"Where's Wednesday?" Enid is saying, wrapped in a pink coat, every inch of her covered in blood and viscera that does not appear to be her own. In truth, she's never looked more beautiful to me. More capable or strong.

"Enid," I call, and she turns in a panic. Our classmates part between us. Our eyes take each other in for a long moment before she runs toward me and throws her arms around me.

There's a moment of shock as I register her body pressed against mine. The first hug I've experienced in . . . well, quite some time. While my normal reaction would be to push the offending hugger away, I find myself hugging her back. Loosening in her embrace, the full weight of all that has befallen me tonight finally given a safe place to land.

Before I know it, my arms are rising, encircling her shoulders and squeezing with everything I have left in me.

EPILOGUE

School is canceled for the rest of the semester. There's hardly anywhere on the Nevermore campus or the city of Jericho that isn't a crime scene. I suppose that will take some time to sort out.

Lurch carries the last of my bags out of Ophelia Hall as I type the final page of my novel. A fitting end to a most surprising year. As I hit those final six keys, I hesitate. THE END. It feels so final. Without overthinking it too much, I add a question mark. What's life without a little mystery, right?

I can't quite bring myself to brave the hormonal goodbye-fest that is the quad, so I make a detour to Weems's office first. It's so quiet without her imposing presence storming around within its walls. It's hard to imagine a principal who could take her place.

It's true, our relationship was complicated, but in the end, I couldn't have discovered Laurel's plot without her. She believed me when it counted. I'll remember her that way.

"I hate to admit it," comes Enid's voice from the doorway, "but I'm gonna miss Principal Weems."

Turning to face her, I hide a small smile. Of course she found exactly where I was hiding. We've been mostly inseparable in the days since the blood moon. Preparing for a long-distance friendship—at least for a while.

"She could be a real pain," I say. "But she gave her life protecting the one thing she truly loved—this school. And for that I have immense respect."

Enid nods. She's wearing an over-the-top pink fleece coat today. It makes her eyes seem even bluer than usual. "She was one of us," she says somberly, and after a moment of silence, she gently guides me out into the hall.

"Now that classes are canceled for the rest of the semester, you've *got* to visit me in San Francisco," she says, clapping her hands at the thought. "I can pretty much guarantee fog and drizzle every day."

"Sounds tempting," I say, except I think I mean it. I have a feeling the Addams Family Mansion is going to feel a little small after this year.

Just then, Bianca passes us, going in the opposite direction with scarcely more than a nod. I still don't know how I feel about her. It's been a roller coaster between us this semester. But one thing is for certain—she saved my life. I can't just let that go.

"Bianca," I call out, feeling, rather than seeing, Enid's eyes widen in shock.

Bianca turns to face me, perfect eyebrows arched in curiosity. "I owe you a thank-you," I say.

She smirks for a moment; then it becomes a genuine smile. "We're getting that fencing title next year," she says with that air of aloof superiority that used to bother me so much. "Don't let killing one supernatural pilgrim get to your head."

Enid squeezes my arm before skipping over to say goodbye to some of the Nightshades girls. I'm considering making my way out when I see Xavier in the gallery. My shoulder is still sore where the arrow went in, but we haven't spoken since.

I make my way up the stairs slowly, wondering what kind of reception I can expect. If my relationship with Bianca was a roller coaster, my relationship with Xavier was more like a plane crash.

"I hear you're officially a free man," I say when he doesn't immediately flee.

"Yeah," he says, spreading his arms like wings. "All charges dismissed."

I nod, unsure what to say next. Of course I feel guilty for what I did, and what happened to him.

"Listen," he says when I don't immediately come up with a new topic of conversation. "When you came to my cell, I said a lot of things." He takes a deep breath, then plows on. "Being your friend should come with a warning label, but I don't know a lot of people who would take an arrow for me, so . . ."

He takes a small black box out of his coat pocket and hands it to me. I take it hesitantly.

"Welcome to the twenty-first century, Addams."

I open the top to reveal a shiny black smartphone.

"My number is in there already," he says with a cocky smirk.

"That's a bold move," I say. "I hope you aren't expecting me to call."

"No, never," he says. "I'd settle for a text, though." My glowering look clearly doesn't produce the desired effect, because he's smirking again in a moment. "You do know what a text is, don't you?"

I roll my eyes, putting the box into my bag. I can always toss it into the lake on the way out of town. Lurch won't mind pulling over.

"Goodbye, Xavier," I say.

"Hey," he calls as I turn for the stairs. "Are you gonna be back next semester?"

I don't bother to answer. Like I said, what's life without a little mystery?

Snow is falling as the Addams family hearse makes its way down the Nevermore Academy drive. Only then do I power up the phone. To my surprise, I already have a new message, from an unknown sender.

When I open it, I see a grainy, zoomed-in photo of myself at the Weathervane a few weeks ago, across the booth from Tyler, before I knew the truth. A second photo must have been taken just an hour ago, as I spoke with Xavier in the gallery.

A little animation pops up next. It's unmistakably me, with the pigtails and the dark uniform. As I watch, a little cartoon knife flies out and buries itself in my skull, turning my eyes to Xs.

The text below reads simply: *I'm watching you.*

My first stalker, I think, more intrigued than afraid. Maybe this forced vacation will be more interesting than I imagined.

I give the phone to Thing, who tucks it into my bag and closes it. I suppose we don't have time for any unplanned stops at the lake after all. More's the pity.

As I stare out the window, the snow flurrying past, I think of everything that's come to pass in my time at Nevermore Academy. Everything that could still be lurking ahead. Unlike my novel, not every thread has been tied up. Nor every question answered. Secrets are still hiding in the dark corners of Jericho.

Enid told me Sheriff Galpin broke up the werewolf/Hyde showdown by firing a bullet into Tyler's shoulder. Enid fled, but there's no doubt that if the sheriff didn't know about Tyler before, he knows now. The question is: What is he going to do about it? Who is the greater loyalty to—his son or the badge?

And what about Laurel and Tyler? Were they just pawns in a bigger game?

Does this stalker have anything to do with them? Or is it a brand-new threat waiting to be investigated?

I know the suspense is killing you.

The End . . . ?

TEHLOR KAY MEJIA is the author of the critically acclaimed young adult fantasy novel *We Set the Dark on Fire* and the Paola Santiago trilogy from Rick Riordan Presents, as well as several more books for all age groups. Tehlor lives with his child, his partner, and an ever-growing pack of dogs in his home state of Oregon.